I0748429

THE AMISH MENORAH AND OTHER STORIES

ENDORSEMENTS

Rich in history and issues of life, this Amish anthology collection is a winsome read! The settings from Germany to the Midwest and various states brought picturesque scenes along with detailed dialog and unique dealings the characters were faced with. The characters were dimensional with flaws but had fortitude, tenacity, spirit, and faith to overcome their challenges.
—**Marilyn Ridgway**, Amish book reviewer

Each tale penned in the author's unique style gave way to emotions and seeing the struggles of life throughout history of the Amish and currently with misunderstandings of their practices. These men of Amish fiction know how to reel a reader into their story and keep them spellbound till the end, while weaving in romance and faith.

Six talented authors (all men!) provide very enjoyable stories with just enough twists, turns, and romance to delight any Amish reader.
—**Kate Lloyd**, Bestselling Author

Amish fiction fans will love this set. These stories are as unique and individual as the men who wrote them. Apart from the enjoyment I got from reading, I learned something, was moved to laughter in some places, and to tears in others. An Amish book lover's delight.
—**Samantha Price**, *USA Today* Bestselling Author.

Ah, the joys of slowing down life's pace with a delightful collection of stories! The *Amish Menorah and Other Stories* is written for those of us who love to settle into a big, comfy chair with a good book. From the moment Patrick Craig opens with his tale of an Amish man and a Jewish girl thrown together in the last Amish community in Europe in 1936, each novella stirred up deep emotions. One after another the tales prompt insight into how multifaceted the human experience can be. Congratulations to Patrick E. Craig, Thomas Nye, Amos Wyse, Murray Pura, Willard Carpenter, and Jerry Eicher for pulling together a collection of delightful, entertaining stories!"
—**Cathy Primer Krafve**, Host of Fireside Talk Radio, Blogger, and Author

THE AMISH MENORAH AND OTHER STORIES

by

THE MEN OF AMISH FICTION

WILLARD CARPENTER † PATRICK E. CRAIG

JERRY EICHER † THOMAS NYE

MURRAY PURA † AMOS WYSE

Cover and Interior Design: Cora Graphics, Derinda Babcock

Editor: Deb Haggerty

PUBLISHED BY: Elk Lake Publishing, Inc., 35 Dogwood Drive, Plymouth, MA 02360, 2020

Library Cataloging Data

Names: Carpenter, Willard (Willard Carpenter), Craig, Patrick E. (Patrick E. Craig), Eicher, Jerry (Jerry Eicher), Nye, Thomas (Thomas Nye), Pura, Murray (Murray Pura), and Wyse, Amos (Amos Wyse)

The Amish Menorah and Other Stories] / Willard Carpenter, Patrick E. Smith, Jerry Eicher, Thomas Nye, Murray Pura, and Amos Wyse

420p. 23cm × 15cm (9in × 6 in.)

Identifiers: ISBN-13: 978-1-951970-59-8 (paperback) | 978-1-951970-60-4 (trade paperback)

| 978-1-951970-61-1 (e-book)

978-1-64949-232-6 (Case)

Key Words: Amish, Mennonite, alternate life style, short stories, anthology, family, relationships, values & virtues.

LCCN: 2020938653 Fiction

This book is dedicated to Amish author Sicily Yoder (Teresa Ann Phillips). You were always there to help those of us who were just beginning the Amish Fiction adventure.

TABLE OF CONTENTS

THE AMISH MENORAH BY PATRICK CRAIG 3

A CLOUDY DAY BY WILLARD CARPENTER . . . 101

WHEN HEARTS BREAK BY JERRY EICHER . . . 167

THE SILO BY THOMAS NYE. 185

LONE STAR BY MURRAY PURA 279

AMISH FOR THE SUMMER BY AMOS WYSE. . . 341

ACKNOWLEDGMENTS

To Deb Ogle Haggerty, who helped us turn a bright idea into a readable book.

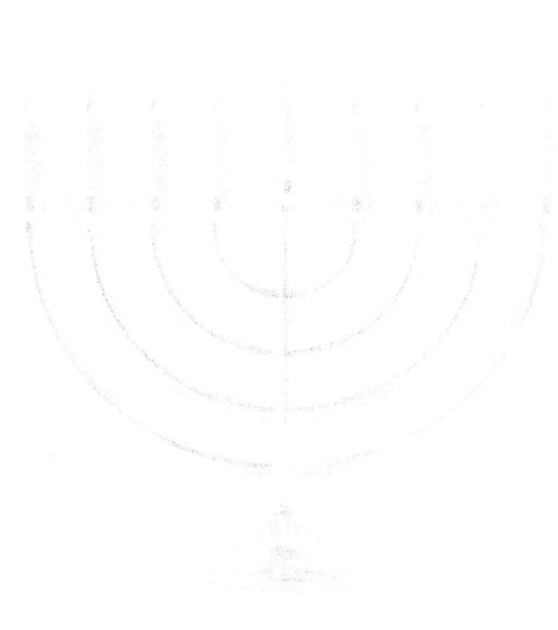

THE AMISH MENORAH

Patrick E. Craig

A NOTE FROM PATRICK E. CRAIG

I have been writing Amish fiction for nine years. During that time, I have published six Amish books and written about the Amish in many blogs and posts. When I began this very interesting journey, I knew two things: one, Amish fiction was the best-selling Christian genre by far and had been for many years; and two, I knew nothing about the Amish.

In 2011, my friend Nick Harrison prompted me to send him a one-sheet with a story idea for what I thought would be an anthology of short stories. He hinted he liked Amish stories and quilting stories, so I sent him an idea for a story titled *A Quilt for Jenna.* To my surprise, Nick liked the idea and encouraged me to turn it into a novel. After I finished the book, Nick's company, Harvest House Publishers, liked the story enough to offer me a contract for *Jenna* and two more books. Thus Apple Creek Dreams was born, followed by The Paradise Chronicles and now, *The Amish Menorah*, being published by Elk Lake Publishing, Inc.

Knowing nothing about the Amish forced me to research (thank goodness for Google) and ask other Amish authors many questions. I'm sure I was like an annoying gnat for many of them. In 2012, I met Sicily Yoder, an Amish author raised in the Amish church and now a Mennonite. Sicily was a gold mine of information. She was always patient and gracious with me and would answer the simplest question with volumes. Sicily wrote books about the Amish, but she had a problem with many of the books written by *Englischers,* folks who had climbed onto the Amish fiction bandwagon and were writing overly romanticized "Happily Ever After" novels where everything turned out wonderfully only because the protagonists were Amish. She warned me that there was a dark side to the Amish myth. The Amish are real people, they go through the same problems and desperate situations that non-Amish do, and they have one problem that broke Sicily's heart. Many of the Amish people do not know Christ as their personal savior. They follow the Dordrecht Confession of Faith, a Dutch Mennonite composition written in 1632. You can read Article 6 of this document in a manner that emphasizes faith and regeneration and sees repentance and the total reformation of life as the result that will always come from this. Everyone who believes in Christ becomes a new creation and this regeneration saves him or her. However, one can also read this paragraph to say that, besides faith and regeneration, one must also repent and reform their life as a separate and additional requirement to attain eternal life.

What I discovered was that like the non-messianic observant Jew, many Amish live their lives trying to attain salvation through good works by following the *Ordnung*, the orally transmitted rules that govern Amish life, a practice at odds with the wonderful statements of Romans and Ephesians concerning justification by faith alone. Sicily warned me of this and encouraged me to make sure all my books stated clearly somewhere in the story that the law does not save you, only Jesus Christ can do so. I have kept that directive as best I can.

Now I am writing the "Amish Menorah" as an expository on this subject—an Amish man and a Jewish girl thrown together in the last Amish community in Europe in 1936—both of them under the law but neither knowing their Messiah. I have used the real Amish village of Ixheim, Germany, as the setting and, as is my practice, have inserted fictional characters into this setting. At the end of the story, the Amish of Ixheim disband their church and become Mennonites, thus ending the long presence of the Amish in Europe. This is a historical fact, but, as I noted, most of the characters in "The Amish Menorah" are fictional, and I have taken some liberties with those who are not. I have done this to create a setting and a story that examines the two big questions of life: what is the key to salvation for humanity—works or faith, and who do you say Jesus is. At the end of the story, you may have to answer these questions for yourself.

—Patrick E. Craig

CHAPTER ONE

Dust and Thunder—1936

"Brrrr, Gunnar!" The huge *Suddeutsches Kaltblut* stopped in his tracks and looked around at Gerd. The horse pawed and snorted, eager to get on with the plowing. "*Beruhigen Sie sich, Gunnar! Seien Sie ruhig."* As the horse quieted, Gerd took the traces off his shoulders and listened.

There! Thunder!

He looked up at the sky, but the calm blue heaven smiled back at him in perfect stillness.

Then again! A low rumbling in the distance, this time accompanied by the slightest shaking of the ground.

"Aufenthalt hier, Gunnar." Gerd left Gunnar standing in the uncompleted row and walked to the top of the knoll that rose in the center of his fields. His eyes followed the line of the road winding off to the east toward Ixheim, then lifted to the low ridge beyond. He frowned. A huge cloud of dust drifted above the ridge. It seemed to move toward him. Gerd took off his hat and wiped his brow. The spring sun was hot on his back and sweat stained his shirt, but the soil beneath his feet was damp and held in place by the unplowed winter vetch.

There should not be any dust storms this time of the year, and not until the harvested fields are dry at the end of summer.

From below Gunnar nickered, calling his master back to the field.

"Bleiben Sie Dort, Gunnar," Gerd called down to the horse. He looked again. Now the dust had come almost to the outskirts of the village, and he could see something

emerging from the cloud. Gerd widened his eyes, and his hand lifted to shade them and get a better look. But he was not mistaken.

Tanks! Armored tanks. What are they doing here?

And then, out of the cloud, row upon row of marching, uniformed men with rifles over their shoulders and packs on their backs following the tanks. As they drew closer, Gerd could see small armored half-tracks and *Kübelwagens* driving between the regiments. As he stood in bewilderment, he saw his neighbor Ernst Troyer coming down the road on the run on the back of a saddleless horse. The young man galloped off the road and through the field, paying no attention to Gerd's plowed rows. He jerked the horse to a stop and catapulted off its back in front of Gerd.

"Gerd, Gerd …" For a moment the lad could not catch his breath.

Gerd grabbed the boy by the shoulders. "What is it Ernst, what's happening."

"The Germans, the army, Gerd …"

"Ernst! Calm down. What about the army?"

"They've come, Gerd, they've come back to the Rhineland. I was outside the village when they marched by. They were cheering and waving and shouting about saving Germany's pride. I came to get you, the Elders want you to come."

"But the army cannot come here. The Allies demilitarized the Rhineland. No one can bring an army in here. It is against the treaty."

Ernst shook his head. "I am afraid Herr Hitler does not believe in treaties."

Gerd Hirschberg stood in front of the fountain that faced St.-Martins-Platz. Beside him stood Christian Guth, the elder of the Amish community in Ixheim, and Otto Schertz and Georg Nafziger, the two preachers. Around and behind them the villagers of Ixheim gathered, a low murmur of anxious voices filling the air. Uniformed German soldiers jammed the plaza. Armored vehicles blocked the entrances into the square except for one road, and Gerd watched as a large black German touring car with Nazi flags on the front fenders entered the town and motored toward them. The driver pulled to a stop in front of them, got out, raced around to the passenger side and opened the rear door. A short, fat man got out. He looked almost clownish in his grey topcoat, which hung to the ground—and the tight collar of his black uniform blouse made his fat neck bulge, which squeezed his eyes into a pig-like stare.

The fat little man looked around at the simple farmers with obvious disdain. He saw the four men standing in front of the villagers and strutted up to them.

"Why are you not cheering and celebrating? This is a historic day for Germany. Our great Fuhrer has put Germany into our rightful place among the nations of the world once again."

Christian Guth reached out his hand to shake the German officer's, but the man ignored the hand and looked at him with the same piggish expression.

"I am sorry, Herr … Herr …?"

"*SS-Oberführer* Heinrich Glauss. I am now in charge of this entire district. You are the Mayor?"

"No, Herr Glauss—"

"Oberführer, *bitte!*

"Yes, Oberführer. No, I am not the mayor. This is a village of Amish farmers, and I am the elder of the village."

"Amish? Amish? You are the cowards who refuse to fight for our country?"

"We believe in the teachings of Jesus in the Bible, when he says that if your enemy smite you, turn the other cheek."

The fat little man looked hard at Christian and then, stepped forward and slapped him hard across the face.

"And I say you are cowards."

Gerd started forward, but he felt Otto's hand hard on his arm. The movement did not miss the Nazi's notice. He turned. "So, this strapping fellow is not so ready to turn the other cheek, eh?"

He stepped up to Gerd, put his hands on his hips and stared up at the young farmer. "Why do you not wear the uniform of the Wehrmacht? You are sound and strong, you would make a good soldier."

Gerd remained silent. Otto spoke. "Please excuse my young friend, your honor. He is impetuous, but he loves his country. We are not at war, your honor, and there is no conscription."

"I am not talking to you, be quiet. I am talking to this fellow." Glauss turned back to Gerd. "If there were a war, would you fight? You seemed ready a moment ago."

Gerd swallowed. He could see danger in the German's eyes. "I apologize, your honor. It's just that Herr Guth is like a father to me and I … I—"

"You did not wish to see him insulted, no? Well, the day is coming when you might wish you had the same feelings for the Fatherland as you do for this man. I ask again, would you fight?"

Gerd shook his head. "No, your honor, I would not."

Glauss stared at Gerd for a long time. Then he smiled. The smile was not friendly. "We shall see, my young friend, we shall see." The German officer took a few steps and faced the villagers. He lifted his arm in a victorious straight-arm salute and shouted. "Today is a great day for Germany. We have come back to the Rhineland, the heart of our country.

Our great Führer has ordered the reoccupation of this region to show the world that we are not toadies and lickspittles who lesser men or lesser countries can push around. We are Aryans, the purest race on earth. The world will soon find out they should not have humiliated Germany. Germany should have dictated the terms of that treaty of Versailles but the traitorous Jews and Communists betrayed us. Chancellor Hitler has cancelled all the reparation payments to the so-called allies, and now, we stand as the one nation that can light a beacon for the rest of the world to follow. Today is a great day; I wish you all to celebrate. Give praise to our victorious German army and our great Führer. *Seig Heil!*"

There was a moment of shocked silence. Glauss reached down, pulled his pistol from its holster and fired a shot into the air.

"Give praise, I said!"

The people jumped in surprise, and a few toward the back of the crowd raised a weak cheer.

"*Seig, Heil!*"

The *Oberführer's* arm snapped up, and he screamed along. "*Seig, Heil!*" All the soldiers in the square followed, roaring their approval. The arms of the non-Amish villagers lifted into the Nazi salute, and they began to shout along with the soldiers. "*Seig, Heil! Seig, Heil! Seig, Heil!*"

The Amish men stared at each other in horror. In a moment, the Germans had transformed their peaceful village into a Nazi rally. Glauss marched up to Christian and placed the pistol to his head. He glared at the others. "You Amish people will give praise to Germany or your elder will die."

The Amish looked at Christian who stared straight ahead. Otto stepped forward and nodded to the villagers, who hesitantly lifted their arms and began to chant along. Gerd was the last to raise his hand. Glauss smiled, waited for a moment and then holstered his pistol. He turned toward the car, but before he left, he took Gerd by the arm and said again, "You will fight, my young friend, I promise you." Then he swaggered back to the car where the driver was waiting to open the door. He climbed into the back seat, but before he did, he turned to Gerd once more and mouthed the words, "You will fight." He began to laugh as he signaled the driver to leave.

The door slammed, and the car departed in a cloud of dust, Glauss laughing in the back seat. The chants of "*Seig Heil*," slowly faded and the citizens of Ixheim stood looking at each other in shame.

Gerd sat on the rough bench in Christian Guth's barn with the two preachers. Christian was reading from the Bible.

Aber ich sage euch: Liebt eure Feinde, segne tauft euch, tut Gutes denen, die euch hassen, und betet für die, die euch trotzig gebrauchen, und verfolgt euch.

Guth closed the book, then looked up and smiled at Gerd. "You were ready to fight for me, my son?"

Gerd nodded. "The man had no right to strike you."

"*Ja*, maybe he did not. But as I read, the words of our Lord remind us always to pray for those who use us evilly. Besides the fact that the Bible and our *Ordnung* teach us the ways of peace, it would have been very dangerous for you to assault the Oberführer. You would be dead now, and we cannot have that because you mean too much to Ixheim. You are the future of this congregation. I have been the elder here for a long time. Any days I have left are a gift from *du leiber Gott.*"

Gerd shrugged. "But I am a simple farmer, and I am too young. I am not made to lead."

Otto turned to him. "The people of the village look up to you. You have great wisdom already. You will be the next elder. So let us say no more about it. *Das ist ein Streit um des Kaiser's Bart.*"

Gerd smiled despite himself. "*Sie müssen einen Vogel haben.*"

The three older men looked at Gerd and begin laughing. Gerd shook his head as he thought about the events of the day.

Perhaps the Nazi was right. Maybe I will fight, if it is against such fools as him.

CHAPTER TWO

Gefährliche Tage

Gerd sat in the kitchen thinking over the troubling day. An oil lantern burned on the stand by the door and shadows flickered on the walls, dancing a strange, silent, *Zweifacher*. His mother poured him a cup of coffee and set it on the table.

"We have fresh cream, Gerd."

Gerd nodded as she set the pitcher next to his coffee.

"What will happen, Gerd? What will Hitler do next?"

"I do not know, *Mütti*. From what I hear, he is a very determined man—determined to erase the shame of Germany's loss to the French and their allies in the war. He wants to make Germany into a great country again, but I do not know how that will affect us."

"I wish your father were here, Gerd. He would know what to do."

"*Ja, Mütti,* he would know."

There was a knock at the door that startled them.

"Who would come at this hour?" his mother asked.

Shrugging, Gerd stood and went to the door. Christian Guth stood there. The old man looked haggard and worn, and his appearance surprised Gerd.

"What is it, Brother Guth?"

"May I come in, Gerd?"

"Yes, yes. Please forgive my rudeness."

Gerd ushered the old man into the kitchen. His mother bustled up another cup, but Christian shook his head.

"I had a visit from the head of the Gestapo after you left."

"The Gestapo? What is that?"

"The Gestapo is Herr Hitler's *Geheimstaatspolizei,* his secret state police. They have taken over Zweibrücken—moved into the Mayor's office, and they have moved troops to the border and closed it."

"Closed it? But how will our people from Lorraine be able to attend church?"

"They will need a special pass, and they will have to cross at a checkpoint near Saarbrücken. But that is not all." The elder looked down.

"What Christian? What else?"

"Hitler's Nazis have been using racial biologists since 1933 to examine the Mennonites and every other people group in Germany for racial purity. The consensus was uniform," Christian said. "Mennonites, according to these scientists, were more Aryan than the average German."

Gerd nodded. "That's not surprising. Swiss Mennonites began coming to Zweibrücken in the 1600s. And since then they have emigrated all over Germany."

"And France," said Christian.

"What does that have to do with us?"

"The Gestapo chief, a Major Steinmann, said that because of our racial purity, the Mennonites and the Amish are crucial to the German war effort."

"War effort! But we are not at war, Christian."

"Steinmann must have trusted me for he used that phrase and intimated the reoccupation of the Rhineland is just the first step in Hitler's plans for Germany."

"But how will we serve the war effort … if a war comes?"

"Steinmann told me that Anabaptists, the Amish and the Mennonites, are the most competent of all German farmers, and they are very obedient to the law. He thinks, given our racial purity, obedience, and loyalty, they could use us to lead other German farmers in a great agrarian revolution, so that the coming *Reich* would have more than enough food to supply the population if difficult times came."

"But … but, Christian, does he understand we will not lead an effort to support great violence?"

"Yes, Gerd, I explained that to him, but he is certain that when the time comes, we will understand our duty."

"What are we to do, Christian?"

Christian stood and shook his head. "I have been the elder of this congregation since 1907. I shepherded it through the Great War, and we faced persecution for our anti-violence stance then. Now will be no different. We will just have to obey Christ, no matter what." He shrugged.

"But, Christian, these men are different, I could see it in that fat *Oberführer* Glauss's eyes. These men are evil, evil to the core. We will despair the day they came goose-stepping into our quiet village. Only bad will come of this, and turning the other cheek will not change that. I do not think our people can bear what is coming."

"It is not only our people I fear for, Gerd. There are those among us who these men do not consider racially pure enough to be part of this great new German kingdom."

"Who are they, Christian?"

"Well, and again only because he considered me his equal as a German, he began to name them: Gypsies, homosexuals, the retarded, communists, the unproductive … but their greatest target is the Jews."

"The Jews? But the Jews have been in our country for centuries. They have assimilated. How many of Germany's great musicians, doctors, teachers, or businessmen are Jews? There are Jews in every village and city. Tov Weiss in Zweibrücken helped my father with a loan to get us by in a bad year. Our family considers him a friend."

"We are isolated here in Ixheim, Gerd. We have not seen what the Nazis are doing. They have used propaganda campaigns to promote hatred of the Jews. They convinced the public it was Jews and communists who sold Germany out, and that is why we lost the war. Now, Hitler is using them as a scapegoat, blaming them for Germany's economic and social problems. Most Germans believe him, and that is one reason the Nazis rose to power."

"But why did he tell you all this?"

"It was a tip-off and a warning, I think. The Nazis are hunting Jews, particularly those Jews who are communists, and sending them to camps. They are confiscating Jewish property and issuing anti-Jewish decrees, which have eliminated the rights of Jews.

"But Christian, this is terrible. Why did we not know of this?"

"We are in the world, Gerd, but not of it. Ixheim is far from the centers of power. And there was one last thing."

"What?"

"Again, I think he was sharing as one Aryan to another, but there was a threat there, too. They will consider anyone who befriends a Jew or helps them a traitor to Germany and that person will suffer the same fate as the Jew they help."

The two men looked at each other with a dawning horror.

The golden edge of the sun was just flashing over the far hills and brilliant rays reached up, turning the indigo of night into the rose of dawn. Gerd walked out into the cold March morning. Christian's words had kept him from sleep the whole night.

What are we coming to? Gefährliche Tage I think, dangerous days.

The bite of a fading winter gnawed at him as Gerd picked up his hoe and began to dig the early spring weeds out of his mother's garden plot. As the sun crept higher in the sky, he warmed to his task, and soon, he stripped off his shirt. He stood there in the sunlight, tall and bronzed, his muscles rippling like ropes as he attacked the wet dirt, partly in anger but mostly in disgust at what he had heard the night before. Streams of sweat ran down his back and shoulders—soon his skin was steaming in the brisk air.

"Working hard, again, Gerd?"

The voice startled him, and he pivoted to find Hilda Knepp standing at the corner of the house, a basket under her arm. He could not mistake the unbridled interest in the young woman's eyes, as she looked him over like she would a young horse.

"I brought some *eier* from our chickens for your *mütter.* I hope I am not disturbing you." Hilda edged a little closer. "You seemed deep in thought. Is something troubling you?"

Gerd had known Hilda all his life. Over the years, they had fallen into an unspoken understanding that one day Gerd would court her. But as Gerd grew older, he began to see things with an eye tempered by the realities of life. He was not sure Hilda was right for him, if only in temperament. Gerd was a serious young man, with the responsibility on his young shoulders for managing the large farm his father had left him when he died in a logging accident. Hilda was mischievous, outspoken, and even brazen in her attention to Gerd. When they were younger, she had driven many an innocent Amish girl away from Gerd's attention. Gerd had puffed up to think a girl as pretty and buxom as Hilda was so interested in him, but as he grew older and wiser, Hilda's possessiveness began to wear on him.

Then other hands began to apply pressure on Gerd to court Hilda. Hilda's father was poor in land, and the thought of his daughter being brought into the family of the man who owned the largest farm in the area prompted him to speak to Gerd's mother about a marriage. But Magda knew her son would make his own decision in his own time. She just shook her head at Jakob Knepp's importuning.

"Gerd will come courting when he's ready, Jakob. He has much responsibility, and I think he has not yet made time for other things in his life—things like a wife and *kînder*. He will come around soon, give him time."

"But Mother Hirschberg, Hilda is not getting any younger. It is time for her to go out from under my roof and into the house … and bed … of her own husband." He shrugged and smiled a deprecating smile. "Don't you want *enkelkinder*? I do."

Gerd's mother shook her head. "In the Lord's time, Jakob, in his time."

Unable to enlist Magda Hirschberg's help, Jakob had sent Hilda by the Hirschberg place every day on the smallest of pretexts, a transparent ploy that was becoming more obvious to Gerd each time Hilda came.

"Gerd?"

Gerd shook his head and smiled at the girl. "Oh, *entschuldigen Sie*, Hilda. My mind wandered. The coming of the Army has changed many things in Ixheim already, and I fear for the future of our community. There are bad days ahead, I am thinking."

Hilda flushed and then stepped closer. "*Ja,* Gerd, I think you are right. Even I can see that." She put down the basket of eggs and twisted her hands. "That is why I must speak my mind. I know you will think me *aufdringlich,* too forward, but I thought we understood that when you accepted baptism into the church, you would ask my father for permission to court me. Well, you are almost twenty years old and your baptism is soon. I am already nineteen, and as you say, the coming of the Germans brings great uncertainty. Don't you think it is time for us … I mean, well, time for you …" She trailed off.

"… to come courting?" He looked at the girl who stood before him. Hilda was beautiful in her own way, curvaceous, with flaxen hair and cornflower eyes—a picture of the idealized German woman.

If I could tame your tongue and your jealousy …

"Can you not speak? Before I shame myself?"

Gerd nodded. "You are right, Hilda, you are right. Give me a few days, and then I will come see your father."

Hilda's face lit up, and she took two quick steps toward Gerd, but he held up his hands. "We shouldn't even be alone together like this. Go home now. I will see you in a few days."

She nodded, then threw her apron up over her burning face, turned and ran down the path to the road.

Gerd shook his head.

I don't know, Gott. I suppose this is the right thing to do, but you must show me if I am right.

CHAPTER THREE

EMILY

It was dusk, and Gerd was walking his fields as he always did when he needed to think something through. To the east, the twinkling lights of Ixheim sparkled like fireflies among the rills and swales that marked the sloping hills of the Saar valley. Below him spread the Amish farms of Ixheim. From his knoll, he could see the lantern light coming on in the windows of the Oesch farm, and on the farm just below, Hans Gingerich led his team of black Friesians toward his ancient barn.

Gerd chuckled.

Hans's blacks are a good team but my Gunnar can out-pull both of them together, Ja!

His steps turned toward his own barn for his nightly check of all his animals. The old door creaked open at his push, and he stepped into the dark mustiness of the rambling structure. His great-great-great-grandfather Hirschberg had built the barn when Gerd's ancestors first came from Switzerland almost two hundred years before to settle in the *Rheinland-Pfalz*. Huge, hand-adzed beams held up the walls and the loft, and many stalls and storage rooms stretched back into the darkness. He took the lantern from the shelf by the door, struck a match and lit the wick. The soft light spread into the gloom where he could see his cows chewing their cuds in their pen. Back to the left, he saw Zwingli the goat's horns peeking up over the boards of her stall, and he heard the tiny bleats of the new kids as they nursed.

When he came to Gunnar's stall, the great horse was standing still with his ears up. Instead of nuzzling up to Gerd looking for the apple Gerd kept in his pocket, he snorted and stamped.

"What is it, Gunnar?"

Gerd looked around, then reached up to stroke the animal's neck, but Gunnar pulled his head up and stared into the darkness at the back of the barn.

Gerd heard a small sound, like the rustle of mice in the corn bin. "Mice again, Gunnar, *Ja*? I thought my traps had rid us of those pests." Gerd turned and walked to the corn bin. He waited, then jerked open the lid, hoping to catch the little *störenfriede* at work, but the bin was clear, full to the brim with last fall's harvest and not one dropping to mark the presence of field mice.

Hmmmm, what was that noise?

Then Gerd heard it again, a movement in the hay, back in the dark.

Cat, maybe …

"Hansli? Hansli, are you hunting for dinner?" But no answering yowl came from his mother's big tomcat.

He walked toward the back of the barn, lifting the lantern and looking in each stall. Nothing. He was about to turn back when he heard another sound, like the whimper of a small, trapped animal about to meet the hunter. Gerd walked around the last stall and lifted the lantern again. There—a movement in the hay mound, something dark, almost hidden by the pale straw. Gerd stepped forward, holding the lamp high.

"I see you in there, come out."

There was a sigh of resignation, the hay stirred and a face looked up at him. Long dark hair with bits of straw stuck in it, large luminous green eyes, pale lips, a slender neck rising out of a dark sweater.

A girl!

The girl stood. She drew her shoulders back. Gerd could see she was trying not to be afraid. Her chin lifted, her eyes blazed up as though a fire had been lit behind them. Her thick black sweater clung to her trim form, rolling down over her hips and hiding the top of her black skirt, which reached down to the tops of her walking shoes. She was lovely.

"Come out of there."

The girl stepped into the light, her movements graceful …

Like a dancer!

"Who are you? What are you doing in my barn?"

"I am Emily. I am hiding."

"Emily who? And who are you hiding from?"

"Emily Weissbach. I am hiding from the Gestapo."

"But why?"

"I am a Jew."

Gerd stared at the girl for a long moment. Christian's words from the night before came back to him and he felt a strange rush of … fear … premonition?

At last he spoke, almost to himself. "A Jew! But I am forbidden to associate with Jews."

A wince passed over the girl's face, and she shrugged. "I know you are. That is why I am hiding."

"Where did you come from?

"Munich. I am trying to get to France."

"You cannot get out of Germany. The border is closed. You need a pass."

"I was hoping to sneak across."

"Impossible. The Germans have already strung barbed wire, and they started patrolling the border day and night. They do not want the French army to come in and throw them out of the Rhineland, so they are extra vigilant. No one can get through."

For the first time, the girl's face lost its bravado, and she stared at Gerd with those enormous eyes, as though beseeching him for something. Without a sound she sank back down in the straw and put her hands over her face. She was quiet for a moment before her muffled words came out from behind her hands, a whisper, a sob.

"What am I to do?"

Gerd stared down at her. Then he crouched down beside her. "Where is your family? Father … mother?"

Her face hardened for a moment, then tears came. She reached up and wiped them away with an abrupt move of her hand. "They are in Dachau camp. My father is a communist, and they rounded him up. They took my mother with him. They killed my brother."

"But that is terrible. You are alone?"

"Yes, I have no one to help me." She reached under the straw and pulled out a cloth suitcase. "I only have these few things. Three days ago, I was coming home from the store, and I saw all the cars in front of our house. The soldiers dragged my father out. His face was bloody, and he had no coat. They threw him in the back of the car. After that, they dragged my mother out and put her in with him. My brother came running out and tried to get my father out of the car …"

"What?"

She brushed more tears away. "The office in charge shot him in the head. They left him lying dead in the street. I could hear my mother screaming as they drove away."

"Mein Gott!"

"I waited until it got dark and went in the back door, got some things and some money and took the bus to Saarbrücken."

Gerd shook his head in disbelief. *"Kumm."* He helped the girl up and led her to a bench along the wall. She sank down on it, her face pale.

"Have you eaten anything, Emily?"

"Not for a day. We were part way to Saarbrücken when several army trucks and soldiers on motorcycles passed the bus. I heard one passenger say the Nazis were sweeping the countryside looking for collaborators, enemies of the Reich. The man said there would be roadblocks and checkpoints, so when we stopped to use the restrooms in Landstuhl, I slipped away and I've been walking ever since, hiding in the woods and keeping out of sight."

"But that's thirty kilometers, and you walked it? Come in the house and eat."

Emily's face went white. "No, I must not. You are already in danger for seeing me. Anyone else who does is also in danger. Just let me hide in the barn for a while and rest."

"I'll go get some food from the kitchen then. Stay here. I'll be back soon."

The girl started up from the bench, her face ashen-hued. Gerd put his hand on her shoulder and smiled. "Do not be afraid. You are safe here, I promise." He went to a shelf and pulled down a thick woolen blanket. "Wrap yourself in this. It still gets cold at night in these parts."

Emily took the blanket with a grateful glance.

"Stay here, I will return."

Gerd went into the house. Magda was in the living room sewing on a quilt. She looked up as he passed. "There is hot soup on the stove and fresh bread on the table. Sit and eat."

Gerd shook his head. "I will take something out to the barn. One kid is very thin, and I want to make sure it is nursing. I will eat there."

Magda shook her head and smiled. "Maybe Jakob Knepp was right. Maybe you need a family so you could take care of your *kinder* the way you take care of those goats."

Gerd went on into the kitchen and poured hot soup into a tin. He cut some slices of bread and cheese and grabbed an apple from the barrel. "Don't wait up, *Mütti,* I may be late coming to bed."

"All right, son, all right."

Gerd went out the back door and made his way to the barn. The girl jumped up when the door opened, but she sank back down when she saw it was Gerd. He brought her the food and placed it beside her. She looked up, the blanket wrapped around her, her hair disheveled, her face drawn, but to Gerd, she was beautiful.

"There is a barrel of fresh water by the door and a basin if you wish to freshen up first."

She smiled a shy smile and went to the barrel. Her movements were sure and smooth, and she carried herself with poise. "Don't look, please," she said. "I need to take my sweater off." Gerd turned away. Her heard the rustle of her sweater slipping off and the splash of the water as she filled the basin. Gerd could hear her slosh the water on her face with a gasp. He smiled.

"I forgot to warn you, it is cold."

"Cold? It is like a Greenland glacier."

She washed for a few more minutes, and then Gerd heard the rustle of the sweater sliding back on. "I'm decent now."

Gerd turned. Emily was standing in the lantern's light, the straw brushed from her hair and her face brighter, more alive. She twisted her long black hair up in a bun behind her head, and the strong lines of her face were now very prominent.

Her deep green eyes were almost unworldly—her nose was straight and her jawline firm. She smiled, and her teeth were straight and white. He stared at her.

"What?"

He turned away, embarrassed he was blushing. "Come, Emily. Eat the soup while it is hot. You must get your strength back."

She sat down on the bench and began to eat. She ate as she had done everything else, with poise and grace, no movement wasted.

Gerd got up his courage. "Excuse me, but may I ask you something?"

"Yes?"

"Are you a dancer?"

Emily looked at him with a curious smile on her face. "Yes, but how did you know?"

"Just the way you carry yourself. I saw a ballet dancer once and you remind me … I snuck away to watch a troupe when they came to Zweibrücken, I should not have done so."

"*Ja*, why not?"

"I am Amish, we try to keep ourselves from the world as much as possible. We follow the *Ordnung* and we—"

She looked at him and laughed. The sound was bells and fireflies and a brook splashing down a mountain cliff.

"Why do you laugh?"

"Because you are telling me everything about yourself, but you have not even told me your name."

He felt the heat of another blush.

This is foolishness. I have never blushed in my life. I am …

"Gerd. Gerd Hirschberg. That is who I am. This is my farm. I live here with my mother. But tell me about your dancing."

"It might be too worldly for you." She laughed again.

"No, please."

"I am nineteen. I began dancing ballet when I was five. When I was thirteen, Mary Wigman chose me to be her protégé. I danced in a company that featured *Ausdruckstanz,* Expression Dancing. I worked with choreographers like Rudolph von Laban and Mary, and our company was just beginning to gain international recognition when the Nazis came to power. They deemed our style of dance degenerate and disbanded our company. All dancing in Germany was now to be for the glory of the Nazis, but Mary would not go along. Rudolph, however, adhered to the Nazi ideals and become director of the national company. I traveled to America with Mary in 1933, but when we returned, it was to a different Germany. Mary still dances and choreographs under the Ministry of Propaganda, but she is not a Nazi." She picked up the bread. "Do you wish to know more?"

"I'm sorry, please finish your dinner."

She took bites of the bread and then went back to the soup with relish while Gerd sat without speaking. The girl eyed him while she ate. At last, she set the tin aside, wiped her mouth with a cloth and looked up. She started to say something but stopped.

"What is it?"

She drew a deep breath. "I need help. I need to get out of Germany. I have money, and I can pay you. If what money I have is not enough, I have something else of great value I will give you if you help me." She turned and reached into her bag. She pulled out a strange looking object that was golden and gleamed in the lantern light. She handed the golden thing to Gerd. It looked like a candlestick but had eight branches with cups on the ends and a ninth in the center.

"What is it? Gerd asked.

"It is a *menorat hanukkah,* a Menorah. It is pure gold. If you will help me, I will give it to you. My great-grandfather, who was a renowned goldsmith in Poland, made it."

Gerd stared down at the golden Menorah. The light from the lantern reflected off the many facets of the beautiful craftsmanship. It seemed almost alive in his hands.

Come to the light, Gerd, I am here. I am the light.

Gerd looked up, startled. "What did you say?"

Emily shook her head. "I said nothing."

Gerd shook his head. The warnings about Jews thundered in his head, but as he sat with this beautiful girl he did not care. He handed the Menorah back to Emily.

"I … I will help you … but I do not want your money."

Is this you, Gott? Is this you?

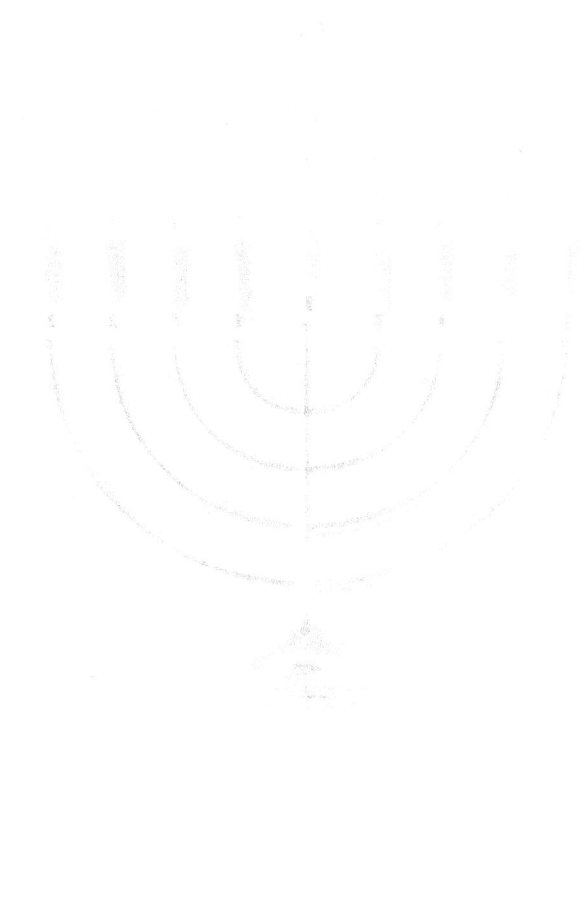

CHAPTER FOUR

A Refuge

After their conversation, Gerd made a bed for Emily in the hay and went into the house. His mother was in her room, and Gerd heard her praying as he passed the door. That night, phantoms filled his dreams—Men in tight-fitting black leather jackets with no faces chased him through the fields waving guns, shouting at him.

"Where is she, where is she?"

He woke before dawn, his sheets soaked in sweat and his stomach churning. He swung his legs over the side of the bed and sat with his head in his hands. The girl flustered him. She was a Jew, an enemy of the German nation—or so they said. He should report her. But she was also lovely, intelligent, and she needed help, his help.

I don't believe in accidents, Gott. You must have something in mind. Of all the farms in the Saar valley, she chose my barn to hide in. She could have picked Hans's barn or Ernst's but she is here, in my barn.

Gerd sighed, stood up and found his clothes in the semi-darkness. On most mornings like this, the first rays of the sun peeking over the eastern hills delighted him, and he loved the light fragrance of forsythia flavoring the day like a small spoon of sugar in a cup of black coffee, the eager greeting of his animals as he laid the hay and grain in their feeders. But today he was in a dark mood.

If I am caught harboring her, it will mean the camps for my mütter and me. I should give her some food and a map and send her on her way. Her being here can only mean trouble.

He remembered her eyes as she crawled in between the blankets he laid out for her—he had seen gratitude and hope in them before they closed and she was asleep. He stood for a very long time staring down at her face. In repose, she was exquisite—her face was a carved marble mask, symmetrical, perfect, but she was alive and her soft breath stirred a piece of straw beside her mouth. At last, he knew if he stayed, he would stay all night, just looking at her, drinking her in. He blew out the lamp and turned toward the door. As he laid his hand on the latch, a small voice came out of the darkness and stirred a fire in him he had never known.

"Good night, Gerd. Thank you."

Now he walked back and forth in front of the barn, thinking. He looked up at the sky. "What should I do, *Gott*?" he cried.

"Do about what?"

Gerd jerked around. Hilda Knepp stood there, looking at him. She had a shawl over her shoulders and a basket in her hand.

"Hilda! What are you doing here?"

She stepped back, a quizzical look on her face. "I come every day with something for your *Mütter*. Papa slaughtered hogs yesterday, and I have brought some hocks for her to make *Schweinshaxe* with. What's wrong with that?"

Gerd shook his head. "Nothing, nothing, except I thought we agreed you should stay home for now, until … until I come to speak to your father. We do not want to start gossip among the villagers."

Hilda laughed. Next to Emily's laugh, her sounded coarse and brazen, like a mule braying in a barn. "They are already gossiping, Gerd. They are wondering when you will visit our house in your courting clothes." She smirked.

"*Ja, Ja*, Hilda, I will come, but until then I think it is best that you stay home."

"What were you asking *Gott* about?"

"Uh … oh, that. It's personal."

"Don't you think we should share our personal things now? I mean, after all …"

"When we marry, Hilda, you will learn everything about me. I warn you though, you may not like what you find out."

Hilda shook her head. "What's wrong with you today? You are not like yourself."

Gerd was silent for a moment, staring at Hilda. The buxom blonde girl, who had once seemed attractive, now looked blowsy and cheap.

"Look, Hilda. The coming of the Nazis has changed everything. Christian has told me when he passes the village will make me the elder. I do not think I am ready for that. It troubles me, the responsibility."

"But all you need is a good wife by your side, a wife to help you and … give you children." She smirked again, and Gerd felt sick inside. *And lord it over the other women in the village because you are the wife of the elder and the mistress of the largest farm in Ixheim.*

"Hilda, give me the basket. I will give it to *Mütter*. Thank you and thank your father for us. I ask you to return home. I will come see your father soon."

Hilda frowned and handed over the basket. "When you come to see him, please bring the old Gerd." She turned and walked away with her nose in the air.

Gerd went into the house with the basket, his emotions in turmoil. His mother was preparing breakfast for him, some *Schwarzwaelderschinken*, some sliced Gouda cheese, and a large cup of coffee. She was slicing a large piece of pumpernickel bread. He hesitated as he sat down at the table.

"*Mütti,* I need to tell you something."

"What, Gerd?"

He looked up and hesitated.

"What is it, Gerd?"

"Someone is hiding in the barn."

She turned. "What! In our barn?"

"Yes, *Mütti.*"

His mother went back to the bread. "Well, tell them to leave. People can't just come and stay in our barn."

"I can't make her leave."

This time his mother turned clear around and looked. "Her?"

"It is a young girl, and she is a Jew."

Gerd's mother put down the knife she was using and moved to the table. "A Jew! But Gerd, you told me the Nazis forbid us to associate with Jews. She puts us in danger, she must leave."

Gerd shook his head. "There is more to it, *Mütti.* She needs help. The Nazis will send her to Dachau if they find her. They will kill her … or worse."

Magda looked hard at her son. Then she noticed something in his face. "Gerd?"

"I cannot send her away, *Mütti,* I must help her."

Magda sat down beside her son. "Gerd, what is it?" She took Gerd's face in her hands. He looked away, but she drew him back and stared into his eyes. "Look at me, son."

He struggled, but her hands were insistent so he surrendered. "*Mütti* … "

Magda gasped. "Gerd! What has happened to you?"

"I don't know, *Mütti*, I don't know."

"But you only met her last night."

"Yes, but … but … Oh, I don't know what happened. She is beautiful and intelligent and, I … I …"

Magda took Gerd by the hand. "Take me to see her."

"But *Mütti,* I promised …"

"Nonsense. I live here too. If we are to save this young woman, we cannot have secrets." She pulled him to his feet. "*Kumm.*"

Together, they went out to the barn. When Gerd entered, Emily was just coming to the door, her suitcase in her hand. "Gerd, I …" Then she saw Magda and stepped back. Gerd saw the fear in her face.

"I am sorry, but my mother—"

Magda stepped past Gerd and over to Emily. "Do not be afraid, my child. I am Magda, Gerd's mother. I made him bring me. We will help you, but you must withhold nothing from me."

"Help me?"

Magda chuckled. "My son hides nothing from me. He never has, and he never will. When I looked into his eyes, I knew he would help you, no matter what the cost. So, I will help too. What is your name? Where are you from?"

The girl hesitated and answered in a quiet voice. "Emily, Emily Weissbach." She looked at Gerd and then at Magda. "I am from Munich. My father is a lawyer, but he was involved with the Communist Party, and the Nazis came for him. They took him and my mother away and killed my brother."

Magda looked at Emily, then stretched out her arms. Emily hesitated and then stepped into the circle of love, tears streaming down her face. She sobbed as Magda held her.

"There, there, *mein kleines Mädchen,* it will be all right. You are safe here."

Gerd stood, shifting from one foot to the other, at once embarrassed and yet grateful to his mother. The sobs subsided. Magda reached into her pocket and pulled out a clean linen handkerchief. Emily wiped her eyes and blew her nose. She looked at Gerd.

"I will leave. I have put you in danger, and I do not want any harm to come to you … or your mother." She glanced at Magda.

Gerd shook his head. "You cannot leave now, it is too dangerous. You should stay here for a week, two perhaps. The French will not come—they are afraid of the Germans. If they weren't, they would be here already. Soon, the Germans will know this and will not be so vigilant. Then we can get you into France."

"But you can't hide me from your neighbors for two weeks."

Magda smiled and took the girl by the arm. "Yes, we can, but if anyone asks, you are my cousin Freda's daughter, Emily, and you are here to visit us for a fortnight. You are from Weisbaden, not Munich, and here to visit your Amish kin. Your family is Mennonite, so Gerd will tell you about us—who we are and what we believe. Gerd is right. The Germans will relax their guard in a few weeks, and we will be able to get you across the border. Until then you will stay with us."

Emily looked at Gerd. "But … but …"

Magda took her by the arm. "It is settled. Now come and eat breakfast."

CHAPTER FIVE

A Light For The Darkness

Emily sat at the table and ate quietly. When she finished she looked up at Gerd. "Are you sure this is what you want to do?"

Gerd nodded. "I think Gott has brought you to us for protection. Beyond that, I only know our faith tells us to strengthen the weak hands and the knees that are feeble, and make straight paths for your feet, so the limb which is lame may not be put out of joint, but be healed."

Emily looked surprised. "You know the *Mikra?*"

"What is the Mikra?"

Emily smiled. "It is the Jewish holy book. It contains the *Torah*, which are the teachings of Moses, the *Nevi'im*, the books of the Prophets, and the *Ketuvim*, the writings, what you call the Psalms and the Proverbs."

"I do not know Mikra," said Gerd. "That verse is in the New Testament of the Bible, in the Book of Hebrews."

"Book of Hebrews? I have read a little of your Bible, but not this Hebrews. That verse is in Isaiah the prophet's writings. He says, 'Strengthen ye the weak hands, and confirm the feeble knees. Say to them *that are* of a fearful heart, be strong, fear not: behold, your God will come *with a* vengeance, *even* God *with* a recompense; he will come and save you.'"

Magda laughed. "I can see you two will have much to talk over. But first, we must do something about you. You cannot say you are Mennonite if you do not look Mennonite. I have some old clothes that will fit you. I wore them when I was a young girl. In those days, I was as shapely as you are, Emily, but the years have added some padding here and there."

To his surprise, Gerd blushed again.

"*Kumm,* Emily. Let us be about your transformation."

An hour later, Emily was a Mennonite girl. Magda had given her some things and sent her into the guest bedroom to change. When she emerged, she was no longer the modern-looking girl of the night before. In place of the dark sweater, skirt, and hiking shoes was a long, pale-blue skirt buttoned up at the side, a plain dark-blue blouse with long sleeves, and a dark scarf.

Gerd noticed the clothing did nothing to hide her beauty.

You could dress her in a pair of overalls and she would still be lovely.

"I found no zippers anywhere, Magda," she said as she adjusted her skirt.

Magda laughed. "And you will not. Although we abandoned hooks and eyes long ago, the non-Amish still call us *Häftler*. You will only find buttons." She handed Emily a pair of wool shoes. "And these will keep your feet warm, but they are not for outdoors. I have some rubber boots for that. Now, go sit with Gerd. He will tell you of our ways."

Gerd and Emily sat at the kitchen table together. Gerd started. "My family came to Ixheim in 1648 from Switzerland. Back then, we were Mennonites. My great-great-great-grandfather built this house and the barn where I found you. We have farmed here ever since. We were Mennonites when we came, but now, we are Amish. We are still Anabaptists, in that we do not believe in infant baptism, but we follow Jakob Amman, not Menno Simons. We have set ourselves apart from the world, and we have a very strict set of guidelines we follow to keep us on the right path. We call them the *Ordnung,* and we have passed them down from generation to generation.

Emily nodded. "Much like the Law of Moses in the Torah. Are your laws written in a book?"

"No, but our elders have been very careful to keep the *Ordnung* pure, because they provide our community's foundation."

"What are some of these rules?" Emily asked.

"Well, Amish men do not wear beards until they are married, marriage can only take place between baptized members of the church, we do not use modern conveniences such as automobiles or gasoline engines, we do not get involved in politics, and we cannot divorce our spouses. But the most important thing is we do not take part in any form of violence."

Emily nodded. "What happens if you violate these laws?"

"If the offender will not repent of their sin, we excommunicate them—what we call *Meidung* or shunning. Then they are in the *Bann.*"

"What happens to them?"

"We keep them separate from the community. We may not eat with them or ride with them or accept gifts from them. They cannot attend church. The community will still give them help if they need it, and we can converse with them, but until they repent, they cannot be a part of community life."

Emily frowned. "This sounds very harsh."

Gerd laughed. "That is what the Mennonites say, and that is why we are no longer part of the same church." He paused. "But these are simple rules, and no one will question you on the articles of your faith. Now tell me about you."

Emily's eyes flashed. "What do you want to know?"

"Well, for one, I want to know about that candlestick, it's beautiful."

"It's not a candlestick, it's a lampstand. The Menorah uses oil instead of candles. This is a *menorat hanukkah,* a Hanukkah Menorah."

"Hanukkah?"

Emily laughed at Gerd's struggle with the word. "Hebrew can sound harsh, Gerd. Many of the words sound like the speaker has a bone caught in his throat. It's spelled with an 'h' but you pronounce it as though it has a 'ch' in the beginning."

"What is … Chanukah?"

Emily laughed again. "That's closer. Hanukkah is the Festival of Rededication. It celebrates the cleansing of the Temple in Jerusalem after its defilement by the Syrian Greeks under Antiochus Epiphanes. It's also called the Festival of Lights. The Menorah is the lampstand God commanded Moses to put into the Tabernacle, which later became the Temple. Most Menorahs only have seven branches, but you see this one has nine. That is to commemorate a great miracle associated with Hanukkah."

"Miracle?"

"I would have to tell you the whole story, Gerd."

Gerd looked at the girl. In that moment, he realized he wanted to know everything about her—her childhood, her family, her religion, if she belonged to anyone …

I don't want her to belong to anyone; I want her to belong to …

"Gerd?"

"Please tell me the story, Emily."

She cocked her head with a quizzical look on her face, a gesture that Gerd would come to know well.

"Please."

Emily sighed and nodded. She rose from the table and went into her room. She returned in a moment with the

Menorah and set it on the table between them. A stray beam of sunlight filtered through the window curtains and fell upon the lamp. The gold surface reflected the beam in a flash of light.

I am the light of this world!

"What?"

"I said nothing, Gerd."

She cocked her head again, and he realized she captivated him—the way she moved, the beauty of her face, the light in her eyes.

"Shall I go on?"

Gerd nodded.

Emily picked up the lamp and revolved it slowly in her hand. "Ever since the days of the Babylonian captivity, one country after another conquered Israel. In 329, Alexander the Great conquered the Jews. After he died, his generals divided his empire into four parts, and Israel became a pawn between the Egyptians and the Syrians. In 167 BC, the Jews of Judea rose in revolt against the Syrians who were the current overlords. The Syrians tried to eradicate the Jews and all their customs including keeping the temple holy. They vandalized it and even sacrificed a pig on the great altar in the Holy of Holies. This enraged the Jews, and under Judah Maccabee, the Jews conquered the city. They set about to cleanse the temple, a process that took eight days. But they only had enough consecrated oil for one day. As the story goes, the Menorah kept burning for all eight days. They say it was a miracle of God."

"Do you believe the story, Emily?"

"Well, I am not so sure, but I know enough of my people believed to make the eight days into a festival of its own, even though Moses did not include it in the Torah. And they created the *menorat hanukkah* with its nine branches to commemorate the eight-day miracle."

Gerd took the lamp and stared at it. "But what is the ninth cup for?"

"It is the servant cup. You light it first, then light each of the others from it. Each night another cup is lit until all of them are burning on the eighth night."

"So this feast of Dedication, it is in December?"

"Yes. We have observed the Feast of Dedication for thousands of years celebrating God's protection and the victory he gives his faithful people who continue to worship him in the face of persecution."

"Such a time as this, perhaps?"

Emily's face paled. "Yes, such a time as this."

"In our Bible, there is a mention of the Feast of Dedication—in the Gospel of John, the tenth chapter." Gerd rose and fetched his Bible off the bookshelf. Thumbing through the pages, he came to John and turned to the tenth chapter. "Ah, here it is. 'Then came the Festival of Dedication at Jerusalem. It was winter, and Jesus was in the temple courts walking in Solomon's Colonnade.' This is the chapter where Jesus claims to be one with the Father."

Emily's eyes widened. "Such a claim is blasphemy to the Jew. The Torah is very clear. 'Hear, O Israel: The Lord our God, the Lord *is* one!' This Jesus cannot also be God."

Emily's face was lit with an inner fire as she spoke. Gerd could not take his eyes away. Finally, he spoke. "May I ask a question?

"Yes."

"You said your father was a communist, yet you know so much about the Torah and your faith. How is this?"

"My father decided that to be German, he must put away his Jewishness. He wanted to become 'assimilated.' During the Weimar Republic, he associated with Walter Sholem, intrigued by the communist theories Sholem was putting forth. The Nazis arrested Sholem as soon as they came to power, but my father had not been high in the party, so they did not come after him right away. If he had not continued speaking out against the Nazis …" She paused and looked away for a moment. When she turned back, there was a glint of tears in her eyes. "My mother tried to go along with Papa in his beliefs but in her heart she was an observant Jew. So despite my father's objections, she taught me about my faith."

"So she taught you about Hanukkah?"

"Yes, and we celebrated every year. For my father, the occasion was more cultural, but the celebration held deep meaning for my mother. She used to say, 'The miracle of Hanukkah shows that Israel is the light of the world.' My mother firmly believed the nation of Israel will be born again, which will be proof to the world that the Jews are God's chosen people." Emily picked up the Menorah and stood up. Her face was haggard. "I am tired, Gerd, I did not sleep well last night. I think I will lie down for a while."

Gerd nodded. He watched as Emily walked away.

I am the light of the world. Jesus said that of himself. Perhaps the Jews and the Amish are much closer than we know.

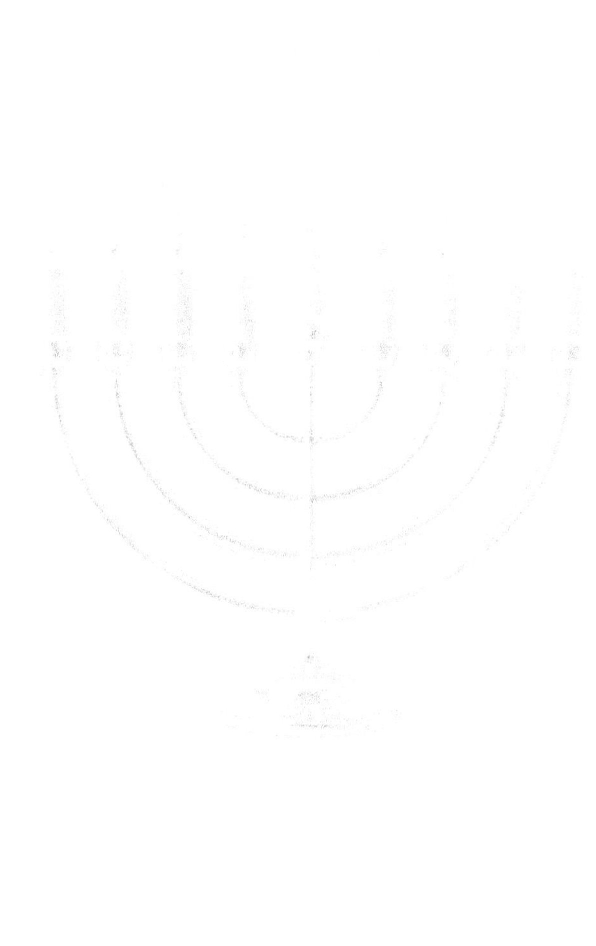

CHAPTER SIX

Hearts Entwined

Now the days passed in a blur. To Gerd, it was as if Emily had always been there. Her smile, her voice, the lithe and lovely movements of her body, the way she cocked her head when she was thinking, all this filled Gerd's waking thoughts and swept through his dreams. He went about his work, but it no longer was the routine of drudgery he once faced each morning, but in every task he saw meaning and purpose. Gerd became more in tune with the cycle of the land and watched with newfound joy as his crops began to burst forth from the ground. His thoughts became focused on the Creator of the universe at work all around him, and they quickened him with a new understanding of his place in the great warp and weft of the days flowing around him like a river.

And instead of finishing his work in the quiet moments of a simple meal with his *mütter* and then the quick fall into an exhausted sleep, he came home from the fields to a house filled with laughter and the aroma of dishes Magda had not cooked in years filling the house, as his mother showed Emily how to prepare them. The two women would giggle like schoolgirls sharing secrets, and Gerd wondered if they were talking about him. After supper, Gerd would sit up with Emily and they would converse into the small hours, but when he awoke in the morning, he was refreshed and ready for the day.

Life flowed back into the house, a life that was born and radiated forth from the Jewish girl's innermost being and filled Gerd's days with unimaginable joy and his nights with peaceful repose. The world outside seemed far away, the Nazis and soldiers in the towns and villages were merely unwelcome visitors and his world —the simple ways, the fields, the growing crops, the land itself pulsing with life—became centered in the girl in his home, hidden away and safe.

Though they did not dare go far from the house, Gerd and Emily began walking to the knoll and sitting together as the crisp March evenings passed into the star-filled nights of early April. Often they spoke together, but tonight, they were silent, sharing the moment, yet trembling on the brink of some great turning in their lives. At last, as a dove called a melodious note to warn its mate to return to the nest, Gerd turned to the girl beside him.

"Emily ..."

She turned and her face reflected the growing rose of the clouds above. The luminous green eyes opened wide, set like emeralds in her alabaster face. There was a question in those eyes and on her lips. "What is it, Gerd?"

But he could see she knew what his words would be, for he saw the answer in those wonderful eyes. His strong arms lifted, and she was in them as close to him as she could come. She turned her face to him, the question gone, replaced by a beseeching and a touching of their souls through their eyes. His lips found hers and they were embracing—the fire and smoke that once flowed from newborn mountains at the creator's command enveloped and consumed them.

Hours later they came back to the house, awed by the stillness of the night and the enormity of the road they had stepped upon. She brushed his fingertips with hers and went up to her room. Gerd went into the kitchen. Magda was there, shelling some early peas from the garden. She looked up and smiled. "When will you marry Emily?"

Gerd stopped in surprise, taken aback by her words. He laughed and shook his head. "How well you know me."

"This means you will leave the church. Have you considered that?"

"What if Emily becomes Amish?"

"She is a Jew, Gerd. She loves her faith. She will not convert. You can help her understand her Messiah has already come. But no, she will not convert. So you will go to the elders and tell them you will marry this Jewish girl, and Christian will weep, for you are taking his dream away. You will go to Hilda and tell her, and she will hate you with a burning hate. We may have to leave our farm and find a new life far away. And that is the path you have chosen. But I will walk it with you as long as I am able."

Gerd was silent at his mother's words. The wisdom in them weighed down on him like boulders pressing upon his chest, but the weight was not enough to make him cry out. He knew the hands of this Jewish girl held his life and his future, and he would not turn his back on what *der leiber Gott* had given to him. "Yes, *Mütti,* that is the path I have chosen."

"No, Gerd, you cannot."

The soft voice surprised him, and he turned. Emily was in the doorway, tears upon her face. "I cannot let you give up everything in your life for me—your farm, your faith, your community, your future. I will leave tomorrow, and I will find my way to France."

Gerd stepped toward her but she raised her hands and moved a half-step back. "No Gerd, please …"

Gerd pushed past the upraised hands and took her in his arms. She was trembling like a leaf in a storm and tears ran down her face. "No, Gerd, no …" Her arms came around him, and she was weeping and holding him with a strength that would have crushed a lesser man.

He caressed her hair and kissed her on the cheek. "You will not leave me, Emily. *Gott* has sent you to me. We will find the way through the darkness."

"You what?" said Christian Guth.

"I have met the girl I want to marry."

"Hilda?"

"No, Christian, not Hilda."

Christian Guth rose from the chair he was sitting in. "What do you mean? Is she Amish? Where did you meet her?"

"I found her in my barn. She was hiding from the Gestapo. She is a Jew."

Christian's face paled, and he sank back down. "A Jew," he whispered. "A Jew?" he said again as though he had never spoken such a word.

"Yes, Christian, she is a Jew."

"But … but … you cannot marry a Jew. You know what the Gestapo said. Anyone who aids or harbors a Jew will suffer the same fate as they do. It could bring destruction down on our whole community. And what of the *Ordnung?* It forbids you to marry someone not of our faith." He began wringing his hands. "Gerd, you will go under the *Bann* if you do this."

"I have considered that."

"You would throw away everything you have—your faith, your community, your position as elder?"

"I will have her, and she is enough."

"But if the Nazis find out …"

"How will they find out? Will one of us betray me? She will live under my roof as my wife, and things will go on as they are until it is safe to get across the border. If people ask, I will tell them she is the daughter of my mother's cousin. Then when we can leave, we will go to France."

"Your farm, Gerd. What of your farm?"

"I will sell it to Hans. He has often hinted he would buy it if I ever tired of farming. It would make him the largest landholder in the Saar Valley."

"Your mother?"

"She knows and will go with us. She loves Emily as I do."

"How long has this Jew been with you?" He spit out the word.

"Since the day after the Germans came."

"Three weeks? You have known her three weeks, and you want to marry her? I am not hearing this," said Christian. "This is insanity."

"That may be, but it is what I will do."

Christian tried a different tack. "Ever since your father died, I have been like a father to you. I am asking you not to do this. I have decided you will take my place when I die. Everyone expects it. I expect it."

Gerd shook his head. "You are like a father to me, Christian, and I will always love you for that. But I never agreed to your plan for my life. *Gott* has sent this girl to me and I will not go against his will."

Christian rose from his chair, his face flushed. He shouted at Gerd. "His will! His will! How would an ignorant, stupid boy like you know God's will? I am the elder, and I will tell you what God's will is! You must send this woman away, forget you ever met her and let things go back to the way they were. You will marry Hilda, and you will become the next elder."

Gerd looked at Christian as he ranted. When he finished Gerd stood up. "I cannot put her away. Our love has already gone too far to do that."

"What? You … you … you have been intimate with her?"

"Yes, Christian, I have been intimate with her. That is why we must marry as soon as possible."

"So you add sexual sin to your litany of transgressions? You will repent now and forget this madness or you will go under the *Meidung.*"

"I will not repent."

"But what about your vows?"

"You forget, Christian. I am not yet baptized into the church, and I have not taken those vows. My life goes a different way."

"Well, since I have not baptized you, I cannot place you under the *Bann*. But you will be as a stranger to us. You will have no relationship with the Amish of the village. We will not do business with you, and you will not be part of our community activities."

"But you do business with the other non-Amish. Why will you treat me so?"

"To teach you a lesson. You know the *Ordnung*, and you are violating it."

"That is too bad, Christian. I hoped you would help me with this."

Christian stood and went to the window. "Violation of our laws separates you from Gott, with no hope of redemption."

The law does not save you, Gerd.

"What?"

Christian turned. "I said …"

"Not what you said, Christian, what *Gott* said."

"And now you are a prophet?"

"The *Ordnung* does not save you, Christian. Only Jesus can do that."

"What!"

"The righteous shall live by faith. It's in the Old Testament and the New. There is no difference between the Amish and the Jews who try to keep the Law of Moses. We all need a Messiah, Christian."

Christian began trembling, and he choked out his words. "This Jew has bewitched you, Gerd. You have lost your mind. Get out of my house!"

Gerd felt a great sadness rise in him—sadness because he was leaving the things of his boyhood behind, because he was giving up his home and community, and because he had lost the friendship of someone he thought would always love him.

If any man will come after me, let him deny himself, and take up his cross, and follow me.

Gerd stood at the door and looked back one more time at the old man who stood with his back turned.

I will follow you, Lord, though I do not know the way.

Then he stepped through the door and out into the world.

CHAPTER SEVEN

New Life

"So you wish to marry?" The gray-haired man smiled up at Gerd and Emily from behind his cluttered desk. He had a kind face.

"Yes, Pastor Jügens." Gerd looked at Emily, and she smiled and nodded.

"Well, Gerd, I am surprised you come to me. Won't you marry in the Amish church?"

"I have decided not to continue in the Amish faith."

A look of concern crossed the Pastor's face. "I have known your family all my life, Gerd. Your father and grandfather were friends of mine. I cannot imagine a Hirschberg who is not Amish in Ixheim."

"Yes, Pastor, but that is what I have chosen."

"Does it have anything to do with …" he looked over at the girl.

"Emily, Pastor. My name is Emily, and yes, the problem is me. I am not Amish."

"Oh, I see now, Gerd. Emily is not Amish and Elder Guth refuses to marry you?"

"Yes, Pastor, that is the heart of it. I have come to you because you have always been a good friend to our family and I know I can trust you."

"Trust me with what?"

"Emily is Jewish."

The words crashed like heavy stones onto a metal floor. The pastor looked down, took off his glasses and passed his hand over his eyes. Then he looked back up. "You were right to come to me." He got up and went to the door and checked and then paused at the window and looked out. "The Nazi regime has not assimilated all the Protestant churches. Since you have trusted me, I will trust you. I am a member of the Confessing Church. Deitrich Bonhoeffer is one of our leaders. We decry the populism, the *Deutchland über alles* heresy that has overtaken the German church. Anti-Semitism is everywhere in Germany now and contradicts what the apostle Paul says about the Jews." Pastor Jügens sat down at his desk. "I will help you, Gerd. Though you put us in great danger. If the Nazis find the girl, they will take her to the camps, and you will go too." He shrugged, "And me."

Emily spoke up. "How do we get around the Nuremberg laws forbidding mixed marriage?"

The pastor smiled. "Actually, I think God has given you a window of opportunity. The Germans are preparing for the Olympics—scheduled for Berlin this summer. Foreign reporters and observers have flooded the country. Hitler is trying to make it look like Germany is peaceful and everything is perfect, a German utopia. He has ordered his officials to relax the discriminatory laws and remove all anti-Semitic signage and newspapers from public places. If we go today, we can get the license. I have a good friend at the city office—he will not be so particular with his questions."

"Won't we need birth certificates?" Gerd asked.

"Yes, do you have them?"

"Mine is at home, but Emily …"

"I brought mine when I left Munich," Emily said. "I thought I might need it when I got to France. I have my passport too, from when my dance troupe went to America."

Pastor Jügens nodded. "Excellent, excellent. We should have no problems. Get your birth certificates and meet me at the *Standesamt.* You must marry before the official, and then, we can have a private ceremony in my church …" he paused and looked at Emily. "If it is all right with you."

Emily paled.

"What is it, Emily?"

"Nothing. It's just I always hoped my father and mother would be at my wedding, and I would watch my husband smash the glass at the end of the ceremony."

Gerd moved to Emily's side. "What is this smash the glass?"

Emily wiped a tear from her eye. "In a Jewish wedding at the end of the ceremony, we wrap a glass in a cloth, and the husband steps on it. It symbolizes the Roman destruction of the Temple in 60 AD. It is a reminder that even amid joy, we recall the pain and losses suffered by the Jewish people. And there is more. Marriage is a covenant. In Judaism, we make a covenant by cutting or breaking something. At Sinai the tablets were broken—at the wedding, broken glass cuts the covenant."

Pastor Jügens nodded. "I have been to Jewish weddings, and I always wondered." He stood and put his arms around Gerd and Emily. "*Kumm, meine Kinder,* we have things to do."

Three days later, Gerd Hirschberg and Emily Weisbach stood in the small chapel of Pastor Jügens's church and repeated their vows. Magda stood beaming by the pastor's wife. At the end of the ceremony, Gerd took Emily in his arms and held her as though he would never let go. "*Du bist ein Geschenk Gottes,* a gift from *Gott,* and his goodness amazes me."

Emily kissed him on the cheek. "And you have saved me. I was lost, and you found me. Thank you, Gerd. I will always love you." She kissed him and held him, and in that moment, he knew a great love that burned him with ferocious heat but did not destroy him.

Like Moses at the burning bush ...

He nodded to his mother, who handed him something wrapped in a cloth. Gerd put it on the floor, raised his heel and smashed the glass hidden in the folds of the cloth. Emily gasped and began to cry.

"What is it, my love?" Gerd asked.

"You, Gerd. You are so kind. This makes the day perfect—well, almost perfect."

"What is missing, Emily?"

"Just this," Emily said, and she stood on her tiptoes to whisper in his ear.

"What?"

Emily blushed and nodded. Gerd felt tears start in his eyes. He said nothing but his heart was bursting with the blessings of this day.

Hilda Knepp stood outside the church in a drizzling rain. Through the window, she could see the happy couple embracing, and the few guests gathering around to offer congratulations.

This Jew witch thinks she can come into my world and steal the man I was to marry? But she does not know me. I will not go without a fight. She will regret the day she ever set eyes on Gerd Hirschberg.

Hilda turned and walked away into the gray drizzle.

That evening Gerd and Emily walked together, their hands entwined and their shoulders touching. The rain had stopped, and the world seemed fresh and alive with sounds and fragrances Gerd had never noticed before. They passed a brilliant yellow bush and the light fragrance lifted to Gerd's nose like a passing thought. Emily smiled. "The forsythia only smell that way after a rain. They were my mother's favorite plant."

The green low hills of the Saar basin rolled away on all sides. Gerd's gaze took in the Hirschberg farm—the house, set in a sheltered swale, the barn behind it, the knoll that had become their special place.

"Gerd?"

"Yes, my love?"

"Can't we stay here? I love this land."

Gerd looked around him—this farm was all he had ever known. As a young boy, he had followed his father from place to place, learning every aspect of the work—the plowing of the fields, the care of the animals, harvesting the crops. And as he pictured his childhood, the thought came to him he had never really loved the work, but work was the way he garnered his father's approval and recognition. When he failed at something, his father was harsh in his quick condemnation, so Gerd had learned to focus, to concentrate on his tasks and in that way to draw forth his father's meager approval …

Like poison from a wound …

He shook his head. "I don't think it will be possible. When I looked in the *Oberführer's* eyes the day the German army came to Ixheim, I saw evil. The Jews have already had their rights taken away, and although Hitler has relaxed his anti-Jewish ranting for the moment, I do not think this time of grace will last. But we still cannot cross into France for we have my *mütter* to consider, and it has only been six weeks since the Germans came. They are strutting along the border daring the French army to push them out of *das Rhineland.* But I do not think the French will come. So we will wait until the Germans are less vigilant and then we will go."

"But this is your home, Gerd."

"My home is where you are, Emily." He paused and turned to her. "I must confess to you I have only been a farmer because my father and grandfather and their fathers before them farmed this land. I only stayed here, stayed Amish, because I wanted to please my *Daad.* And when he died, I had to provide for my mother. But I have other dreams."

A look of surprise crossed Emily's face. "Other dreams?"

Gerd paused, and he was suddenly shy. He had never shared his heart with anyone in this way, not even his *mütter.* He took a deep breath. "Yes, I want to raise and breed horses. That is all I have ever wanted to do, but my father rejected the idea as too worldly. He told me I had to concentrate on farming because I was a farmer, and Amish, and that was all I ever would or could be. I raised Gunnar from a tiny colt. His mother died when he was born. He has been my only horse. But many times, I have wished I could breed him and populate this land with strong, beautiful horses."

Emily took Gerd's hand and laughed. The sound was a delight to Gerd. "It may take many years to discover everything about you, Gerd Hirschberg." Her face grew thoughtful. "When I was in America with the dance troupe, we traveled to Colorado. Oh, Gerd, you cannot imagine the beauty of the mountains there. It is as though the heavens and earth touch each other everywhere you look. And in the west of America, there are horses, beautiful horses. When we were going on the train, I saw men on horseback driving huge herds of cattle—the horses were small, but so agile, and the men riding them are called cowboys. It was as though adventure stories had come to life. Perhaps we can go to

America and go to the west. It is a big land, and it is a place where dreams can take root and grow."

Gerd took his wife in his arms. "Yes, Emily. Let us leave this place of war and beating drums and marching armies and go into the west. We will find a new life and we will build our dreams, you and me and … and …"

"Our baby?"

"Yes, beloved, our baby." They turned back toward the house, and as they did, the gray clouds opened and a dazzling sunset spread before their eyes. The moisture in the air reflected the light in a beautiful prism of color.

"Look, husband. God's promise is there before us. We will go into the west."

Gerd's heart beat fast and his body was alive as it had never been before.

Yes my love. We will go into the west …

CHAPTER EIGHT

I Am The Light

The next morning, Gerd told Magda the news of her coming grandchild. Magda went off humming an old German lullaby with a broad smile on her face. Emily came into the kitchen and sat down with Gerd. "Your *mütter* is happy, *Ja*? She is not ashamed of me?"

Gerd reached over and caressed the alabaster skin of her face. "She is your mother now too, and she loves you almost as much as I do. She knew from the first day I told her of you I had fallen in love with you. The night," Gerd blushed … "That night, when we came home from the hill, she asked me when I would marry you. She somehow knew we were already one in our hearts. No, she is not ashamed."

"And I love her too …" Emily hesitated, then put her hand on Gerd's arm. "Do you think she would mind if I put my Menorah on the kitchen shelf? It is the only thing I have to remind me of my home."

"Please, bring it out. We will give it a place of honor."

Emily went into her room and came out with the Menorah. Gerd placed it on the high shelf between his Mother's good china pieces. The morning sun coming in through the window caught the facets of the beautiful Menorah and lit the walls with golden diamonds. Emily sat next to Gerd as he sipped his morning coffee. As he gazed at the lampstand, he closed his Bible and looked at Emily. "Tell me more about the celebration that this candle …" he paused, "I mean, lampstand, represents."

Emily smiled. "The feast is Hanukkah, the festival of lights, and we pattern it after the Feast of Tabernacles. Tabernacles is one of the seven feasts of the Lord given to Israel to mark the important events of the year. The feasts start at Passover, which marks the day the Lord sent the destroyer angel over Egypt and killed all the first born in the land as a warning to Pharaoh."

Gerd nodded. "Yes, I've read about that. The Israelites marked their doors with the blood of a lamb and the destroyer passed over."

"Yes, that is right. There are five more feasts—Unleavened Bread, where devout Jews only eat the same bread the Jews ate when they came out of Egypt, The Feast of First Fruits when the people of Israel brought their first harvest to the priests at the temple and waved it before the Lord, and the Feast of Harvest, which celebrated the summer harvest. I think Christians call it Pentecost."

Fifty days after I rose from the dead …

"Fifty days after First Fruits?"

Emily cocked her head. "Yes, how did you know that?"

Gerd shrugged. "I must have read it somewhere…"

Emily went on. "After that come the three most important feasts in September or the Jewish month of *Tishri*. First is the Feast of Trumpets, what we call *Rosh Hashana*. It marks the first day of the Jewish New Year, and the Rabbis blow the Shofar. Beginning on *Rosh Hashana*, there is a ten-day period known as the *Yamim Nora-im,* Days of Awe. Nine days after the first day we observe *Yom Kippur,* the Day of Atonement. That is the day where Jews ask for forgiveness of sins committed during the year. When the temple still existed, this was the day that the High Priest entered the Holiest place and brought the blood of a sacrifice and asked God to forgive all the sins of Israel."

Without the shedding of blood there is no remission of sins.

"That reminds me of a Scripture from the Book of Hebrews."

Emily smiled at Gerd. "You mention this Book of Hebrews often. I think I must read it."

"What about the Feast of Tabernacles?"

"The Feast of Tabernacles often goes by another name, 'The Season of Our Joy.' The feast reminds us that God is the Great Shepherd who dwelt among his people, to protect and bless them wherever they wandered. Every Jew looks for the day when God will come back to his people and save them, as he did in the days of Moses. We chant the *Hallel*, the psalm of praise, during the celebration in the synagogue and wave palm branches."

"Palm branches?"

Emily nodded. "Yes."

Like Palm Sunday when Christ rode into Jerusalem …

"How do those psalms go?"

Emily thought for a moment. "Well, I don't have them all memorized, but the ones I like are 'Save now, I beseech thee, O Lord: O Lord, I beseech thee, send now prosperity. Blessed be he that cometh in the name of the Lord: we have blessed you out of the house of the Lord.'"

For I say unto you, ye shall not see me henceforth, till ye shall say, blessed is he that cometh in the name of the Lord …

This intrigued Gerd. "I know that Scripture, but it is in the book of Matthew. So why is Hanukkah patterned after this feast?"

"During the time of the Maccabee revolt, Antiochus defiled the temple and no Jew could go into it to celebrate Tabernacles in September. So two months later, when they recaptured Jerusalem, the Jews celebrated Tabernacles in December. They spent eight days cleansing the Temple, and then celebrated *Sukkot* by waving palm branches and chanting the Hallel. Ever since then Jews celebrate Hanukkah and the Feast of Tabernacles in much the same way. **The** *menorat hanukkah* is lit in the homes of observant Jews to commemorate the miracle of the lights when the Maccabees restored this important Feast."

Gerd sat for a moment. "I think we have much in common, wife, though our worlds are so far apart."

Emily blushed and lowered her eyes. "Wife," she whispered.

Gerd took her hand and bowed his head. When he lifted it, he could feel tears on his face. "I am thanking God for you, today and every day, my Emily. You have given me much to think about. For the first time in my life I feel that *Gott* himself is speaking to me—through you."

A week after the wedding, Gerd went to Hans Gingerich. Hans saw him coming through the field between their farms and motioned him into the house. He looked nervous. "Gerd, it is good to see you. I … I …"

"You don't want any of the village to see me here, right?"

Hans shrugged. "Christian has forbidden all of us to speak to you, but you have been my best friend since we played in my father's apple orchard, so I welcome you. Sit down, I will get us some coffee."

Hans brought coffee and sat across from Gerd. "Do you remember sitting here waiting for a piece of my mother's *Stöllen?"*

Gerd smiled at the memory. "So you know what has happened, Hans?"

"You will marry the Jewish girl? Christian told us."

"We married a week ago." Gerd saw the look of dismay on Hans's face. "Do not worry, Hans, we are leaving in a few days. That is why I have come. I want to sell you my farm."

"Your farm? But Gerd, there have been Hirschbergs on that farm since the 1500s."

"Yes, and now there will not be Hirschbergs there." He shrugged. "Things change, Hans. *Gott* has sent me a wife, and he is moving me out of the rut I have lived in all my days. He is opening up something new and wonderful in me. Every day I am with Emily, I discover how little I know about him. I feel like nothing in my life has been real until now." He looked at Hans. "Do you want the farm? I give you a fair price."

Hans nodded. "I will buy the farm. Gunnar too?"

Gerd hesitated. Gunnar? Gunnar was the best horse in the Saar valley, but there was no way to get him to America. "Yes, Gunnar too, Hans."

Hans shook his head. "Now I know you are going away, or you would not sell Gunnar. Where do you go?"

"We will go to America."

"America? But this is so far. How will you get there?"

"I do not know yet. I must get to France first. Once we are there, we will be safe and can figure everything else out."

"What will you do without land?"

"I will go into the west of America, find some land, some good horses, and raise them."

"Horses! *Ja,* Gerd, you have always loved them." Hans reached across the table and took Gerd's hand. "I will miss you."

"Ah, but Hans, now you will have the biggest farm in the whole valley, and your dream will come true. You will have a second house where your sons and grandsons can live."

Hans laughed out loud. "If I ever find a wife that is." He shook his head. "No one knows me like you, Gerd."

Gerd stood. "I am only taking a few things. I am leaving the furniture so you can do with it as you wish. All the tools are in the barn—you know where they are. I must go now."

"I will bring the money tomorrow, Gerd."

"*Ja, Gut.* Tomorrow then." Gerd rose and turned to go.

"Gerd?"

"You must be careful."

"Careful? *Ja*, the Soldiers…"

"Not of the soldiers, Gerd, but of the Amish." Gerd turned back in surprise.

"The Amish?"

"Ja, Gerd. The Nazis think the Amish and the Mennonites are the purest Aryans of all the Germans…"

"Because we come from Switzerland, *Ja?*"

"Ja. So they have held a few meetings where they have been shouting about the superiority of the German nation, how we are the highest race of men, and the Mennonites are at the top. Many of the pompous asses in the village have swallowed the bait, hook and line. Now, they go about with swelled heads looking down their noses at anyone who is lesser than themselves. They have already driven the Gypsies out of the valley."

"But the gypsies are the best people with horses. Who will shoe the farmer's teams?"

"They will have to figure that out, for the Gypsies are gone. The Nazis called them subhuman, so the Mennonites joined in driving the *Romani* out. Now they are looking for Jews."

"Do you think they would betray me? These are people I have known all my life."

Hans hesitated. "Hilda Knepp …"

"What about Hilda?"

"I have seen her in the *Oberführer's* company."

"The fat one?"

Hans nodded.

Gerd laughed despite the tightening in his stomach. "I would expect no less of her. She will find a bed to sleep in where she can trade her body for a place of importance. But the *Oberführer?"* He laughed again.

"But she hates you now, Gerd, and she has made that plain. She has been planting seeds among the villagers who sympathize with the Nazis. I will come as early as I can. You must not wait a few days, for that will be too late, I think. You must be ready to go as soon as I bring the money. It is no longer safe for you in Ixheim."

No longer safe in Ixheim? How can this be?

"Thank you, Hans. I will be ready."

CHAPTER NINE

Betrayed

The next morning, Hans came to the house early. "We must go into the village to sign the papers, Gerd. It should not take long."

Gerd went inside to get the deed to his land and told Emily and Magda to finish packing. "We will leave tonight when it is dark. Take only what you can carry. I will return soon." He went out to find Hans looking over the fields.

"Are you sure about this, Gerd?"

"*Ja*, Hans. It is time for me to go."

The two men walked down the path to the village where they went to the office of Johann Schweitzer, an attorney who had handled Gerd's legal matters for years. After an hour, the transfer of property was complete, the money exchanged. Gerd pulled his attorney aside. "Johann, I am leaving Germany. I want you to keep the money until I contact you from France. Then you can wire it to me."

Johann put his hand on Gerd's shoulder. "I have known you since you were a small boy. I will miss you. I hope you find happiness in your new life, and I will do everything you ask."

"Thank you, Johann. I will contact you soon."

The two men embraced, and then, Gerd left the office headed toward the farm. As he crossed Han's field, he saw a caravan of black cars accompanied by a truck full of German troops moving up the road toward his house.

Emily!

Gerd ran through the field, jumped the fence, hurried up the path and burst into the house. Emily and Magda were standing ashen-faced in the front room. Gerd grabbed them. "The Germans, the Germans are coming up the road. We must leave."

"I'm afraid it is too late for that, *Mein Herr.*"

Gerd jerked around. *Oberführer* Heinrich Glauss walked out of the kitchen, a smirk on his face. "Sooooo! The man who will not fight has committed treason against the Third Reich. To marry a Jew …" he gestured at Emily, "… is not allowed. Now your idyllic days as an Amish farmer working for the glory of Germany are over, *Herr* Hirschberg. And it is such a shame, for your race is pure, and you could have been in the forefront of a ruling race of men. But …" he shrugged, "… you and your wife will take a journey. We have a camp at Dachau that is full of people just like you." His face bulged and flamed red. "Traitors! Cowards! Sub-humans and filth. The world will be better off when we are rid of you." He advanced toward Emily and grabbed her arm. "Too bad, for you are beautiful. If I didn't want to foul myself, I would bed you …"

"Take your filthy hands off my wife or I'll kill you."

Glauss turned in surprise. "*Und zo!* I thought the Amish were pacifists. Amish do not fight."

Gerd stepped up and delivered a powerful blow to Glauss's face, knocking him to the floor. He stood over the man, flexing his hands. "That's true, but I am no longer Amish."

Glauss screamed from the floor. "Guards! Guards!" Blood was streaming from his broken nose. Soldiers came running into the room. "Take them to Saarbrücken and put them on the train to Dachau."

"What about my mother?"

Glauss pulled a handkerchief from his pocket and dabbed his nose. "You have proved me right. I said you would fight, and you did." He glanced at Magda. "I am not a cruel man. I have need of someone to cook and clean for me, and since your mother is not the one who married the Jew, I will show mercy by giving her a place in my house."

You mean by making her your slave!

Gerd looked at his mother. As Glauss turned away, he mouthed the words, "I will come back …"

Magda nodded. The soldiers grabbed Gerd and Emily and shoved them out the door. As Gerd passed the *Oberführer's* car he saw Hilda Knepp sitting in the back seat, a look of raw hatred on her face.

If I could reach you now, Hilda …

Gerd and Emily stood on the platform of the Saarbrücken train station with a group of haggard looking people. Soldiers carrying guns surrounded them on all sides. A light rain had come through an hour before, and Emily shivered next to him. They had been there for hours and now at last, around midnight, a train with four or five boxcars was pulling in. Next to Gerd stood a tall, husky man in a ragged coat with an unkempt black beard. His hair was uncombed and wild, and he was missing some teeth. A strange odor arose from his clothes. Emily grimaced when he came and stood next to them. He smiled, but Gerd looked away.

He looks crazy.

The man smiled again. "I know I don't look so good. I looked better before the Nazis threw me in jail … and smelled better, too. And I had all my teeth then."

Gerd looked back. The man, despite his wild appearance, had a kind face and piercing eyes. Gerd swallowed his distaste and reached out his hand. "I am Gerd Hirschberg. This is my wife, Emily."

"I am Joshua, Joshua Rosen."

Emily looked up. "You are Jewish?

Joshua nodded. "*Ja.*" He looked around. "Most of these people are Jews also, and many of them are communists. *Herr* Hitler has little tolerance for either, I'm afraid."

Emily looked closer. "You are Joshua Rosen from Munich?"

"*Ja,* the very one."

"You know my father, Émile Weissbach?"

Joshua looked closer and a broad grin creased his battered face. "Why, it's little Emily all grown up. Yes, I know Émile. We were comrades together on the front lines of the Revolution with Werner Sholem. I have been to your house in Munich often, but long ago, and you were much younger. Also, I have not been a Communist for many years."

Emily cocked her head. "You haven't? I thought you all swore to die for the revolution."

Joshua smiled. "Yes, but I found another way, a better way."

Gerd looked at the man. His face lit up and what had been a marred landscape seemed to shine with an unearthly light. "Yes, I found …"

There was a shouted command, and the doors on the boxcars up and down the line slid open with a crash. The soldiers began to shout. "*Reinkommen. Beeil dich. Schnell nein.* Get in! Get in! Hurry!" The soldiers behind them began to herd them toward the boxcars. Many in the crowd cried out, but the soldiers kept shoving. When they got to the boxcar, Joshua jumped up into the open doorway, then turned around and gave his hand to Emily as Gerd boosted her up. When they finished loading everyone onto the cars, the soldiers slammed the doors shut. Bodies jammed together in the darkness, but Joshua wrapped his arms around Gerd and Emily and herded them to a corner where they slumped down with their backs to the wall. The train whistle blew several short blasts and began to move, at first slow, then faster as they pulled out of the station. They were on their way to Dachau.

The train traveled through the night. After a few hours, the faint light of dawn came through some cracks in the walls of the car. The train began slowing and blasting its whistle. Gerd rose and squinted through a crack. "We are coming into Stuttgart. I saw the sign. The train looks like it is pulling off onto a siding."

The train stopped with a jerk. There was a rattling at the door, it slid open and a guard stuck his head in. He grimaced and leaned back. "You stink like animals," he shouted, "but what can you expect of Jews? *Raus mit dir. machen Sie es schnell.* Everyone out! The commander gives you ten minutes to do your business."

The people in the cars clambered down, and the soldiers herded them off a few yards onto the dirt. "Go," shouted one soldier.

Emily blushed. "Here? But they will all see."

Joshua took off his coat and made a shield, and Gerd stood on the other side. When Emily finished, they did the same. Then the soldiers herded them back onto the train. But they remained on the siding. Soon, Gerd could hear another train coming, going the opposite direction.

"It is a troop train," he said. "It is full of soldiers probably headed for the German border."

They sat on the siding for many hours as more troops and equipment clattered by headed west. At one point, the guards opened the doors and handed in big milk pails full of water and some tin cups. The people in the boxcar shared the water and then handed the pails back out. They were let out to stretch their legs.

Gerd watched as the young soldiers laughed among themselves and made fun of the prisoners. "These soldiers seem friendlier than the ones I met in Ixheim."

"Look at them," said Joshua. "They are only boys. This is all a lark for them, a picnic. They are the vanguard of the great Germanic kingdom, and they are all puffed up with themselves."

"They do not fear a war?"

Joshua shrugged. "They do not understand. Most of them weren't even born when the Great War ended. They never saw the death and destruction, the millions killed. I was in the infantry. I saw the horror of the Somme firsthand. Thousands of men being blown to bits, parts of bodies everywhere in the mud." He shook his head. "These children knew the hard times of the Weimar, but then Hitler came and everything got better. He is a God to them. He is restoring Germany to greatness. They are Germans and easily pushed into arrogance. They will all have a sad end, I am thinking."

Soon the sun went down and darkness began to grow. As a final train went by, two trucks rolled up. Soldiers in black uniforms got out. A man in an overcoat with a death's head emblem on his cap walked up to the commander of the guards and spoke rapidly in German. The commander saluted and shouted orders to his men, who went to the trucks and got in.

"Shutzstaffel," hissed Joshua, "SS. "This is not good."

The man with the death's head shouted at his men, and the SS troops began pushing everyone back into the cars. The doors slammed shut, and the train began to roll. Joshua was silent.

Emily whispered to Gerd. "I feel sick. It is probably the pregnancy. I will try not to throw up."

Joshua looked at them. “She is not feeling well?”

Gerd shook his head. “She is nauseous. I think it is the baby.”

“You will have a baby?”

Emily smiled. “Yes, but not for a while.”

Joshua looked at Gerd. “You are not Jewish?”

Gerd shook his head. “No I am … I was Amish.”

Joshua smiled. “Now, that’s something. A Jewish girl and an Amish Christian, both under the law, both going to Dachau, and their law cannot save them.” He laughed uproariously.

Gerd frowned. “I don’t see what is funny.”

Joshua calmed down and put his hand on Gerd’s shoulder. “I’m sorry, I did not mean to offend. It seemed funny at the moment.”

Emily spoke up. “You said you are not a communist anymore. Are you a practicing Jew?”

Joshua hesitated. “Well, yes and no.”

“What does that mean?”

“I am still a Jew, and I am observant. I celebrate all the feasts and long to go to Jerusalem. But I have added something.”

Just then the whistle blew, and the train jerked. As the train began to pick up speed, Emily shouted over the noise. “What have you added?”

Joshua grinned. “I have found my Messiah.”

The train sped on through the darkness.

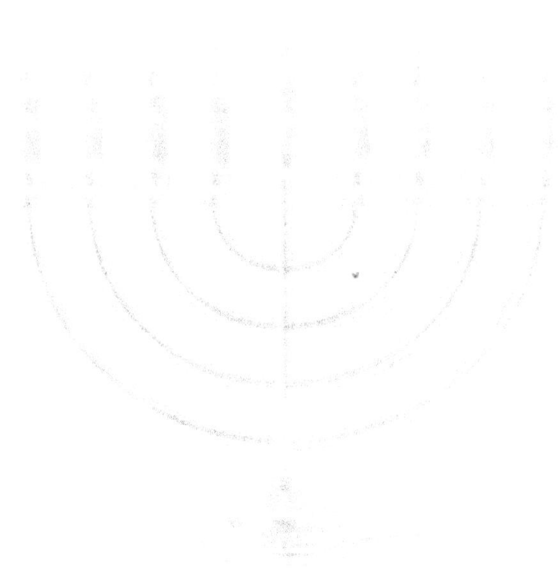

CHAPTER TEN

Who Has Believed Our Report?

It was late in the night when a hoarse whisper followed by a hand shaking his shoulder awakened Gerd. "Gerd? Gerd?"

He had been dreaming of horses. He was astride a huge black stallion running like the wind down a gravel road, the horse's hooves pounding out a relentless rhythm. He awoke to the clacking of the train wheels on the track.

"Gerd?" It was Joshua. "I found something. I was sitting here and something kept poking my backside. When I looked, I found water has rotted a big section of the floorboards. I worked at it and got a big chunk out. I think we can pull up enough of the floor to crawl out."

"Crawl out?"

"Yes. We must escape, and soon. I do not feel good about these SS troops. Something bad will happen I think. You don't want your wife and baby to end their days in a Nazi concentration camp or worse, do you?"

"No."

"Then help me pull these boards up. We must do it while the train is moving or the guards will hear." Joshua scooted over and showed Gerd the place where the floor was rotten. It looked like the floor had been getting wet for a long time. There was a hole where Joshua had broken some pieces out.

"Here, pull up hard on this one. Wait until the wheels hit a joint in the track." The two men waited until they hit a joint and then pulled. The board came up.

"*Gut!* Now this one."

Again the two men waited until they hit a joint and then jerked. This time an even bigger piece came out. Three more times they waited and pulled, waited and pulled. Gerd looked at their handiwork. There was a large hole, big enough for even Joshua to crawl through, torn in the floor.

"*Sehr gut*, Gerd. The Lord is with us. Now we must pray the train will stop one more time before we get to the camp."

Gerd hesitated.

Throughout all of this, I have not even asked you for help, and now a Jew reminds me …

Gerd bowed his head. "*Du leiber Gott.* We ask you to stop the train one more time so we may escape."

"And we ask it in the name of *Yeshua Hamashiach,"* whispered Joshua.

Gerd started to ask him who that was, when there was a blast on the whistle and the train began to slow.

"Thank you, Lord," whispered Joshua. "Gerd, wake Emily!"

Gerd shook Emily awake. "What, Gerd …?" but Gerd put his hand on her lips.

"Shhh, Emily. Make no sound," he whispered. "We are going. You must be silent and do as I say. Joshua has found a way for us."

The train came to a halt. Gerd could hear the SS guards gathering on the door side of the train. Joshua grabbed his arm. "Now, Gerd. Climb through and help Emily. Roll to the dark side of the train and then head for the nearest cover you can see. Just get away. I will be right behind you."

Gerd swung his legs over the edge and Joshua lowered him until his feet touched the gravel bed. Emily came right behind, and he lifted her down. They rolled away from the light and stood up once they were out from under the train.

"This way, Gerd." Joshua's voice almost pushed them in the dark. His hands were strong on them as he guided them toward a clump of trees. They slid down the bank and crawled into the tall grass under the branches and lay there for a moment. They could see the legs of the prisoners as they climbed out on the other side of the train. Commanders shouted orders as the soldiers lined up all the prisoners. Gerd caught his breath and started to get up when there was a burst of machine gun fire. Joshua grabbed him and pulled him back down. All up and down the line of train cars, machine guns burst into action. Gerd could hear the people screaming, see them falling. Emily gasped and put her hands over her face. Joshua held them both down.

"Do not move, or we will meet the same fate."

In a few moments there was silence, broken by an occasional moan followed by the quick bark of a pistol. A light rain began to fall, muffling the gunshots.

Emily sobbed. "They were never taking us to the camp. They were bringing us here to kill us."

Joshua nodded his head behind them. "We must get further into the trees and run. We have to get as far away as we can."

They wiggled backward through the grass and the low-hanging branches until they could not see the train. Then they stood and ran through the woods.

After an hour, they came out of the woods into a clearing. The rain had ceased, and the moon had come out from behind the clouds. Gerd saw a building looming up in front of them. In the moonlight, he could see it was a barn—the door hung on one hinge and there were holes in the shingled roof. Joshua motioned for Gerd and Emily to stay. He crept forward across the clearing until he reached the side of the barn. Gerd watched as Joshua peeked over the sill of an open window and then, ducked down. Once more he raised his head, but this time he stayed up and motioned for Gerd and Emily to come. They crossed the clearing and stood looking into the barn.

Joshua motioned toward the door. "The barn is empty. We can rest here for a while, but not too long. I don't think the guards would have noticed we were missing, but you never know. And there are plenty of other soldiers around so we have to keep moving."

Gerd pushed the door open, and they went inside. There was a large mound of hay and Emily sank down in it. Joshua placed his coat over her, and in a moment, she was asleep. The two men looked around the barn. On a shelf in the back, Gerd found several candles and some matches. The matches were old, but at last, he got one to ignite and lit a candle. He held the candle up and looked around. Out of the darkness, a hand pulled his arm down. "Be careful with the light, Gerd. We don't know where we are or who could be watching."

Together, the two men searched the barn. In a bin in the back, they found some dried ears of corn, but the real treasure was a cache of canned goods they found hidden in a tool chest.

Joshua held up the cans of stew and vegetables. "Someone did not enjoy being forced by the Nazis to cook an *Eintopf* every Sunday and give the savings from their one-pot meal to charity. Better for us. But we need something to open it."

Gerd reached in his pocket and pulled out a small clasp knife. "Glauss was so angry after I hit him he did not search me." He took a can, punched a hole in the lid and widened it until he could get the contents out." Come, let's wake Emily and eat. Then we must go."

"Where will we go, Gerd?"

"We return to Ixheim, get my mother and sneak into France."

"That's your plan?"

"If you have better, tell me."

Joshua shrugged. "I guess that's the plan."

Gerd went over to Emily and roused her. The three fugitives sat on the floor and shared a small meal.

Joshua handed them each two ears of the corn. "Take the dried corn in your pocket. You can suck on the kernels, and they will soften."

After they finished, Emily spoke to Joshua. "In the train, you said you had found your Messiah. What did you mean?"

Gerd nodded. "Yes, and you prayed in the name of Yeshua Hama … hama …"

"*Yeshua Hamashiach,*" said Joshua.

The words puzzled Gerd. "Who is that?"

Joshua smiled and reached in his pocket. He pulled out a folded piece of paper and spread it open. "Let me read you something." He peered at the paper. "Who hath believed our report? And to whom is the arm of the Lord revealed? For he shall grow up before him as a tender plant, and as a root out of a dry ground: he hath no form, nor comeliness; and when we shall see him, there is no beauty that we should desire him. He is despised and rejected of men; a man of sorrows and acquainted with grief: and we hid as it were our faces from him; he was despised, and we esteemed him not."

Gerd stopped him. "I have heard this Scripture. It is from Isaiah."

Emily shook her head. "I know Isaiah well, this is not from Isaiah."

Joshua smiled at Emily. "Yes, Emily, it is. It is Isaiah, chapter fifty-three."

Emily frowned. "But I know Isaiah, and I have never heard this."

"That, my dear, is because your rabbi never read it in the synagogue. Chapter fifty-three is called the forbidden chapter.

When they come to Isaiah 52:13, they end the service. The next *Shabbat* they start at Isaiah 54."

Gerd looked at Emily. There was a strange expression on her face he could not read.

"But why," she said.

"Because, Emily, it tells us who our Messiah is."

"What?"

"Yes, I was like you. I was waiting for Messiah. When I was in prison, they put me in a cell with a pastor from the Confessing Church. He shared this with me and wrote the words on this paper. When I heard, and he explained it to me, I knew that I, along with all of Israel, had missed a Messiah who was right before our eyes. Now, I carry this with me always. Listen, and tell me who you think this describes." He continued. "Surely he hath borne our griefs, and carried our sorrows: yet we did esteem him stricken, smitten of God, and afflicted. But he was wounded for our transgressions, he was bruised for our iniquities: the chastisement of our peace was upon him; and with his stripes we are healed."

Gerd felt something like a shock run down his spine.

No one ever explained this to me.

Joshua went on. "All we like sheep have gone astray; we have turned every one to his own way; and the Lord hath laid on him the iniquity of us all. He was oppressed, and he was afflicted, yet he opened not his mouth: he is brought as a lamb to the slaughter, and as a sheep before her shearers is dumb, so he openeth not his mouth. He was taken from prison and from judgment: and who shall declare his generation? For he was cut off out of the land of the living: for the transgression of my people was he stricken. And he made his grave with the wicked, and with the rich in his death; because he had done no violence, neither was any deceit in his mouth.

A light was dawning in Gerd's heart. "But this describes Jesus Christ, his suffering, and his death. I have never seen this before."

Emily frowned. "You said this Jesus claimed to be one with God. That cannot be! It is blasphemy. Our Rabbi called Jesus, Yeshu, the Christian."

Joshua nodded. "Yes, Emily, but he was not a Christian, he was a Jew. There were no Christians before 300 AD. He is Jesus the Messiah, *Yeshua Hamashiach*."

Gerd remembered a verse. "I am not sent but unto the lost sheep of the house of Israel."

"Yes," said Joshua. "God sent him to the House of Israel. He was their Messiah. In Daniel chapter nine, it is very clear the Messiah would ride into Jerusalem before they destroyed the second Temple and suffered death. That had to happen before 70 AD. Only Jesus fits."

Emily cocked her head. "Is there more?"

Joshua smiled and read on. "Yet it pleased the Lord to bruise him; he hath put him to grief: when thou shalt make his soul an offering for sin, he shall see his seed, he shall prolong his days, and the pleasure of the Lord shall prosper in his hand. He shall see of the travail of his soul, and shall be satisfied: by his knowledge shall my righteous servant justify many; for he shall bear their iniquities. Therefore will I divide him a portion with the great, and he shall divide the spoil with the strong; because he hath poured out his soul unto death: and he was numbered with the transgressors; and he bare the sin of many and made intercession for the transgressors."

Gerd stared at Joshua.

Seeing then that you have a great high priest, that is passed into the heavens, come unto God by him, seeing he ever liveth to make intercession for you, Gerd ...

"What?"

Joshua looked up. “I said nothing, Gerd.”

Then from outside, they heard a truck rumbling up the road.

“It is the Nazis,” cried Emily.

“Someone saw our candle and told them,” said Joshua.

The three fugitives jumped to their feet. The sound of the truck grew louder …

CHAPTER ELEVEN

Hear, Oh Israel

The roar of the truck grew louder. Emily grabbed Gerd's arm. "What must we do, Gerd?"

Joshua took the two of them by the arms and dragged them to the back of the barn where there was a small door. "I will go out the front. When you hear them give chase, go out the back as quickly as you can. Run, like the wind."

Gerd shook his head. "No, Joshua, I cannot leave you. They will kill you."

"And if you stay, they will kill you too, and Emily and Adina."

"Adina?"

"Your little girl. I have no one. My wife and children are gone. I have only *Yeshua*, and I will go with him." He handed Gerd the folded piece of paper. "Take this and go!"

Joshua went to the barn door and waited until he heard the truck slowing. He turned and smiled. His broken face was beautiful to Gerd. Joshua raised his hand. "The Lord bless you and keep you; the Lord make his face to shine upon you and be gracious to you; the Lord lift up his countenance upon you and give you peace." And then he was gone.

They heard someone outside shout. "*Halten! Stoppen Sie. Hände hoch.*"

Gerd opened the back door. No one was there. "Come, Emily, run!"

Together, they ran out the back toward the woods. In the distance they heard shouts and the sound of many running feet. Then there was a shot … another … then a burst of shots … then … silence.

Gerd ran with Emily, not knowing where they were going, not caring. Tears streamed down his face. They burst through a tangle of brush and onto a road. "Which way, Gerd?" Emily whispered.

"West. I think it is this way." Gerd led her down the road. In about fifteen minutes, they came to a farmhouse. A box truck stood in the road in front of the house. An old man was loading some bags from a cart into the back. They tried to walk past, but he called out. "Are you lost?"

Gerd hesitated, but Emily answered. "Yes. We were on a motor trip, but we followed the wrong road. Our car broke down. We left it down the road and are trying to find a town …"

The old man stopped what he was doing and walked over. He looked at them for a long moment and smiled. "Not a likely story, *jünge Dame*. Perhaps you are lost in another way—from the Nazis, maybe? I saw them driving by."

Gerd's heart leaped, and he looked around for a way to escape. The old man put his hand on Gerd's arm. "Do not be afraid. No one in this whole area hates the Nazis more than I do. How can I help?"

Gerd looked at Emily. "We need to get to Ixheim."

The old man laughed. "*Gott ist gut.* I am taking this feed to Saarbrücken. I go right through Zweibrücken. I can drop you outside town, and you can walk to the village." He nodded toward the back of the truck. "Why don't you ride in the back? There's a pile of hay and your …"

"My wife," Gerd said.

The old man smiled. "Your wife can sleep in the hay."

Gerd hesitated, but the old man pushed them toward the truck. "If you walk, they will catch you. If they don't, it will still take you two days to get where you are going. Don't worry. I will get you there safely."

Emily took the old man's hand. "How can we thank you."

"Get away from the Nazis."

Emily lay in Gerd's arms as the truck rumbled down the road. Gerd glanced down and saw tears running down her face. "Joshua?"

"Yes. He gave his life so we could live. He disgusted me when I saw him on the train platform. He smelled, and his face was so ugly. I did not even recognize him, though I saw him many times in Munich."

He hath no form nor comeliness; and when we shall see him, there is no beauty that we should desire him …

"What?"

"I said nothing, Gerd."

"Wait." Gerd reached into his pocket and pulled out the piece of paper. "Listen to this, Emily." He began to read. "He hath no form nor comeliness; and when we shall see him, there is no beauty that we should desire him. He is despised and rejected of men; a man of sorrows, and acquainted with grief: and we hid as it were our faces from him; he was despised, and we esteemed him not."

"Joshua disgusted me when I saw him. I turned away, I … despised him, Emily. And yet …"

Emily took the paper. "Surely he has borne our griefs and carried our sorrows. He was wounded for our transgressions, he was bruised for our iniquities; the chastisement of our peace was upon him and …" Emily began to weep.

Gerd finished. "… And by his stripes we are healed."

Emily looked up. "Do you know what the Hebrew pronunciation of Joshua is, Gerd?"

"No."

"Yeshua. Joshua's name in Hebrew is *Yeshua*."

The words struck Gerd's mind like a blinding light. "Emily. *Du leiber Gott* sent a Jewish man named Yeshua to die for us. We despised him when we saw him, but it did not matter to him. He sacrificed himself so that we might live."

"*Gott* sent him? But why?"

Gerd pulled Emily closer. "All my life, I have tried to obey the rules. First, my father's rules, and when I was older, the *Ordnung*. I thought my obedience would give me right standing with God. I thought being Amish was my ticket to heaven. But it was not. I did not have peace or joy in my life, at least not until I met you. But being with you did not solve my problems either, and we found ourselves in a desperate situation. Ever since I met you *Gott* was trying to get our attention."

Emily nodded her head slowly. She looked up at her husband. "I was the same as you, Gerd. I learned the Law of Moses from my mother, but though I knew it, I could not live it. So I flung myself into the things of the world, dancing, entertainment, education …"

"The night you showed me the Menorah, Emily, I heard his voice. "He said 'I am the light of the world.' This Jesus, whom I have always seen as a stern judge, relentless in his criticism, was waiting for me always with grace and mercy extended. And he was waiting for you."

"Is it … could it be …"

"Yes, Emily. That is why *Gott* sent Joshua to us—to show us that Jesus is your messiah—and mine."

Hours later, they stopped. The old man came around and opened the canvas flap covering the back. "We are outside Zweibrücken. The way is clear. Go with Gott."

Gerd helped Emily down and led her off the road to a familiar path. It was dark when they reached the village, and Gerd could see a light burning in Christian's window. A woman came to the window and glanced out.

Hilda!

Gerd turned to Emily. "Wait here."

"Where are you going?"

I have some unfinished business with Christian and …"

"Hilda?"

"Yes."

"I am coming with you."

Gerd nodded. They went to the door, and Gerd pushed inside. Christian saw him and rose from his chair, his face pale. Hilda saw the look on Christian's face and turned. She threw her hands up and scrambled behind Christian. "Gerd! What are you doing here?"

Gerd walked into the room. There was no one else there. "Where is my *Mütter?*"

Christian pointed. "Still at your house."

Hilda was shaking. Her face was bloodless. "Don't kill me, Gerd. Heinrich plied me with wine and I …"

"Heinrich? You mean the fat little man who thinks he is *Gott?* You make me sick, Hilda. You have sold yourself, and you betrayed me for what? Thirty pieces of silver?" Hilda backed up as he approached. "No, Gerd …"

Emily came behind Gerd and took his arm. "No, Gerd."

Gerd shook his head. "No, I will not hurt her. She deserves to die, but instead, I will forgive her." He turned to Hilda, whose mouth was gaping open. "Yes, Hilda, I forgive you. Not because you deserve it, but because my Messiah commands me."

"Your Messiah?" Christian asked.

"Yes, Christian, my Messiah. His name is Jesus. For Emily, he is *Yeshua Hamashiach.*"

"Yes, of course, Jesus. He is the Savior."

"No, Christian. You do not know him as the Savior. You know the *Ordnung* as the Savior. All your life you have believed and taught that besides accepting Jesus, one must also repent and reform their life as a separate and additional requirement to attain eternal life."

"Yes, Gerd, that is the truth."

"No, Christian, it is not. There are no additional requirements. 'Believe on the Lord Jesus Christ, that he rose from the dead and you shall be saved.' Don't you understand?"

"But we need the *Ordnung.*"

"As a roadmap, perhaps, a guide. But it is not the light. He is the light. He always was and he always will be."

Christian stared at Gerd, his mouth open. At last he whispered. "What will you do, Gerd? The Nazis will find you."

"I am taking my wife and my mother, and we are going into the west. After tonight, you will never see us again. You can stay here and wallow in your racial superiority with this Nazi filth, but you will never find the Kingdom if you believe Herr Hitler is the king."

Christian stood. "Please, Gerd. Don't leave. I am an old man. There is no one to take my place. If you go …"

"And under what condition could I stay?"

"You must put away this woman, repent, and return to the fold. We will forgive you, and all will be well again."

"What, and marry her?" Gerd nodded at Hilda.

"Yes, or whomever, just as long as they are Amish."

Gerd stared at Christian for a long moment. He shook his head. "No, I will never do that. You see, Christian, in the end it's a grace issue. God sent his Son and through him bestowed his infinite, amazing grace on us. By grace we are saved, and that by faith. And yet you, with your conditions and rules and hardened heart, would take the grace away, and it would be amazing no more. No, Christian. I go where perhaps I can see grace at work again. I know it is not here." He turned to go but then turned back and pointed to Hilda. "You will keep her here. If she makes a sound or tries to leave before I am gone, I will forget my words."

Christian nodded.

Gerd took Emily's hand. "*Kumm mit mir, Frau.*"

They turned and walked into the night.

EPILOGUE

Four months later in early 1937, with no hope for someone to carry on as elder, the Ixheim Amish and the Ersntweiller Mennonites met and agreed to merge and establish a single congregation called Mennonitengemeinde Zweibrücken, the Mennonite Community of Zweibrücken, and the last Amish congregation in Europe ceased to exist. Gerd and Emily escaped to France with Magd,a and in the spring of 1937, Emily gave birth to Adina Hirschberg. Three years later in the summer of 1940, Gerd and Emily Hirschberg, their daughter, Adina, and Gerd's mother, Magda, came to the San Luis Valley in southern Colorado …

Gerd pulled off the road to watch a blood red sun sinking behind the mountains, mountains that touched the sky.

"You see, Gerd, the mountains …"

"*Ja,* Emily, just as you said. And look. There are the cowboys."

A group of men on horseback herded a band of small, wild-looking horses toward them. Gerd stood on the running board of their truck and watched the horses as they walked. Though small, he could see the strength in them. Their leader, a powerful looking red stallion, nipped at the mares, reared up and whistled a challenge. As he watched, enthralled, a man rode up to the truck on a rangy sorrel horse.

"Howdy, stranger. I can see by your truck that you're moving. Coming here?"

"*Ja,* I will purchase the Anderson ranch."

"That's a nice piece, partner. My place is just over that hill." The tall man leaned down. "Billy Roberts."

Gerd took his hand. "Gerd Hirschberg. A pleasure to meet."

"Say, are you German?"

Gerd nodded.

"I guessed by your accent. Some of your folks have a village near here. Nice people and good farmers. They call themselves Amish." Billy pronounced it 'Aaymish.'

Gerd looked in at his mother. "The Amish are here *Mütti.* Well, perhaps they are not as unforgiving as those in Ixheim. Maybe you will have friends in this valley."

"We'll see, Gerd, we'll see. *Ja?*"

Billy's horse nickered and Gerd thought of Gunnar.

"You going to farm?"

Gerd turned back to the cowboy and smiled. "*Nein*, no farming. We will raise fine horses."

Billy smiled. "Wal, ya come to the right place."

Gerd pointed at the herd. "Maybe horses like those. What are they?"

"Those are Mustangs. They may be little, but they are the toughest critter on four legs. They can go for days without water and bring a dead man home out of the desert."

Gerd laughed. He opened the door, took Emily by the hand and helped her out of the truck. Gerd and Emily walked together into the tall grass beside the road and looked at the land that spread before him. An evening zephyr rippled the prairie and moved away over a rise.

"Look, Gerd. It is like the ocean."

"We will put our roots down in this place, Emily. I will be a cowboy and we will raise these Moostang horses and also a fine family."

He chuckled as Emily blushed.

"And we will put your Menorah on our mantle, my wife. It will remind us that Yeshua is the light of the world, and that his light has guided us to this place. And at Christmas we will light the *menorat hanukkah*, and we will remember your people and think of the Jewish men who gave their lives so we might live."

The End

A CLOUDY DAY

WILLARD CARPENTER

AUTHOR NOTE

The journey begins on a very warm Tennessee day when I am asked, "Would you be interested in being in an anthology of Amish male authors"? My interest is piqued, and I find myself in a world of "contrasts" and "contradictions," mostly "contrasts."

I feel the sting of heat from the light tan of concrete under my bare feet. Bending over, I help Bud, my grandson, with his floats. I'm baking inside of my T-shirt and can't wait to get into the relative cool of the pool.

Down the stairs and relief. A quick dunk, I look around keeping the two boys in sight. My wife is nearby with my daughter, whose husband is deployed to Ukraine. My mind whirls at the ambiguity of the task at hand.

I look up at the clouding skies, my grandchildren splashing around me in the blue of the swimming pool at Fort Campbell. The contrasts become clear as a Blackhawk passes above, just below the gray, which is crowding out the light blue haze.

Contrasts—horses and buggies and Blackhawks. Thinking about a peaceful people, the Amish, on a post dedicated to keeping the peace through the art and science of warfare. I think of children in straw hats and bonnets versus swimming trunks and war machines. The list can go on.

Above me, the gray clouds birth a title for the story as I go to that special place no one knows about but those who write. In that place, my characters come alive—a study in contrasts. Jacob and Isaac, Amish farmers, meeting in a half-plowed field. Jacob and Isaac have discovered Jesus Christ, grace and salvation, and they are caught up in the contrasts of the reality of the *Ordnung*, the Old Order laws within the church, and their new awakening.

The Ordnung forbids the belief in salvation by faith alone, because to assume something of God's is considered proud and boastful. What has them in even greater trouble is the evangelizing. Sharing the good news of Christ and the *Englisch* Bible has caused the *Bischof* to become upset with them. He is locked in the old ways and permits only the Old German dialect and Bible . His congregation sings the hymns in the same old German. Works are the path to right standing with Gott.

With the threat of being shunned or being thrown out of the church and community on the horizon, they must decide—deny Christ or face a life alone without their church and community. Standing with the mule hee-hawing in the background, storm clouds pass over them. What will happen?

Hannah, daughter of Jacob faces her own contrasts and contradictions. Hannah is nearing the end of her Rumspringa *or "running around years." She has been free to "test" the world and has met and fallen in love with James, an* Englischer, *a boy outside the Amish faith. Her father and mother know very little about James. They don't know he is a soldier. To complicate matters, both her father and his friend Isaac expect she will settle down with Isaac's son, Abram.*

Hannah and Abram have been friends since childhood. The Amish have expectations of their women once they are baptized—become part of the community, marry and obey their husbands, bear many children.

Walking in a quiet wood, Hannah feels the warmth of James's hand in hers—James, who cares about what she thinks and her dreams. The warm Pennsylvania day in the small town of Honey Brook cools as a cloud darkens their sun. What is she to do?

I return to the reality of the sun stinging my back. I look around taking in all that is beautiful—the green of the grass just beyond the fence, the blue of the sky just above the trees.

I hear children playing, laughing and calling out. "Marco … Polo!" A lifeguard's whistle sounds as she calls out, "No running!"

Another dunk. Wiping away the water from my face, I pick up Bud and lift him high into the air. He laughs.

For a moment, as the gray gathers above, I think of the coming task. "A Cloudy Day."

CHAPTER ONE

Spring's Unplowed Fields

Under the pale yellow of his straw hat, Jacob is a man torn. Torn from community, church, family, and earth. As he tastes the salt of the sweat from his brow, he snaps the reins up in one brisk motion "He-ahh, go on there, Daisy!" The mule pulls hard and the plow cuts into the unturned earth of Jacob's tobacco field.

For the second year, Jacob is planting Connecticut broad leaf tobacco, used as wrappers for premium cigars. The planting always begins in late April or early May. The difficulties he is having with the Bischof are pushing his planting later into May, and he is still turning fields in mid-month.

Digging deep, the plow moves the earth aside in deep furrows. Straight lines prepare the fields for the crop destined to bring the cash to feed his family through another fall and winter and spring. Jacob looks ahead at the coming turn, then to his left at the unturned earth, which is but a moment away.

Jacob looks up at the scorching sun and wipes his brow. On the road by the fence, his friend Isaac is watching him. "Jacob," yells Isaac. He yells again, but louder, "Jacob!"

Looking over, Jacob returns the greeting, "Isaac, *Gut morgan!*" and he continues, "*Wie geht's?*"

The broken German passes between them as Isaac climbs the stile.

"*Gut morgan, gut, vera gut!*"

The two men greet each other with a holy kiss. "*Gott is gut*, Jacob!"

"*Ja*, he is," responds Jacob, steadying the mule. He wraps the reins around the plow handle. The shade of a nearby tree is inviting in the hot sun. A large red cooler waits beneath it. "I brought an extra sandwich, Isaac, I thought I would see you today."

The two men throw their straw hats on the grass under the maple tree, sit down and lean against it, the cooler between them.

"So, Jacob, what do you think will come of this meeting with the *Bischof*?"

Jacob looks at his mule, then peers into the distance, "I don't know. How could loving our Lord and Savior get us into so much trouble with the community, with the *Bischof*? How can our belief in salvation bring so much turmoil within our families?"

Isaac shrugs, Jacob goes on. "Mary has been very quiet, and Hannah also. Wife and daughter, they both don't understand, I do not wish to leave our church and community. I believe in the order of the *Ordnung*. I am happy being Amish. It is who I am."

Isaac wipes the sweat from his face. "It also tears Sarah. She fears the *Meidung*." The men open the cooler and take out sandwiches wrapped in wax paper. They share a thermos of cold water.

"Did I tell you about David?" asks Jacob.

"*Ne*," responds Isaac, "what of him?"

"He has accepted Christ as his Savior."

"Well, this is *gut, vera gut*!" Isaac looks over at his friend.

Jacob shakes his head, as his eyes glisten and a single tear rolls down his cheek, he whispers, "Jesus is *gut*, his will be done."

"*Was* are you planting, Jacob? Tobacco again?"

Jacob smiles. "Tobacco and a home garden for canning in the fall. Two rows of tomatoes, half of beans, corn, pumpkin, squash, beets, some flowers for sale, and lettuce. I'll get this done, and Mary will take care of it with the *kinder*. I can go back to the leather, then."

"Tobacco, pays well, Jacob?"

"*Ja*, there is a big demand for the Connecticut broad leaf for cigars. I don't see what they see in the liking of cigars, but it pays well. You should think on it, Isaac."

"Don't have time, the builder I work for is busy. I work morning to night with overtime on Saturdays now."

Isaac pulls an apple from the cooler and bites down. The crunch breaks the silence between the men. In the field, Daisy shakes off flies. The plowed earth has an essence all its own that only a farmer can understand. For the old order community, it takes on an even more significance as a gift from God.

The sun is high at noon. The two men look into the distant unknown.

Jacob stirs. "I have a field to finish plowing, Isaac, back to *Gott's gut* earth."

"*Ja, gut* day, and God's blessings to you, Jacob, and your family."

"*Danke*, Isaac, and you and your family also, blessings."

They both pick up their hats. Jacob shakes off a bug, one of many to come.

As Isaac walks off towards his buggy, Jacob unwraps the reins from the plow's handle, looks over his left shoulder. "Hee-ahh, Work to do, Daisy," as the reins snap again.

The mule lunges forward and in the distance, thunder cracks. A few clouds darken the otherwise bright blue skies.

The beauty of the past winter's grays and whites have long since disappeared, making room for the freshness of green buds on the tall great oaks and wide maples of Honey Brook. Just outside of town, a young girl with long blonde hair walks a well-known path. Because she is on her *Rumspringa,* Hannah wears jeans and a T-shirt to the nearby meeting place. Ahead, James comes into view.

They run towards each other, the gray twigs and crunching of crimson leaves cracking beneath their feet.

Hannah smiles as they come together in a warm embrace. It is late morning on Saturday, the same hot day her father is plowing the field. She leans back, looking into James's eyes and kisses him.

"James, *meine leibe*, I have missed you!"

James pausing, looks at Hannah, takes her gently by the sides of her head, looks deeply into her eyes, "I love you too, you!"

She looks down and sighs, as if relieved. She holds his hands with her own as she gazes back up into his eyes. "What are we to do, James?"

"Is something wrong? What do you mean?" James responds with a concerned look on his face.

"The time is nearing when I have to return to my community. My *rumspringa* is almost over." The smile has turned to a frown. Wrinkles furrow the sides of Hannah's down-turned mouth.

James frowns too. "Hannah, I have a commitment now that school is over. I have to report in October to Fort Sam Houston in Texas. We have spoken about this."

"*Ach!* Why is life so difficult? Why can't we just be together? You can't leave where you are going. I can't leave the community." Hannah throws her hands up in frustration!

"Hannah, never mind that now. I have a surprise. In a little while, I want you to meet me at the back of the firehouse in town."

"Ja?" Hannah's face lights. "*Was?* What are we doing?"

James pulls her close, whispers in her ear. "How about dinner at my home tonight? Meet my family?"

"Your family? Why?" Hannah's face brightens.

"Well, maybe they can help. Maybe they have some ideas we haven't thought of. Besides, they know about you, just haven't met you. They also don't know about you being Amish."

"This will come as a shock to them! I will be dressed plain." She hesitates. "*Maem* and *Daed* should let me go. I will say that we are going to dinner." Hannah looks up at James, smiling. She reaches around his neck, kisses him. "I just won't say where! What time?"

"Is five, ok?"

"*Ja!* Five is *gut!*"

James takes her by the hand and leads her through the woods. A tiny warm breeze moves the green of the trees about them. Birds chirp. The sound of a helicopter brings James to a stop. He looks up, smiles and squeezes Hannah's hand.

She smiles back. "*Was*?"

"I will fly one of those someday!"

They continue on through the woods. The cracking of the helicopter blades fades in the distance. James nods his head. "Yep!"

"How are you going to do that?"

"The Army has twenty slots every year where they allow MSC officers to go to flight school. I have one of those slots."

"What does that mean?" Hannah asks. "What is MSC?"

"MSC is Medical Service Corps Officer. Medical Service Corps Officers act as managers of medical facilities within the Army. I am on my way to flight school. When I have completed my training, I will fly medevacs. I will also be in charge of the men and woman who make up a medevac platoon.

Hannah's look speaks volumes to James.

She doesn't understand what I'm talking about!

"Hannah, if people are hurt, I fly to them, the medical personnel help them and put them into the helicopter, and I fly them to the hospital."

"*Ach!* Now I understand! You will do this for the Army, *ja?*"

"*Ja.*" He gets a playful smack on the arm.

They see his car ahead, his pace quickens as he pulls her the last couple of feet, flinging her around and against the white Honda. He presses himself into her and kisses her deep as she presses back into him.

"I love you, Hannah."

Hannah, breathless, responds in a whisper, "I love you, too."

From the barn, Jacob sees Hannah getting out of the car. As he brushes and cools down Daisy, he watches Hannah walk towards the house.

"Hannah! *Kumme bitte!*" He calls to her while pulling Daisy by the lead.

"*Ja, Daed,* I'm coming!" Hannah smiles as she runs towards him.

"*Ja, Daed. Was?*"

"Is this James, your friend, who just dropped you off?"

"*Ja.*"

"You are seeing a lot of him, are you not?"

"*Ja.*" She stiffens. "I have done nothing wrong!"

"I didn't say that you had. Only I noticed you spend much of your free time with him."

"*Ja. Und zo*?"

"Hannah, you are coming of age. It will soon be time to end your *rumspringa,* be baptized, find a husband, and begin your own life."

"*Ja, Daed*, I know!"

"Have you thought of this?"

"*Ja*, a lot!" She tries to change the subject. "*Daed*, can I ask what is going on with the church?"

"*Ne*! This is for me to deal with. None of your concern! Now about this James …"

"Yes, *Daed!* James would like to take me out to dinner tonight. Is it ok? I have so very little time left on my running around."

"Ok, don't be late! Tell your *mamm*."

"*Ja, Daed! Danke*!"

CHAPTER TWO

Solstice Longed For

The sun was edging toward the horizon as Hannah waited in the fire company's back parking lot for James. She wore a plain blue dress with a white apron and cape. She had her hair pulled back, covered by a simple white *kapp*. A bright smile showed as James's white car turned the corner onto Railroad Avenue and crawled the few feet to where she was standing.

As the car pulls into a space behind the firehouse, Hannah makes her way toward the now parked car

She throws her arms around James. "It's only been three hours, and I missed you so."

James nods. "Me too, Hannah, me too.".

Hand in hand, an older couple walking their dog pause as Hannah wraps her arms around her *liebe*. They smile as James kisses Hannah on the neck burying his face into some flyaway wisps of hair.

"You ready," he asks.

"Hmm, yes, I am." She looks up at the blue.

The white Honda pulls out onto Horseshoe Pike headed west. A short distance and they are passing Wimpy and Dee's, a little 50s diner. On any given Sunday, Amish teens can be seen in courting buggies making their way down the Pike to a singing.

They pass the diner with the old 1950s Chevy out front, and turn left onto Whitehorse Drive. James's house is two blocks down.

"James, James! Can you pull over for a second?"

"Sure, what's up?" James pulls to the side on a tree-lined stretch.

"James, I have dreams."

"I am certain you do. I hope you do. Are you ok? What do you want to say?"

"I liked school *vera* much, and I like to learn. I want what you have. I want to experience college also!"

James laughs. "You don't want to experience my college!"

Hannah turns to him. "You know what I mean, I'm serious."

"I see that!"

"I know I will have children, but I want to work. Not baking and keeping house. I want a career. I would like to become a nurse." She looks down and whispers, "*Ja*, I want to be a nurse." She looks up, bolder now that she has bared her heart. "I can't stand the thought of having to settle into the life expected of me. My father just reminded me of what is coming. *Ne! Ne*, not me!"

"You should be able to do whatever you want, Hannah, anything."

"We have been together for two years now, James." She looks down and James sees the tears on her cheek. "James, I love you. Can you see us together?"

James leans over the console and kisses her cheeks, reaches up and cupping her face wipes the trail of her tears with his thumbs.

"No more tears now. These things will work out," he reassures her, taking her into his outstretched arms burying his face into the top of her *kapp* again, whispering, "These things will work out."

"We're here!" James yells as he enters the front door with Hannah right behind him. A flurry as the family enters the foyer from the kitchen.

A woman, his mother. "James!" She turns to the girl. "And you must be Hannah. It is so nice to meet you. I'm Eileen. We have heard a lot of wonderful things about you. I don't understand why he hasn't brought you here earlier."

A man, his father. "James, why is that?" He takes in Hannah's plain dress. "Hannah, are you Mennonite?"

"No, I'm *Amisch*."

He turns to James. "She's beautiful. Very nice."

James looks at Hannah. "You are."

James's dad pats Hannah's shoulder. "You can call me Michael. Come into the living room. Let's get to know you better. Would you like anything to drink? Coke, ice water, tea, lemon aid? We have everything."

"No. Thank you, sir," responds Hannah formally.

"Dinner will be done shortly. Your father made pork on the grill, James."

James turns to his mother. "Thanks, Mom!"

Screams from the top of the stairs. Hannah looks up as two girls come bouncing down.

"Hannah! Hi. I'm Cecelia. I'm, or we're James's sisters. This is—"

The second girl interrupts. "… Constance, you can call me Connie. You are so pretty. James, why haven't we met her earlier?"

Cecelia makes a face at her older brother.

Connie joins in. "Yes, James, why is that?"

"But …" The hubbub flusters James.

The two sisters sit on the floor in front of the fireplace crossing their legs. Sandy blond hair and hazel eyes make them almost identical. They smile, looking at Hannah, then their father, then James.

The sunlight fades. Hannah looks at James's family.

They have endeared themselves to me already.

"Dinner is ready," James's mother calls out from the dining room.

"James, sit here with Hannah." They sit at his father's left. His sisters sit together on the opposite side, while his mother sits opposite his father.

"Shall we say grace?" James's dad begins.

All together, they begin, and Hannah, hands folded, bows her head and listens.

"Bless us, O Lord and these thy gifts which we are about to receive from thy plentiful bounty, through Christ our Lord, Amen. Lord, please bring peace upon Hannah while she is both here with us and away. Let her realize our love for her and bless her."

"Amen!" Everyone says one more time, smiling at Hannah.

"I'll have two of those dinner rolls, Sis!"

"Dinner rolls it is," acknowledges Cecelia, passing the rolls over to her brother, then looking up and smiling at her father.

Hannah interrupts, "Thank you."

"For what?" James' father wears a smile, his full attention focused on Hannah.

Smiling back, Hannah responds simply, "Your blessings."

"Oh, you are most welcome."

"Hannah, I want to hear all about your family," Connie begins while pulling a piece of pork onto her plate, "Ahh, a charred one, I love it that way. Yes!"

Eileen chimes in, concerned. "Connie, she just got here, let her catch her breath and take a bite of her food."

"It's OK, I don't mind. Our last name is Zook, my father is Jacob, and my mother is Mary. I have four brothers and sisters. Two brothers and two sisters."

"Are you the oldest, Hannah?"

"Yes, Mr. Longacre."

"Hannah's father is a leather smith." James adds.

"A leather smith? That's very interesting! Does he own his own business?" James's father asks.

"*Ja*. It's called Zook's Bridles. That's because most of what he makes are bridles for horses. My *mamm* makes baked goods and sells them at a local store along with flowers in the summer and fall. She also quilts. My younger *schwester*, my sister, Sarah, she helps my mother. She is just finished school. And my *bruder* Joseph, helps my *daed*. Sarah is beginning her *Rumspringa*."

Cecelia asks, "What is rum … rum …?"

Hannah smiles. "*Rumspringa*. It is the running around years. Amish children, before we baptize them into the church, get to go out in the world to see if they would like it better than being Amish. Most do not." She glanced at James.

As dinner ends, a quiet light rapid tapping comes from Hannah's plate. Everyone pauses and watches. The fork moves around the plate, collecting every bit of food, crumbs, and fluid. Except for the clicking of the fork, the table is silent. Hannah slows to an uncertain stop. She looks up and sees everyone gazing at her and smiles. As quickly as the smile appears, it goes. Hannah lays her fork down. She looks down at her hands in her lap.

"Hannah, it's OK," says James's mother

"I'm so embarrassed."

"Nonsense! Don't be! Your parents taught you very well to not leave food on your plate. We have German friends, and we know it is a German tradition. That's the first time we have seen it, though. Don't be embarrassed."

"I didn't know it was German. I know we do this. It is sinful to waste." Hannah looks up smiling. "*Danke,* the dinner, *vera gut, Danke*!"

"You are so welcome, Hannah," says Eileen with a smile. She looks at her son. "I like this girl, James.

James's dad rings out from the table's head. "We have dessert tonight. Chocolate ice cream and homemade chocolate chunk cookies."

"I helped mom make the cookies," Connie adds.

Eileen beams. "Yes, you did. That is why they are loaded with chunks of Hershey bars.

The gooey morphed chocolate cookies, small mountains of cake and chocolate bits, take center stage. Warmed, they melt the chocolate ice cream. There is silence as the cookies disappear, and then, the family pushes back from the table, groaning and smiling.

Saturday, the 18th of May. The full moon highlights Hannah's face as she steps out of her James's car. James gets out and walks around to her. The moonlight casts his shadow on the car. She looks at her future.

James moves her away from the door, closing it and pressing against her. Hannah rests her head back against the car smiling.

"Want to *kumme* in?"

"I can?"

"*Ja*, everyone is in bed, we are dating, and we can sit together on the sofa. I don't want tonight to end."

"OK," says, James.

A quick kiss and Hannah takes James by the hand and leads him up the steps and inside. The porch steps creak. James notices there are no locks on the door. The door creaks open.

"Shhh," says Hannah smiling back at James. "*Kummen si*," she whispers. She draws him into the sitting room and gives him a friendly push as he collapses on the sofa.

"Okay!" responds James, pulling her down onto his lap. They kiss only once before Hannah rests her head onto James' shoulder closing her eyes.

"I so love you, James."

"I love you too," whispers James.

"James!" A quick shake. "James, wake up!"

"What time is it?" James is groggy.

With a little laugh she responds, "It's a little after midnight."

"Hannah," a quiet voice comes from the stairway.

"*Ja, mamm*?"

"Your friend must go now."

James hears the sternness. "I better get going."

A quick kiss and Hannah walks him to the door. She opens the door and follows James outside onto the stoop. Hannah takes James by the arm from behind and turns him towards her, wrapping her arms around his neck, saying only, "James."

James holds her. "Oh, I wish we had longer days."

It is Sunday, the 19th of May, and another rain passes. Then the day is sunny again with some clouds on the horizon. Jacob and his *frau* leave their house with their five children. They open the back of the gray-over-black buggy. The children scramble in and settle on the benches as their parents climb into the front.

As they canter along the highway, impatient drivers speed by. The unwavering horse continues its practiced journey. Jacob does not look at the passing gawkers. He and Mary don't show concern for they do not want their *kinder* to think there is any peril, though Jacob knows that is always a possibility with the uncaring *Englisch*. He sighs. *Gott* watches over them. A truck rushes past them with horn blowing, startling the horse. A hand gesture from the truck driver goes unseen. Down the road, the truck makes a hurried turn into a driveway. Barreling past the horse and buggy bought the man five seconds.

Arriving at Isaac's home, Jacob sees Isaac and his wife, Anne, waiting for them. It is Isaac and his family's turn to hold church. All who come share a common meal. In two weeks, church will be at Jacob's home.

The two families are standing together in the driveway when another horse and buggy turn off the road unto Isaac's driveway.

"*Ach*, it is the *Bischof*," says Isaac, his face ashen. He looks at Jacob, then turns to his wife shaking his head.

The *Bischof* is early. He gets out of his gray buggy and walks his horse over to a rail near the barn to tie him off.

"*Gut Morgan, Bischof*," says Isaac. "The blessings of our Lord and Savior Jesus Christ be with you"

A stern look from the *Bischof* silences Jacob. "There will be no talk of Jesus or the *Englisch* Bible today, Isaac and Jacob. You should know better. Better to think what is *gut* for your family. My advice? Follow the *ordnung*. That will keep you both out of trouble with the elders.

"Let us go in," Isaac takes Anne's hand and leads the way, silent. His kinsmen follow him toward the house.

"Jesus loves you," says Jacob, to the *Bischof.* His reward for the heart felt love is a scowl.

After the service, the *Bischof* waits for them. "Jacob and Isaac, *kumme* to my home tomorrow." The Old German hymns and preaching had occupied the morning and with the common meal, it was midafternoon. All day Jacob and Isaac received cold looks from their kinsmen. Everyone knows about their new beliefs.

"Ten in the morning, we will have one last talk," says the *Bischof.*

Jacob watches the *Bischof* walk away. "Well, there we have it, Isaac,"

"*Ja*, I don't like it," Isaac responds, "I don't like it at all."

"What is to come of this," Mary asks.

Anne takes Isaac's arm. "*Ja*, husband, what?"

"*Frau*, we will talk of this at home," Jacob admonishes.

The wives, quiet with heads down, walk to the buggies where their children await.

Isaac pulls Jacob aside. "Jacob, there is a whisper that Hannah is seeing an *Englisch* boy."

"*Ach*, I will speak to her of this. I think nothing of it. Just a friend. I believe she will be with Abram. Won't be long they will baptize her into the faith and she will marry Abram, then they will have many *bopplis.*"

Isaac moves Jacob's horse away from the rail. "The sun will go down all too soon, Jacob, then tomorrow will *kumme.*"

"Ja, tomorrow will kumme too soon, Isaac. It would be nice to have those longer days."

CHAPTER THREE

CLOUDS OF STRIFE

Clouds, dark, threatening, hang over Honey Brook as two gray horse-drawn buggies with bearded kinsman, brothers in the Lord Jesus Christ, make their way to the *Bischof's* home. They come from different directions and meet at the entrance to the drive which leads up to the *Bischof*'s farm.

The men tie their horses and greet each other with a holy kiss, shaking hands. They proceed to the front door where a rich and provocative smell greets them. Jacob, looks at Isaac. "*Kaffi*?"

Jacob knocks. "*Ja*, maybe it is a sign he will listen to what we have to say." Lilly, the *Bischof's* wife, answers the door. "*Gut Morgan*," says Lilly with a concerned look.

"Or maybe not," responds Isaac. He smiles at Jacob and then greets Lilly. "Our Lord's blessing to you."

"Kumme!" A yell from the kitchen. The two men walk in. The *Bischof*, stern, asks, *"Kaffi?"*

"*Ja, danke*," say both men simultaneously. The *Bischof* looks at the coffee pot and nods to his wife. Lilly pours three cups and brings them to the table.

"*Danke*, Lilly." the *Bischof* says. *"Gut! Ja, gut!"*

Both of the visitors take turns with the sugar, Jacob reaches for the fresh cream.

"Let us pray," the *Bischof* begins, as the two guests bow their head. After thirty seconds, the *Bischof* concludes with an "Amen."

"We have spoken of this *Englisch* bible and speaking of it ..." begins the *Bischof.*

Jacob breaks in. "*Ja*, you have spoken of it."

"Have you read God's word, brother?" asks Isaac bringing out his copy of the *Englisch* Bible. "It is the same Bible we read, just in *Englisch*. It is filled with *vera gut* news!"

Jacob pulls out his own Bible. "It says here in John the third chapter, sixteenth verse, that God so loved the world that whoever believes in him will not die but have everlasting life."

"You dare to disrespect me in my own home bringing *Englisch* Bibles here after I told you that this will end?" The *Bischof's* voice rises to a peak. His hand slams down, as he stares from one man to the other. His wife jumps.

"We mean only to spread the *gu*t news of Jesus's love for you brother ... *Bischof,*" says Isaac quietly. "We cannot turn or deny our Lord, it says here about denying ..."

"Enough!" yells the *Bischof.* "We have our way of following *Gott* which we have done for hundreds of years. I ask you. Will you stop spreading this *Englisch* Bible, and will you stop bringing division within the community?"

"We cannot by that same *Gott's* command, deny him who has saved us," says Jacob resolutely. "*Ne*, I cannot make this promise to you nor any other man"

Isaac follows, with tears in his eyes. "*Ne*, I also cannot make this promise."

"Will you think of looking for another community then?" asks the *Bischof.*

"*Ne*," says Jacob, "this is my community."

Isaac looks at Jacob and shakes his head.

The *Bischof* rises from the table and points at the two men. "You leave me no choice than to separate you from this community. You are *shunned,* under the *Meidung*. You cannot—"

Jacob interrupts. "If we are *shunned*, then you have nothing more to say to us. We have tried to share the love of Jesus, *Gott's* son, that same *Gott* that you speak of, with you, and you have met us with wrath we do not deserve. *You* have divided the community in this one act."

"We may be finished here," says Isaac, "but we will continue to spread the good news!"

One last time, the *Bischof* tries to interrupt, "leave the commun—"

"Ne!" says Jacob sternly. "We are *shunned,* we are separated from you. We speak to who we want to."

"They will be *shunned* also!" The *Bischof's* face is turning red.

"From you, not from *Gott,*" adds Isaac.

Holding up his coffee, Jacob says, *"Danke!"*

"Ja, danke!" Isaac says, then looks over at Jacob, asking, *"Gut?"*

Jacob nods, *"Ja, vera gut!"*

The two men stand, and Jacob follows Isaac out the door. Lilly turns her back on the men as they leave, as does the *Bischof.* Isaac and Jacob look at each other and smile, shaking their heads in disbelief.

As they walk out onto the porch, a light rain falls. Looking out into the distant horizon, they see a double rainbow. They look at each other with relief on both their faces. An era has come to an end. Another era begins. With only faith to guide them now, they walk down the steps and into an unknown future.

In the sky, the sun is now shining brightly, but on the horizon more clouds are coming, clouds of strife, yet to be realized. As they walk, the two men ponder the future. A future without the community they grew up in. A future without the support of family and loved ones.

The shunning has deep ramifications for a man. No one in the community who is aware of this shunning can do business with a shunned man. They cannot speak to him. Technically, his family should not either. But Isaac's family supports him, and with this support, Isaac will now go off on his own.

A carpenter by trade, he works for the *Englisch*. He has one other friend from his community that also works with him. It presents a problem. They have to work together and communicate on the job to accomplish it. Jacob wonders if his friend will bow to the *Bischof* or act sensibly.

Home from his meeting with the *Bischof*, Isaac is having lunch with his family, trying to plan what to do.

Ach, what will my children's lives be like now? Sarah, how will her life be? They are not shunned, Will they be part and I not? They are all looking to me for answers.

Looking over at his wife he asks, *"Wie geht's, lieb?"*

"Kinner, Kumme!" His voice booming, Jacob brings his family to the table. He sits them down and looks around the table. "Mary, I have been shunned. Isaac and I, we are both shunned."

"What do we do now, Jacob?"

"We begin again with the Lord on our side. We are no longer welcomed to church. We will begin thinking of other ways. Ways based on the *Englisch* Bible and Jesus Christ."

"*Ja*, we go where you go, Jacob."

"We have a few who have come to Jesus, we will all meet and decide what to do. Isaac has to return to work tomorrow. We are going to bring everyone together soon."

Mary nods. "*Ja, gut*, Jacob."

Once the word got out, Jacob and Isaac found they were not alone—there were likeminded brethren who met together, more than they had known of. The families of King, Lapp, Troyer, and Fisher—all families of the old order, but now renewed in Christ, promised to gather with them. On their first Sunday together, Jacob addressed them.

"My idea is to continue our lives as always, only now Christ is with us."

Isaac affirmed his words. "*Ja*, Jacob and I have discussed what direction to go. We begin our own community and continue our services every other Sunday as we have in the past."

Jacob continued, "David King, would you like to have worship at your home next Sunday?"

David smiled, "*Ja*! We will follow with a common meal, everyone to bring something," says David, smiling broadly showing a missing front tooth.

"What do we do with the *Englisch* brothers and sisters who want to come to our service?" Jacob asked.

Samuel Lapp stands. "We don't encourage this, nor do we deny our brothers and sisters. After all, would Christ deny them? *Ne!* All are welcome, but we stay to ourselves. Nothing should change but our worship."

Samuel goes on. "With this meeting, we now separate ourselves from our brethren. We will be *shunned*. We should consider ourselves *shunned*."

Joseph Troyer raises his hand. "What of the old German? We read the *Englisch* Bible. It makes no sense to do sermons the old way. We never knew who Christ was based on what we did. Our children should grow in Christ. They cannot do this by what we have done in the past."

"We will do our service in the *Englisch*, anyone visiting from the *Englisch* will understand us," Jacob states with finality.

"Who will be the minister? David asks.

Isaac smiles. "We shall all take turns as the Lord gives us the words, I am prepared as well as Jacob. You all should be also."

"*Ja*, Isaac and I can begin next week," volunteers Jacob.

The men nod. "*Ja!* OK."

"What will we be known as in this new church, when we are asked?" Joseph Troyer asks.

Jacob thinks for a moment. "Amish Pentecostal, if anyone should ask, though it is not important. Our beliefs are of the literal bible with all the gifts. *Ja*, we are Pentecostal."

The quiet voice of Zeb King, a farmer, asks, "My *kinder* like music. I see no reason why they can't learn music for worship."

Jacob nods affirmation. "This is *wunderbar!* What gifts they have, we will encourage. We will look for a new hymnbook in *Englisch*.

And so a new church takes hold within the small Old Order Amish community outside of Lancaster. Tracts now are handed out in earnest—invitations go out to the community. The small church is established. Christ is the center of their lives. The *Ordnung* in respect to faith had now been changed.

Hannah stands in the woods, the blue sky bright above her. She does not see the new storm clouds far away on the horizon. The sound of footsteps. James!

He comes and rushes to him. She embraces him, her heart beating with wild excitement, her mouth forming the words of freedom. "James! I have such great news! James! "

James stares in amazement.

She grasps her beloved around the neck and whispers, "James, we can be together. The *Ordnung* has changed. We no longer are as we were. We are no longer under the *Bischof*. My papa says we are now free in Christ."

"What are you saying, Hannah?"

"We are shunned for believing that salvation is a free gift of *Gott* and not something we earn by keeping the law, the *Ordnung*. We are no longer part of the old way. We are free to live our own lives."

James holds Hannah at arm's length. "Seriously, Hannah, we can be together? Do you know what this means? It means . . ."

"*Ja*, it means we don't have to be apart," she said, finishing James's words in a single breath.

"When can I see your father, Hannah?"

"He usually is in his workshop during the day, why?"

"I tire of hiding. I want him to know how I feel about you. I love you! I want to spend the rest of my life with you!"

James squeezes her close as Hannah nuzzles her face into the side of his neck. Her breath burns his neck. James kisses her head, then lifting her by the chin, kisses her tenderly on her lips. "I love you so much."

They go for a drive. Dusk comes early with the darkening overcast. Hannah is unaware of anything, but James and his love for her. Happy dreams envelop her senses, happy tears fall. She reaches over and touches him. "I am so happy."

CHAPTER 4

Of Ganders and Geese

Monday, May 20. James tosses and turns throughout the night. He wakes, rolls over, stares at the clock.

0600.

He goes to the window and opens it. A chill bites in the air, and clouds hang low in a foggy blanket.

Stumbling his way back to the bathroom, he reaches for the handles of the faucet and turns on both, feeling for the right temperature. He begins throwing water on his face and rubbing out the night's sleep from his eyes, thinking about the coming day.

He hears his mother downstairs. Her voice floats up the stairs.

"James, you have mail. It looks important—from the government."

"OK!"

"I wonder what that can be. I spoke with my branch manager."

One more splash on his face, more to wake up than prepare, then the shaving cream—the first swipe of the razor.

"I'm due to report in October for training at Fort Sam Houston, Texas. What can be going on? Fort Rucker, Alabama is January. Hmm …

He stumbles downstairs. His mother is waiting with coffee.

"You're up early, James. Couldn't sleep?"

"I slept good, Mom! Mom, I'm going to speak with Hannah's dad today."

Eileen cocks her head.

"Oh?"

"Mom, I love her, Hannah is the girl for me. I want to spend the rest of my life with her."

An earnest James stands solemnly looking at his mother.

Eileen wipes a tear. "My baby boy has grown—too fast, too fast. Where has the time gone?" She busies herself removing bacon from the baking sheet.

James sits and opens letter envelope and begins reading.

"James, eat your breakfast, it's getting cold."

Taking a bite, he continues to read, "Oh no, this changes everything."

"What, sweetheart?"

"My orders have changed."

"Well, what has changed?"

"The Army has changed my active duty and training status. I now go to Texas in September. I have to speak with Hannah." James sighs as he picks up his cup of coffee and shakes his head.

"*Mamm*, James is coming over to speak with you and *Daed*," begins Hannah. The early morning clouds are now a partly cloudy day over Honey Brook. It's 9:00 a.m. Hannah, up for three hours, has completed her chores. Looking forward to a short break, she sits at the table with her *mamm,* enjoying *kaffi.*

"Hannah, *was*?"

"James, is speaking to *Daed* today."

"What for?"

Hannah returns her mother's troubled stare.

Mary bored in. "Your *daed* has got a lot on his mind. James is not coming to upset him?"

"*Ne, Mamm! Mamm*," Hannah smiles broadly, "James and I …"

"*Ne! Ne!* There is no James and I!" Hannah's mother is visibly upset and her voice rises.

"*Mamm,* James and I!"

"*Ne!* The *Ordnung* strictly forbids this! I know what you are going to say, Hannah! *Ne!* He is not *Amisch!* Everyone talks of you being with Abram. You have spent a lot of time together."

"Until I met James, *Mamm.* We have been together for almost two years. Abram and I only see each other at church or singing. Now, even church has changed! The rules are changing! No more *Ordnung*!"

"*Ne*, the *Ordnung* has not changed! Your *daed* does not want to leave! Nothing has changed but the manner in which we worship *Gott*!"

With tears in her eyes, Hannah proclaims, "I love James. Nothing will change that!"

"The *Ordnung* has not changed nor has your *daed,* either!"

Hannah turns away and pours herself a cup of *kaffi*. Her hands are trembling as she pours in fresh cream and spoons in sugar. Staring, she looks at the AP cake and Funny cake sitting on the counter.

I like AP cake with kaffi but then there is the chocolate in the funny cake. I am so depressed, funny cake it is!

She reaches for a butter knife leaning against a nearby plate. With some anger she stabs the funny cake, cutting the dryness of the top and burying the knife deep into the chocolate gooiness below.

A big piece, a very big piece. Fork or no fork, I'll eat it by hand. My daed is not the only one who reads the Bible. What does the Bible say about not tempting your children to anger?

With the last bite of funny cake, Hannah wipes away tears from both cheeks and sniffles. Lucky can be heard barking from a distance. A car is making its way over the gravel of the driveway.

James! James!

"James!"

Bounding from the chair, Hannah runs her hands down the back of her skirt from behind as her *mamm* yells, "Hannah, *ach*, Hannah!" *The kinner have grown so fast!*

Hannah is out the door as James is closing the door to his car. Hannah's *daed* walks out of the leather shop, taking in the scene in the driveway, a frown on his face.

Hannah and James kiss, and Jacob's face becomes grim. "Hannah, *was es das*?"

He walks toward the couple, but they are not paying attention to him.

James breaks away, turns to Jacob. "Sir, my name is James, James Longacre, I'm here to speak with you, if I may, please, sir."

"*Ja*, so speak," Jacob responds curtly. He remembers himself. "*Kaffi*?" He climbs the steps to the back door of the house motioning James to follow.

"Coffee? Yes, thank you, sir." With his arm around Hannah's waist, he follows Jacob. He holds the door for Hannah and sneaks a kiss on the back her neck, lingering momentarily, and taking in her fragrance of lilacs.

Hannah turns around with sparkling eyes and mouths, "I love you!" Then as quickly as the smile came, it vanishes with the reality of her *daed* in front of her and her *mamm* coming into view. An embarrassed flush covers her face.

Ach, was es to become of us.

"Mamm and Daed, this is James."

James reaches out to shake their hands and is met with a cool hello. Putting his hand down, he isn't smiling now either. He takes a deep breath as he smells the fresh bread sitting on the counter top covered with towels.

"Sit!" Hannah's father booms.

James pulls a chair out.

This isn't going to be easy. Why did I even think that it would be?

"What do you want, James?" Jacob begins.

Steeling himself, James answers. "I was going to speak to you regarding Hannah and I and the differences in our culture and to try understand you better. I would like to share with you who I am, as well. It would make planning easier. I want to do the right thing. Not offend anyone."

James looks around the table with his hands folded in front of him. He sees Hannah looking down at the table, her hands folded too, and her mother, then her father just staring at him. He picks up his cup and sips at the rich black coffee.

Well, this is going south quickly, James. Just go for the whole thing. We really don't want to do this again! Do we?

Hannah jumps in. "James, would you like a piece of cake? We have AP cake or Funny cake. That's what I like—funny cake when I am stressed!" She looks at her *mamm* and *daed* sitting at either side of the table.

"Funny cake," comes the quick response from James. He takes a deep breath. "Well, this isn't going to be easy, so I will just speak plainly, politely but plainly. Hannah and I, as you may know, have been seeing each other for a couple of years. We have become, no, we are in love with each other. I would like your blessing to ask Hannah to marry me."

James stops and looks over at Hannah.

This is not how I planned this.

"Hannah, I love you and want to spend the rest of my life with you. I want to help make your dreams reality." As he looks at Hannah, he sees tears come down her face. A small, sad smile breaks the grim set of her face. He continues, "Hannah, will you marry me?"

As Hannah begins to nod yes, a loud "*Ne!*" rings out in unison from both her mother and father.

"*Ach*! This is not possible," her mother begins, shaking her head no. "Hannah, I told you before …"

Jacob raises his hand, cutting off Mary.

"I will speak at this table, *frau*."

Ignoring James, he speaks to his daughter. "Hannah, is it not enough that your mother and I are now shunned? People who once spoke to us now turn their backs. We deal with a lot gladly, but this … you are *Amisch!* James is *Englisch*. You cannot stay here and marry the *Englisch*. You cannot have both. *Ne!* You marry outside, you will stay outside."

Hannah, trembling, responds. "You are saying if I marry James I cannot be part of this family? Is this the love spoken about in the Bible, *Daed*? The same *Englisch* Bible you read now. Is this the freedom in Christ that you and Isaac shout from the rooftops?"

"What do you know of the *Englisch* Bible? What do you know of Christ? You are to leave what is spoken and taught to the men of this community."

"What community, *Daed*? The new community begun by you and Isaac because you learned the *Ordnung* is wrong? The Bible says we should love one another, that love is born of *Gott* and those that love know *Gott*. How is it love that you will shun me by the same law that you disagree with—the law that now shuns you?"

"You are not to interpret what that verse means." Jacob's face is grim. "We the elders of the community will decide what the law is." Jacob smacks his hand down on the table.

James responds forcefully.

"I'm a man, and I have studied God's word. It tells me you are to be respected—not obeyed without question, but respected, and also in the same verse you have a responsibility not to tempt your children to anger."

"You will not tell me how to raise my children or how to care for my family. What do you know of the Bible? You at your age, and *Englisch* besides. You can go now."

James starts to rise. "I see, I see how it is, thank you for your time."

Speaking excitedly and above the din, Hannah calls out, "Yes … James, yes."

James confused, asks, "What's that, Hannah?"

"You asked me a question, James. My answer to you is yes. Yes, I will marry you."

"*Englischer*, go now!"

"Coffee, thanks for the coffee," smiles James, shaking his head in disbelief. Heading to the door, he turns, looks at Hannah, "I love you, Hannah."

"I love you, too. You are my fiancée now! *Ja, das es gut!* "

Hannah follows James out to the car. Two worlds blend as James opens his window and Hannah reaches her head in and kisses her future deeply.

Mary is on the steps, waving frantically. "Hannah! *Kumme! Bitte!*

James and Hannah smile at each other. As they smile, they don't know what lies before them. A distant honking breaks their reverie as the Canadian geese fly overhead, geese and gander heading north for the summer.

The last weekend of the month, Sunday, May 26. The courting buggies can be seen going up Horseshoe Pike past Wimpy and Dee's. Sometimes one buggy, sometimes a line filled with young Amish. Open carriages with couples riding together line the side of the Pike. Sometimes another girl can be seen sitting on the floor of the buggy in front of the two facing them and talking.

Abram, Isaac's son, is alone in his buggy as he passes down the road. He turns down state Route 10 and pulls into the stone driveway just before the Amish market.

Slowing to a stop in the middle of the drive he faces a white Honda and looks into the passenger seat at Hannah. She is dressed in a blue dress and black apron.

He sees Hannah smile at the young man next to her and say something, and then she climbs out.

"Abram, hi! What are you doing here?"

"I have come to pick you up and bring you to the singing." He does not speak his question. "Your *daed* told me you had left early, and I should come right over to pick you up."

"Abram, I'm sorry, but James and I have plans. Did my father tell you that we are to be married?"

"How is that possible, Hannah? He is *Englisch*."

"Being *Englisch* is not a disease, Abram."

"But the *Ordnung*?"

"Abram, why don't you go around us and turn around at the barn. It was nice to see you, Abram."

Abram snaps the reins hard as the horse lurches forward pulling the courting buggy around the car. James drives out onto the road as Abram looks behind him one last time as he pulls hard left on the rein.

"Church, next weekend?" James asks as they head up the road towards his house.

"*Ja,* as usual, James."

"We have been going to church together for a long time. Something tells me your parents don't care about anything I do or my beliefs," says James, his disappointment evident.

"It doesn't matter, James. What matters is our future."

"Hannah, I was brought up Lutheran, and I would like to make Living God Lutheran church our church. Is that OK with you? If it isn't, we can start over and go to a nondenominational church."

"We have been coming to church together for a while. I like it here or anywhere you are. I am just glad you are a believer, James," smiles Hannah, looking over at James.

"Mom and Dad—we're home." James yells as he opens the door and ushers Hannah ahead.

"Hannah, hi," says Cecelia as she enters the room from the kitchen. Constance piles into the room from outside. "Hannah!"

The scent of bacon and hot rolls in the oven wafts through the house.

"Well, you two, how are you, Hannah?" James' father enters the foyer behind Cecelia. He is drying his hands with a dishtowel. "Here, let me give you a hug."

"Hi, Hannah." Eileen joins the hug.

"Hi, everyone. It is good to see all of you." Hannah nervously fidgets with the small bag in her hand.

"Hannah needs to change," cuts in James.

"Oh, Hannah, please come up to my room." Cecelia takes her by the hand up the stairs and into her room. Cecelia smiles at Hannah removing her *kapp,* then unpinning her hair and letting it fall

"Hannah?"

"*Ja*?"

"You two are getting serious."

Hannah smiles softly back. She doesn't say a word.

Cecelia takes Hannah by the shoulders and looks deeply into her face.

"Uh-huh, something's up. I know something is up." Cecelia smiles, shaking her head.

Hannah pulls out her jeans.

"Is this what you're wearing? Here, want to do something different? Knock James' socks off?"

Cecelia goes to her closet and pulls out a yellow spring dress with spaghetti straps. "You will need a strapless for this. I think we are the same size. Try this on." Hannah shyly turns around and, after taking off her apron and blue dress, puts on the strapless bra.

"Here let me get that!" Cecelia reaches out and fastens the back, then hands her the dress. "Wow, that is so nice. Look here in the mirror."

Hannah likes what she sees. "We don't have mirrors. It's looked at as vain, but I like it. I like how I look. Is this bad?"

"No. Why shouldn't you look nice?" Cecelia is reassuring.

"Ready, let's go show you off." She takes Hannah's hand again leading her out the bedroom door and down the stairs.

"Presenting the new Hannah," calls out Cecelia.

"Wow!" says James walking over to her. "I have something that will go with that very well." He takes Hannah by the hand.

"Hannah and I have something to tell you."

"I knew it," smiles Cecelia. Hannah looks at her and smiles, looking at the family shyly.

Everyone gathers as James begins. "As you know I went over to Hannah's to speak with her father. It did not go well, but we'll speak about that later. Here's the good news. I have asked Hannah to marry me, and she has said yes.

Constance was the first to scream. "We're going to be sisters."

"I knew it." says Cecelia not to be outdone. "I knew it. I told her upstairs something was up. Yes, I knew it."

"Hannah, I know you don't do this, but we 'English' do." He reaches into his suit jacket pocket pulling out a small box.

Constance shrieks, "Oh my gosh!"

Cecelia holds her folded hands in front of her face whispering to herself just loud enough to be heard, "The perfect day."

James pulls the ring out of the box. He lifts Hannah's hand and slides the ring on.

"It's only a tad bit loose. Good," he says, relief in his voice.

Hannah stares. "James, it's an engagement ring?"

"*Ja*," kids James then holding her face gently kisses her softly. "It's only a quarter carat, but I have been dreaming of putting an engagement ring on your finger for a long time."

"Our boy has grown up," Eileen says crying. She hugs Hannah. "You call me Mom now, ok?"

Michael steps in. "Congratulations you two. Give me another hug. Hannah, call me Dad, ok?"

"Ok, I shall like this, I shall like this a lot," Hannah says. She brushes a tear away.

"Sis, we are three now," smiles Cecelia. "Welcome to the family."

The morning brunch turns into a celebratory brunch. Hannah is introduced to Mimosas. She makes a face as she sips.

"This has alcohol, *Ach,* don't tell my *daed* or *mamm.* I will for sure and for certain be shunned."

Everyone laughs.

Hannah devours extra potatoes and bacon with breakfast. Nothing negative is mentioned. It is a day of celebration.

Geese and Gander have traveled on this day, continuing to fly north. The sun has come up and is bright. No clouds on the horizon.

CHAPTER FIVE

Rain Kissed Leaves

Saturday, June 1, a mostly cloudy day. For James, time to get serious about his future. There are two months left before he departs for Ft. Sam Houston in Texas, and Hannah doesn't know. There are two months to plan, two months to dream. James'a reporting date is Monday, September 9th. He won't be back until the middle of November.

For Hannah, things have settled into quiet—not shunned, just quiet. A kind of quiet that is unspoken and uneasy. She hides her engagement ring when home, bringing it out only when with James and his family. Home is still pleasant for Hannah—pleasant enough for her to speak with her *mamm, daed, bruders* and *schweschders,* pleasant when she does what is expected at home, pleasant when she participates in the new church where the membership now ebbs and flows.

One family, in particular, found that they could not live outside of the old community they had left. Walking the proverbial line, they now hold on to their new found Christ—they just don't talk about him and have asked the *Bischof's* forgiveness and have repented.

It has not been easy for the families in the new church to do business. Where once they went to the Amish-owned grocery store, they are now not welcomed and are ignored. Instead they go to the *Englisch* grocery store around the corner on Horseshoe Pike.

Isaac speaks with the men who work with the construction company as far as what business needs to be done, but lunchtime has become lonely and uncomfortable. The Amish men avoid him because not only is he *shunned,* but he always wants to speak to them about Christ. After all, it is what brought him to this place to begin with.

Abram continues to go to singings alone and spends time with a mix of friends. He holds out hope Hannah will not marry, choosing instead to remain in the community in the good graces of her family and the new community begun by both of their *daeds.* He feels confident that *Gott* will lead her to reject the *Englisch.*

James is at the little diner on Horseshoe Pike. It has been raining and the leaves of the trees outside glint with the drops of water. Sitting back in the front corner of the diner adorned in 50s antiques, he awaits Hannah. In the distance, he sees a gray buggy pulled by a black horse. The clip clop of the hooves ring on the asphalt as the buggy turns into the parking lot.

James watches as Hannah climbs out of the buggy. She stops to speak to the young Amish woman who is driving. They both are smiling and chatting, the woman driving the buggy shaking her head up and down as if agreeing. He sees her slip her ring on and, holding her *kapp,* run towards the diner.

As she comes in the door, James stands. "Hannah! Back here,"

"*Liebe!*" responds Hannah, a glint in her eyes.

James is aware everyone around him is staring, but English and Amish embrace—first a long hug and then, a quick kiss. James pulls Hannah down into the booth.

"We are waiting for my sisters," he says.

"*Ach*, we are? Why?"

"I asked for them to be here, but before they arrive, I want to speak to you about the Army's plan for me. It has changed."

"*Ach*, no more trouble, James. Please, no more," Hannah pleads.

James takes a breath, then continues. "I wouldn't do anything to hurt you." He reaches out and takes hold of her hands. "My orders have changed. I have to report September 9th. Which means I will be leaving the 7th to give myself time to settle in. But I will be back in time for Thanksgiving, and I don't have to be in Alabama until January 6th."

Hannah frowns. "What does this mean for us, James?"

"I want you to come with me to Alabama. I want us to start our lives together," answers James.

"I can't move in with you. This I will not do."

"You can if we are married."

"Married? Really? Now?"

"No, not now, now we plan." I, I mean we … my family … we want you to have a wedding to remember."

"My family will not allow this. I will be cast out. You know this, James. *Ach*, what am I to do?"

"I have spoken to my family, and they will help us. That is why my sisters are coming."

"Your family wants to do this?"

James watches as the reality sinks in. Hannah is crying now.

"I will be shunned. I knew this day was coming. It is just coming so soon. But I also want it so bad."

James pulls Hannah close. "I love you, and I will spend the rest of my life loving you and caring for you. As long as God gives me breath, I will love you, not just feel love, but do love." She nuzzles her face into his chest. Her *kapp* comes loose, Her hair is a mess from the wind and rain.

Cecelia arrives first. Hannah looks up, her face stained by tears. "James. Hannah, what's the matter?"

Eileen and Constance are right behind. "Cecelia, Hannah. My goodness, what is going on?" Eileen pulls Hannah up from her seat and hugs her. "Everything, and I mean everything, that is a problem can and will be handled. I know what's happening with your family. Dad and I are going to take care of you. Don't you go fretting now." She holds Hannah away and lifts her chin. "Young lady, do you understand?"

"*Ja*," says Hannah with a whimper—squeezing out a smile.

"Hannah, you're a mess." Constance blurts out breaking the mood and Hannah laughs. She grabs the girls by the hands. "Squeeze in there so I can sit with you two."

"We are going to plan a wedding," Eileen says. "Now that we are back on track, where is the menu? I'm starved."

"Mom, thanks for coming," says James. He grins and hands his mother a menu.

Brunch is long with light talk of dreams and what ifs. With James's family around her, Hannah's spirits lift. In the safety of their love, she speaks of all that she used to dream of as a child. Hannah wonders if she should hold onto as many Amish traditions as possible or completely let go of the past, but in the end they put off those decisions. For now, they speak of dreams—dreams of being happy and having babies and where they will live. What life will be like.

Life at home becomes awkward for Hannah. Her new secrets are troublesome, and she debates whether to draw her *mamm* and *daed* into her plans or leave them out. One morning as she helps her *mamm* with the baking, she ventures to try. "*Mamm …*"

Mary does not let her continue. "Hannah, we have decided to send you to our family in Michigan. My *schweschder* has a child ill. Your cousin, Lillian, is ill, and they need our help. You need time away. It is settled. Your train leaves from Lancaster tomorrow. You have to be there at 1:30 in the afternoon."

"*Ne! Ne!*" Hannah shouts in response.

"*Ja,* I have packed your clothes. You are leaving. We will wait at the train station with you until you are on the train."

Hannah runs from the house, tears pouring down her face.

Her *mamm* comes to the back door. "Hannah, *kumme hier.*" but Hannah is already out of the driveway and down the road. The phone shack is outside the Amish store. She rushes in and pulls the little piece of paper from her pocket. She picks up the phone and dials the number.

Please, James, be there!

More uncontrollable sobbing. She bends over holding onto her stomach. "*Neeee!*"

She takes a deep breath.

Settle down now, slow down, dial correctly, there. James be there.

"Hi, this is James. Sorry I can't take your call. Please leave a message at the sound of the beep."

Ne, ne, ne. Jame,s you aren't there.

"James, this is …" Hannah sobs. "… James, why aren't you there? My *mamm* and *daed* are sending me to Michigan. They have packed my bags and …"

"Hannah!"

Hannah hears the sound of her father yelling. Looking around, she sees him at the end of the driveway coming onto the street. She speaks hurriedly into the phone.

"James, my father is coming. I am leaving on the train from Lancaster tomorrow. My train is at 2 p.m. I will be there earlier at 1:30 pm. I don't know …"

"Hannah, *was es das?*" Her father nears. He is angry.

"I love you so very much and don't want to go. I don't know when I will see you …" *beep*. "Aahhh!" she screams and drops to her knees.

"*Kumme, dochder*. In time, all will be well again." Her father lifts her to her feet and steadies her.

Monday the 3rd of June. Jacob and Isaac meet in the now planted tobacco field. It is late in the afternoon. Isaac's horse and his clean gray buggy are tied to the nearby fence.

"Jacob!"

"Isaac, hello, *Wie Gehts*?"

"*Gut!* It is done?

Jacob nods. "*Ja*, she leaves tomorrow."

"Abram is happy. He is leaving the day after to stay with his uncle and help out on the farm. They will be only ten minutes apart from each other. *Gott es gut.* "

James looks down at his phone.

I have new messages—those two are from the phone shack. Hannah!

He enters his password and punches the pound sign.

She never leaves me messages. What's going on? Her parents again?

Beep!

"James, this is …"

She is sobbing!

"… James, why aren't you there? My *mamm* and *daed* are sending me to Michigan. They have packed my bags and …"

"Hannah!"

That's her father's voice. She's in trouble!

"James, my father is coming. I am leaving on the train from Lancaster tomorrow! My train is at 2 p.m. I will be there at the station at 1:30. I don't know …"

Oh my dear Lord, help me! Please help me.

"Hannah, *was es das?*"

Her father again. He is so controlling. I'm so sorry I wasn't there for you, Hannah.

I have to get hold of my sister.

The message beeps off. James dials his sister's number.

Safari, let's see, Amtrack! There we go! Stops? Next stop? Harrisburg, Pennsylvania. That's it.

"Hi, James!"

"Cee! I need your help. Hannah's parents are moving her to Michigan. Can you help me?

"Of course, James. What do you need?"

"They will probably be with her at the station. I won't be able to get close enough to speak to her. They don't know you. Do you think you can get a message to her?

"Absolutely! I'm in," says Cecelia excitedly.

"I'm headed home, I have to speak with Mom and Dad," says James, now thinking aloud.

"Yes, life is going to change! Better bring them into this," agrees Cecelia.

June 4th. Cecelia is at the train station early, 1:15, sitting in her car.

I'll recognize Hannah, don't know if I can recognize her parents. Just look for someone Amish, Cecelia. Too far for a buggy, maybe a car? Here comes a car, Amish! They're stopping! They're getting out. There's Hannah. Good, lower my window and listen.

Cecelia listens as Jacob speaks to the driver. "Wait for us, we will be out when the train leaves."

"Yeah, sure, Jacob," says the driver

Poor Hannah, she looks awful. Is she still crying? Ok, now, when to make my move?

"Hannah, get your bags," mother says. Hannah obeys.

My turn, time to make my move.

Cecelia leaves the car, slams her door, drawing Hannah's attention. Cecelia, holds a finger up to her nose, motioning quiet. Hannah, at the trunk, excitedly mouths to her, "Cecelia!" Hannah's father calls. "Hannah, *kumme*!" He motions toward the station doors.

"*Ja, Daed!*"

Cecelia follows the family inside, watching, waiting. She studies the three at the counter and listens.

"One ticket for Lansing, Michigan," Hannah's father says. He passes the two pieces of luggage to the woman at the counter.

Mary takes Hannah's arm. "Your aunt will pick you up in Lansing, *dochder*"

"*Ja, mamm.*" She hangs her head. As she does, she looks behind her for reassurance. Cecelia nods her head towards the woman's restroom.

She moves toward the Ladies room.

"*Mamm,* I need to go to the toilet"

Good girl, Hannah.

"*Ja*, OK, go, Hannah."

Hannah walks to the Ladies room. Cecelia is waiting inside. She grabs Hannah and whispers in her ear.

"Hannah, he loves you,"

Cecelia hands Hannah an envelope. "Here, read this on the train."

Cecelia leaves. Hannah puts the note in her pocket and washes her hands and face. Looking in the mirror, she smiles at herself.

It's okay to look in the mirror, It's not a sin. Cecelia showed me.

She dries her face, thinking about all that has transpired in the past twenty-four hours.

Ach, what is happening to my life?

The train arrives, and Hannah boards with only a small bag in hand. She sits in a bench seat across from a mother and child. She looks at the sealed envelope in her hand turning it over and over. She opens the envelope and pulls out the card.

> Dear Hannah,
>
> If you see this, then Cecelia has made it to the station. I am so sorry I wasn't there for you when you called. You were so upset. It hurts me to think of the pain you are in.
>
> Well then, here we are. We have spoken about this. You called it, "jumping the fence." This is the crossroad we have come to. We both know if you get off the train, then you will be jumping the fence. You will be turning your back on your family.
>
> I don't believe though, anything is permanent. Not today. Things change, even people, even your parents.
>
> If you choose to jump the fence and come home with me, my parents are on our side and will take you in. Yes, they love you and want you in their lives as much as I do.
>
> Here's the plan. Take your bag and get off at the Harrisburg stop. I'll be waiting
>
> If I don't see you, I know that you have decided not to "jump" and as much as it will hurt, I will understand.

I love you always,

James

The conductor passes through Hannah's car. "Harrisburg! Next stop, Harrisburg!" His voice rings out. Hannah sits with tears in her eyes.

"Are you OK?" the young mother across from her asks.

Hannah nods, then shakes her head no. "*Ja* … well, no."

A gut *man. James is a* gut *man. I have known this since I met him. Why do my mamm and daed not understand this? I am not a child. I can make decisions for my own life. To put me on a train. My daed picks and choses what to believe, what to obey. Well, now I am still not with them. I am already shunned, am I not? So, I will go with James.*

She looks up at the young mother. "*Ja*, I'm good, *danke*, thank you."

The train station in Harrisburg is not very busy this Tuesday afternoon. James hears a train horn in the distance. Uncertainty comes.

What if she doesn't get off?

Again, the train horn sounds as it approaches the station.

Coming into view, the diesel locomotive is now close as squealing can be heard coming from the brakes. The doors of the cars open, and people begin to get off as others wait to get on. Within the small flurry of people, James looks around and not seeing Hannah turns towards the doors of the station, thinking to himself, *she isn't here, she isn't here, she must be so scared.*

"James!"

He turns quickly to see Hannah making her way through a throng of people.

"James!"

"Hannah," yells James. She jumps into his arms. They hold each other.

"Hold me, James, hold me and never let me go."

"I'm never leaving you go, never." James buries his face into the side of her neck. "Come we're going home."

Hannah watches porters retrieving bags from the baggage car.

"My things, I can't get them off the train."

"What's in there?" asks James.

"Clothes my mother packed. Anything of importance is in this."

Hannah holds up her handbag.

"OK. A lot to do here," James says. "You're starting your life over again. You ready for this?"

"Yes, I have never been so ready. James, I have jumped the fence. I have never felt so free."

"Give yourself room. A lot of changes going on in your life. There will be times when you feel off, but I will be here for you."

"And your family, James?"

"Yes, dearest, all my family."

CHAPTER SIX

Love's Warmth

Life happens quickly. Only twenty-four hours have passed from the moment James heard about Hannah leaving to now, when she is safely back in his car traveling home to Honey Brook.

Left hand on the wheel, James holds Hannah's hand tightly. Occasionally, he looks over, and she meets his gaze and smiles. Sometimes quiet speaks volumes. Quiet speaks to the soul. It has words not yet known. A language unto itself, it moves the spirit as music, deeper, with more emotion. It stores for the future, it longs, it gives, it takes in its own fragrance, it listens, it touches, it feels, it tastes sweetness, it sees a kaleidoscope of color in its own brightness and pales in pastels of beauty.

James pushes through the door, pulling Hannah with him. "Mom and Dad, we're home." Cecelia calls from the kitchen. "We're in here."

"We're in the kitchen, Bud! Bring that young lady in here!" Dad is standing at the kitchen table. Everyone is seated, coffee on the table in front of them. As Hannah enters the kitchen, they all stand smiling at her. No words, many smiles, hugs, kisses, tenderness, affection.

Hannah looks overwhelmed. "I've not known this. I know my *mamm* and *daed* love me, but I have missed … touching."

James pulls out a chair for her.

Hannah sits. "I hope I have not brought trouble to your home."

Michael shakes his head. "No, we have talked it over while we were waiting for you to get here. This is the way we see it. You two are obviously in love, and though this is not the ideal situation you want to be in, it is what it is. We want nothing more than for the both of you to be happy and to support you. Now we have a lot to plan and prepare."

Hannah looks at Michael. A frown mars her lovely face. "But I have no clothes."

Everyone laughs. Constance reaches across the table and takes Hannah's hand, shaking her head.

Eileen chuckles. "Well, if that's the biggest concern you have, then we have no real concerns."

"Nope, that's easy," says Constance, looking at her sister. "Ce Ce has a department store in that room of hers!" More chuckles fill the room.

James interrupts. "I have the money to help with this," he begins. "Cecelia, can you and Connie take her out? Maybe to the outlets in Limerick? Remember? We've been there a few times, you like those stores. How about a thousand to get her squared away?"

The whole family looks at him, their mouths open.

"Where is that kind of money coming from, son?" James's dad asks.

Grinning, James responds, "My bank has starter low-cost loans. It helps new Army officers get started in life. I, we have twenty-five thousand to get us started, though we will appreciate any help you can give. I don't think this money will cover everything."

Michael nods. "No, absolutely. We want to help. James, this is why we are here. OK, girls?"

Constance grins. "I think we can help James spend a thousand dollars on Hannah."

"No problem," agrees Ce Ce, smiling and shaking her head. "I guess we're going shopping, Sis!"

"Hannah, do your parents know you are here?" Eileen asks. "From what I understand from Cecelia, you may not have had time to tell them, but I thought I would ask."

"*Ne*, no. I will speak to them, so they don't worry, but I have done what the Amish call jumping the fence." Hannah shrugs. "Right now, they will not want to hear from me."

The table grows quiet. Michael frowns. "I'm sorry I don't understand a culture that doesn't support and embrace their children."

"No! I don't either," Eileen agrees, looking at her husband, then at Hannah. "We also understand you want to complete your education, Hannah. Perhaps we can do some online classes and you can study for your GED. I understand you want to become a nurse?".

"*Ja,* more than anything!"

"Well, that's another easy one then!" Michael says. "Okay, that's all settled. Now where will Hannah sleep and what will she wear? For tonight …"

Cecelia interrupts. "I can take care of that, Dad! We wear the same size, and I have lots of clothes.

"And I'll help her get set up in the guest room, Dad," Connie volunteers. "I'll head up now and check the bed and get her towels and toiletries."

Michael smiles. "Good, good! That's great, girls, thank you." He turns to Hannah. "Hannah, welcome to your new life. Everything will be all right. It won't be without its obvious hurts and emotional pain, but we are here for you and I can promise we can and will work through all of whatever may come your way."

"Thank you," Hannah says. "I don't know what to say but thank you."

"You said it all. Now to get on with it."

There is a knock on Jacob's door. A neighbor's son tells them there is a phone call from Michigan at the phone shack by the road. Jacob walks down. He is expecting to hear that Hannah is now in Greenville, Michigan.

"This is Jacob Zook,"

"Jacob, this is Mary's sister Anne. We came to the train station in Lansing and she did not arrive. I spoke to the conductor, and they remember a young *Amisch* girl leaving the train in Pennsylvania. They don't remember where."

"Hannah not there? *Was es das?*"

"Jacob, please let me know when you find out where she is. I will be going now. We have a bit of a drive back. Abram is here with us as well. Let Isaac know he is *gut!* He is disappointed at the moment. Bye now."

"Bye, Anne, I will let Mary know we have spoken."

Ach! I know it is her boyfriend. She left but hasn't left. Where is she? She will contact us. Then we will talk. She will have no place to stay with us anymore. Ne!

When he returns to the house, Jacob is angry he was not obeyed and snaps at the other *kinder.*

"Get your *mamm*! *Schnell*!"

Mary comes in from the kitchen.

"Mary, I spoke with your sister. Hannah has not arrived in Michigan. Anne thinks she got off the train in Pennsylvania. It is that *Englisch,* he has her. He took her."

"Jacob, she got off the train on her own. Don't you think she has something to do with this?"

Jacob bellows. "I want him out of her life …"

Mary breaks in. "Jacob, are you thinking maybe she has jumped the fence? Why wouldn't she? She does love him. She has told us many times. We never listen."

"Not up to us to listen! She is supposed to obey."

"*Ne*, she is on her *Rumpringa*, she has this time to decide. She has decided. Now she is out of our lives. Why? Because of the *Ordnung?* The same *Ordnung* you decided is wrong in how we worship and believe?

"*Ne!* I wanted us to stay. It was the *Bischof* who decided that we should choose."

"Just as you had decided for our *dochder*. You left her no choice. I left her no choice. They will one day have *bopplis*. Will I ever see them?

In the background, Hannah's siblings begin crying.

The youngest sister cries out. "Is Hannah not coming home?"

Her little brother tries to reason. "*Ne*, Hannah is in Michigan, and she is coming home."

"*Ne*, *Daed* says she is not in Michigan, and she is not coming home!"

"Shh, there now, we will see her again, *Ja,* we will see Hannah again," says Sarah the oldest, as she stares at her *daed*.

Mary Zook has opened up a stand at the end of their drive. She sells baked goods there as well as some vegetables and flowers in season. The Lord does provide as the traffic from tourists, the curious, and the knowing stop, buying anything that she may have out.

Time has slipped past, June is gone and July, with its forest greens edged by the pink and white of dogwoods, is welcomed. Flowers are in full bloom as lilys, dahlias, and Gerber daisies pepper the Zook garden. The essence of roses perfumes the summer air, and mint, which lies next to the fence behind Zook's roadside shack, fills the air with its sharp tang.

This day, a car pulls in and stops in the trampled grass at the side of the road. Eileen Longacre, feeling the longing of a mother, makes a trip to visit Hannah's mother. Walking around to the front of the shack where a wagon rests, she is welcomed by a young girl, a teenager, a little younger than Hannah.

"Hello."

"Hello," Eileen smiles. "Is your mother close by?"

Sarah points to a woman pulling a cart toward them.

"*Ja*, that is her pulling the other wagon with baked goods." Is there something you are looking for?"

"Well, yes, I am looking for Funny cake? Is there such a thing?"

"*Ja*," Sarah responds with a chuckle. "Right here. My sister loves funny cake."

"I know. I think Hannah would also like Whoopie pies, what do you think?"

"You know my *schweschder?*"

"Yes, I do. She has spoken about you. You must be Sarah. How are you, Sarah?

"I'm *gut*, how do you know Hannah?"

"I am James's mother. I am Eileen," she answers as she counts out cash.

Mary arrives with the cart. "Sarah, *Wer ist das*?" She smiles at Eileen.

"Hello, Mary? My name is Eileen Longacre. I'm James's mother." She holds out her hand as she smiles warmly.

"Hannah's James?" Mary slowly holds out her hand accepting the warmth of friendship offered by Eileen. "Hannah is with you, *Ja?*" Mary asks, though she knows the answer.

"Yes, she is. I'm here as a mother visiting another mother. It's been a few weeks, and Hannah is beginning to feel better. She was very hurt. Now she is doing better. I feel you should have some idea where and how your daughter is doing."

Mary takes out a handkerchief and dabs her eyes. Her voice is quiet, her head bowed. "We thought it would do her *gut t*o be away. My husband does not want Hannah outside the community. We expect for our *kinder t*o follow us all the time and stay. We forget they have minds of their own."

"Well, I'm here to let you know she is well. She is happy, but she is also sad. She does not want to leave her brother, sisters, and you. But she is in love."

Mary looks up. She smiles a little. "I know. It would help if my husband also understood this,"

"Well, husbands, right?" Eileen smiles.

With a chuckle, Mary shakes her head and looks into Eileen's eyes "*Ja*."

Sarah has finished bagging the funny cake and whoopie pies and is standing behind the makeshift counter, her hands folded in front of her, resting against the white apron.

Mary puts her hand on Sarah's shoulder. "Oh, this is Sarah, Hannah's sister."

"I know. We met. You have wonderful children, Mary. Hannah is a wonderful girl, and we welcomed her into our family with a lot of love …" She pauses, then goes on. "Mary, our son James is in the Army. He is an Army officer in the

Medical Service Corp. He, one day, will be a pilot. Hannah knows all this. James will leave for his initial training in the end of August."

"Hannah is OK with him being in the Army?" questions Mary.

"Yes, she is looking forward to and planning their new life."

"Are you OK with your son being in the Army?"

"Well, as any mother we will always worry about our children, Mary. But it is his life and calling," responds Eileen again with confidence.

Mary shakes her head. "Calling, how can the Army be a calling?"

Eileen ignores the abrupt question and brushes aside any theological debate. "Our children are going to be married this fall. James will be back on leave at the end of October. The wedding day is on the 9th of November. Just after Thanksgiving, they will move to Alabama. There is a small town, Enterprise. It is a military town.

"Hannah is moving away?"

"Yes, they will move a lot. But they will come home also. It would be good if they can see you those times they are home. Maybe you can come to the wedding. It would make your daughter so happy."

"I would like this, but my husband still obeys the *Ordnung*."

"Speak to him, if not him, maybe yourself and the children. I will mail invitations to you. All of you are invited. Mary, we are in town, not far from here. You are welcome at any time to visit." Eileen smiles, looking up at the gray clouds gathering above.

The warmth of the day envelops them, but Mary and Eileen feel something else—love's warmth. As they both look up Mary responds with a smile,

"*Danke*, Eileen. I feel much better and will tell the *kinder* of your visit. Please tell Hannah we love her." Mary hands Eileen bag of treats. "She should like these." Mary looks up and then at Eileen. She smiles. "It is warm, for a cloudy day."

WHEN HEARTS BREAK

JERRY EICHER

PROLOGUE

Lily

I stared at the pages of the notebook Barbara had written. I didn't stay for the funeral, but left Walter's body washed, not a crevice of his skin untouched by my hands. As the tree falls, it lies. So went the familiar saying in the community. I stared at the notebook again. Barbara left me her story. She trusted me, so I will write mine, and together we will share the tale of what came before the falling.

SECTION ONE:1903 TO 1910

BARBARA

CHAPTER ONE

The community was little more than dusty framed wood buildings, rough and weather-beaten if you saw them during the day, or a softer touch when outlined against the starry skies at night. This was Indiana's southernmost Amish settlement, the beginning a mile or so below the small town of Odon, along County Road 1200 and south from there.

I am an old woman now. I rarely venture out on the roads alone without Walter driving. Automobiles whizz past making dull whooshes sounds, as if to suck the air right out of the buggy. I thought I was used to the modern world, but old age travels one backwards, I have been told. I saw Lily's face in the clouds the other day—not simply a rough outline, either.

"Look," I told Walter.

"A cloud," he said.

I didn't argue with him. I know what I saw. Before the calendar turns twice again, fifty years will have passed since my sister left the community for the last time. Walter's son will be approaching the same age—a son, to replace the one I gave Walter and lost. Lily will come back when I am gone. I will have left her Walter. A shell of a man she once knew, but Lily accepted this inevitable end when we parted.

I could seek to justify myself in this telling of my tale. I will try not to, but I suppose I will. We all labor under some form of self-delusion. I wish I had always been right. I wish desperately as I see the waters of the dark river approaching.

I would ride triumphant into heaven. Yet, I will not. If God understands what I have done and how I have lived my life, I will be satisfied if his hand can reach me, as I know his mercy has—for Walter has loved me. I will ask for no more.

We were born long before automobiles clogged the roads, Lily and I. Daett was a short man, while Mamm was lean and lithe. On Sundays, the top of Daett's black hat barely cleared Mamm's bonnet.

Lily was a wisp of a girl compared to my stocky frame. She had taken after Mamm and her sisters while I had inherited all my genes from Daett's side of the family. At least I thought so for a long time—about Lily getting only Mamm's genes, and me getting Daett's. Time would reveal another reason, a dark secret which had frozen the hearts of my parents into icy pillars. Lily would get the worst of the fallout, from Grandpa's transgressions, and from Mamm's. I am tempted to use the sins of the fathers to justify my own behavior, but I will not. I never suffered what Lily suffered.

Lily looked over at me from her side of the bed one evening, "Grandpa gave me a kiss again today."

"I don't care," I said.

"Grandpa likes me." She looked dreamy eyed at the ceiling.

"Maybe you should worry more about what Daett thinks of you," I shot back.

"I like Grandpa," she said, as if the pleasant fact canceled out any unpleasant ones.

Lily dropped off to sleep instantly. She always did. I, on the other hand, lay awake thinking, and hearing the sounds which came from Mamm and Daett's bedroom after we had gone to bed. Voices were often raised. Mamm begging and pleading and Daett's lower harsh tones. I could never understand what they said. I didn't really want to know, or why the rapid squeaking of the bed followed these exchanges.

I awoke one morning to Mamm shaking my shoulder.

"Get dressed and come downstairs. We're leaving for Aunt Nancy's place." She whispered.

I sat up and rubbed my eyes. The world was completely dark outside the plain, dark bedroom curtains. I got out of bed and dressed by the flickering light of the kerosene lamp Mamm had left behind on the dresser top.

"Get up." I told Lily.

She groaned but didn't move.

"Mamm wants us up," I said, louder this time.

Lily finally stirred and I helped her dress. She stayed close to me, with one hand on my sleeve, as we made our way downstairs and into the kitchen, where a meager breakfast sat on the table.

"Sit down and eat," Daett ordered. His bowl of oatmeal and toast half eaten.

"Why are we going to Aunt Nancy so early?" I asked.

"Just eat," Daett said.

We ate, the usual prayer of thanks after breakfast skipped. Daett left for the barn the moment he had scraped the last bite of oatmeal from his bowl. We left the dishes unwashed, once Daett had the horse and surrey ready. Mamm hustled us out, holding our hands, and we climbed into the buggy. Aunt Nancy's home soon appeared in the distance. I couldn't see the line of buggies already parked in the yard, until Daett whirled into the driveway. Maiden had barely come to a halt by the hitching rail before Mamm hopped down the buggy step. The barn door swung open in front of us, and soft lantern light spread across the driveway stones. Aunt Nancy's husband, John hurried out, with Grandpa Yoder by his side. Both men had their black brimmed hats pulled low over their faces. "You should both go into the house," John said to Mamm, and placed his hand on Maiden's bridle. "We'll take care of the horse and bring the girls in when you've had a few moments alone."

Mamm made her way slowly up the sidewalks with Daett walking behind her. I was ready to climb down when Grandpa appeared in the buggy door.

"Shall I help you?" He offered his hand.

Before I could answer, Lily piped up. "What's wrong?"

"Your Aunt Nancy will soon be with Jesus," Grandpa said.

I exited the buggy, while behind me Lily clung to Grandpa's neck.

"It'll be okay, sweetheart," Grandpa whispered. "Everything will be okay."

"I'm glad to see you." Lily cooed.

Grandpa patted Lily on the head. "And I'm glad to see you."

"I'm taking the horse into the stalls." Uncle John hollered. "You should bring the girls into the barn for a few minutes."

We followed Uncle John. The musty odor of cows and milk greeted us, with soft bellows from the cows coming from the barnyard in the back.

"We'll wait here," Grandpa said.

He gave us little stools to sit on until they took us up to the house, where Grandma Yoder met us at the front door.

"You can't hide these things from the little ones," she said.

Uncle John set his lips and didn't answer.

"Death is what it is," Grandma continued.

Uncle John's face twitched. "We will say no more about this. Nancy may be your daughter, but she is my wife who is being taken away from me in the prime of her youth. The Lord may have forgiven, but the pain stings deeply."

"You think our hearts don't also hurt?" Grandma asked.

"I said, we will say no more about this." Uncle John turned on his heels and disappeared into the kitchen.

"Come here, Lily," Grandpa said, and sat down on the rocking chair to pull Lily up into his lap. He appeared old and tired.

The other adults left for the bedroom. Their soft cries drifted out of the open door, rising and falling against the living room walls. I waited silently with Cousin Heidi, as the sun began to rise outside, the first rays bursting through the window, and diming the light of the lanterns.

The adults drifted back from the bedroom one by one, and a meeting was soon called with Uncle John in charge. "My heart is broken this morning," he began, "knowing Nancy's crossing is at hand, and yes, there is anger over what is happening, yet we are still family, and we must make the best of things. The Lord will see us through this trial. Somehow he will."

"I have to speak," Grandpa said. "What you say about my sins following me home into the community from my rumspringa is not right. I have begged both the Lord and the church for forgiveness. I know I fought as a solider in the great war between the states, and so committed a great evil by killing men by my own hand. Yet, what is happening here is what happens to many a family. We cannot draw conclusions about the Lord's judgment because of the ill which befalls us. Otherwise, Job would not have been left to us as an example."

"Job was a perfect man," Uncle Mose said, "which you are not. I agree with what they are saying in the community about the Lord's judgment. These are not old wives' tales. The sins of the fathers are visited to the third and fourth generation. I have repented often I was not more careful before I married into this family."

Aunt Malinda leaped up to rush from the room. Mamm stared after her sister but didn't move.

"I accept blame for what I have done," Grandpa said. "I did a great evil in my younger days, but this is not an evil I have brought on my family."

"There is no benefit in this discussion." Daett spoke up. "What is just is. We will have to live with them and make the best of things."

The men stirred restlessly. Outside, the sun continued to rise, pushing its warmth past the window drapes. Deacon Miller arrived with his wife, Lavina. Bishop Mast and his wife, Esther, came in the buggy behind them. The glum faces in the house were not questioned. There was a mother and wife dying in the bedroom.

More of the cousins had joined us and we whispered together planning out escape. No one was paying attention so with Heidi in the lead we slipped outside. Lily and I hung to the back of the group, the hush from the house still on us.

CHAPTER 2

We crept past the long lines of buggies, a few somber faced men standing around, chatting. They looked at us, but no one objected to our leaving. Children were supposed to play, even when their relatives lay dying in the house.

I didn't know where we were headed. It was enough we were released from the house. In the summertime, there would have been green pastures growing on either side of us, with ragged grass growing down the middle of the cow path leading back to the creek behind Uncle John's barn. In this weather, the brown grass was bent and matted and there would be ice along the edges of the creek below us, the water cold to the touch. There would be no wading along the shallow shores, but we still ran down the cow path.

I was panting when we reached the edge of creek and petted the nose of Uncle John's pony, named Brownie, to cover for my deficiency. Lily climbed on his back and stroked his nose. Several of the cousins pressed on down the stream bed. Their cries soon reached us. "We've found something!"

Lily turned away from the pony and ran along the bank.

I followed more slowly, the pony staring after us. Lily was pointing towards a low branch of a tall oak tree when I arrived. Someone had tied a pair of red shoes to the tree limb. They had straps over the top and had open sides which would obviously display the wearer's bare feet. Their sheer audacity held us spellbound, as they glittered in the sunlight.

"Who could have put them there?" Heidi asked.

We stared silently.

Lily was the first to move, reaching for them, and untying the strings. She held them up, one in each hand. "Aren't these pretty shoes!"

"Those are English things." I found my voice. "We shouldn't take them, even if the owner doesn't want them anymore."

Lily appeared unfazed as she allowed Heidi to examine the shoes.

"You should try them on," Lily offered, her eyes shining.

Heidi did, slipping off her boots, and sliding into the shoes in her stocking feet, their redness a stark contrast to any color Heidi was wearing.

"They are so beautiful!" Lily gushed.

Heidi turned her feet first one way, and then the other.

"Those are English shoes," I tried again. "They don't belong on our feet."

Heidi took them off and handed them back to Lily.

"Leave them," I ordered.

"I'm wearing them when we ride Brownie back to the barn!" Lily declared.

And Lily did, alone on the pony, as if Heidi knew I was right, and wanted no part in the action Lily had taken.

We followed, and arrived at the barnyard to find Walter, the boy from next door holding Brownie's bridle. He was admiring Lily's shoes.

"Aren't these pretty." Lily was waving her feet about.

"Were did you find them?" he asked.

"Hanging on a tree branch."

"Really? I wonder who left them."

"I wouldn't know," she said. "Can you help me down?"

Lily was perfectly capable of sliding off the pony on her own, but she liked Walter, as she liked Grandpa. Walter barely noticed me, especially when Lily was around.

Walter was grinning as he took Lily's hand and helped her down from Brownie's back.

"Lily shouldn't be wearing those red shoes." I spoke again.

Walter finally looked at me. "Be quiet, Barbara. No one else is complaining."

Which was true. My cousins appeared dumbfounded. Only Lily blossomed in his presence. I opened my mouth to object further but shut it again. Walter was on his knees in front of Lily running his fingers playfully over the red straps.

Lily lifted one foot high in the air. "I'm wearing these for the rest of the day."

Walter chuckled. "You'll be a pretty English girl until bedtime."

"Yes, I will be." Lily beamed. "I'll be an English girl all day today."

"Why are you here?" I demanded of Walter, mostly because I couldn't stand his fussing over Lily.

He stood to his feet and didn't answer. He was watching Lily disappear around the corner of the barn, with several of the cousins in tow.

"There goes nothing but trouble," I said.

He turned back to look at me. "What is wrong with you? Leave your sister alone."

"Why are you here?" I asked again.

"Daett wants me to help with the Byler's chores tonight." He was staring after Lily again.

"She shouldn't have worn those shoes," I said.

"Lily is lots of fun," he said. "Lots"

"Lily is different," I muttered.

He wasn't listening.

I turned to the pony who lingered by the fence. I felt like climbing on his back and riding furiously across the pasture with my dress pulled up well past my knees, and my head scarf thrown from my head. I had beautiful long black hair. What a sight I would make with my hair blowing in the wind. Maybe Walter would see me then. Instead, he was moving towards the barn, still staring at the corner around which my sister had disappeared.

AFTERWORD BY AUTHOR

This is a two-chapter excerpt from, "When Hearts Break," due for release soon by Elk Publishing. A story of abuse in the Amish community and the far-reaching effects on the lives of two sisters. Purchase your copy for the full tale.

THE SILO

THOMAS NYE

AUTHOR'S NOTE

Allow me to share a few important notes about this story. You will notice I don't use "Amish words" in this novella. Most conversations between Amish family members would be spoken in Pennsylvania Dutch. I think of the story as having been initially told in the Amish dialect of German and then translated into English. For that reason, I chose not to use occasional German words. The Amish families I know speak English about as I do. Many of my Amish friends have an accent, but that is difficult to show without becoming a distraction.

Another important note: This story has many characters. To simplify, I let the Father and Mother in the story be known mostly as Dad and Mom. The youngest daughter is referred to as the baby. (This is not to say an Amish family would do this. It's only to take away another name.) I will share a list of names with you as an aid. I know many large Amish families, and I often write lists of their children's names as a reminder. It is common for Amish children to be shy when meeting strangers but quite open once they get to know you. They, like all of us, like it when someone takes the time to remember their names.

The Chupp family:

Lavern, known as Dad
Harvey, 14
Orva, 11
Ada Fern, 6
Leroy, 4
Baby

Emily, known as Mom
Edith Rose, 13
Mary Elizabeth, 8
Myron, 5
Charlie, 2

CHAPTER ONE

Friends and Rivals

A silo stood ominously in the middle of the Chupp family's Amish farm. To those who lived there, the silo marked the epicenter of everything significant. One year, when birds returned to the Midwest to nest, a series of events shook the Chupp family and their Amish community. Reverberations trembled out into the larger non-Amish neighborhoods for miles around. The Chupp family's troubles began during spring plowing when Amish children had time away from school to help with fieldwork.

Every spring, storm systems follow the Mississippi up from the Gulf into the heartlands and bring flocks of birds with them. After dumping their rain, thunderheads roll back like a scroll revealing blue skies and birds are everywhere. They swoop to-and-fro, fluttering about, and fighting for nesting materials.

A group of starlings came in chattering wildly and rested atop the Chupp's silo for a spell. They all jumped to flight at the same instant and brought their mayhem to a section of plowed ground not far away. Out in that field, near the silo, fourteen-year-old Harvey held tight to a set of leather driving lines. He sat behind six massive workhorses as they stomped, snorted, and pulled a two-bottom plow. His horses were hitched six abreast. When Harvey and his dad led them out of the barn that morning, Harvey asked, "Can we hitch them in two rows of three?"

His dad answered, "No—you're not old enough yet. It's much safer to drive them this way."

Harvey bit his lip for a moment before pushing the topic. "It's so much faster that way. As it is, two horses have to walk in the plowed ground."

"We're in no hurry. Just be sure you take breaks up by the fence and down under the oak on every round."

Harvey couldn't tell his dad why he wanted to speed up the plowing. He thought about ways to cut corners as he watched the sod split open under his leather boots. Usually, Harvey preferred to go barefoot, as did all of his younger siblings. However, his dad bought him new boots for spring fieldwork, so he ignored how uncomfortable and confining boots felt.

The plowshares gleamed silver as they cut into the earth and turned over four-inch-thick slabs of dirt. Grasses squeaked as the shares sliced through them and into the ground. A rich scent of freshly opened soil and sweating horses filled the air. A battle raged between two of the horses directly in front of Harvey. Cello, a coal-black Percheron, worked the spot on the right side of the plow tongue. Brick, a sorrel Belgian, had been hitched on the left. Only during spring fieldwork were those two horses used side-by-side, when the two strongest horses worked in the center. Harnessing them together seemed to prompt the question of which would be the lead horse. The jury was still out.

Most of the time, Harvey's dad preferred to use matching horses on his wagons and farm equipment. Not that a black horse couldn't be hitched with a sorrel. Dad always said, "Horses look smarter when they match their teammates."

Harvey watched Brick and Cello push forward like a clash of titans in an epic battle to outdo each other. He himself understood the urge to take on a challenge. In the next field over, Harvey's best friend and rival, Joe, also plowed ten-acres with six horses. Joe and Harvey never actually acknowledged the contest between them, but it went without words.

Brick and Cello's rivalry played right into Harvey's hand, and he let them surge forward in their quest to be the lead horse. The other four horses were mostly along for the ride. Two of them were young horses beginning their spring training. The other two, Butte, a blond Belgian, and Viola, a gray Percheron, were both older than Harvey. They had always been used as a team even though their bloodlines were so different. They matched in height and weight, and both had a low-slung belly from raising so many foals.

Harvey kept a watchful eye on his horse's legs and feet as they powered over the field, his brow shadowed from the bright sun by the brim of a straw hat. His narrowed eyes revealed how seriously he approached life. He did enjoy humor, though.

Laughing and teasing had always been a part of the Chupp household, as with almost every Amish family. However, Harvey, the eldest of nine children, usually wasn't the instigator of laughing and teasing. His personality tended toward smiling at what the others said. When his eyes twinkled, his siblings were quite pleased to have brought that reaction out of him.

Already, at fourteen, Harvey stood nearly six feet tall. His size was inherited from his dad, a large, rangy man with big bones. His mother looked small next to her husband, but she wasn't. Harvey had his mother's sandy-brown hair and his father's blue eyes. His mother's compassion and his father's grit. Sometimes, his determination grew beyond the boundaries of hard work. Hard workers were well respected among the Chupp's Amish community. Determination to outdo others was viewed as something that might become a vice and grow into pride.

Brick and Cello surged up the gently sloping ground with the gumption Harvey admired in them. All six horses maneuvered gracefully to turn the plow one hundred eighty degrees. All twenty-four heavy-boned legs sidestepped in perfect time, swinging to the left. Their massive hooves swished through tall grasses along the fencerow. Once they made the complete turn, Harvey said a single, "Whoa." All six horses froze in place and rested.

Harvey tied the driving lines to a handle on the plow and stepped down from his seat to look over the fence. A bluebird swooped out of the cloudless sky and sat on the barbed wire a few rods beyond him and sang bright notes. While the horses caught their breath, Harvey checked on his rivals in the next field over. He could see Joe and his team down in a low spot near a creek. Lush grass strips outlined both farms. Trees with budding leaves stood in rows along field edges. The unplowed ground lay flat and drab brown. Where Joe and his horses had passed with the plow appeared black. Rich topsoil looked wet and thick.

Harvey turned and leaned back against the fence to survey his own family's farm. The first thing anyone would notice while pulling into the Chupp's lane would be the silo. The white farmhouse and barns stood on a hill off to Harvey's right.

To Harvey's left, on a slightly higher hill, a neighboring house overlooked their farm. Harvey and his siblings called it "The Mansion." The exterior appeared to be of white marble, the house had a row of columns in front and back and windows everywhere. The mansion had been vacant for years, but recently Harvey and his family heard rumors someone had bought the place. While he looked at the mansion, a light came on in one window.

Harvey looked away from the mansion and toward his own home. From that distance, his house looked like a two-story cardboard box. A small orchard of apple trees blossoming between the house and barn added color to the scene. Laughter echoed off the barn and silo. Harvey's little brothers scampered under the trees with a pack of puppies at their heels. Suddenly, movement in the branches of one apple tree caught Harvey's eye, and he realized a person was there. He considered the possibilities and concluded his eight-year-old sister, Mary Elizabeth, was in the tree. The Chupp's didn't believe in having favorites, but if they did, Mary Elizabeth would have been the one. Everyone loved her smile, especially the way her thick eyelashes squinted together, concealing her eyes completely, when she laughed.

Harvey smiled as he thought about how cute she was until he noticed her little body tumbling out of the limbs and falling to the ground. He jumped forward as if somehow, he could reach out and catch her. The echoing laughter of his little brothers went silent, and they all rushed to her and stood gawking. Harvey yelled across the field, "Go get Mom!"

He turned to look at his horses, trying to decide if he could leave them standing and run to help, or if he should tie them first. He looked back toward the apple tree and saw Mary Elizabeth stand up. Harvey stood spellbound, holding his breath until his little sister took off running with her brothers. Their echoing laughter resumed.

Harvey checked his horse's sides to be sure they were all breathing slow and even—a sign Dad had taught him at an early age. They seemed refreshed. Harvey took his seat, untied his driving lines, and clucked. The horses all raised their heads from a resting position and flicked their ears back to be sure they heard correctly. With a single command, "Get up," Harvey's horses leaned into their thickly padded black collars and shoved off. Their heel-chains jingled merrily as the plowshares sank back into the soil and resumed carving a shallow ditch. Overturned slabs of earth tumbled onto the crevasse created on their last pass downhill.

The horses' downhill task wasn't as strenuous because they had gravity on their side, and each horse had almost two thousand pounds of body weight to push into their collars. Starlings followed the plow, chattering as they fell onto worms and bugs that were thrust out of hiding. The parade of horses, plow, and birds crept across the field, heading directly toward the massive oak near the road, where Dad had instructed Harvey to rest his horses after each pass. Brick and Cello surged forward. Not because they wanted to get to the shade, but because they both wanted to outdo the other no matter what. When they stepped under the tree, Harvey said, "Whoa." All six horses blew and snorted.

Orva, the only blond child in the Chupp family, stumbled over the plowed ground and joined Harvey under the tree. His morning job entailed clearing weeds near the creek with a hand scythe. Whenever the horses rested under the oak, Orva came over and took a break too. Harvey smiled at his eleven-year-old brother and said, "You ought to watch Cello and Brick plow. I've never seen two stronger horses in my life!"

Harvey and Orva stood behind the row of workhorses. The tops of the boys' straw hats didn't reach the height of the rumps on their massive steeds. Suspenders hung on the boys' shoulders just as the harnesses crisscrossed over the horses' backs. Oak leaves were dainty in the spring, but the towering arms of the mighty tree were so numerous that darkness shadowed the brothers and horses.

Orva pointed at the middle two. "Cello and Brick look odd working side-by-side." And then he glanced up at his older brother to see his reaction.

"I don't mind them not matching at all. If I were the dad on this farm, I'd drive those two together all the time. Then we'd get some real work done!"

Orva laughed. "If you were the dad here, our horses would get run into the ground, overworked."

"I'd rest 'em—just not as much as Dad does. I think these horses want to work harder than we let them."

Orva picked up a clod of dirt and threw it at a fencepost. He always threw dirt clods at posts because he loved playing baseball, and throwing clods was about the next best thing. After hitting it a few times, he turned to Harvey and said, "You're letting these horses push each other so ya can outdo your buddy, Joe."

"I didn't start it, Joe did." Harvey checked his horses and harness while he talked. "Joe always tells the other guys how much plowing he gets done. He knows my field is ten acres, just like his. He watches to see how much we get plowed every day, and he tells all the other guys how much faster he is, and how much better his horses are." Harvey reached up and rubbed a hand on Cello's hip. "I wouldn't trade these two horses for all six of his matching Belgians."

"Be careful," Orva said. Harvey was surprised to see his brother's eleven-year-old face suddenly take on the soberness of an Amish preacher. "If you're too proud, God may have to take ya down a notch."

CHAPTER TWO

Silhouettes and Shadows

Harvey clucked. His six huge horses raised their heads and flicked their ears. "Get up," he called, and the horses stepped forward, drawing the plow back down into the ground. Cello, being on the right side of the plow, had to walk in the furrow. He didn't seem to mind being the one in the trench—he happened to be the tallest of the six horses anyway. The two horses to Cello's right walked in the plowed ground. While they chugged their way uphill, Harvey noticed some tree limbs had blown onto the field's edge during a spring storm. He made a mental note to move them off the ground the next time his horses rested under the oak. He would save time if he got them out of the way during a break.

Movement near the mansion caught Harvey's eye. A person with short, silvery hair walked from the house to the mailbox. Harvey couldn't tell from that distance if he saw a man or woman. The whole Chupp family had high hopes for friendly and exciting new neighbors. Rumors said that a single older woman had moved in.

His team marched up the slope with Harvey leaning forward on his seat, almost willing them to walk faster. At the fence, Harvey let them relax while he checked on his rival. Joe's horses, visible in the valley on the other side, were six perfectly matched Belgians. They worked in two rows of three, the way Harvey wanted to hitch his team. More driving skill was needed to hitch horses that way because the horses could step over their heel-chains easier. The front three horses were way out in front of the driver and hidden by the back three, therefore more difficult to keep an eye on. Dad's top concern was always safety for his horses and children, *not* with keeping up with the neighbors. As a result, Harvey had to swallow his pride and drive his horses six-abreast like a little boy.

He scoffed, "They are getting further ahead on each round!" His horses jerked their heads up from their resting pose at his words. Harvey didn't wait long to put his horses back to work. On their way down the slope, a thought came to Harvey. *This end of the field is shorter than the far end because of the creek. I could skip one break and catch up with Joe.*

Brick and Cello didn't hesitate when Harvey chose to break his father's rule. He turned his team away from the oak resting spot and back uphill. Butte tried to go toward the shade at first, anticipating their pattern. She didn't resist when Harvey made his wishes clear with the driving lines. The horses all seemed quite sound, and their wind looked good as they moved ahead. Harvey told them, "Don't worry—I'll give you a few minutes at the hilltop by the fence while I check on Joe. When we get back down under the shade tree, you will have a longer break while I move some limbs off the field."

On the hilltop, his horses made their one-eighty turn, and Harvey kept his word. He called "Whoa," allowing them a chance to catch their breath. Harvey hurried to the fence and visually measured Joe's progress again, estimating his total plowed ground around five acres. He checked his field. His heart sank at the sight of his two rectangular sections of black, plow-turned soil, which appeared smaller than Joe's. He growled to himself, "I've gotta find a way to catch up with them no matter what." He headed over to put his horses back to plowing and heard a voice behind him.

"Do you know there is a story in the Bible about a donkey that speaks to his master?"

Harvey turned sharply, surprised to hear his father's voice. He didn't answer, but let a slight smile form on his lips, hoping his dad was making a joke.

Dad's face didn't soften. He continued, "Balaam is riding his donkey to a place he knew he shouldn't go. Three times an angel with a drawn sword stands in the road ahead of the donkey. The donkey sees the angel and halts, but Balaam doesn't know why his donkey is stopping. He can't see the angel, so each time he strikes his faithful old donkey for being stubborn.

The third time the donkey sees the angel, she falls under her master, and Balaam gets off his donkey and lets her have it. At that moment, God gave the donkey power to speak, and she says, 'What have I done unto thee, that thou hast smitten me these three times?' After the donkey speaks, Balaam's eyes are opened, and he can see the angel. Then the Lord spoke to Balaam and told him, 'If she hadn't stopped, I would have slain you and kept the donkey alive.'"

Harvey studied his father's features as he told the story. A thick black beard framed his dad's handsome face and moved against his broad chest as he spoke. His clear blue eyes visible, although shaded by a broad-brimmed hat. Harvey began to dread what intention his dad had in telling the Bible story. Inside he knew. He squinted into the sun until the story ended. Harvey let his eyes lower to Butte's heels. She stood with sides heaving to catch her wind.

"What would Butte say if God suddenly gave her the power to speak?"

His dad's words cut into his heart. He wanted to cry, but he was too old for that. He thought of saying, *I'm sorry*, but he knew his father always said, "Show by your actions that you are sorry—actions speak louder than words." So, he nodded that he understood.

"Harvey—did I see you make two rounds without stopping in the shade?"

Harvey nodded again. He thought about explaining, *this end of the field is narrower*. He knew his father was aware of that. His scolding revealed the narrowness of the section wouldn't be an excuse for disobeying. He answered, "It won't happen again."

His father placed a hand on Harvey's shoulder and gave it a gentle squeeze. That touch stung Harvey's heart more than the scolding. He knew his dad's hand passed forgiveness to him with an action that spoke louder than words.

His horses' breathing quieted again, and Harvey clucked. They obediently leaned into their collars and pushed downhill. His ears felt hot with shame. On his way, he looked at the limbs that had fallen on the edge of the field. Even after being admonished by his dad, he still wanted to find a way to keep up with Joe.

About halfway down the slope, a shadow came over Harvey, and he looked back. The late morning sun hid behind the silo, casting darkness across the lower part of the field. The sight of his father walking in the dark shadow sent a shudder through Harvey. He suddenly remembered something the minister had said last Sunday at church. "Respect your earthly parents, you never know when you might lose them, and you don't want to regret how you treated them."

Those words and the sight of his dad walking in the shadow-filled Harvey with remorse. He wanted to run and hug his dad. Instead, he resolved in his heart to show him respect by his actions. The only thing in the world Harvey wanted more than plowing ten acres faster than Joe was to be like his dad. His dad was good-natured enough to roll around on the ground like a grizzly when playing with Harvey's little brothers and sisters. When he was in public, he stood tall, confident, and only spoke when he had well-thought-out words. Harvey always tried to emulate his father's way of standing and talking.

The shadow stayed on Harvey as he continued plowing toward the oak. The boy turned to look at his father again, and movement on the silhouetted silo caught his eye. A large bird or something clung onto the cylinder, its wings flapping. Harvey stopped his horses and stared at the strange sight. Whatever it was, it slowly descended to the ground, wings flapping as it moved.

With a cluck, Harvey sent his horses plowing again. He couldn't shake the strange image imprinted on his mind's eye. Once they reached the shade of the oak tree, Harvey headed over to tie his horses to the fence near the road. Just then, Orva stepped out from behind the tree, "What did Dad say to you?"

Orva's voice didn't startle Harvey. He knew his brother would be joining him for a break. They took turns drinking cool water from a jug that had been stashed in a cold gurgling creek a short distance from the tree.

When Harvey didn't respond, Orva asked again, "What'd Dad say?"

"He saw that I didn't rest the horses on my last round. He wasn't happy."

Orva finished taking a sip from the jug and used his sleeve to wipe his mouth. His honest brown eyes looked straight in Harvey's as he asked, "Why didn't you?"

"Because this end of the field isn't as wide. I didn't think they needed a rest."

"Did you tell Dad that?" Orva questioned.

"No—I knew he wouldn't agree with me." Harvey nudged his brother. "Hey, Orva. Keep an eye on the horses.

I'm gonna run over and move some branches off the edge of this field."

While Harvey ran, he heard his younger brother yell teasingly, "What's the matter—trying to save time so you can beat your friend?"

Harvey didn't waste time defending himself. He ran to where the branches were laying and dragged them aside. One thick limb proved to be a struggle. He thought about calling for Orva to come to help him, but he didn't want to lose time. Instead, he heaved, groaned, and grunted. The branch suddenly snapped in half and slapped Harvey on the back, knocking him to the ground. He jumped up and pulled the two halves until they lay in tall grass out of the way. He ran back and joined Orva in the shade. Both boys sat on overturned five-gallon buckets and relaxed.

"You sure did get all sweated up while moving those limbs," Orva said.

Harvey smiled and answered, "Yeah, but now my horses are nearly rested, and I saved time."

Orva laughed. "You and Joe are as bad as Brick and Cello. You all have yourselves sweated up from trying to outdo each other. One of these days it's gonna come back on ya."

Harvey hoisted up his shirttail. "Maybe it already did? A big limb snapped while I was dragging it and slapped my back. Did it leave a mark?"

His younger brother touched it. "Yeah—two big ones."

The brothers laughed.

Just then, a woman's voice came from beyond the horses and fence. "Hello!"

Harvey and Orva stood out of politeness and peered between their huge horses to see what she wanted. The woman wasn't like anyone they knew personally. Her face contorted, visibly angry. "Come here!"

They maneuvered around their giant horses, reluctant to get close to her but also afraid to disobey. Her silvery hair had been chopped short. She wore a sleeveless T-shirt with writing and cartoon pictures on it and a pair of shorts.

"What are you boys doing here?" she demanded. Her eyes flashed anger, and the boys were scared into silence. They thought what they were doing was obvious. Harvey struggled to think of what she might be asking and why she could be so angry.

"I said, what are you boys doing here with these horses under a tree!"

Harvey concluded she thought they were lazy. He tried to explain himself. "Our dad is very strict. He makes us do it."

The strange woman's eyes flashed sternness. "I'll be talking to your dad about this!"

Orva picked up his scythe and hurried back to his task of clearing weeds. He swung it hardily as if to be sure she noticed his effort. Harvey's horses were well-rested at this point. He turned them out to the field and set them plowing.

That evening, after supper, Harvey's family followed their routine of relaxing on the front porch. From there, they had a magnificent view of a cattle pasture and the road beyond it. Huge trees lined the highway and were full of birds singing spring songs. Harvey's little brothers and sisters were spread out on the porch floorboards. They were on their tummies coloring pictures of farm animals. Dad and Mom sat on the porch swing, their usual spot. Harvey sat on the steps and suddenly announced, "I think I met the woman that moved in next to us. She is strange."

Harvey's mother stopped him. "Harvey—don't jump to conclusions based on how she looks. She may be a nice woman. We don't all have the same upbringing."

Emily, the mother of all the Chupp children, didn't own an angry expression. She only needed to look at a child with her gentle brown eyes, and a feeling of remorse would come over them for whatever naughty thing they had said or done. Her look worked like that on Harvey, and he tried to think of how he could reword his statement about the neighbor. "It's not just the way she looks." He scratched his head and chose his words carefully. "She was walking down the road today and saw Orva and me sitting in the shade resting the horses, and she scolded us."

Mom lowered her knitting to her lap. "What did she see you boys doing?"

"We were sitting on buckets relaxing, and she thought we were acting lazy. She seemed mad and said she was gonna tell our dad."

Orva, who sat on the steps by Harvey, nodded in agreement. "It's true. Harvey tried to tell her Dad wants us to rest the horses, but she thought we were making excuses."

Dad laughed out loud. "If only she knew I had to force you boys to take a break."

Orva added, "Harvey hurt his back, trying to hurry too much."

Mom stood up from her seat beside Dad on the porch swing. "What happened, Harvey?"

Harvey shrugged. "Nothing."

"Show them those marks," Orva insisted.

Mom tugged Harvey's shirt up in the back. "Oh, Harvey, your back looks like someone took after you with a hickory switch."

"It's nothing. It didn't even really hurt," Harvey said, trying to be sturdy like his dad.

Mom went into the house and came out with salve. "Here—let me put some of this on your back." While she rubbed it in, she said, "Be careful what you say to our new neighbor. We don't want to start anything bad."

Harvey said, “Dad—did you see that strange thing on the silo this morning?”

“I didn’t see anything. What did it look like?”

“A huge bird or something. Its wings were flapping in the breeze, and it slowly came down off the silo.”

Dad didn’t look too nervous. “It must have been a crow.”

Eight-year-old Mary Elizabeth, who had been writing in her journal, stopped her pencil and looked at Harvey. Her eyes were filled with terror, so much so that Harvey wished he hadn’t brought it up in front of the little children.

“Yeah—I bet it was a crow,” Harvey said.

Mary Elizabeth’s expression relaxed, and Harvey felt better.

CHAPTER THREE

Mary Elizabeth

The next morning, a blossoming apple tree near the Chupp's garden chimed with cascading notes. A cluster of robins shook the limbs as they hopped from branch to branch singing. One of the robins left the canopy of white flowers and fluttered down near eight-year-old Mary Elizabeth who knelt on the black soil. Earlier that morning, her mother had hoed out long straight rows as a seedbed. Mary Elizabeth carefully tucked pea seeds into the bed and covered them with a blanket of dirt. She stopped her seed planting long enough to watch the robin near her on the ground tug on a worm.

The bird worked for a while, pulling and hopping in a circle. It had to hoist its head high, tugging the worm into a straight line like elastic. The robin's orange breast feathers puffed out while it wrestled with its catch. Finally, the reddish-brown worm popped free of the soil and rolled into a coil trying to escape. The robin tussled with it on the ground until Mary Elizabeth giggled. At that, the bird noticed the little girl watching him. He gathered his meal in his beak and flew off.

Lavern and Emily Chupp's family spent most of their time in the space between the screen door of their back porch and the big barn. The way the Chupp's farm buildings were situated created a courtyard area behind the house, a perfect space for small children to play. Emily could look out her kitchen window and check on her little ones. A small apple orchard occupied one edge of that space. Just below the kitchen window and beyond the screen porch, a vast garden that had been carefully tilled and made ready for spring planting filled another corner of the courtyard. The gravel lane that brought visitors in from the road ended in a large circle drive between the house and barns as well. A long wooden hitching rail ran along in front of the biggest barn and ended near the silo. There had been as many as fifteen buggies lined up along the hitching rack at times.

Mary Elizabeth didn't mind planting seeds. Although it wasn't her favorite job, she gladly did so in anticipation of how fun it would be when everything began to sprout and grow. The little girl kept hiking up her green dress so her bare knees were on the soil instead of getting her dress dirty. A yellow apron had been tied on over her dress. The combination of yellow and green made Mary Elizabeth appear something like a flower. She sat up and tucked a strand of her sandy-brown hair back into her green headscarf. Her dainty nose and chin gave her face an angelic look.

The little girl hummed as she worked, imagining what summer would bring. She and her siblings would walk the garden rows barefoot. They would pick strawberries to can or for putting in pies or to pop in their mouth. When the sweet peas were ready, they also made a nice snack to be enjoyed freely. There were things in the garden like cucumbers and potatoes that didn't make a quick treat. Those types of products were gathered in piles when their season came. Everyone helped gather, process, and eat the bounty.

Mary Elizabeth loved the garden as much or more than anyone in the family. As with other jobs around the farm, Mom and Dad allowed their children to do the chores they enjoyed most, as long as all the work got done. Some tasks nobody wanted to do, like scraping out the hog lot. When it came to jobs like that, they all did it together, to make the work more fun and to finish more quickly.

Thirteen-year-old Edith Rose, raven-headed with glassy-blue eyes, finished hanging clothes on the line and joined her little sister in the garden. "How's it going here?"

"I'm frustrated with my dress," Mary Elizabeth said, and let out an exasperated sigh. "It keeps getting in my way. I don't want to kneel on it, so I have to keep hiking it up."

"Do like this." Edith Rose stood and rolled the middle of her blue dress into the top of her underwear. "Some of the older girls at church told me that they do this to make their dresses shorter while gardening."

Mary Elizabeth's face lit up as she tucked in a roll of her dress. "I never thought of this!"

The sisters got to work pushing peas into the soil. The work moved along much better with their shortened dresses. Mary Elizabeth piped up, "I'm so happy we have a week off from school for spring fieldwork. I like school, but I like gardening better!"

Edith Rose paused in thought. "I wish I could be home when I'm at school, but when I'm home, I miss my school friends."

"I guess that's true," Mary Elizabeth said and giggled.

Six-year-old Ada Fern hopped and then skipped across the driveway and stood watching her older sisters plant peas. She had dark hair, blue eyes, and a blue dress, making her look like a miniature version of her older sister, Edith Rose.

"Can I help?" she asked.

Edith Rose pointed to the last few peas she had tucked into the earth. "You could cover those seeds up like this." She showed her little sister how to smooth a blanket of dirt over the seeds carefully.

Several robins jumped from the blossomy boughs near the garden and took flight. The sisters stopped planting for a moment and watched them soar overhead and across the roof of the big barn.

"I wish I were a bird," Mary Elizabeth announced.

Edith Rose wrinkled up her nose. "Why that?"

"Because it would be so wonderful to be able to fly right over the big barn if you wanted to."

"Not me," Edith Rose said emphatically. "I'd be scared to death to be up that high." After the girls moved forward on their knees, they started planting again. Edith Rose added, "Besides—I wouldn't want to eat worms!"

They all three stopped planting to look at each other with wide eyes. Without knowing the others were going to do it, they all stuck out their tongues and made a gagging sound. The coincidence tickled them, and they laughed until they shook.

The sisters quickly finished planting both rows of peas. Mom came out through the screen-door just as they stood up to admire their work.

"We finished the peas," Mary Elizabeth exclaimed cheerfully.

Mom's face didn't look pleased as they had expected. "What have you girls done with your dresses?"

Edith Rose yanked the roll of her dress out and smoothed it down with her hands.

Mary Elizabeth's eyes squinted in her usual smile, thick lashes hiding her pupils. "We found a way to keep our dresses out from under us while we plant the garden."

Mom stepped over and untucked Mary Elizabeth's dress. "Let's not do that. What if the bishop or someone stops by and sees you girls with your dresses all hiked up?" Mom turned her focus to the garden and smiled. "I'm happy you girls got the peas planted. How about we all wash up, and we'll get started putting lunch together."

While slicing homemade-bread, Mary Elizabeth asked her mom, "Do you think we could work in the garden first thing in the mornings?"

Mom stopped cutting ham long enough to see what her daughter was asking. "It's still spring. We usually don't do that until the middle of summer."

"I know it's not that hot during the day, but I love working in the garden in the morning and evening." She glanced at her mother and sighed. "It's just so fresh outside at those perfect times of the day. We can do our inside things during the boring old afternoon."

"I guess—if that seems so much better to you. Maybe your sisters won't feel like doing it that way?"

Mary Elizabeth shook her head, flopping her headscarf. "I already asked them, and they want to do it that way too!"

Ada Fern nodded in agreement. "I like mornings too!"

The big boys came into the kitchen with the little boys tagging behind them. All three of the little boys looked as if they had been cut out with the same cookie-cutter, except in three sizes. They all shared silky-brown hair, cut in typical Amish bowl fashion. Each wore light-green shirts, and little Amish trousers held up by white suspenders. Myron, the oldest at age five, tugged on his mother's dress. "Us little boys wanna feed the pups."

"That's Orva's job. He's older, and giving puppies food and water is very important." Mom cocked her head and looked at Myron to let him know she cared about him, but the job was over his head.

Leroy, next in age to Myron, turned four that spring. He stepped over beside his slightly older and bigger brother. He and Myron stood tilting their heads up at Mom and gave her pleading eyes. Myron persisted, "But, Mom, we'll all three help get the food and water. We can do it."

Leroy nodded. "We promise."

Mom glanced at Harvey, raising her eyebrows to ask for his opinion. He stepped near her and whispered. "I can double-check every day and make sure they are taken care of."

"Harvey agrees that you little boys can do it. But no tossing dog food about—it's expensive."

Mary Elizabeth watched the whole thing unfold. She admired Harvey almost as much as she did her dad. He seemed like a man to her. After all, he was nearly fifteen, tall and handsome and turning out kind like Daddy. She decided she would write something about him in her diary that evening.

After lunch, Mom said, "Girls—let's walk down the lane together and get the mail." She asked Harvey, "Will you keep an eye on the little boys till we get back."

Harvey nodded.

She told the little boys, "You can play with the puppies. Behave for Harvey."

Myron, Leroy, and Charlie ran for the back door. Mom and the girls headed out the front and down the porch steps. Emily strolled down the lane under spring sunshine, with the natural motion of a woman. Edith Rose, being the oldest sister, pulled the wagon with the baby in it. Mary Elizabeth and Ada Fern walked arm in arm, singing a song together. The lane ran between fencerows. The field Harvey had been plowing was on one side, and on the other, a cow pasture. Large black-and-white spotted cows grazed peacefully along the lane. Birds sang and fluttered about busily finding nesting materials.

When Emily and her daughters reached the mailbox, they saw the new neighbor lady striding toward them on the road. Mary Elizabeth and Ada Fern quit singing and hid behind their mother at the sight of the strange woman.

Mom stepped forward. “Hello—you must be our new neighbor? My name is Emily, and these are my daughters.”

The lady said, “I’m Ms. Mims—is your husband at home?”

“Oh—not at the moment.” Mom looked taken aback at Ms. Mims’s curtness. “He should be home soon. Is there a message I should give him?”

Ms. Mims stood with her hands on her hips as if ready to spout off. “It’s about your boys and horses.”

The baby started crying, so Mom gathered her up out of the wagon and rocked her soothingly. “Is there a problem?”

“I’d rather talk to him about it,” she said and turned to walk away.

“We’ve heard that you’re a nurse!” Mom called after her as if hoping to start a friendlier conversation.

Ms. Mims stopped walking long enough to turn and correct her. “I’m the director of nursing at the university hospital.” Then she marched up the hill toward the mansion.

Emily drew the mail from the box and looked at it while still rocking her crying baby. She acted calm, but the girls knew she was upset. They didn’t say anything. They stood and watched Ms. Mims head uphill until she was out of earshot.

Six-year-old Ada Fern spoke first, “Why doesn’t she say her first name?”

Mom put the mail in the wagon. “I’ll carry the baby,” she said to Edith Rose as if instructing her to get started pulling the wagon and mail back toward the house. After the baby’s crying quieted, Mom said, “It’s our Amish way to call people by their first names, but other people say Mr. and Mrs. this and that.”

Mary Elizabeth asked, “Why does she say Ms. with a Z sound? Does that mean she has a husband or not?”

"I guess she doesn't want people to know for sure. That's the way some do nowadays."

Mom and the girls followed the lane around the house and into the courtyard space. The little boys were busy playing with puppies. Harvey stepped out of the barn leading four horses. Orva followed with two more. They stopped the crowd of massive workhorses just in front of the barn and began to snap driving lines in place.

Mom walked directly toward the big boys, and the girls followed to see what she would say.

"What did you boys do?"

Harvey stepped away from the horses and looked at his mother. "What do you mean?"

The baby started crying again, and Mom swayed to keep her quiet. "Harvey—you might as well tell me what you boys did. Our new neighbor is upset about it, and she's gonna talk to your dad."

"If we did something wrong, we don't know what it is," Harvey said sincerely.

Orva nodded in agreement. "Honest, Mom, we weren't doing anything, and she came by mad as a hornet. Maybe someone else did something, and she thinks it was us?"

Mom checked for truthfulness in Harvey's and Orva's eyes while rocking her baby. Her own eyes welled up, and a few tears trickled down her cheeks.

The boys stood and stared, not sure what to say.

Mom wiped her cheeks with her apron. "Well—please be careful. We don't want trouble with her."

CHAPTER FOUR

Chickens and Sundays

Sunday afternoon, the world seemed perfect. Laverne's best team of perfectly matched driving horses clip-clopped in a happy rhythm along the paved road leading home from church. The big boys, Harvey and Orva, and the two big girls, Edith Rose and Mary Elizabeth, were crowded into the four-foot back seat. Ada Fern leaned over between the front and back seats. Mom held the baby, and Dad held two-year-old Charlie. Myron and Leroy snuggled in around them, standing between their legs, half-on the front bench. Several conversations were going on at once. Mary Elizabeth kept a study barrage of questions running for her older siblings. Her smile-squinted eyes and grin made it impossible to get frustrated with her ways.

The little boys asked Dad about how things were when he was their age. His interesting facts were more numerous than an encyclopedia. He kept his children entertained for hours with hunting and fishing tales from his childhood in Michigan. If that got tedious, he had stories about runaway horses, mean bulls, snakes that drank milk from cows while they rested, crows that stole fish from their set lines, dogs that saved people from a rabid skunk, and a long list of incredible stories that never ran dry. Harvey struggled to answer Mary Elizabeth's questions because of getting distracted by Dad's retelling of a camping adventure.

"Harvey," she started a question with his name to gather all his attention. "How can people like our new neighbor be in such a bad mood when the world is so full of happy things?"

Harvey studied his younger sister's face before answering. He hadn't realized how much she looked like her mother until that moment. Her sandy-brown hair smoothly pulled back under her covering. As with mother, she had a lovely tan complexion with light freckles on her nose and cheeks. Mom's brown eyes were easier to see because they weren't squinted with a smile as often as Mary Elizabeth's. Mom did have the same happy face, though. Her smile just seemed more relaxed and mature than Mary Elizabeth's.

Harvey tried to explain a mystery he couldn't quite fathom himself. "I guess some people have grown up seeing all kinds of scary and horrible things on TV and listening to it on their radios. They are so used to everything being bad in the news they feel sad. They forget to listen to the birds singing or play with kittens and puppies."

Mary Elizabeth's face lost its smile for a fleeting moment. It came back in full force as she lit up with an idea. "Maybe we should invite Ms. Mims over to help feed the calves some morning. How could she be sad when the sun comes out bright red and our rooster crows?"

Harvey nodded in agreement.

Edith Rose's cheeks balled up in a smile of her own. "The puppies come out chasing each other and tripping over chickens. Who couldn't laugh at those silly pups? We could hold Ms. Mims down on the ground like we do with Daddy and let all six pups lick her cheeks until she starts giggling. Who couldn't?"

Mom suddenly leaned over between the front and back. "What's this about holding Ms. Mims down?"

Mary Elizabeth defended Edith Rose. "She meant it in the best way. Really she did."

"What way could that be?" Mom asked seriously.

Edith Rose explained. “We were just saying that Ms. Mims couldn’t help but laugh if all six pups licked her cheeks. I don’t think any person alive could keep a sour face if those pups got to them.”

Mom laughed. Even Dad and Harvey sniffled out a short chuckle.

Mary Elizabeth told Edith Rose, “Look at Harvey’s eyes. We made his eyes twinkle.”

Harvey tried to turn away for a moment. He glanced back and took in the sight of his sister’s smiling faces.

“There it is!” Mary Elizabeth teased.

Orva laughed and elbowed his older brother. Heat rose to Harvey’s cheeks, and he tried to hide his face with his broad-brimmed Sunday hat.

The horses turned into the Chupp family’s lane. They all studied each cow they passed, watching for identifying clues. “That’s Diana!” Mary Elizabeth announced. Little Leroy called from beside Mom’s knees, “That’s number 26 beside her!”

They all laughed because Leroy didn’t know his numbers yet. He knew “number 26” as a name and recognized the cow correctly. The children kept up identifying the cows until the buggy stopped by the barn.

Myron asked his mother, “Can we get the puppies out and play with them now?”

“After you change into your chore clothes. I don’t want you getting your Sunday clothes all dirty.”

Dad stopped unhitching the horses to look at Mom. “They won’t get their clothes dirty just letting the puppies out, will they?”

“Have you seen these children with those pups?” Mom checked Dad’s eyes. “They roll around on the ground with them.”

The little boys all watched Dad and Mom curious to see what they decided. Dad said, "Do like your mom said, change into your chore clothes." He led his team into the horse barn.

Harvey said, "Dad, I'll unharness the horses after I change."

"Go ahead and change," Dad said. "I don't mind taking care of the horses."

All the children hurried in to change. They raced to see who could get back outside first. Harvey and Edith Rose waited by the steps, having realized the little boys were crying because they couldn't get changed as fast. Little Leroy came out smiling with a tear in the corner of his eye, and they all laughed at how cute he looked. They were heading down to the big barn in a happy cluster when a car pulled into the lane.

Ms. Mims parked near the house and headed toward the children. They hushed all their laughter and huddled together when they saw her angry face. Mom stepped out of the house, and the little children hid behind her.

"I'd like to buy some eggs," Ms. Mims said in a cross tone.

Mom's eyes widened in surprise. It was a rare moment when she didn't answer with something. She stood dumbfounded and looked at her children as if they might have an explanation for the neighbor. Ms. Mims's eyes followed, and she glared at the children's clothes.

"We don't…" Mom stammered.

Ms. Mims asserted herself. "I saw your sign on the road. You do have eggs for sale, don't you?"

Mom's face paled. She almost whispered, "The sign says, *No Sunday Sales.*"

"Oh, that's ridiculous," Ms. Mims scoffed. "I only need a few eggs, and I don't want to run into town for them." She held out a five-dollar bill.

Mom's face returned to its natural color, and she smiled. "Mary Elizabeth—run and get a dozen eggs. We can give them to our neighbor."

Mary Elizabeth dashed off until Ms. Mims shouted. "Never mind the eggs!"

Mary Elizabeth froze in her tracks, and the whole family looked to Ms. Mims to see what she would say next. She opened her purse and placed her five-dollar bill back inside. All the while, muttering. "The horses have to pull a buggy on Sunday. The chickens are expected to lay eggs, and the children told to run and fetch eggs on Sunday. But heaven forbid that we could pass a few dollars between us on the Sabbath!"

Mom started toward her, clearly searching for some compromise, but Ms. Mims slammed her car door and drove away. Dad came out of the horse barn and found everyone standing in a gloomy clump.

"What happened to my cheerful family?"

Mom faced Dad and let out her breath slowly. "We had a visit from our new neighbor. It seems we can't do anything right in her eyes."

"What's wrong now?" Dad asked with astonishment.

"She wanted to buy eggs. I told her we don't sell them on Sundays."

Dad shrugged his shoulders. "You should've given her a dozen."

"I tried," Mom said in frustration. "That seemed to make her mad too!"

Dad laughed and tugged on Mom's sleeve. "Don't let her upset you so much. She's one of those people that won't be happy no matter what."

"Well, something set her off. I wish she'd talk to you about whatever it is that's bugging her and get it out in the open." Mom looked up the hill toward the mansion and sighed.

"I can't feel peaceful living here with my closest neighbor looking down on us in anger all the time."

That evening the Chupp family relaxed on the front porch again. Enamel gray floorboards, slick and shiny, ran the full length of the Chupp's large farmhouse. Four simple posts held up the overhang. The ceiling of the porch had a fresh coat of sky-blue paint that glowed off the white wall behind the family. From their porch, the Chupps could watch any traffic that might pass on the road beyond their cattle pasture. Very few cars passed on a Sunday evening. However, numerous buggies rolled by with the faint but pleasant clip-clop of horse hooves and gentle rumble of buggy wheels. The Chupps knew every Amish person that passed their home, and they made a game out of being the first to identify who they saw.

"Here comes Banana Pudding Barbara!" Orva announced. They all looked to the road. "See—that's her bay horse with one long sock." Everyone knew the elderly widow for her delicious pudding and horse with one long sock.

Harvey and Orva whittled on long sticks they found earlier near the road. They planned to carve a morel mushroom on the top and use the sticks for mushroom hunting. Edith Rose dawdled the baby on her lap and kissed her chubby cheeks. Mary Elizabeth sat with her back against the house, writing another private entry in her journal. The little boys played with their toy farm animals in the flower bed near the porch.

Edith Rose looked at Mary Elizabeth and asked, "What got you started with a diary?"

"Our teacher wants us to. She says it will help us remember what our life was like when we were eight." She let her tongue curve out of her mouth as if that helped with her writing. "How do you spell, expected?"

Mom answered, "E-X-P-E-C-T-E-D." After a pause, she asked, "What are you journaling about?"

Mary Elizabeth put her pencil to her mouth. “I’m writing everything.”

Orva laughed. “You can’t write everything.”

Her thick eyelashes batted with her smile. “Everything that happens here— I can.”

CHAPTER FIVE

Flowers and Puppies

A bright red sun glowed through tree limbs east of the Chupp farm on Monday morning. Clouds of fog hung along the creek and other low places. Within a few rooster crows, songbirds awoke, and one by one added a few notes until their symphony reached its full volume. An occasional trumpeting bellow from a cow echoed through the mist and overshadowed the sound of birds. Dad, Harvey, Orva, and Edith Rose milked in the big barn. Tinkling of buckets and soft voices came through the open doorway and reached the calf pen, where Mary Elizabeth and Ada fern bottle-fed calves.

Myron and Leroy let the puppies out of their pen, and Charlie got busy playing with them like it was his job. Mom had already run a basketful of laundry through a ringer-washer, and most of it dangled on the line. The baby cooed in her springy seat near the laundry basket at Mom's feet. Scents of blueberry muffins floated through the screen kitchen windows and made it to Mary Elizabeth's nose.

"Don't you just love mornings," Mary Elizabeth asked Ada Fern.

"Yes—mornings with no school and blueberry muffins."

A calf butted its head against the bottle Mary Elizabeth held and jiggled it out of her hands. She gathered the slippery bottle up off the ground and pushed it back into the hungry calf's mouth. Mary Elizabeth continued, "When I'm a mother, I'm gonna make blueberry muffins every day!"

Ada Fern giggled. "Me too!"

The calves sucked the last drops of milk dry and returned to their bed of straw. Ada Fern ran off to join the little boys and the puppy's playful antics. Mary Elizabeth quickly rinsed out the bottles and rubber nipples with the handpump. She set them in the milk-house where Edith Rose would wash them properly in hot water when she cleaned up the milk buckets.

Happy to have her morning chores out of the way, Mary Elizabeth hurried to do what she loved most, planting flowers. Mom let her choose some annuals at the greenhouse a few days ago, and she couldn't wait to get them in the ground. After gathering the flat of plants from the toolshed, she spread the little plastic pots out in a neat row by the front porch. The little girl carefully alternated the red and pink sets, imagining how beautiful their white house would look in a few weeks.

As she worked, the sun climbed through treetops and chased the fog away. Movement on the road caught Mary Elizabeth's eye, and she noticed Ms. Mims going by on a morning jog. Mary Elizabeth called out a friendly "Hello" and waved at her new neighbor. Ms. Mims returned the wave, which pleased the little girl. She turned her attention back to spacing her flowers out perfectly. She didn't plant one flower until she had stood twenty feet back and made sure the sets were just right.

Dad and Orva came around the corner of the house and headed toward the mailbox.

Mary Elizabeth stood and called to them. "Where are you going? The mail won't be here for hours!"

Orva cupped his hands to his mouth. "We're gonna put a sign on the road. Puppies for sale!"

His words created a strange mixture of excitement and sadness in her heart. She knew they couldn't keep six Burmese

Mountain Dog pups. If they got as big as their mother, Roxy, they would be more like a herd of horses than a pack of dogs. She hated to see them leave the farm. At the same time, it seemed fun that people would come in the lane wanting to buy one of their puppies.

Mary Elizabeth dug holes with a spade exactly where each flower had been placed. By the time Dad and Orva strolled back up the lane, she had her holes ready and most of the flowers in the ground. When Mom called everyone in for breakfast, the sets were all planted, and nothing left to do but water them. While gathering the little plastic pots, she noticed Ms. Mims trotting back past. Ms. Mims stopped at the end of the Chupp lane, and Mary Elizabeth wondered if she might be planning to come to the house. Ms. Mims resumed her trot up the road, and it occurred to Mary Elizabeth that her neighbor had stopped to look at the puppy sign.

After breakfast, Mary Elizabeth watered her flowers and then scoured the vegetable garden for weeds. They were hard to find in Mom's garden. While breaking off thick stems of rhubarb, she found a kitten she hadn't seen before — a faintly marked calico with silvery-blue eyes. The kitten hissed when Mary Elizabeth picked it up but purred once it found itself snuggled in the eight-year-old girl's arms.

"What's that?" Four-year-old Leroy questioned.

"I found a kitten." Mary Elizabeth took the kitten out of the garden and showed Leroy. Soon, all the younger children left their game of pushing each other in a wheelbarrow and came to see the kitten.

"We never see kittens in the house yard," Leroy said.

Mary Elizabeth, being the older sister, explained, "That's because we have Roxy and her six puppies. Those dogs won't let any kittens out of the barn without a chase."

Myron, Leroy and Ada Fern nodded that they understood. Mary Elizabeth said, "Dad and Orva put a sign up this morning that says *Puppies for Sale.* Pretty soon, people will come and buy all the puppies, and then kittens will play in the yard again. The three little children looked at each other soberly.

Leroy spoke up, "I like kittens, but I like puppies better."

"I don't want to sell the puppies," Ada Fern said. Her lower lip protruding.

Mary Elizabeth answered like a little mother, "We can't have seven big dogs, and they are all gonna grow up soon."

At that, the little children resumed their game with the wheelbarrow. Big pawed, Burmese Mountain Dog pups followed the children and nipped at their heels.

Mom stepped out of the screen door. "The milkman will be coming soon. He comes barreling in here with his big truck at full speed. We don't need one of those pups to get run over, and I don't want the milkman to be upset. Let's put the puppies in their pen. They can be in there for a bit until the milkman leaves."

Mary Elizabeth returned the kitten to its hiding place in the garden and joined her little siblings in rounding up the rambunctious puppies. They all enjoyed the job. Partly because it was challenging, but mostly because the chubby pups were so soft and cuddly. They managed to push the last puppy into the pen and shut the gate just as the roar of the milk truck rumbled into the lane. The children all knew their dad's rule. They had to stay in the barn until the truck came to a complete stop. Once he stopped and got out, they were allowed to stand and talk to him until he put the hose away. After that, they had to go into the milk-house or barn while he backed out.

The children stepped out of the milk-house and noticed a car parked near the house. Ms. Mims stood near the garden, talking with their mother. The Chupp children had been enjoying a fun conversation with the milkman and spent the past five minutes laughing about Leroy slipping in the milk-house and sitting down hard. At the sight of the grouchy woman, they all grew silent and gathered behind their mother to see what the matter was. Emily passed a carton of eggs to Ms. Mims and took a few bills from her hand.

"Where are these puppies you have for sale?" Ms. Mims said it as if she was mad.

Mom pointed to the barn. "We have them in a kennel if you want to see them."

Ms. Mims charged forward as if she might be planning to kill the pups instead of buying them. Mom followed, and her children tagged along without making a peep. Mary Elizabeth pushed open the big door to make the puppies visible inside the dark barn. The little dogs all began to yap, thinking they were about to be let out to play. Ms. Mims stood looking at the pups as if appalled. Mary Elizabeth couldn't imagine why the woman didn't like them; they were all so cute and happy. She wondered if the grouchy woman didn't like how happy they were.

Ms. Mims scoffed, "I was here yesterday, and I didn't even hear these puppies. Were they all shut up in the barn then too?"

"I guess they were," Mom said. "They don't make a fuss until we open the door." With that, Mom pulled one of the big pups from the pen and held it out for Ms. Mims to hold. The woman leaned away as if it might contaminate her. "We are asking $400 each for the pups." Mom smiled at her. "I'll ask my husband if we can cut the price in half for you, beings that you're a close neighbor and all."

"You'll ask your husband?" Ms. Mims scoffed.

Mary Elizabeth and her little brothers and sister clumped together, staring at the grouchy woman. They didn't know how she could be so upset while looking at puppies.

Myron piped up, "Us little boys do the dog chores."

Leroy nodded in agreement. "They're our job."

Ms. Mims stared at the children. She scanned their clothes as if disgusted. After a long awkward silence, Ms. Mims met eyes with Mom and said with an angry tone. "I wouldn't give you people a penny after how you treat these pups." With that, she charged out of the barn. They watched her slam the car door. Mom's head jerked with surprise. Edith Rose stepped out of the back door with the baby about the same time, and the baby started crying at the sharp noise. Edith Rose rocked the baby gently and watched Ms. Mims start her car, rev her engine, and turn it around with jerky surges back and forth, then charge out of their lane.

The baby's cries grew louder, and Edith Rose brought her to her mother. "What happened with Ms. Mims?"

Emily soothed her little one by humming and didn't answer right away.

Leroy offered his perspective. "She hates the pups."

"I'm glad she doesn't want one," Myron said. "Dogs don't want to live with a mean lady."

Mom looked at Edith Rose as if she hadn't heard what the little boys said. "She came to get her eggs and wanted to see our pups."

"Why did she leave so mad?" Edith Rose asked with fear in her eyes.

Emily looked at her younger children as if they might have the answer. "I guess I don't know."

CHAPTER SIX

Harvey's Monday

That same Monday morning, Harvey and his team of six horses resumed their plowing. Brick and Cello were in rare form. After a full day of Sabbath rest, they were more than ready to challenge each other to a contest of will and strength again. Harvey had to rein them in during the first two passes across the field. On the third pass, they quieted a little. The two plowshares sliced deep and provided enough drag that the big geldings got a workout.

Harvey rested his horses religiously at the fence on the hill and under the shade tree in the low spot. At the top of the ridge, he looked over the woven-wire to see how Joe's horses were doing. They seemed to be having an issue with their harness. Joe unhitched his team and drove them toward his barn. Harvey felt an excited twinge fill his heart, considering this might be his chance to catch up with Joe. Then he felt guilty for thinking that way.

He checked his team to be sure they were resting and not thinking about leaving without him. Brick and Cello were filled with a driving urge to outdo each other, yet when they were in harness, they wouldn't think of moving forward without being told. They were free to stomp at an occasional fly, and they did. It was permissible to nose-and-nudge each other with their soft muzzles. They nibbled at each other's harnesses, rubbed their ears on the horse next to them, but they stood firm where they were asked to stand. They never moved forward without an explicit command. That was the first rule every horse on the Chupp farm learned.

Dad had explained, “Horses that don’t understand this rule are dangerous to themselves. They also become a risk to their teammates and to the people that work with them.” The older horses understood this. The colts were too young to be trusted alone. While hitched to four older horses, they were not a risk. The older horses demanded that younger ones behaved. Harvey had witnessed Butte and Viola lash out with lightning-quick bites at younger horses for crowding them or for moving out of turn. Harvey didn’t need to do much training with the colts, Butte and Viola took care of most of it.

Stone and Rocky were known as “the colts” by the Chupp family, not because they were babies, but all young horses were known as colts on their farm. They would have that title until they matured and earned everyone’s respect, including the other horses. Cello, the tall black horse on Harvey’s right, happened to be the son of Viola, the gray mare hitched to the right of Cello. Butte was the mother of the Belgians in the hitch, Brick, Stone, and Rocky.

Dad told Harvey once, “My grandpa gave us Viola and Butte as a wedding gift when your mother and I got married. My grandpa raised those two at his place. He told me, ‘I’ll give you a Percheron and a Belgian filly. That way you can decide which breed you like best.’”

“Which do you prefer,” Harvey had asked.

“Can’t decide,” was his answer. “That’s why we have both on our farm.”

On one round, as the horses chugged up the slope toward the fence, Harvey saw it. The sun silhouetted the silo again. Once more, that creature clung on about midway up. Harvey couldn’t take his eyes away. He watched the wings flapping as the strange thing moved down the cylinder toward the ground. Harvey tied his horses to the fence and ran uphill to catch a glimpse of the creature. By the time he scrambled his way near, it had disappeared.

From then on, Harvey couldn't stop glancing at the silo. While the horses plowed, Harvey alternated between keeping an eye on the silo and looking up at the mansion. When he wasn't analyzing what he saw on the silo, his mind wrestled with what might have upset Ms. Mims. He couldn't solve either mystery.

At lunchtime, the dinner bell rang, and Harvey finished his last round of plowing. He unhitched the horses and left the plow on the hill. Dad only let him plow for four hours. He always said, "That's enough for horses. We don't want them getting thin and worked down."

"Couldn't I do three hours in the morning and three in the afternoon?" Harvey asked. "I could use two buggy horses with my afternoon hitch so the colts wouldn't get overworked."

Dad listened as if he might consider it. He pulled on his beard in thought before answering. "Pretty soon one of the other horses would get a sore shoulder, and then you'd have bigger troubles. Let's play it safe."

That noon, after plowing was done, and lunch was out of the way, Harvey's mother sent him to toss some table scraps over the fence. "The barn cats will find it there," she said.

When he came around the barn, movement on the silo caught his eye. He flinched, expecting to see the mysterious descending bird. Instead, he realized Mary Elizabeth was on the ladder. He didn't say anything, afraid he might scare her into falling. He noticed she had tipped a hay-bale against the silo to help her reach the first rung. The first built-in ladder rung had been strategically placed high enough to keep children from climbing the silo.

He watched her jump from the bale to the ground. Her little body shook when she saw Harvey. "I didn't know you were behind me," she said and giggled awkwardly.

"Why would you even think of climbing the silo?"

She cocked her head shyly and said, "I didn't go all the way up." Mary Elizabeth's smiling eyes with thick lashes pleaded with him. "Don't say anything to Dad about it, please."

Harvey wanted to scold her *and* tell their dad, but she was so cute he couldn't. He realized for the first time in his life how difficult being a dad could be. Who would want to be the one to enforce all the safety rules? Yet, it must be done. "What were you doing up the silo?"

She giggled a little. "It's so pretty up there. Please don't tell Daddy."

Harvey tried to scare her. "Mary Elizabeth—do you know I've seen a big scary creature on the silo?"

She didn't look as nervous as he'd hoped. "Dad says it's just a crow."

"We don't know what it is, but if I were you, I wouldn't want to go up there. That big ugly thing might come along, and you wouldn't be able to get down fast enough." When that didn't seem to make her nervous, he added, "Mary Elizabeth—one slip and you may not live to tell about it."

That evening after supper, the whole family sat on the front porch again. Mom and Edith Rose sang hymns as they swung the porch swing gently. Dad sat on a folding chair and stood the baby on his lap. She giggled and tugged on his beard. Ada Fern and the little boys stretched out side-by-side in a row coloring. Four of them shared two pages of one book and a handful of crayons. Harvey and Orva whittled on their mushroom sticks with their pocketknives. Mary Elizabeth made another entry in her diary.

"Harvey, how do you spell hickory switch?"

"What do you wanna know that for?"

"I'm just wondering," Mary Elizabeth said.

"How do you spell Ms. Mims?"

Orva laughed. "Are you gonna chase her off with a hickory switch?"

Mom stopped singing long enough to say, "Orva." They all knew instantly who she was scolding and why.

Ada Fern looked over Mary Elizabeth's shoulder to try and read from her journal. "What are you writing about today?"

"Two things. How Harvey hurt his back and about Ms. Mims and the puppies," Mary Elizabeth said with a smile.

Orva asked, "Can I read it?"

Mary Elizabeth covered it with her hands. "No—diaries are supposed to be private. You put down all your true feelings and read them back to yourself when you get really old. Like eighteen or something."

"We'll find it and read it all," Orva teased.

"Orva," Mom said. "She is right. Nobody needs to read her journal."

"I'm not worried," Mary Elizabeth smiled. "Where I've been hiding it, nobody will ever find it."

CHAPTER SEVEN

A Very Long Day

Mary Elizabeth remembered the warning Harvey gave her about climbing the silo. As she scaled the ladder, his words, said with a very stern face, echoed in her head, "One slip and you may not live to tell about it." She could see his kind blue eyes sparkling below his broad-brimmed Amish hat. She hesitated for a moment ,and then reminded herself out loud, "Dad is at the horse sale today, he won't see me, and Harvey is in the barn unharnessing the horses."

Mary Elizabeth loved climbing trees with her brothers. Every time her family put up hay in the big barn, she scaled mountains of square bales to look out the big door at the mow peak. During haymaking, the big door was unlatched and flopped open, revealing a spectacular view of surrounding farmlands. Amazing views came into sight as she neared her special spot on the silo.

A smile covered the little girl's face as she reached the point she had been climbing to, about one-third of the way up. She took a firm grip on one rung and scanned the horizon. "This must be what it's like to ride in a hot air balloon!" She could see cars on the highway several miles to the east. A horse and buggy trotted along a gravel road to the south. On beyond those spectacles, a huge feed-mill was buzzing with activity. She watched as tractors pulled into the lot and waited their turn to pick up grain.

A few sparrows fluttered around below her, and Mary Elizabeth watched them fly in and land on the ladder beneath her feet. They chirped and argued among themselves and then flew away. She spun around to see where they were heading and lost her grip on the handle. Her eyes opened wide in surprise as she realized she was falling. Her arms flailed as she floated downward. She wanted to cry for help, but there was only time for one word, "Daddy!"

Mary Elizabeth's little brothers were playing near the barn. They heard a thump but didn't know what made the sound. They continued pushing each other around in a wheelbarrow. They ended up coming close to where their big sister lay. Myron said, "Mary Elizabeth, why are you sleeping out here on the ground?" She didn't answer. Myron continued pushing Leroy in circles near the silo. They had a small disagreement about whose turn it was to ride and who should push. Usually, Mary Elizabeth settled their arguments, but she didn't help at all this time. "Mary Elizabeth," Myron called. "It's my turn to ride, and Leroy won't get out of the wheelbarrow!"

Myron stopped pushing his brother and hurried over to his older sister. He crouched down and shook her shoulder. "Mary, wake up! Mary Elizabeth, wake up. Leroy won't get out of the wheelbarrow!" He stood up and looked at her, surprised she wouldn't respond.

Leroy ran to the house, "Mom, Mary Elizabeth is sleeping on the ground, and she won't wake up."

When Mom got there, Myron said, "I saw her climbing the silo, and now she's here on the ground."

Everything after that blurred into chaos. Harvey remembered his mother sending him to Ms. Mims's house. He had just unharnessed the horses and came running out of the barn when he heard his mom scream his name. He stood with all his siblings looking at his sweet little sister lying as still as death.

"Harvey!" Mom yelled as if he wasn't standing there, but he was right there. "Harvey—run to Ms. Mims's house. She's a nurse. Ask her to call 911, and then maybe she'll come here to help."

Harvey started for the horse barn because he thought it might be faster to ride a horse. Getting a horse ready seemed too complicated, so instead, he obeyed his mother and ran. He cut directly across his plowed field. Thick, wet soil clung to his work-boots and turned his feet into globs of lead. His mind raced ahead of him. *This accident is my fault. Why didn't I tell Dad about Mary Elizabeth climbing the silo? Why couldn't I be stern with her?*

The section of unplowed ground that had been a frustration, when Harvey's world centered around his contest with Joe, became a blessing. His feet felt much lighter as he charged over solid ground and neared the creek. The sound of his thumping heart pounded in his ears and the whistle of his labored breathing. Harvey stumbled through the stream. He clambered up the slippery bank on the other side and scrambled up the hill toward the mansion, climbed the fence at the corner post, and fell over the top wire. He pounded on the door with his fist and doubled over sucking wind.

A few seconds and deep gasps for air later, he banged on the door again. He saw Ms. Mims's eyes under the security-chain holding the doors a few inches apart.

"What do you need?"

Harvey choked out, "It's my sister—she fell from the silo. Can you call 911?"

The door shut tight and stayed closed. Harvey wasn't sure what to do next. He stood, looking at the door for a moment, then turned and started running back toward home. At the fence, Harvey changed his mind and returned to bang on the door again. That's when he noticed movement on the garage door. It came up slowly, and Ms. Mims yelled, "Come get in!"

"Please call 911!

"I already did. Now get in the car!"

Harvey ran to the car and jumped in. He stared at Ms. Mims, and she scolded him. "Put on your seatbelt!"

He pulled it on as Ms. Mims revved her engine and her car raced toward his home.

"What was she doing climbing a silo?"

"I'm not sure."

"How old is your sister?"

"Eight."

"And she was climbing a silo? What is wrong with your parents?"

Harvey didn't try to answer. All he could think about was seeing Mary Elizabeth's lifeless body on the ground by the silo. Ms. Mims's car raced into the lane, and they found everyone standing in a clump around Mary Elizabeth. Seemingly, they weren't doing anything, but Harvey knew they were praying. Ms. Mims ran to Mary Elizabeth's side and felt her neck. She put her face close to Mary's. Harvey guessed she was listening for the sound of breathing.

"She has a pulse. Run and get a blanket! Let's cover her to keep her from going into shock."

Harvey started to run, but Edith Rose was already halfway to the house. They seemed to wait forever for an ambulance. Suddenly, there were firemen, policemen, and paramedics everywhere. Red lights pulsed off the silo and barn. Harvey couldn't even see his sister because so many of them were crowding around her. Finally, everyone backed away. Mary Elizabeth lay on a flat board, and firefighters hoisted the board onto a stretcher with wheels. They loaded her into the ambulance.

Mom touched Harvey's arm. "The police are going to find Dad at the sale-barn. He'll meet me at the hospital. People will be here soon to help you with your brothers and sisters."

Harvey looked into his mother's eyes and nodded.

"Keep praying," she said, and got into the ambulance, sirens and lights whirring.

Buggies started filing into the lane as soon as the ambulance left. A few friends and neighbors came at first. By the time an hour had passed, the yard was full of buggies. Women brought plates of food and covered the table and countertop with what they brought. Men stood in circles and talked in hushed tones. Teenage boys stood in circles of their own and chatted quietly. Harvey's little brothers showed the puppies to other little boys. Someone brought news from the hospital, and everyone passed the information, "Mary Elizabeth's not doing well."

Harvey didn't see anyone leave. His thoughts swirled, and he suddenly realized the yard stood empty again. Only a few buggies remained. His uncle and aunt stayed with the children, waiting to hear from the hospital. Harvey looked at the clock when he heard a car coming in the lane, 11:15. He expected someone was bringing Dad, Mom, and hopefully, Mary Elizabeth home. He went to the porch and looked up the lane. Three police cars followed each other toward the house and parked in a line. The officers got out and gathered by one of the cars, talking in hushed tones for a few minutes.

Harvey stepped toward them. "How is my sister?"

An officer motioned toward the house. "Let's go inside and talk for a minute."

Harvey's heart started pounding. He led the way inside, and the policeman followed. Uncle John stood near the table as the officers came in. Only one of them was a man. There were four women officers all dressed in the same garb the policeman wore. Dark blue, so dark it almost looked black.

They all had guns and clubs on their belts, and each wore a shiny badge. They stood in an awkward group near the table.

"What news do you have?" Uncle John asked them. He grimaced as if he didn't want to know what they were going to say.

A female officer stepped forward. "Mary Elizabeth is still fighting for her life." She paused to let the good-news sink in for a moment. "We are here to take the rest of the children with us."

Uncle John didn't seem surprised. He said, "Do you mean, take them to see their sister?"

A woman officer shook her head. She softened her face and spoke in a whisper; her words were barely audible. "We are taking them to safe homes for tonight."

Aunt Linda stepped near her husband, John. "That won't be necessary—we have lots of family members in the area. We can take care of them."

The female cop nodded politely. "I'm sure you do. In this case, we are going to need to take the children to safe homes until we have a chance to examine everything that happened here today." She turned to Harvey. "Can you help me gather some of your little brothers' and sisters' things?"

Harvey nodded and led the way into his little brothers' room. Flashlight beams crisscrossed through the house ahead of him. The little boys were sleeping so soundly they didn't wake up as drawers squeaked opened and shut.

Everything happened like a strange dream. Edith Rose had gathered a few of her dresses and some for Ada Fern. They put everything in paper sacks and set them on the kitchen table. Uncle John and Aunt Linda stood helplessly to one side, speechless. Harvey assumed the officers didn't want to say too much in front of the children.

The male cop took Harvey and Orva toward his car. He opened the back door for the boys. "You guys can have a seat, and I'll be ready in a few minutes."

The brothers sat in silence for a few moments. They gazed over the seat at the shotgun and computer.

Orva looked up at Harvey, "Why are they taking us?"

"I guess they think one of us pushed Mary Elizabeth. Maybe they are gonna take us in for questioning."

One of the woman officers came out with Edith Rose and Ada Fern, and the brothers watched their sisters get in the police car in front of them. The female officer stopped between the cars to speak to the man.

Harvey could almost make out her words. "This is ridic …" She mumbled on for a bit.

The male officer's voice carried a little more. "It's the worst possible setup for neighbors. Over here, they are as old fashioned as it gets. Right up that hill is the new way of thinking. She said she learned about how abusive Amish are on the internet and didn't believe it until she saw it with her own eyes. That woman is a big wig at the hospital, and they took her word for it."

The female cop turned and looked at the boys with pity in her eyes. She motioned for the man to keep his voice down. The other two female officers came out carrying the little boys, who were crying as the officers strapped them in car seats.

Harvey and Orva found themselves escorted into a split-level suburban home in Cash Town. It wasn't more than three or four miles from their home. They had passed the Jones's house many times in a buggy, but it never occurred to the boys that they would someday spend the night there.

The officer rested one hand on each boy's shoulder as he prepared to leave. "The Jones family will take good care of you, boys. They are nice people. If you need anything, ask

Mrs. Jones, and I'm sure she will do whatever she can to make you comfortable."

"Where are our brothers and sisters?" Harvey questioned.

"They are staying in other safe-homes. There are too many children in your family to all stay in one place."

Orva started to sniffle when the cop said it. Harvey put a hand on his younger brother's shoulder and said, "God will be with them."

CHAPTER EIGHT

The Safehouse

Mrs. Jones, a thin and attractive woman, turned out to be very friendly. She had kind dark eyes and long auburn hair tied back into a ponytail. After the officer left, Mrs. Jones showed Harvey and Orva to their room for the night. They both stared at the NFL posters and Spiderman bedsheets. The room also had plenty of stuffed animals and plastic figurines. Everything seemed unusual to them.

"I'm sure you two have had a long day. I'll let you shut the door while you get ready for bed. There is a bathroom right over there, attached to this room. After you turn out the light, please open the door a little. That is our safe house policy."

The Amish boys only nodded that they understood.

Mrs. Jones attempted to look the boys in the eye. "I left some cookies and water bottles on the stand beside the bed if you want them. Otherwise, we'll have breakfast as soon as everyone wakes up tomorrow."

Harvey nodded and said, "Thank you."

Orva echoed, "Thank you."

When they shut the door to change, Orva whispered, "Why are we here?"

"I'm not sure," Harvey answered quietly. "Hopefully, we'll find out more tomorrow."

They tried to get to sleep, but Orva kept wheezing. Finally, Harvey whispered, "Why are you breathing so heavy?"

"They must have a cat," Orva answered matter-of-factly.

The next morning a cat sat on the foot of Orva's bed. Mrs. Jones seemed too young to be the mother of ten- and eleven-year-old sons. They had auburn hair like their mother. Though attractive on her, it didn't help the boys' appearance at all. They didn't have her kind face. Their dad wasn't around for comparison, but Harvey assumed they got their personality from him. They didn't make eye contact with their guests at all. Both looked pudgy like they had never been asked to do a full day's work in their life.

"It turned out lucky that my sons have this week off from school for spring break," Mrs. Jones said. "Maybe you boys can get to be friends."

The TV ran all day, even in a room without people. Shootings, wild car chases, love scenes, and some guys called "Impractical Jokers" played out on the 48" plasma screen all day. Harvey began to worry his little brothers might be subjected to the same garbage wherever they were staying. The Jones boys sat on one couch while Harvey and Orva sat in chairs across from them. The English boys stared at their phone screens for hours while the Amish boys watched them. Sometimes the boys got out their iPads and played games on those. At other times, they used their Xbox. At least then, Harvey and Orva could watch the war games while the Jones boys played.

Mrs. Jones came into the room at regular intervals and moaned. "Are you boys still playing? I asked you to finish that game and empty the dishwasher."

The Jones brothers didn't even so much as look away from the screen. They didn't even grunt an answer to their mother. Instead, they sat like lumps and shook their controllers as if it might help them beat each other. They argued between themselves about things that happened on the screen. From time-to-time, they reached over and poked or slapped at each other. Harvey and Orva sat across from the Jones boys and watched in disbelief. They couldn't imagine ignoring their mother like that. Harvey glanced at his brother. Orva returned a knowing look.

Harvey stood up and went into the kitchen. "Mrs. Jones, I'd be willing to empty the dishwasher if you show me where everything goes."

"Oh, Harvey, that's very nice of you, but my boys need to do their chores. That's all I ask of them—they can do it."

Harvey pulled open the dishwasher. "Really—I don't mind at all. I'm kinda bored anyway."

Mrs. Jones smiled at him and opened the cupboard. "That's where the glasses go. The dish cupboard is right next to it. And the silverware drawer is over there."

Orva appeared and, without words, took the job of putting glasses away while Harvey filled the silverware drawer.

While they were finishing up, Mrs. Jones asked in a friendly way, "What do you boys like to do?"

Orva wasted no time answering, "I like playing baseball."

"Oh, nice," Mrs. Jones said. "I didn't know you boys would be allowed to do that. We have some ball gloves in the garage. You could play catch in the backyard if you want." Orva's face lit up, and Mrs. Jones led the way to the garage and found mitts and a couple of baseballs. "Stay inside the fence. If a ball goes over—tell me, and I'll get it."

The boys didn't throw as hard as they did at home. They tried to be careful, worrying the ball might hit a window or go over the fence. Neither brother dared speak, afraid Mrs. Jones might hear them. After throwing the ball for a while, Harvey said, "This looks like a good climbing tree. Let's go up there for a bit." He hoped that up in the branches, he could talk to Orva without being overheard. In seconds flat, they were up in the tree high enough to be straight across from the bedroom where they had been sleeping. They sat beside each other on a big limb. Maple leaves as big as book pages dangled around them like curtains.

"Are they afraid we'll run off? Orva asked.

"I guess they are. I don't know where Mrs. Jones thinks we'll go—maybe home?"

They sat quietly for a few minutes until Orva asked, "What is going on?"

Harvey didn't want to say what he thought—it sounded too awful to be said. He decided there was no use trying to keep it from his younger brother. "From what those cops were saying, I think they took us away from our parents because they think we are being abused."

Orva's eyes got as big as half-dollars. "We're not—are we?"

"No!" Harvey paused and then scratched above one ear. "Do you know the Bible story about Job?"

Orva shook his head.

"Job was a good man, but the devil told God, 'The only reason Job is good is because you bless him so much. Take all his good things away and he will curse you.' The devil told God to test Job and see."

"Did God test him?"

"No, but God let the devil tempt him. He said, 'You can take away all of his blessings and possessions.' That same day, all of Job's children died."

Orva met eyes with Harvey and asked, "Did Job pass the test?"

"Yeah—he was a good man, and the devil finally gave up."

"Our dad will pass this test too!" Orva said. "He could pass any test."

Harvey nodded, "We need to help our dad get out of this."

A bluejay flew in a few branches above them and fluttered his wings. He added a few angry cries to their conversation.

Harvey started to say, "I sure hope …" His words were interrupted by Mrs. Jones's panicked voice calling, "Harvey! Orva! Where are you?"

"We're up here," Harvey called.

Mrs. Jones shielded her eyes and moved under the tree, searching for the boys. "Oh—you boys scared me. I didn't know where you were."

"We're sorry, Mrs. Jones," Harvey said. "We like to climb trees and things like that."

"Okay—okay—just tell me before you do something like that," she pleaded. Her eyebrows arched with kindness and concern. Harvey felt bad they had scared her. "Please come down now," she said, sounding like she was about to start crying. "It's time to eat, and afterward, you and my sons can watch a movie."

Orva climbed down first, and Harvey followed. At the bottom limb, Harvey's shirt caught on a twig and untucked. Mrs. Jones gasped, "Harvey—what happened to your back?"

"Oh—that's nothing. It just happened the other day."

Mrs. Jones held a hand over her mouth as if afraid she might say the wrong thing. After a moment of looking Harvey directly in his eyes, she said, "Let me see that."

Harvey turned around, and Mrs. Jones lifted his shirt and gasped again.

Orva offered an explanation, "A branch off a tree did it."

"Yeah—a branch off a tree," Harvey confirmed.

Harvey tucked in his shirt and met eyes with Mrs. Jones. It surprised him to see a tear in her eye. "Really—it's nothing. It didn't hurt at all."

Mrs. Jones dabbed at her eye with a finger. "Okay—let's go have some supper." She shifted her voice to sound happy and excited. "After supper, we can watch a movie!"

The boys glanced at each other, thinking the same thing. They had never watched a movie before.

They watched a DVD named Free Willy. Harvey and Orva fell into the story and laughed with the Jones boys during funny parts. All in all, the Amish boys felt guilty for watching when it ended.

After they brushed their teeth, they knelt by the bed to pray, Harvey whispered, "Let's pray for Mary Elizabeth."

Orva said, "And that our dad passes this test quickly so we can go home."

Harvey nodded. They each prayed silently and got into their single beds. A knock on the door sounded, and they heard Mrs. Jones's kind voice. "Are you boys in bed already?"

"Yes," Harvey answered for them both.

Mrs. Jones opened the door. "I'll leave this door slightly open. We'll leave a light on in the hallway again."

"Okay—thanks," Orva said politely.

"And boys …" she hesitated as if thinking out her words. "In the morning, you have an appointment with your caseworker."

Orva spoke up, "What's that?"

"That's your social worker," she paused and then added, "Your caseworker is a therapist. He will talk to you boys about life and important issues. Don't be afraid—just be honest with him. Therapists are people who want to help children and teens. They are on your side—to be sure you are safe and happy."

"Okay—thanks," Harvey said.

Mrs. Jones said, "Goodnight."

Both boys echoed, "Goodnight."

Mrs. Jones's shadow left the doorway, and everything got quiet, except the sound of Orva's wheezing and the Jones boys' cellphones beeping as they played games in the next room over.

After a long silence, Orva said, "I guess you were right."

CHAPTER NINE

Questions and Therapy

Mrs. Jones drove Harvey and Orva to their appointment. The office wasn't what Harvey expected. Mrs. Jones turned at the yellow arches of a McDonalds. She stopped in front of a strip-mall with a coffeehouse, drugstore, and a place named All Day Fitness. In among those shops, they found a small entrance with a door marked, "Skifferton Counseling."

Mrs. Jones gave the boys a reassuring smile. "Now, don't worry. These people are really nice. They want to get to know you a little today." She talked to the lady at the front desk for a moment, and then said, "I'll be back in about an hour to pick you guys up."

Harvey and Orva hung their broad-brimmed hats on the coat hooks and took a seat. A tall, skinny, bald man with a goatee stepped into the room. "Hello—you must be Harvey and Orva?"

Both boys stood.

"I'm Mark Skifferton—you can just call me Mark."

The boys nodded.

"Harvey—I'll have you come into my office first, and then I'll meet with Orva after that."

Orva sat down, and Harvey followed Mark. Mark had a big desk in his office, but he didn't sit behind it. He took a seat in an armchair that looked like it belonged in someone's living room and nodded for Harvey to sit in the comfortable chair across from him.

"So— tell me about yourself."

"I'm Harvey Chupp; I'm almost fifteen. I finished 8th grade a year ago, and I farm with my dad."

"What are your earliest memories?"

"I guess standing between my dad's knees while he let me drive a team of horses?" Harvey paused. "That's the first thing I can remember."

"Do you have any early memories of getting in trouble with your dad?" Mark leaned back in his chair and placed his hands behind his bald head as if he hoped to hear something interesting.

"Not really," Harvey said. He looked out the window as a sparrow flew past. A strange machine sitting on the floor made a whirring sound. Harvey turned to look at it.

"That's a noise-canceling machine," Mark explained. "That way, nobody can hear anything we say in here. This office is a safe place to talk about your feelings and your past." He kept looking at Harvey as if expecting him to talk.

"I guess my dad spanked me as all dads do. Whenever I needed it— I guess."

Mark leaned forward and rubbed his hands together while looking Harvey in the eyes. "Not all dads spank their children," he said in a soft voice.

Harvey didn't know what to say about that.

"Tell me—can you think of one occasion when you got in trouble with your parents?"

Harvey watched the birds flying back and forth outside the window for a moment. "Well—I just got into trouble with my dad the other day."

"Tell me about it."

Harvey looked at Mark for a moment and then out the window as he spoke. "I was plowing with horses the other day. My dad gave me strict orders to rest the horses on every pass of the field. He happened to see me go two rounds without resting the horses."

“Why did you disobey him?”

“Because I was trying to get my field plowed faster than my friend. Joe was plowing with horses in the next field over.”

Mark raised his thick eyebrows as if the story was getting quite interesting. “What did your dad do?”

“He told me a Bible story.” Harvey checked Mark’s face and could see that he wanted him to continue. “Dad told me a story about a man in the Bible who beat his donkey. God gave the donkey the power to speak, and the donkey asked his master, ‘Why are you beating me? I’ve always been a faithful servant.’“

Mark put his index fingers together and touched his chin with them both. “What point do you think your father was making?”

“That I shouldn’t mistreat our animals. That they have feelings even if they can’t talk. If they could talk, they would have something to say if we mistreat them.”

Mark nodded as if he agreed and liked the direction the story was going. “And—Harvey—what would you say to your dad if you could tell him anything you wanted to say to him?”

“I guess I’d say—I’m sorry I disobeyed you.”

Mark rubbed his forehead as if trying to smooth out his wrinkles. “Harvey—your dad is asking way more from you than should be asked of a fourteen-year-old boy. At fourteen, you should be playing ball or riding a bicycle or hanging around with other boys your age.” He studied Harvey’s face for a few moments.

“I don’t wanna play around all day like a little boy,” Harvey said. “I wanna grow up to be just like my dad.”

Mark pursed his lips. He seemed to be thinking of a way to pry the truth out. “What would you say to your dad if you could say anything without him getting mad?”

"I guess I'd tell him I saw Mary Elizabeth climbing the silo the other day." Harvey couldn't stop the tears. They came out in a flood he had been trying to hold back ever since he saw his little sister lying on the ground, silent.

Mark let him cry for a few minutes before he spoke again. "What do you think your dad would say or do if you told him that?"

Harvey wiped his eyes, and Mark handed him a tissue. After he blew his nose, Harvey said, "I don't know, but I'm sure he'd be disappointed in me."

Silence reigned in the room for a short time. Harvey glanced up to see Mark's expression. Mark was staring at him with eyes of compassion. He softened his voice even more and said, "Harvey, your dad is trying to treat you like a grown man. Don't you see he puts way too much on your shoulders?" Mark leaned forward as though encouraging Harvey to see how concerned he was. "Don't you think your dad is strict?"

"No," Harvey said and shook his head.

"Harvey, I have it from a very reliable source that a few days ago you said, 'Our dad is very strict.'"

"What?" Harvey scrunched his nose for a moment and then raised his eyebrows. "Oh, I was just saying that Dad is strict about resting the horses."

Mark cocked his head. "Could it be that you are trying to protect your dad?"

Harvey shook his head. He couldn't help remembering he told Orva, "We need to help our dad get out of this."

Mark continued, "I understand you see the best in your father. We all want to think the best of our parents. I know you want to protect him." Mark sat quietly until Harvey met eyes with him. "It's hard for you to compare your experience with other boys your age because you have only had this one home. I'm an experienced therapist, and I've talked to boys your age from hundreds of homes."

Harvey squinted at Mark, trying to understand what he was getting at.

"I'm not trying to make your father guilty of anything here, Harvey. I want to help you and your dad to have a healthy relationship. I need you to be completely honest with me. I promise—you don't need to worry about me telling your dad what you say in here. This office is a safe place."

Harvey didn't know what to say. All he wanted was to go back home, and for life to go back to normal.

After another long silence, Mark said, "Mrs. Jones mentioned that you have some ..." he hesitated, "marks on your back. Do you mind showing me those?"

"It's just these scratches," Harvey said as he stood and twisted while lifting the back of his shirt. "I got them while dragging a big branch off a field."

Mark sat upright and let out a long breath. "Okay, Harvey. I'll let you think about what we've gone over here today. We'll schedule an appointment for you to come to talk to me again in a couple of days. In the meantime, I want you to think about my questions. It will be best for everyone if you can be perfectly open and honest with me."

Harvey nodded and tucked his shirt back in around his suspenders as Mark got out of his chair.

They stepped out into the office and found a policeman talking to Orva. He almost looked too old to be an officer. His balding head had a ring of spiky, buzzed, gray hair. His chin had been shaved nice and clean, but his upper lip sported a thin gray mustache. The policeman looked directly at Harvey and said, "Young man, I'd like to ask you a few questions if you are feeling up to it?"

The officer turned to Mark for the answer. Mark met eyes with Harvey. "You'd be okay with that, wouldn't you?"

Harvey nodded.

The officer opened the door for Harvey. "Let's go out to my car for a bit."

Orva's eyes got wide, and the officer must have noticed. He said, "Don't worry, son. I'm just gonna ask your brother a few questions, and he'll be back inside when you finish talking to the counselor here."

Harvey followed the officer outside. The policeman opened his passenger door and said, "You can sit up here. We won't take long." They both got situated in the car, and the officer said, "I'm Captain O'Malley, but you can call me Bud, that's what all my friends call me." He didn't look at Harvey while he talked, but straight ahead as if watching for bad guys. "I just need to ask you a few questions about how your dad handles the livestock."

"Okay," Harvey said, hesitantly.

"Does your family keep the puppies in a small pen in a dark barn?"

"Only at night. We let them out when we get up to do chores at 5:00 a.m. and put them back in at dark. We don't want the coyotes to get them."

Bud nodded but didn't turn to face Harvey. "Do you put them in the kennel any other time?"

"Yeah—Mom wants them in there when the milk-truck comes. So, the driver doesn't get mad." Harvey hesitated, then added. "The puppies get in his way and slow him down, but the milk driver is a nice guy. We also put them inside if we are all going away. It doesn't happen very often."

Bud chuckled. "Okay, okay, that all makes sense. "How about your horses—do you ever see your dad hit them or anything?"

Harvey squinted, trying to remember if he ever saw his dad hit a horse.

Bud glanced over. "Does he ever lose his temper and let them really have it?"

"No—never!" Harvey considered retelling the Bible story about the donkey, but, instead, he just said, "My dad would get pretty upset if he saw one of us hit a horse."

At that, Bud finally turned and looked Harvey in the eyes. His kind expression surprised Harvey because the man seemed so tough. "Harvey, I've seen abused animals before. I know nobody is abusing animals at your place. These town people have no idea about livestock." He chuckled and looked over the dashboard again. "I've had people call us at the station to report a horse that has snow on its back. I wanna ask them if they'd mind taking the horse into their living room until spring."

They laughed together for a moment. It was the first time Harvey had laughed since his sister fell from the silo.

"How's it going in there with your counselor?" Bud asked.

"Not that good," Harvey confided. For some reason, he suddenly felt that he could trust the officer. "He thinks I'm lying when I tell him that our dad is good to us. He says I'm trying to protect him by not telling everything."

The officer locked eyes with Harvey. "You are telling everything?"

"Yes," Harvey said emphatically.

"And you have nothing to hide about your home life?"

Harvey shook his head. "Nothing."

Bud put his hands on the steering wheel as if he planned to drive off. "Well, your new neighbor gave us a whole list of abuses she witnessed." He glanced at Harvey and winked. "Before I rattle them off—I wanna say—I don't think she knows what she's talking about."

Harvey let his lips curve into a smile and nodded.

"She said you and your brother were way too young to be driving multiple draft horses. She also thought your horses were being overworked and looked overheated. That your family had a puppy mill going and the puppies are always inside a dark barn. Your little sister was forced to work in the garden from sunup till sundown. All of you children were made to work without shoes. And the Chupp children had dirty, worn-out clothes on, even when she stopped in on a Sunday. However, she noticed your mother and father had nice clean clothes. And above all else—an eight-year-old girl was expected to climb a silo and fell."

Harvey's jaw dropped as Bud shared the list. When it became clear Bud had finished speaking, Harvey said, "I could explain away all of that. Especially about Mary Elizabeth climbing the silo. My parents would never let her climb it, and for sure, never asked her to do it."

Bud looked over the dashboard again and made a disgusted face. "That's what I told the other guys at the station. These people that move in here don't know anything about you Amish. They don't take time to get to know ya, and they assume the worst."

Harvey felt a tear trickle down his cheek. He tried to wipe it off before the tough man saw it. "What's gonna happen to us?"

Bud shook his head. "Don't you worry, son. We'll get this straightened out yet. I'm gonna talk to police chiefs from some other towns and see how they handle this kind of thing." He scratched his head. "I don't know if I can explain the difference between having working animals and abusing animals to these modern-thinking town people, but I'm gonna try." The policeman shook his head and let out a long, slow breath. "I grew up on a farm. I know what it means to work with and around livestock. I can see that your family is doing a fine job of it. If only everyone out there took as good of care of their horses as your dad does, we'd be fine."

Harvey nodded. The sensation of hope welled up deep inside and made another tear stream down his cheek.

"Okay," Bud said, "In the meantime, see if you can think of something you can do to prove that you are telling the truth. I'll work on things from my end."

"Thanks," Harvey managed to say without crying.

"Your dad needs you to be strong. He won't defend himself."

Harvey drew in a deep breath, "What do you mean by that?"

"He says it's in the Lord's hands."

Bud opened his door, then paused. "Is there anything else I can help you with?"

"Do you know how my sister, Mary Elizabeth, is doing?"

"Oh, yeah, I've heard she's doing a little better. I don't think she's talking yet."

As Harvey stepped out of the squad car, an idea popped into his head. He leaned in and told the officer, "Mary Elizabeth has been keeping a journal of everything that happens at our place. Maybe if we could get that, we could prove the truth?"

"Great idea," Bud said. "I'll ask your parents to bring it in."

CHAPTER TEN

The Journal

Mrs. Jones brought the boys back to her house after the appointment. The rest of the day seemed long and boring. Mrs. Jones asked, "Would you boys like to watch another movie?"

Harvey shook his head. He didn't know how to explain that his family didn't believe in watching movies. "We don't wanna be rude, but we would rather do things instead of watching other people do them."

"Oh—I like that, Harvey," Mrs. Jones said. "I wish my boys thought more like that. Do you boys want to play catch in the back yard again?"

"Sure," Orva answered.

"We might wanna climb the tree again," Harvey added.

Mrs. Jones smiled and said, "That would be fine."

The brothers tossed the ball back and forth for a while. They watched some ants carry a dead cricket and try to pull it into a tiny hole in their anthill. After that, they climbed the tree again. The brothers each took a seat on the same thick limb that hung near the porch roof.

Orva pointed to their room. "I bet we could climb right off this limb onto that porch and into our bedroom."

Harvey let out a snicker. "That would surprise the Jones boys if we came back downstairs after they saw us go outside."

"Let's do it," Orva said.

Harvey shook his head. "No, it might upset Mrs. Jones. She's such a nice lady we don't wanna scare her. She might think we'd crawl out during the night and worry herself sick."

Orva nodded but seemed disappointed. He asked, "Did that counselor guy ask you all kinds of questions about how Dad treats us?"

"Yeah. I told him the truth, but he didn't believe me."

"Me too," Orva said. "That Mark acted like our dad makes us work too hard. What do they think we'd do all day?"

Harvey told Orva, "They want us to be like these English kids—sitting around playing video games. That's what they think is normal."

After supper that night, there was a knock on the door. Mrs. Jones answered, and they were surprised to see Bud, the policeman standing there. "Could I have a few words with Harvey?"

Mrs. Jones motioned for Harvey to come to the door. "Of course."

Bud nodded for Harvey to step outside, and Mrs. Jones shut the door behind him.

"I talked to your dad about that journal of Mary Elizabeth's. Your parents searched the house and couldn't find it. Do you have any idea of where she might be hiding it?"

Harvey shook his head. "I just assumed it'd be in her dresser drawer." He hesitated for a moment and then added, "Just the other day I heard her say, 'Nobody will ever find it where I'm keeping it.'"

Bud scratched his balding head. "Well, that was a great idea to have a journal to prove things." He shook Harvey's hand. "If you think of anything else, have Mrs. Jones call me."

Harvey nodded. "Thanks for helping us."

The officer put a hand on Harvey's shoulder. "Don't worry, son. We'll get this figured out."

At bedtime, Harvey stared at the dark ceiling, wondering how this would all end. He tried to guess as he listened to Orva wheeze. His eyelids felt heavy and closed. Suddenly, he saw the image of that strange bird with flapping wings on the silo. He sat straight up and shook his head. He lowered himself back to the pillow and tried to get the image out of his mind. He went over ideas, searching for an explanation of what he saw, and nothing came. Finally, his eyes closed, and he drifted off again. The image returned, only more vividly than before. He thought about the flapping wings, and he sat back up and whispered as loud as he could. "That's it!"

Orva rolled over. "What's it?"

"I know where Mary Elizabeth is keeping her journal."

"Where?"

"Somewhere on the silo," Harvey said beneath his breath.

"What makes you think that?"

"I just realized I've seen her climb up the silo every day." Harvey tiptoed over and knelt beside Orva's bed so he could keep his voice down. "Remember me saying I saw a bird or something on the silo? I just realized it must have been Mary Elizabeth. Her apron and dress blowing in the wind looked like wings."

Orva rose up on his elbows. "Seems like an odd place to hide a journal."

"I'm sure that's where it is. Let's go look for it tonight."

"How could we get out of here without Mrs. Jones knowing?"

Harvey put a finger to his lips. "Quiet. We'll wait about an hour until everyone's sound asleep. We can climb out the window onto that roof and down that tree."

Harvey could almost see Orva nodding. "We could put stuffed animals under the blankets to look like we are still sleeping."

The boys waited until everything had been quiet for a long time. Harvey stood up first and gently slid open the window. Orva took the stuffed animals from the closet as they had planned. They each made their bed look as if they were still under the covers. Harvey went out first and carefully tiptoed to the tree. He got a firm grip on a higher branch and stepped over onto the thick limb they had been sitting on earlier. It worked as slickly as he had imagined. Orva slowly closed the window and followed.

Harvey held out a hand to his younger brother. He whispered, "If you slip, I'll be in more trouble than Dad is."

Orva snickered and reached for Harvey's hand and made his way over onto the limb. They sat for a while to be sure nobody heard them. The house was quiet. They took their time and quietly maneuvered down to the bottom limb and jumped to the ground with a soft thud. A neighbor dog barked, and a light went on over the fence.

Harvey whispered, "We'd better climb over that other side. We can go around and back east after we get onto the street. The neighbor dog continued barking until a man opened a door and shouted, "Georgy—shut up!"

The boys slipped carefully over the fence and slinked along in the shadows. They avoided areas lit up by streetlamps. Once they made their way past the last cluster of houses, they could breathe easier. They began to visit as freely as they used to be able to do.

Harvey confessed, "I feel like all of this is my fault."

"Why would you think that?"

"I saw Mary Elizabeth climbing the silo the other day, and I should have told her she had to quit, or I'd tell Dad."

Orva panted as he hurried to keep up with Harvey's longer stride. He puffed out, "Has she been climbing it all the time?"

"Yeah—like I told you—she must keep her diary up there. She writes in that thing every day. I guess she's been climbing up there twice a day. Once to get it down and then again to put it back."

"Funny such a little girl wouldn't be afraid of climbing up there," Orva said.

"I know, but sometimes little children don't comprehend how dangerous something can be."

Orva's shoulder nudged Harvey. "Do you think Mary Elizabeth will be mad if we let people read her journal?"

"No. I believe she would want to help Dad and Mom and our whole family." Harvey bit his lip and then said, "I should have been more like Dad."

"What do you mean by that?"

"Dad does what's right no matter how hard it is. Mary Elizabeth's face was so cute I just couldn't tell her no. That's why it's all my fault. I let her sway me into doing the wrong thing, and now maybe she's going to die. And then all of this happened to our family."

Car lights appeared on the road ahead of them. The boys both hurried down the sloping side of the ditch. As the car got closer, they lay against the shady side of the ditch bank. When they started walking on the dark road again, Orva spoke. "I still don't think it's all your fault. That Ms. Mims had it in her mind we were bad people."

"I know, but I'm partly to blame."

They passed by Ms. Mims's house silently. They looked in and could see some lights were on, though no movement.

"It feels so good to be this close to home," Orva said. "I wish we could just go inside and talk to Dad and Mom."

"We don't know if they are at home or not," Harvey reminded his brother. "They could be at the hospital with Mary Elizabeth. Either way, we can't talk to them, or we could get them in more trouble."

"I just don't get it," Orva said.

"I know. None of it makes sense. It's just the devil putting our dad to the test."

They started up the lane—everything felt so familiar and wonderful. At the same time, something felt odd and terrible.

"It's so quiet," Orva said.

"Yeah, I was worried that we'd have trouble keeping Roxy from barking, but she hasn't heard us yet." Harvey let out a quiet whistle that a dog might hear but not a person. The dog didn't come. "We'll have to speak to her if she comes out barking, and let her know it's us."

The dog never did come out. Everything looked so dark in the house and barns, which almost seemed natural on an Amish farm. Harvey whispered, "Let's get right to the silo first thing and find Mary Elizabeth's journal. No messing around with the pups or anything."

"All right," Orva said, sounding a bit disappointed.

Something still seemed wrong, but Harvey couldn't place what. They slipped past the house and made their way to the silo. Orva stood beside the ladder while Harvey climbed up. He whispered, "I sure hope the journal is up here." He climbed up further, feeling around the steel ladder and in the cracks of the old concrete silo. Orva turned on the flashlight he borrowed from the Jones' family.

"Shut that off!" Harvey said in as loud of a whisper as he could muster.

He climbed down and joined Orva on the ground for a moment. "I'm afraid someone will see that light. Let me have that, and I'll take it up with me. Maybe I can cover it with my hand and still see to find the spot where Mary Elizabeth has been hiding her diary."

Harvey made his way up the ladder again. He remembered how far up he had seen her that day, but it seemed higher when he was on the ladder himself. A red light began to flash on the concrete in front of him, and Harvey turned to see the source. For some reason, a red light seemed to be shining on the road coming from town. Harvey climbed higher using one hand to hang on and the other to hold a flashlight. The red lights grew brighter, and Orva called up to Harvey, "I think the cops are coming."

Harvey turned his flashlight off. Fortunately, the flashing lights of the police car created a glow on the silo. He found a shelf-like ledge and reached behind the ladder bars. His hand found what felt like a notepad, and he tugged on it. The pad slipped through the rungs of the ladder and fell to the ground. Harvey looked down at Orva. He couldn't believe how high up it felt.

Orva called up, "I've got it! But you'd better hurry—the cops are coming in our lane."

Harvey descended as fast as he felt was safe. "Let's hide in the barn near the horse stalls. We can't be out in the open."

Orva hurried inside, and Harvey followed at his heels. He heard Orva say, "I've been hankering to see the horses anyway."

"Me too," Harvey agreed.

CHAPTER ELEVEN

The Truth

The flashlight beam glowed in the horse stalls, but they were empty and quiet. Harvey whispered, "Dad must have put them all out to pasture since I'm not here to do the plowing." The boys slipped out the backway and tried to adjust their eyes to see without using the flashlight. Everything seemed empty and completely quiet.

Harvey reached over and felt his brother's arm. "Let me see that flashlight. I wanna be careful we don't shine it too much, but I've gotta see where the horses are."

He made a quick pass over the horse pasture with the light and found nothing but an empty lot. A lone rabbit scampered away under the far fence. Harvey turned the light back toward Orva. Just before he shut the flashlight off, he saw Orva fall to his knees.

Orva sobbed out, "What's happening to our family?"

Harvey rubbed his younger brother's back. "Don't worry. It's gonna be okay."

"No, nothing is okay. It's just like that Bible story you told me about. The devil is taking everything away from Dad." Orva's back shook with sobs under Harvey's hand.

Harvey tried to soothe his little brother by rubbing his back while he cried it out. Meanwhile, Harvey felt thankful that it was dark enough the tears streaming down his own cheeks weren't visible. As soon as Orva calmed down a little, Harvey said, "Come on. We have Mary Elizabeth's diary.

Let's get back and show it to our caseworker and the police. Maybe it'll help."

They watched the cop car speed back up the road toward town. Orva asked, "What do ya think the cops wanted."

"I don't know," Harvey answered truthfully. "This whole thing is so crazy it could be anything. Hopefully, they weren't looking for us."

They took the shortest route, cutting kitty-corner across the field. They stumbled over the plowed ground. Harvey bumped into Orva by accident and said, "I think all ten acres are plowed. People must have come and plowed it since our family has an emergency."

Orva didn't speak until after they had trudged another twenty, or so, steps. "What do you think they did with our horses and dogs?"

"I don't know. Maybe Uncle John has them until we all get back home."

Orva started sniffling again, "What if they sold them?"

The boys saw headlights coming up the road. Harvey told Orva, "Stand still. That car will go on by on the road, and they won't see us out in this field."

They stood like statues while the car crested the hill. However, the vehicle turned into Ms. Mims's driveway. As it did, the headlights flashed over the field in one fell swoop.

"Do you think they saw us?" Orva asked.

The car backed up and aimed the lights directly at the boys. They stood there frozen like deer in the headlights. They heard a car door open, and Ms. Mims grouchy voice. "Come here, boys!"

They didn't dare disobey her. Orva followed Harvey over the fence in the glow of headlights. Once they stepped out of the brilliant beams, they could see Ms. Mims with her hands on her hips. "Where are you boys supposed to be?"

"At the Jones's safehouse, "Harvey answered meekly.

"And what are you doing here?" she demanded.

"We wanted to get something from our house," Orva explained. "We were just heading back to Mrs. Jones's house."

Ms. Mims drew out her cell phone and made a call. "This is Ms. Mims, head of nursing at the university. I want to report that I've found the Chupp boys over here by my house." She hesitated for a moment. "Okay, do you want me to bring them in or come and get them?"

Harvey and Orva met eyes and waited to hear the answer.

"Okay, we'll be there in a few minutes." She put her phone in her purse and opened her car door. "All right, boys," she said. "Get in. That was the police department. Mrs. Jones reported you missing, and that poor lady has been worried sick about what happened to you. I agreed to take you to the station, and she is going to meet us there."

Harvey took the passenger seat, and Orva climbed into the back. They rode silently in the glow of dashboard lights until Ms. Mims said, "That wasn't very nice of you boys to scare everyone like that. We are all trying to help you, and is this the thanks we get?"

"We didn't mean to scare anyone," Orva offered from the backseat. "We thought we could get back before anyone knew we were gone."

"Half the town is out looking for you," she said as if thoroughly disgusted.

They stepped into the brilliant lights of a brick police station. The station looked like it was built in 1950, and nothing had changed since. They were met immediately by a tearful Mrs. Jones. Her pretty auburn hair and kind dark eyes were a welcome sight. She hugged Harvey and Orva and said, "You boys had me worried sick."

"I'm so sorry," Harvey said. "I thought of something that could help sort all of this out."

Bud, the police chief, came over and put a hand on Harvey's shoulder. "You'd better have something good after all the trouble you caused here tonight."

Harvey couldn't believe his eyes when he saw Mark, his therapist, come through the doors.

Orva asked him, "Are you a policeman?"

Mark's thick eyebrows sagged as if he had just woke up from a long dream. "No, I'm a therapist. The police called me in desperation, thinking I may have a clue to where you boys might be."

Bud said, "We went to your house and looked around but couldn't find you there."

Harvey nodded, "We didn't go into the house. We didn't want to upset Mom and Dad. We just went to the silo, because I thought my sister's diary might be there."

"Did you find it?" Mrs. Jones asked.

Harvey untucked his shirt and pulled out a spiral-bound notebook. "Yep." He set Mary Elizabeth's journal on an empty table under a bright light, and everyone gathered around it.

Bud looked at Harvey, "Have you read it yet?"

"No. We just found it in the dark. We were going to look at it after we got back to Mrs. Jones's house."

Mark looked at the police chief. "Would it be okay if we have a look?"

"That's up to Harvey," Bud said. "Do you feel confident about what's in there?"

"Yes—for sure. Mary Elizabeth is very kind and honest."

Bud, Mark, Ms. Mims, and Mrs. Jones all stood around the table, looking at the journal. Orva leaned against Harvey, looking over his shoulder as he opened it. The bright lights of the no-nonsense police station emanated a sensation that nothing mattered but the people, the law, and the truth.

Harvey scanned the pages for the day he and Orva met Ms. Mims. He couldn't believe how neatly Mary Elizabeth had recorded everything. He started reading, "My brother Harvey got into trouble with Dad today. Dad wants us and the horses to be safe, but Harvey let the horses race each other. Ms. Mims thought my brothers were lazy because they were sitting in the shade. Dad laughed about that because he has to make Harvey take a break. Harvey hurt his back, pulling a branch off the field. Mom said it looks like he got hit with a hickory switch." Harvey checked the faces of those around him.

Everyone looked surprised, but Bud. He said, "Why don't you read something about your puppies?"

Harvey turned the pages. "Mom made us change clothes after church before we let the pups out. We play with them all day and get so dirty. Ms. Mims came to buy eggs before we got the pups out, and she didn't know it was Sunday." Bud started laughing at that. Harvey continued, "Ms. Mims was so mad that she forgot it was Sunday she left before we could give her some eggs."

Harvey wanted to look at Ms. Mims to see her expression, but he didn't dare. He turned the page. "On Monday, Ms. Mims came to buy a puppy. The puppies tried to lick her and make her happy, but she didn't like them."

Bud cleared his throat. "Does it say anything about the girls working in the garden?"

Harvey flipped through a few pages. He started reading again, "Mom didn't like it because me and Edith Rose tucked our dresses in the top of our underwear to make them shorter." Everyone laughed, even Ms. Mims. Harvey cleared his throat and started again, "I asked my mom if I could plant flowers first thing in the morning. She is so nice she said yes! I love to be barefoot in the garden."

Mark asked, "Does she say anything about climbing the silo?"

Harvey pointed to the bottom of the page. "Right here it says, my brother, Harvey caught me climbing the silo today. He didn't see me hiding my diary up there. He's so nice he didn't tell Daddy." Harvey's voice caught, and he couldn't make himself read anymore.

Bud put a hand on Harvey's shoulder and squeezed it. "That's enough, Son. I think we all get the picture that you, your brothers, and sisters are telling the truth. Do you mind if I keep the journal and double-check a few things?"

Harvey nodded. "We'd like it back after you finish with it, in case our sister doesn't …"

"Your sister is doing better," Bud said. "I stopped by the hospital earlier this evening and checked with your folks. They said she is starting to talk again."

Harvey and Orva looked at each other and smiled together for the first time in days.

Mark Skiffington, their caseworker, had been leaning over the table across from Harvey. He stood, folded his arms, and let his thick eyebrows arch with sincerity. "Our foster-care system is full of children suffering from abuse and needing safe homes. It seems ridiculous and unnecessary to take up space with the Chupp family. I've already interviewed seven Chupp children and find no indication of anything suspicious. It is my professional opinion they should go home."

Bud, the police chief asked, "Today?"

Mark didn't unfold his arms. "We are doing more damage to these children by keeping them from their parents than good. Yes. Today!"

Ms. Mims didn't speak. Something about her looked rather less pompous.

Bud smiled at Harvey. "I'll stop by the hospital and have a conversation with your parents. We'll make arrangements to get your family back home."

Mrs. Jones wiped a tear from her eye. “I’d love to drive Harvey and Orva to their home. It’d be good for my sons to see the farm.”

“Thanks,” Bud offered. “I’ll give you a call when everything clears at the station.”

On the way back to the Jones safehouse, Harvey looked at Mrs. Jones and offered an apology. “I’m really sorry we scared you. You’ve been so nice to us.”

Her face glowed in the dashboard lights revealing her kind smile. “I’m not upset with you now. It makes sense you two boys wanted to help your family.”

“How did you know we snuck out?”

Mrs. Jones let out a little chuckle. “You almost fooled me with those stuffed animals, but I couldn’t hear Orva’s normal wheeze.” She turned into her garage and said, “Let’s get some sleep and see what tomorrow brings.”

CHAPTER TWELVE

Home

Right after lunch, Mrs. Jones got the call the Chupp family could go home at 1:00. Harvey rode in the front seat. Orva sat between the Jones boys in the middle of the van. The Jones boys fought about what DVD they wanted to watch, all ten minutes getting to the Chupp farm took.

As they drove into the lane, the silo stood like a watchman on guard high over the neat white house and farm buildings. Sunlight broke through gray clouds and shot a column of light toward the house. Mary Elizabeth's flowers were blooming with brilliant reds and pinks. Birds crisscrossed from every tree and bush singing bright notes.

When the van rounded the house and entered the courtyard, they found two pickup trucks with horse trailers parked near the silo. A friendly older lady with curly hair and a pair of dirty jeans said, "I'm Ms. Miller from the animal rescue farm. I sure could use a hand unloading all these horses."

Orva climbed over the Jones boys and ran to unlatch the trailer door. Harvey followed at his heels.

A young-looking woman with tight jeans got out of the other truck. She opened the passenger door, and Roxy jumped out and almost knocked Harvey down in her excitement. The young woman with tight jeans laughed. "I'll need a little help unloading these puppies too!"

"All the heavy horses are in that trailer," the woman said. "I've got the buggy horses in the smaller one. We'd better lead in these horses before we release the puppy chaos."

The puppies all yipped in excitement while Harvey untied Brick and led him out. The Jones boys set down their iPads and stood with mouths hanging open when they saw the massive horse. Orva followed with the old mares, Viola and Butte. The woman came behind, leading Rocky and Stone. Mrs. Jones and her boys followed the stately procession into the barn. Harvey opened a fresh bale of hay, and Orva filled their bunks.

They hurried back to the trailer, and Harvey's face paled. "Where's Cello, our black Percheron?"

The curly-headed woman chuckled. "He's in with the buggy horses. I had to keep him and that big sorrel separate. They seem to think they have to outdo each other all the time."

As Harvey led Cello out of the trailer, a taxicab pulled into the drive with two police cars following. Harvey and Cello stood like a statue of an Amishman and his horse. He watched his mother gather her baby out of a car seat. Dad stepped out with Mary Elizabeth in his arms. She leaned weakly against his chest, but her eyelashes were squinting shut with a smile. Dad and Mom looked so much thinner than the last time Harvey saw them.

Edith Rose and Ada Fern jumped out of one squad car and ran to help the woman in tight jeans let the puppies lose. Three little Amish boys with straw hats came bumbling out of the other vehicle and collided with excited puppies. All of them tumbled into a heap of puppy licks and boy's giggles. The flock of robins in the apple trees seemed to sense all the excitement. The branches shook as they jumped from limb-to-limb, singing happy notes.

Leroy stood up out of the pile of puppies and exclaimed, "Mom, we stayed with an old grandma, and she had a huge sandbox with lots of toys!"

Mom's face glowed with a smile. Dad held Mary Elizabeth close and wiped a tear from his eye.

Later that evening, Harvey headed to the barn to see his horses again. He stood in the stall next to Cello and smoothed a hand along his massive neck. The smell of horses and hay had never seemed so divine before. "I'm so happy we're all home again. Let's not try to outdo our friends anymore." He moved over to where Brick stood and ran a hand on his broad forehead. Brick let out a warm nicker. "You and Cello don't need to be better than each other. I like that you are not the same—that's what makes you equally valuable to me."

Harvey gave the horses each a handful of grain as a snack. He stepped outside. The Milky Way hung like a cloud made of a million twinkling stars around the silo. An owl hooted. The sound seemed to come from the oak down in the valley where the creek met the road. Harvey turned to go back into the house and realized his dad was walking out toward him.

Harvey said, "Do you see these stars?"

Dad stood so close Harvey could feel his body heat. They gazed up at the silo standing firm in a night-sky full of sparkling stars. Dad said, "Thank you, Harvey, for all you did for our family."

Harvey bowed his head. "This whole thing was my fault."

"What are you talking about—none of it was your fault."

"It was. The whole thing started because I was trying to plow my ten acres faster than Joe. I let Cello and Brick challenge each other into working too hard. It was right after I skipped their break, and I pulled those limbs off the field that Ms. Mims saw us all sweated up."

"Harvey, Ms. Mims had a whole list of complaints. That thing with the horses was just one of them."

"There's more," Harvey took a deep breath before confessing. "I caught Mary Elizabeth climbing the silo one day, and I didn't tell you."

"Why not?"

"Because she begged me not to tell." Harvey pulled out a hankie to wipe his eyes and blow his nose. "She looked so cute, and I wanted my little sister to like me. Now, I wanna be like you and always do the right thing."

Dad wrapped his arms around Harvey and gave him a bearhug. "Harvey, you are exactly like me. We both make mistakes, and we both put too much on ourselves."

Harvey had been wanting to hug his dad ever since he saw him walking in the shadow of the silo. He held him tight and said, "If I'm like you, I'm happy."

Dad said, "I think you're a better man than me."

"Being like you is good enough for me."

A bright lantern shot inviting rays between the house and barn. Harvey and his Dad followed the light inside.

The next morning, Mom said, "I made a strawberry pie, and I want everyone to go with me to take it to Ms. Mims."

Dad cocked his head. "Are you sure that's a good idea?"

"I have something to say to Ms. Mims, and I want you all to be there when I do."

Dad loaded Mary Elizabeth into the wagon with the baby beside her. Everyone else walked along following Mom down the lane. On one side, the dairy cows grazed peacefully beyond the fence. On the other side, Harvey's field of ten acres lay completely plowed and drying.

Orva said, "Well, I guess you got your ten acres plowed before Joe did."

Harvey looked at his field. "I wonder who plowed it?"

Dad answered, "Your friend Joe brought his six Belgians over the day after Mary Elizabeth's accident. He worked on it every day while you were gone."

Harvey stopped and looked at the field. "Now that's a true friend." He shrugged. "It was super nice of him, but I wanted to do it myself. Plowing is one of my favorite things."

"Don't worry, Harvey," Dad said with a chuckle. "You'll have plenty more chances to plow in your life."

Harvey didn't laugh. He thought for a moment before adding, "It's not just that, I really like driving Cello and Brick together. Now the plowing is all done, I won't get to again until next spring."

Dad stopped, and the whole family paused along with him. "Harvey, if you really want to drive those two together—go ahead. I don't mind. After all, I've always hitched Butte and Viola together, and they aren't the same breed."

A smile spread out on Harvey's face. "Do you mean it?"

"Absolutely."

They resumed their trek up the hill toward the mansion. The little children chit-chatted the rest of the way to Ms. Mims's door. When Mom knocked, they all fell silent, not sure what to expect.

Ms. Mims looked surprised to find the whole Chupp family standing on her stoop. "Would you like to come in?"

Mom held up her pie. "No, our children would probably get your nice clean floors dirty. We got our first strawberries out of the garden this morning, and we thought maybe we should make you a pie."

Mom's face looked like an angel to Harvey. Ms. Mims stood there, speechless. Mom continued holding the pie out. "Do you like strawberry pie?"

Ms. Mims reached out to take it. "It's my favorite."

The children all looked at their mother to see what thing she planned to say, knowing this would be the moment.

"We all wanted to thank you for coming to help us when Mary Elizabeth had her accident."

The family all nodded in agreement with their mother.

Ms. Mims leaned down and asked, "How are you doing, Mary Elizabeth?"

Mary Elizabeth smiled. Her eyelashes so thick they hid her pupils. "I'm feeling better every day! Tomorrow morning Mom is gonna let me go into my flower garden again."

Mom nodded and continued, "We also wanted to thank you for looking out for our children's welfare. It makes me feel blessed to have a neighbor who cares so much about children."

Ms. Mims turned white. She looked at Mom to see if she meant her comment in sarcasm. The children all turned to look at their mother's face and saw tears streaming down her cheeks. Ms. Mims set the pie down on a chair near the door and gave Mom a big hug.

After Mom regained her composure, she added. "We'd like to give you a puppy if you're still interested."

"Maybe I am." Ms. Mims said with a smile.

Myron was never the shy one. He looked up at Ms. Mims and said, "My sisters wanna hold you down on the gr … gr—." He stammered and restarted his sentence. "They wanna hold you down like we do our dad so the puppies can lick your face. It makes our dad laugh, and it will you too."

They all laughed together. Ms. Mims said, "I think I'd like that."

THE END

LONE STAR

MURRAY PURA

CHAPTER ONE

Kansas—Spring and Summer 1874

Saul Miller was driving his wagon into town for supplies. Passing his freshly planted cornfields, he thanked God they were already sprouting in the warm, wet spring weather. He also thanked God he was not just going into town for flour and salt and tools. He was having lunch with a lovely young woman named Eve Sorensen. They had met on several occasions but never really talked. She had told him she was interested in learning more about his Amish faith. Whether that was true or not, he had no idea. He was just grateful she wanted to dine with him.

He had been a happier man once. Always ready with a smile or a cheerful laugh. Until his young wife had been in a wagon rollover. Killed along with their unborn child. This grief had not robbed him of his faith. Indeed, his faith had helped him survive the loss of his wife and child. But his smiles became few and far between. And his laugh ceased to exist.

Eve Sorensen made him smile more often. She was like a sunny day without a cloud in sight. And no twister brooding on the horizon either. Her beauty, as far as he was concerned, was beyond description. One minute in her company made him feel glad to be alive. Something he did not feel very much anymore.

Saul realized he could be imposing. He was six-six, broad-shouldered and dark complexioned. His somber disposition didn't help any. He regretted the unpleasant effect he could have on people. But he saw no change in the road ahead. A man of sorrows and acquainted with grief. Isaiah's description of Jesus was how he saw himself. At twenty-five, life was hard labor, hard prayer, and hard hope. Eve, although not of his faith, was a candle in a very dark room. Perhaps her light would grow. Perhaps diminish.

About the time he could see a formation of boulders up ahead, he also saw a large herd of beef cattle being moved across the plains towards town. Lone Star was a railhead. Cattle were shipped from here through neighboring Missouri to the slaughterhouses in Chicago, Illinois. There wouldn't be a freight train till that afternoon, but stock pens would hold them securely till then. The cowboys could relax, get baths, and collect their wages. Whether they wasted their money on cards, gambling, and liquor was up to them.

What Saul hated to see were fistfights and gunplay. However, those were inevitable in any cow town. That's why they had a marshal and deputies. Regrettable, for they often had to resort to violence to keep the peace, and violence was something the Amish would not countenance among themselves. But even though the county had many Mennonites and Pennsylvania Quakers and a sprinkling of Amish, it was far from being a haven of law and order where swords were turned into ploughshares.

So, an eruption of gunfire was not unexpected in Lone Star, Kansas. And Saul was not so much startled, as he turned away from the hitching post to see what had happened, as disappointed. Others were running away or ducking into shop fronts. The thought did not occur to Saul. Outside of outright foolhardiness or recklessness, when your time was up it was up. God made the arrangements, not man or woman.

He did not want to see what his eyes showed him. Marshal Steiner and one of his deputies, Sid White, were face down in the dirt of Main Street. Blood was seeping out of the holes in their bodies. The cowboy who had shot them, obviously liquored up, was standing over them and hollering gibberish at the top of his lungs. He fired into the air. Three little boys, unaccompanied by any adult, stood frozen on the boardwalk across the street from Saul, only a few feet from the drunken cowboy and the smoking pistol he was still waving around.

Saul made no actual decision he could recall later. He just walked towards the cowboy, all six-six of him, well over seven foot in boots and a creased, rim-rolled Boss of the Plains Stetson. When he reached the cowboy, he stretched out his left hand. "That's enough. There are women and children on the street. Give me your pistol, sir."

The cowboy looked up at Saul with wild eyes. "Women and children? What?"

"Do you shoot women and children?"

"No!"

"Then give me your gun, so you don't start today."

The man stared another moment, apparently trying to figure out who Saul was, why he was so tall, and if he should surrender his weapon. Then he put the gun in Saul's hand. "No women. No children. I don't do that. I've never done that. I've been on the trail for three months."

Two deputies ran up, pistols out. Saul handed one of them the cowboy's gun. The other deputy cracked his revolver against the side of the cowboy's head. The shooter went down. Saul hung his head, said a prayer over the bodies of Marshal Steiner and Deputy White, and made his way back across the street to McCarthy's General Store. By the time he'd finished his business an hour later, the two deputies had quit, and the drunken cowboy was locked up with no one to keep an eye on him. The town needed new lawmen fast.

Saul shrugged when Eve Sorensen told him this over lunch at the Emporium. She looked stunning in her green dress and hat, her blazing blonde hair pinned up to perfection, and he preferred to gaze at her and think about her. And discuss her life at the boarding house her mother ran where Eve helped with meals and entertainment—her piano playing of Bach and Mozart and Beethoven, as many had said, was worthy of New York and Philadelphia. But Eve kept turning the conversation back to the shooting and, in particular, to the role Saul had played in disarming the drunken cowboy.

"The entire town and I'm sure the county is buzzing about the murders," Eve said, "and how you made the shooter back down."

"It was nothing," Saul insisted. "He handed his pistol to me without an argument. I simply made him aware he could shoot children by accident."

She leaned over the table and touched his hand with hers. "He would have if you hadn't intervened."

"Well, it was too late for the marshal and his deputy."

"That's not your fault. They'll hang him for that. I don't even think there will be a trial."

"It is up to the mayor and town council."

Her green eyes were lit as if by a lantern inside. "Couldn't you do something, Saul?"

He raised his eyebrows as he raised his cup of coffee to his lips. "Me? What could I do?"

"Get a rifle from the town. Gather up some men who would be worthy deputies. Guard the jail until the judge convenes the court. Attorney Tick Morley says he will represent the cowpoke."

"I'm sure Tick will. And get him off by arguing the cowboy was drunk and didn't know what he was doing."

Eve brought her golden eyebrows down into a sharp frown. "Well …"

Saul finished up his omelet. "In any case, you know I am Amish, and that is not the Amish way, Eve. We don't bear arms against people. We don't punch them or kick them or buffalo them. Amish don't join the army or cavalry, and we don't pin on tin stars and become lawmen. In the old country, it was the police and the soldiers who persecuted us. So, we have nothing to do with any of that."

"No guns? Ever?"

"Never. Firearms are forbidden to us."

"Why, even the Methodists wear pistols on their belts, Saul."

"That is between them and John Wesley and God. It is not for me." He wiped the corners of his mouth with a white napkin. "Now. May we please talk about something else?"

But apparently, there was nothing else to talk about in the entire town. Including Saul's intervention in the affair, which he found was getting increasingly embellished. He could not even get free of the matter when he climbed onto the seat of his wagon and steered his horses for home. To his astonishment, the mayor appeared and asked him to consider taking on the position of town marshal. Saul shook his head.

"You do not know me or my faith, Mr. Mayor," he replied. "This is something the Amish do not do. Find a Methodist. I will not wear a gun."

The mayor nodded. "I know that, Mr. Miller. You need not. Your deputies can do that."

"Neither me or my deputies. I'm sorry. I cannot be your marshal. It's impossible."

"Mr. Miller. You disarmed one cowboy. You can disarm others. You can bring our town peace."

"Not I. You must find another."

"There is no other."

"There has to be. Good day, Mr. Mayor."

"Think of the women and children."

"Good day."

SHERIFF

CHAPTER TWO

Saul was sure that would be the end of it and that his church would support him in his decision. At first, it was so. But after a week of incidents in town, including the wounding of a young girl, and with matters getting increasingly out of hand, the bishop approached Saul and asked him to reconsider. Did he need guns to be a peace officer? Had not the Lord been enough for the apostles? Who would be his strong right arm but God?

"This is something you can do," the bishop insisted. "It is not as it was with our forefathers on the other side of the ocean. You do not come as a lawman to persecute and harass. You come to protect and defend. Without violence or weapons. It is a good thing. Mary would have asked you to do exactly what I am asking now."

"I'm sure that is true," Saul admitted. "But my wife is not here. So. I have cornfields and horses to tend to."

"We will care for your farm, Brother Saul."

Saul shrugged. "Then there are the goats, and the vegetables, and the wells. And don't you agree I must have my time of prayer about what you suggest?"

The bishop handed him a slip of paper folded in half. "This was delivered to me to pass on to you."

Saul unfolded the note. There was only one word, penned in an elegant female hand.

Please.

Two young Amish men in their twenties were permitted to join Saul as unarmed deputies. They were prayed over and sent out by the church as if they were on a mission.

Saul picked up a third man in town he felt he could trust. The lawmen were given the rooms above the marshal's office and jailhouse and free meals at the Emporium. Saul had one room to himself and the others bunked together in the second. Each room had a water basin, pitcher, and mirror. Their wages, by arrangement, were given to the support of the orphanage that was overseen by the town and the bordello, Flamingo. There was one toilet in the hall.

Everyone was infallibly polite to Marshal Saul Miller and his men. Not just townspeople and churchgoers. Rough and ready cowboys too. Saul knew why. It wasn't his imposing presence. At least, that wasn't the whole reason. The town had hired locals to lurk in doorways and on roofs and down back alleys, carbines in their hands, watching every move the new marshal and his deputies made, keeping an eye on their backs, ready to intervene if anyone should try to shoot the unarmed lawmen down. Everyone knew the men with guns were there and newcomers to Lone Star soon found out. It was the locals with carbines who kept the peace, not Saul and his young deputies.

He permitted it for three weeks to help everything settle in. Especially the new ordinance against wearing or carrying guns in town, a restriction growing in popularity across the West. Cowpokes who might be inclined to argue against giving up their rifles and pistols were well aware carbines were aimed at their backs. They gave up their weapons without a cross word. Once Saul felt enough water had flowed under the bridge, he asked the mayor to call off the gunmen the town had hired. It was time for the Amish marshal and his three men to make peace on their own.

Of course, it soon got around the carbines were no longer there. This put beef back in some of the cowboys who rode into Lone Star with the herds. Saul had to handle quite a few hotheads who had no intention of handing over their firearms. Most of the time, other cowhands helped out, particularly those who rode for the brand and didn't want their ranches to get a bad rep as troublemakers. Trail bosses often intervened for the same reason. So, Saul found the job doable.

Except for owlhoots. They could be rancorous. And none of the ones who rode into Lone Star had warrants on their heads. Saul had no authority to arrest them outright. He had to put up with their rough and tumble ways.

Yet even there, gang leaders would step in and tell one or more of their men to settle down. They'd come to town to gamble and drink and enjoy the services offered by the bordello. They didn't want their night on the town to get ruined by gunplay. The outlaws were well aware federal marshals could be brought in from Wichita with one telegram. So could bounty hunters, and they were worse. It was much better to be in a town where no one had guns, and therefore, no one had to be ready to shoot someone who had one. A town with a firearms restriction and an unarmed marshal could be a sweet deal.

Though everyone, including Saul, knew there were men and women who came into town by stagecoach or steam train or on horseback who said they'd surrendered all their firearms, but hadn't. They concealed the weapons on their bodies against a moment when they felt they must defend themselves from a threat an unarmed marshal could never stop. It was human nature to do this, Saul explained to his young men. Broken, recalcitrant human nature. "It will always be with us, like a curse."

Guns and gunplay weren't the only issues the lawmen had to deal with. Even devoid of firearms, Lone Star had its drama. Fistfights in the saloon, knife fights in back alleys, complaints from the Madame at Flamingo about rough customers, horse theft, house fires, even rustlers who tried to spirit away a dozen head from the stock pens in the dead of night. Having muscle came in handy more than once and at least the marshal and his boys had plenty of that.

"After all, Jesus did hustle those ne'er do wells out of the Temple, didn't he?" Nate grinned. "We can't do any less, can we, Marshal?"

Saul smiled his infrequent smile back. "No, we sure can't."

CHAPTER THREE

Nevertheless, despite the help of ranch hands and trail bosses and wranglers, the support of the town, the churches, the Amish, and the very vocal support of the Flamingo bordello, tense confrontations did not cease. Saul had not expected they would. He didn't confide to anyone, certainly not Eve, that he was sure the day would come when a bullet found its way into his heart or his brain. As he had said, human nature was what it was. It would not be quelled by an Amish marshal or by a thousand guns. One day someone would shoot, and Saul Miller would be in the path of the shot.

But before that came the day of Lucky Jack Stranger.

There was a gunslinger in the street twirling both of his silver-plated revolvers. Several men were standing there with him, guns out. Every now and then the gunslinger fired into the air. Saul's deputies were elsewhere. He walked from his office without his hat and went directly towards the man. The gunslinger spotted his approach and laughed. He pointed both pistols at Saul.

"Not another step!" he warned.

Saul kept coming.

"Hey, you! You deaf? I said, *not another step!*"

Saul kept walking until he was right on top of the man.

"You don't hear too good, do ya?" the man snapped. He cocked both revolvers. "I'll only surrender my guns to the law. And even then, I probably won't do it."

Saul gave the man his hardest stare. "I am the law."

"You? You're not even wearing a gun."

"But I'm wearing the star."

"Which means what?"

"You can do as I say, and we can deal with this like men. Or you can refuse to listen. Then other men will come who have guns. And rope. And you'll have to deal with them instead. Which would you prefer?"

The gunslinger hesitated. "I heard about Mike Dooney in Wichita. He shot the county sheriff in the back while Jackson was having dinner at a saloon. Dooney was acquitted in a jury trial two days later. Rode into another county where he was recognized. News about his acquittal had spread. But the next county saw things differently than the jury in Wichita. They strung Dooney up from a tall tree."

Saul's eyes didn't flicker. "I wouldn't do it. But others might. Especially if you'd shot me dead, and I wasn't able to lift a finger to help you."

The man turned it over another second or two. Then he uncocked his pistols, holstered them, unbuckled his gun belt and handed it to Saul. "I won't be no trouble. Neither will my men." He stuck out his hand. "Jack Stranger. Most call me Lucky Jack. I admire your sand."

Saul took the hand and the gun belt. "Much obliged. They'll be waiting at my office for you when you leave town."

"I like it here. Maybe me and the boys will stick around for a while."

"You're welcome to stay as long as you like. Unarmed."

Lucky Jack grinned. "You bet. Hand the marshal your guns, boys. We're gonna take a vacation from gun slinging while we're here in Lone Star."

It worked out well with Lucky Jack and his gang. The next day, it didn't work out so well with another group of cowboys that rode in. They shot up the signs at both ends of Main Street that said all guns had to be left with the marshal. When Saul walked out of his office to confront them, all still on horseback, one of the cowboys, obviously liquored up, pointed his Colt 45 at Saul's head.

"We don't take orders from two-bit tin stars," he laughed. "Need another hole in your head? You've only got seven if you count your nose as two. Could probably use eight, couldn't you, Marshal?"

Saul didn't flinch. He stared at the man for several long seconds. The cowboy began to look puzzled and confused. Saul reached up for the Colt.

"What does the Good Book say?" asked Saul. "What did your mother teach you?" He gently pried the gun out of the young cowboy's hand. "You don't need a gun to get a shave and a haircut in this town. Or a hot bath. Or to protect yourself. No one carries a gun in Lone Star. Not even the law."

The leader grunted. "I'd heard a rumor the new marshal here had guts. Now I see the rumors were true. I don't mind surrendering my guns to a brave and honest man." He unbuckled his gun belt and handed it down to one of the deputies who had joined Saul. "Let go of your iron, boys. I swear to the good Lord I'll always honor a man with intestinal fortitude. There ain't too many of them."

That afternoon Lucky Jack came into Saul's office and propped his feet up on the cast iron stove. It was cold as snow, unusual during the hot Kansas summer. Saul offered him a mug of coffee. Jack took it.

Saul had a cup himself. He nodded toward his three deputies who had come in once they'd seen Lucky Jack enter the office. "Nate's the redhead. The tall skinny one is Zacchaeus. Sam's the blond."

Jack smiled and sipped his coffee. "You all Amish?"

"Not Sam," replied Saul.

"What do you put in this coffee, Marshal?" Jack asked. "Horseshoes?"

Saul smiled his quiet smile. "That. And turpentine."

Nate grinned. "You didn't mention the rusty nails."

"Or the old boots," added Sam.

Zacchaeus was whittling a stick with a small knife. "It's the coal that gives it the flavor. That and railroad ties."

Jack laughed. "You have a merry crew, Marshal. That sits well with me. I was raised Methodist, and Pa was forever quoting John Wesley. One of the quotes stuck though. *Sour godliness is the devil's religion.* I still believe that."

"Good," replied Saul.

Jack took a long drink and grimaced. "Whew. The devil's brew. What do you believe, Marshal?"

"About what?"

"The Bible. God. Jesus Christ. Heaven and Hell."

Saul shrugged and took a pull from his coffee. It was still so hot steam continued to curl up from the tin mug. "Amish don't have three heads and a tail, Lucky. We're Christians like everybody else. What you hear preached in most churches is what we believe too. God is strong. God is love. Jesus is what deity looks like when you're staring into the blue eyes of God—he took iron at the Cross to save our skins and save our souls.

"Where we differ is when it comes to gun play and fists. Jesus was strong enough without resorting to that. His body was strong—he was a carpenter who had to fell, haul, saw, and dry his own trees and lumber before he could make tables and chests and wagons. His heart was strong—he knew right from wrong. His soul was strong—he knew what he had to do, and he did it. Nothing made him swerve from his purpose. He came to deliver freedom. He did that by taking the bullets meant for us. Not dishing them out. He's not a killer, Lucky. Satan is. So, we Amish toss our hats and spurs in with Jesus. You know the hymn "Strong Son of God, Immortal Love?" We don't need guns and fistfights to keep the peace. Just the spirit the Lord puts in those who believe. It makes us more solid than your Colt 45, Lucky."

"I carry a 44, Marshal," Lucky Jack quipped. Then he sobered up. "You're saying strong like a son of God?"

"We try."

"But in the Bible, the Lord pulls his gun sometimes and lays the bad men low."

"That's his call. I don't have his jurisdiction." Saul drained his cup, steam and all. "You one of the bad men, Lucky?"

"Nah." Lucky smiled. "Mischievous maybe. A little unruly. I break the rules now and then. But I've only killed in self-defense. And I haven't killed much."

"No?"

"No, sir. Ask God. He'll tell you. I know he keeps track." Jack handed his empty mug back to Saul and stood up. "So. A man doesn't need to be Amish to be deputized?"

Saul nodded. "That's right. Just a Christian man who promises me he won't resort to gunplay or his fists to keep the peace."

"I know a lot of the ranch hands in these parts. Lots of the cattle drivers. Lots of the owlhoots too, to be square. I reckon I can help you out. Backing your play to keep this town a safe place for women and kids is something I'd like to do. I know a lot of men will respect my stand or at least not go against it."

"Why, Lucky? Why do you want to take a stand with me?"

"I told you from the first, Marshal. I admire your grit. And maybe I admire Jesus's grit too."

Saul pulled a thick black Bible from a drawer. "Take the oath."

Lucky Jack did that. Saul fished a star out of the drawer in his desk, stood up and pinned it on Jack's shirt. They shook hands. Jack looked at the star and laughed.

"The boys will never believe this," he said.

"So long as the men you have to confront do," Saul replied.

Jack instantly sobered up again. "They will."

CHAPTER FOUR

Lucky Jack Stranger was true to his word. Weeks rolled by, and every day, Jack was at Saul's side whether the marshal had to face cowboys down in the saloon, the barber shop or on the dusty streets of Lone Star. A lot of the men knew who Jack was on sight. Others knew of his reputation. Still others were impressed by Jack's and Saul's nerve—a peace officer and gunslinger standing together to maintain law and order without firearms. Guns, gun belts, and rifles were always forthcoming.

It lasted a long time, the town's peace and quiet. Cowpokes drifted in and out with the cattle drives to the railhead. A few caused trouble and had to cool their heels in jail. Most surrendered their guns. The mayor and council were pleased. Churchgoers were pleased. Regular townsfolk and the families who drove in to purchase supplies and conduct their business were pleased. The whole county, a county replete with Amish and Mennonites and Pennsylvania Quakers, was ecstatic. Word got around Kansas that Lone Star was a safe and lucrative place to be. To some, this made the town the star of Bethlehem. To others, it became a temptation. "We can thank our lucky stars there's a plum ripe for the picking like Lone Star."

But when outlaws heard Lucky Jack Stranger was a deputy in the town, they reconsidered. It was well-known Jack had ridden with the Texan John Wesley Hardin for a time, and Hardin was a cold-blooded killer still on the loose. No one wanted a confrontation with Lucky Jack or Hardin. And no one believed Lucky Jack was enforcing the peace in Kansas without a 44 on his hip. "That's like saying the rattler left his hole without packing his venom. Lucky Jack always packs his venom."

So, most outlaws reconsidered about plucking the town's feathers. Not all. One group went to rob the bank in Lone Star. The bank was rumored to be thick with gold from the many cattle drives that ended at the stock pens and railyards outside of town. The would-be robbers never even got to the bank because they were ambushed by lawmen about a half-mile from town. Federal marshals had gotten a tip that proved to be true and wiped the owlhoots out in a gunfight that took place in a location favorable to the US marshals—the pile of huge boulders. The lawmen were hidden among them with brand new Winchester 73s and the outlaws were down below with no cover at all. The word was the marshals dispatched the gang within two sweeps of the second hand. The gunfire could be heard in Lone Star less than a thousand yards away.

Another bunch got a bit farther. By five hundred yards. A rider came out to warn them that both John Wesley Hardin and Lucky Jack Stranger were in Lone Star. He said both were packing iron, both had their gunmen with them, and both had grudges to settle with members of the gang. That was a lie Lucky Jack had sent the rider to spread when he spotted the mob approaching. He'd recognized gang leader Skink Whittier's bright yellow bandana he used as a hat band. The outlaws knew the rider, Nine Lives Skillett, because he rode with Lucky Jack. They believed him, thanked him and turned aside.

But one man made it in. On his own. Not to rob banks or scare the locals. To settle a score. Which he did in a back alley in the broad light of day. Lucky Jack ran to the smoke and gunshots. He found attorney Tick Morley flat dead in the dust with four bullets in his heart. Scott McCabe made no effort to conceal his pistol or what he'd done. And he knew Jack Stranger and knew he was a deputy in Lone Star. "You've killed skunks in your time, Lucky. Now I've killed mine. Tick made sure I went behind bars for a crime he knew I never committed. I've paid him back in full."

"You're aware there's an ordinance against guns in town, McCabe?" demanded Jack.

"I could've used a knife, I suppose. But four aces to the heart seemed more poetic."

"Did he draw?"

"Who knows? I hauled him by the scruff of the neck to this alley here behind his office. I told him I was going to shoot him. Then I shot him."

"All right. A jury will have to decide your fate."

McCabe scoffed. He still hadn't holstered his revolver. "A jury? You mean a jury like all the juries you've never faced, Lucky? I don't think so."

Jack planted his hands on his hips. "My rep's on the line. I swore to uphold the law in this town and stand by the marshal. And I intend to keep my word. I'm known for that, McCabe."

"Yeah. You and Hardin are both known for keeping your word to the men you've killed."

Jack stretched out his hand. "Give me your pistol, McCabe. And come along."

"Come along?" McCabe whipped up his gun. "I load with six. Not five. Two shots are more than enough to plant you firmly in Boot Hill, Lucky. No one will cry. No one will care."

Saul and Nate arrived on the run just in time to see Jack hurl himself headlong at McCabe. McCabe fired once, but he fired wild. Jack slugged him in the head and pried the revolver from his hand. McCabe swore and yanked a derringer from his pocket. McCabe's revolver was in Jack's hand, and he smashed McCabe across the face with it. McCabe was a tough nut. He shook off the blow, nose bleeding, and smacked Jack on the side of the head with the derringer twice. When Jack fell back, stunned, McCabe jumped to his feet and pointed the derringer down at him. He laughed.

"Who knew it would end for Lucky Jack Stranger like this? The bullet of a derringer borrowed from a painted lady who resides in San Francisco. How humiliating. How fitting."

Saul threw a handful of dirt and stones into McCabe's face. The man cursed and staggered back a step, swiping at his eyes. He fired the derringer blindly at the same time as Lucky Jack shot him from the ground with McCabe's own revolver. It sounded like just one gunshot. McCabe flew backwards as the bullet from the 44 struck his chest. He hit the wall of the law office, hung there a moment looking at everyone with wide eyes, then he slid down into the dirt.

Saul went to one knee at Lucky Jack's side. "Are you all right? Were you shot?"

The derringer bullet had found Jack's shoulder. "It's just a small bullet, Marshal. But it stings."

"We weren't supposed to use guns. We weren't supposed to use fists."

"We didn't have much choice, did we? I didn't even see him ride into town. First I knew he was around was when I heard the four shots and saw the gun smoke."

"Let's get you to Doc Greenfall. We'll have to explain to the mayor and council what happened and why."

"God saw what happened, marshal."

"But they didn't."

CHAPTER FIVE

No one had a problem with it. Once the mayor and council heard the story from Saul and Nate and Jack, and an unexpected witness peering through the window of the general store who saw the whole thing, they absolved their lawmen from any wrongdoing. Things carried on as before. The result at the town meeting at the Methodist church was much the same. The citizens heard, the citizens understood, the citizens applauded the efforts of their lawmen. It was understood the use of force had been more of an accident than a deliberate action. It was not likely to happen again. No one had a problem with the shooting.

Except Marshal Saul Miller. He brooded in his office and in his room above the office. He brooded a lot. No one bothered talking to him about it. There was nothing to say. Either he accepted what had happened in the grace of his good God or he didn't.

He took to whittling like Zacchaeus. Which was how Eve Sorensen found him four days after the shooting. Three days after the meeting with the mayor and council. Two days after Boot Hill. And one day after the town meeting at the Methodist church.

"Good day, Marshal Miller. How is your deputy's arm?" she asked. "And … how are you?"

"Hello, Eve." Saul stood up when she entered his office in her fancy blue dress and wide-brimmed hat, then sat down again. "Lucky Jack really is lucky. Or blessed. Doc got the bullet out and all the putrefaction too. His arm should be like new in a month or two."

"I'm heartily glad to hear it. When are you going to be like new, do you suppose?"

"I'm fine," Saul replied, returning to his whittling.

"Twice you have turned down my dinner invitations."

"It's been busy."

"Still a man must eat."

Saul shrugged. "Coffee and apples. I didn't want to put you and your mother to all the trouble."

"All the trouble? She cooks for ten at our boarding house. What is one more? Even a rather large one more?"

Saul smiled. "Next invitation."

Eve smiled. When she smiled, rooms lit up with lanterns, and men noticed. Even men who were whittling like Saul Miller. He put down his stick and pocket knife.

Her beauty, all golden-skinned, golden-haired and green-eyed, with six feet of height, and arms and legs stronger than most men's, was exceptional. He had seen her dressed in a man's shirt and pants chopping wood behind her mother's boarding house where no one was supposed to see her. He'd seen her strength and, even in that garb, her spectacular feminine loveliness. Any number of men would have given their eye teeth to have done the chopping on her behalf. Her father and brothers were dead, killed in the war, so men of all ages volunteered.

She never said yes. Sometimes, she was rude if a man persisted. "I am stronger than you, why would I need your help?" If a man persisted past her cutting remarks, she'd roll up her sleeve and challenge him to an arm wrestle. She always won. "I'm of good Danish and Norwegian stock, little man," she'd taunt with a huge sparkling grin, enjoying his discomfiture after she'd decisively pinned his arm. "And you? You bring nothing to the table at all. Not even manhood apparently."

Eve was laughing at Saul. "What on earth are you thinking about, sir? You're gazing at me as if you're moonstruck. Am I a species of creature you've never seen before?"

He laughed back, tugging himself out of his reverie. "In truth, you are, Miss Sorensen."

"Oh? How is that?"

"On the one hand, you look like a sunny Sunday morning at church. On the other." He paused, wondering if he should risk it. Then decided he was in the sort of mood that didn't care one way or the other. "On the other, I've seen you chopping wood in men's clothing. Your sleeves were rolled up. You never missed a strike."

"I see." She smiled. "And how long did you have to watch to ascertain that?"

Saul shrugged his shrug. "Half an hour."

Her green eyes widened. "Half an hour!"

"You often spilled the dippers of water you took from the barrel to your mouth."

"You must have thought me clumsy, sir."

"I found you charming, miss. Especially when you poured the contents of the dipper over your head."

"I see." Her eyes were dancing with a sharp green mischief. "And what did you think of my manly attire?"

He smiled the quiet smile. "That it looked better on you than any man."

She turned her face away, but he saw the crimson blush.

"And," he added, hoping to see more blush, "no woman looked more womanly, in any attire, or at any activity, than you did in that shirt and those pants swinging away with that Swedish axe."

He did gain another blush. She kept her face down and averted. "I see." She cleared her throat, still refusing to look up. "I … I only came … uh … to try and invite you to our dinner table one more time."

"When?"

"Tonight. This evening. At five."

He nodded. "Very well. I'll be there."

Her head came up sharply, even though it was still mottled red and white. "You will?"

"I will."

"That's astonishing."

"It is."

"At five? You'll be there?"

"I so intend."

CHAPTER SIX

His intentions proved true. He arrived ahead of grace and sat next to a traveler from New York, a pocket watch salesman, who was passing through. Saul needed a watch, so they carried out a brief transaction before the meal. On Saul's left was another drummer. This one dealt in jewelry that glittered with rubies and diamonds. Whether they were authentic or not, who could say? Saul toyed with the thought of buying a brooch for Eve. Then he dismissed the temptation. It was not the Amish way to hang baubles on a woman you admired.

Still. He had heard the story of a man at table with John Wesley a century before, much as he was at table now at the Western Skies boarding house. The table, like this one, had been seated round with many guests. Wanting to ingratiate himself with the famous preacher, the man had seized the hand of a pretty woman sitting across from him and thrust it under Wesley's eyes. "And what do you think of that for the hand of a Methodist, sir?" The hand was rich with silver rings and bright gemstones. Wesley had looked and kept on eating. "I think it is an uncommonly beautiful hand," he had replied.

So, perhaps there was a place for putting a small bit of shine on a woman's hand or dress or at her neck. He felt Eve's eyes on him as bowls of food were passed, and he dished modest portions onto his plate. He did not look up or meet her gaze. Nor did he engage in the table talk that ranged from weather, to crops, to Washington and President Grant, the kidnapping of four-year-old Charley Ross in Philadelphia, trouble with various Indian tribes, General Custer and the Black Hills Gold Rush in South Dakota he had instigated, the wild and lawless town of Deadwood that had arisen out of that gold rush, and trade that was booming with the Kingdom of Hawaii in the Pacific Ocean.

The only thing that actually caused Saul to engage was an announcement by a third drummer at the far end of the table. He had hundreds of the new and durable Levi Strauss and Jacob Davies blue jeans with copper rivets for sale. Saul knew of the pants and their reputation for rugged wear and longevity. He told the man he would like to purchase several after dinner. They were thirteen dollars and fifty cents a dozen.

"Well, you have finally found your voice, sir," teased Eve, arching her golden eyebrows at him. "I am very glad to discover you are still among us."

Saul smiled and sipped the fresh coffee that had just been poured by a young boy. "I was famished."

"And has that issue been resolved?"

"It has." He nodded at Eve's mother. "My compliments, ma'am. I can't recall the last time I had so pleasant a dinner. Everything was delicious."

Eve's mother shone with the compliment. "Thank you, Marshal. I hope you will have some pie?"

"I'd like nothing better, Mrs. Sorensen."

"Anyone else?" she asked.

All those seated at the table murmured their assent.

Eve pressed her advantage. "I'm sure our guests would love to hear your account of how you govern a cow town without resorting to firearms or violence, Marshal Miller."

Saul glanced around. All eyes were fixed on him. Well, he supposed he had already been anti-social enough by only commenting on the Levi Strauss blue jeans over the past half-hour. He took another drink from his coffee mug.

"There is not a lot to say," he told the table, permitting himself the happy indulgence of looking at Eve and into her dazzling emerald eyes without others thinking she fascinated him. "My faith eschews firearms and the use of force. The only time you will see an Amish man or woman with a rifle or shotgun is when they are hunting. This is how we have always understood the followers of our Lord were to behave. For where do we see him with a knife or sword and threatening bodily harm? Only at the cleansing of the Temple was he a bit rough. He cracked a whip to get animals and sellers out of the holy place. But he did not inflict harm."

"Have you found it necessary to crack the whip in Lone Star, marshal?" asked Eve with a sly smile.

"Sometimes I have found it necessary to imitate our Lord in this regard," Saul admitted. "But not by using pistols or fists. Or bullwhips."

The Strauss jeans salesman leaned forward. "But surely you respect the role of the military in our national affairs, Marshal."

Saul nodded. "We appreciate our God has put certain things in place to aid in maintaining law and order within the nations of the earth. I do not argue that point. However, we Amish see our role is to balance such an unfortunate necessity with a peaceful approach. That God has called upon us to do things differently. Without bloodshed or killing of any sort. We would beat our swords into ploughshares. Our guns into pruning hooks and hoes and spades. Blessed are the peacemakers for they shall be called the children of God."

The jewelry drummer spoke up. "Yet sometimes peace is achieved or sustained by force of arms."

"Not here. And not by the Amish or Quakers or Mennonites. God has called upon us to exhibit a different way."

"How is it you have been able to carry this off in a rough and ready cow town, Marshal? Abilene cannot do it. Neither can Newton or Ellsworth or Wichita."

Saul shrugged with one shoulder. "Citizens respect my stance and that of my deputies. It was understood from the beginning that if I were to be marshal here, I would be a lawman who never resorted to a Colt 45 or a Winchester 73. Word has spread. Those who come here, even outlaws, do not expect trouble or gunplay. No doubt many harbor concealed weapons. But everyone has left well enough alone."

The jewelry salesman lifted a fork to his slice of dried apple pie. "It seems then that Lone Star is a town where "let bygones are bygones" is not simply a sentiment, but the actual rule of law. Where grievances are set aside and the lion lies down with the lamb."

Saul chewed and swallowed a piece of pie. "Fair enough."

An elderly woman seated near Eve laughed happily. "You ought to consider renaming your town Burns after the Scottish poet. Or "Auld Lang Syne." For your town sounds like his song." She began to sing the words and carried the tune well. "Should auld acquaintance be forgot and never brought to mind? Should auld acquaintance be forgot and auld lang syne?" The guests clapped and she clapped too.

"We must never forget old friendships or times we were close with others," she went on. "At the same time, we can hope for more such pleasant friendships to form in a community like this. Friendships we can sing about ten years from now in some other part of America." She lifted a glass of wine by her hand. "A toast to friendship and peace in Lone Star and *auld lang syne*."

Everyone at the table lifted their glasses. Saul's was filled with water. Nevertheless, he made the toast. "Friendship and peace in Lone Star and *auld lang syne*.

CHAPTER SEVEN

Eve coaxed Saul into escorting her on a stroll about town after the meal. He did not offer much resistance. At first, they were both quiet. Then, on an empty side street, she suddenly hugged his arm. "What did you think about the Scottish song?"

He smiled. "Oh, I am fine with it. It would be an answer to prayer if Lone Star came to be known as a place where broken friendships were restored and new ones forged. Where hatred and gang rivalries did not reign. Where revenge was laid aside for good and new lives and beginnings sought. But that sounds too much like heaven and not much like earth. This is an imperfect world, Eve. Indeed, it can be a murderous world. Look how terrible our last war was. Brother against brother, father against son, family against family. What we are enjoying here in Lone Star cannot last much longer."

"Please. Don't say that." She stopped walking and looked up into his face with a childlike earnestness. "Don't say that, Saul."

He took in her beauty and hopefulness along with her yellow dress that reminded him of dandelions and buttercups. She was not wearing a hat and an evening breeze stirred the dress as well as the long bright hair she had pinned up. The hair began to unravel, strand by strand. He did not tell her because he liked the effect.

"That is the first time you have used my Christian name," he said.

"I pray not the last." She did not smile. "I believe in you, and I believe in what you are doing here. I want to be like you. I want to join you."

"Eve—"

"I know you do not move quickly. You don't need to. I'm not going to run away, and there's no man I would rather be with. You have no rival." She glanced around to be sure the street was still deserted and raised a hand to gently stroke his face. "If you want to court me, you can. My mother approves, and I certainly will not say no. And to make all of it even simpler, I want to be Amish, just as you are. I want to be part of your faith."

A thrill of new life swept through Saul, the sensation he had when a foal was being born in all its lively, gawky beauty. He hesitated, then saw the "yes" in her eyes and touched her cheek as she had touched his. "Are sure? Are you very sure?"

She smiled and folded her fingers over the hand he had placed on her cheek. "Well, I haven't fasted and prayed about it for two years. But you lit a candle in my heart with your courage weeks and weeks ago, and it's never gone out. I sense it never will. I more than admire you, Saul. My feelings have grown much stronger than that."

He did not know how to respond. "I see."

"Do you? And what do you feel about me?"

"I think that's obvious."

"Oh? Then think again."

"I … " he stumbled.

She waited.

"I would like nothing better than to have you at my side," he finally got out. "Nothing better."

"Well, that is something. Thank you."

"You have surprised me, Eve. Surprised and delighted me. I am afraid to believe it. Afraid it is not true and that this is some sort of hallucination. Perhaps I drank too much of your mother's wild cherry wine."

She laughed. "You didn't drink any of it."

"Are you sure?"

"Very sure. I never took my eyes off you all night. I treated myself." She laughed again and took to hugging his arm once more. "Don't look so sheepish. It's all right for a woman to like you. My question is, when may I speak with your bishop? When may I begin instruction in the Amish way?"

"You are so eager?"

"Yes, I am. I've turned it over in my mind long enough. Tonight's table talk sealed your fate. I want to see the bishop."

"I shall speak with him. I'm sure I can arrange something for tomorrow."

"Good." She slipped her arm through his. "Now, let's continue walking. Please take me to the orphanage."

"The orphanage?"

"Yes. How long has it been since you visited? A long time. I know that, because I volunteer there. The children adore you, you know. They've heard all about how brave you are—and kind. They know you and your deputies protect the town and protect them. You and your men are their heroes. Do you mind dropping in on them before they're tucked in for the night?"

"Of course not. Just don't make too much of me."

"Oh, I won't. But I can guarantee you the boys and girls will."

"All right."

"Tell me something," she asked him as they made their way to the orphanage at the edge of town. "Does it trouble you that ladies from the bordello volunteer there?"

"No."

"Is that why you avoid visiting the children?"

"I don't avoid visiting the children, Eve."

"I just know most of those who are members of churches in Lone Star won't help out at the orphanage because they know women from the Flamingo are often present."

"Serving meals. Drying tears. Doing laundry. Playing games with the children. Yes, I know that, Eve. I also know they dress modestly when they are at the orphanage. Our Lord befriended many women like the ladies at the Flamingo. He did not condemn them. Instead, he showed them a God of love and mercy and redemption. Soiled doves flew free and cleansed once again."

"That's sweetly put," Eve responded. "How remarkable you are."

He shook his head. "I'm not remarkable, Eve. If anyone is remarkable, it is our Lord himself."

"Yes. That's true. Along with those who emulate him."

As Eve had expected, once they arrived and the orphans recognized him, Saul was swarmed. Finally, he took a chair and sat down among them, holding two of the youngest in his lap. He began to tell the children stories from the Bible as well as stories about being a marshal in Lone Star. From the Bible came the tale of the boy with his loaves and fishes that fed so many hungry people. And the story of girls and boys trying to get through to Jesus, but being blocked by the adults, and Jesus seeing this and ordering the grownups to let the children through.

"You must not stop them," Saul related the story with far more animation than he displayed at any other time. "The kingdom of heaven belongs to such as these. Yes, to children like all of you. Each one of you is special to God. His love for you is without bounds." His smile was rich and warm. "That means God doesn't put fences up between you and him. You are always welcome in his pastures, children. Always welcome to play there, and do somersaults, try to skip stones on the creek, chase butterflies, or climb the tallest tree. Always."

Eve wondered if he noticed the ladies from the Flamingo who hovered at the edge of the group of orphans. The madame was there as well. Yes, all of them were dressed modestly, and a great deal of their makeup had been washed away, but still, you could tell who they were by looking in their eyes. In a way, Eve thought, they were as much orphans as the children, and they too hungered for family, love, and kindness, not only from people but from God.

"Did you see them?" asked Eve as he walked her back to the Western Skies boarding house. "Did you?"

Saul nodded, his eyes admiring the gold and scarlet of the sunset and how it mingled with her hair, hair the color of ripe corn. "I saw. So did God. So did the angels."

SHERIFF

CHAPTER EIGHT

Saul was not a man given to qualms or superstitions or premonitions. Yet as July slipped into August and bright Kansas light poured over the town, he began to experience a feeling of unease. He could not understand it nor could he see any reason for it.

Eve was being instructed in the Amish way by the bishop and his wife. When the church met in one of the Amish homes every second Sunday, she met with them, and brought wonderful baskets of food to the lunches that followed every service. Several evenings a week, they drove out together to enjoy the beauty of the ripening crops. Often enough, she leaned her head on his shoulder. He sensed she would not say no if he tilted her chin towards him and asked to kiss her. In addition, Lone Star was experiencing a particularly long stretch of peace and calm. God was in his heaven, all was right with the world, as the poet had said.

And yet, strange dreams would disturb Saul's sleep, dreams he never remembered but which left their mark upon him as a knife blade would leave a mark upon his skin. All too often the vivid sunsets of August made him think of blood and fire without him willing such thoughts. When his patrols of the town took him past the graveyard no more than a hundred yards west of the last buildings and streets, he would pause and contemplate the wooden crosses and marble tombstones—and wonder about the people who had been placed in the ground and where they were now. Ravens or crows perched on the stones, and the one mausoleum in the cemetery, put a darkness in him stronger than the darkness that still lingered over the death of his wife and child.

He could not shake the feeling something was coming. As if he could see black clouds gathering on the horizon that presaged hail and the destruction of his crops. Or the buildup of massive thunderheads that warned of lightning storms and the ugly threat of twisters. There had been no gunplay in town of late, no knife fights, not even any particularly vicious fistfights. But Saul felt as if a fuse had been lit somewhere, somehow, that would reach a keg of powder and blast the town and his well-ordered life sky high.

Eve noticed his mood. So did his deputies. But she was the one to address the matter.

"It's as if you're a storm brewing," she told him one evening on a wagon ride. "What's troubling you?"

He shook his head, gazing at a neighbor's tall field of wheat. "I wish I could put my finger on it."

"Is it me, Saul?"

"No. Absolutely not."

"Something I said or did?"

"It isn't, Eve. You are a light in the night."

"So, then what has put a darkness in your life?"

"It used to be I could not shake the pain and gloom of my wife and child being killed. But you changed all that. You and your smile. Your beauty and your warmth. Your prayers, Eve, for I know you have prayed for me. The light in your eyes burned the ill haze off my soul. God's will was it should be so. For my wife and child are in heaven, and the Lord desires I have a family on earth as well."

Eve curled her fingers through his and drew closer. "You cannot even guess what is cutting at you?"

"It is nameless. But not the same as the dread I knew before. That came about because of something bad that had already happened. Now my mind and body are cringing in anticipation of something bad that is on its way."

"It is not like you, Saul."

"No. No, it is not."

"What can I do to help?"

His smiles had become rarer again. But now he offered her one. "You are Eve. All that you are blesses me tremendously. It used to be I roughed things through without you. Now I can no longer do that. I must have you near me. I must have your words and your prayers. Your beauty. I must have Eve in the same way a day must have sunrise and the night moonrise and constellations."

A tear cut a path through the dust on her cheek. "You say such sweet things. I don't know that I deserve them. But I'm so grateful for the way you feel about me. You are so sad these days. Yet I am so happy."

"You should be happy. I want you to be happy. You are one of the few things that gives me any sort of happiness these days."

"And the orphans."

"Yes." His smile. "The orphans. All the orphans."

"All the orphans." She kissed his hand. "When the boy asked you last night if you would protect them, you promised him you would. You said you would protect all the orphans. The madame of the Flamingo was there and knew exactly what you meant. So did her girls who were serving the children that birthday cake. And it's true. You have protected them, all of them, all these months."

"It's coming to an end!" Saul suddenly blurted, making the horses start.

Eve recoiled from him. "Saul! What's gotten into you?"

His face was set in stone. "I believe that. I wish it were otherwise. But a season of grace has been extended to us. We have basked in it. At no time did I or you or the Amish or any of the townspeople take it for granted. But now it is ending. As August presages September and harvest and the dying of the leaves. We cannot escape it. Summer is ending."

"Saul. Please. You're frightening me."

He quickly wrapped his arms about her and kissed the top of her head, holding her as tightly as possible. She placed her own arms around Saul and began to cry. She had no idea why. Only that it helped.

"Don't be alarmed," he said. "It is not the end of the world. Just the end of peace. That is the impression I have. Haven't I told you before? Lone Star cannot long remain a heaven on earth. It cannot long remain the Garden of Eden, the Garden as it was before the Fall. This is not Beulah Land. Not Zion. Not the Promised Land. Not Paradise. Jesus walks with us through a vale of tears. Sometimes there is respite. Sometimes there are great hazards. We go through them all in the strength and grace God provides. Not every outcome is to our liking. Nevertheless, we do not lose hope. God is greater than heaven and earth."

She was trembling within the strong circle of his embrace. "What is going to happen to change everything, Saul? I don't understand what you think is going to descend upon us."

"I don't know, Eve. I cannot put a face to it. But the gate is open. The gate has always been open. And they are coming through it. The Lord be with us and be gracious unto us. They are coming through it."

CHAPTER NINE

A week later, just before dawn on a Sunday morning in late August, the deputies came to Saul's bedroom with a lantern burning in Jack Stranger's hand. He shook Saul by the shoulder. Saul's eyes immediately blinked open. "What is it?"

"We have a boy with us, Marshal. About fourteen. He's ridden most of the night. He's been shot, but we got Doc Greenfall to patch him up so's he wouldn't bleed out. You ought to hear what he has to say for yourself."

Saul sat up in bed. "Where is he?"

"Step forward, boy," Stranger said quietly. "Tell Marshal Miller exactly what you told us. More, if you remember more."

A tall, skinny boy who looked more sixteen than fourteen shuffled into the lantern light. Fear pinched his long face. And pain too, Saul decided. He saw that one arm was in a sling. The boy's eyes were impossibly wide.

"Rest easy, son," Saul said softly. "You'll come to no harm here. What is it you have to say to me?"

"I hardly know how to put it," the boy half-whispered.

"Do your best," Saul encouraged him.

"One of your deputies shot a man to death here."

Saul glanced at Jack Stranger and thought of the incident with Scott McCabe. "That's true. In self-defense."

"I been riding with Buck O'Shea. The Irish Gang. All we ever done was rob trains and stagecoaches. Sure, we scared people, but we never killed no one. Swear to god. McCabe, now he was a stone killer. And a lone wolf. That's why no gang ever came to avenge his death. But his pa in Boston got wind of it. He's convinced his son was murdered. Been spreading money around. A lot of money. Even silver. Not to law. He don't trust law to deal with law. He wants McCabe's killer dead. And the marshal and deputies of Lone Star."

Saul nodded. "How'd you get shot?"

"Buck was thinking of taking some of Old Man McCabe's silver. It's not just you and your deputies, Marshal. McCabe wants the town gone. And everyone in it. Women. Children. Grandmas and grandpas. Makes no difference. Burn it, dynamite it, he doesn't care how. Just needs photographs proving it was done and needs to read about it in the newspapers. Then he'll shell out even more money to those that done it." It was like the boy had been holding his breath. Now he let it all out in a big gust. "I couldn't abide by that. About two this morning, I lit out. One of the guys on guard duty winged me. I made my own tourniquet outta my shirt sleeve while I rode. That's why I made it."

"You're a brave lad," Saul responded. "Are they coming?"

"Oh, yessir, they'll come. Buck wants the silver like he's got the devil's itch. The gang won't be in too much of a rush though. They know you can't get help from Wichita in time. I expect the only thing that'll worry them is another gang getting here first, blasting the town all to heck, and getting the payout."

"They know this is a gun-free town?"

The boy shrugged. "Everyone knows it. There was a time Buck and the gang respected it. Other gangs too. Not anymore. They figure it'll just make their job that much easier. They got the shine in their eyes, Marshal. Even with the train, you won't get US marshals here in time."

"How long?"

"I consider they headed after me no more than an hour later. They won't ride as hard. What o'clock is it?"

"You come in about quarter after five," said Jack. "Brought you up to see the marshal right after Doc gave you your sling. It's just after six now."

"They'll be here at dawn," the boy replied. "Seven. Sure, no later than seven-thirty."

"All right." Saul climbed out of bed and pulled his Levi Strauss blue jeans on over his long johns. "You'd better get some rest, son. What's your name?"

"Andy, sir. I don't want to rest, Marshal. I want to help. I got a gun. A good one too. A Henry Rifle."

"No guns, Andy," Saul responded. "We'll talk our way out of this."

Andy's eyes jumped. "They're not gonna talk, marshal. They got the shine in their eyes. They'll just cut you down."

"They'll talk."

"They won't."

Lucky Jack broke in. "You played this hand long enough, Marshal. You got more jackpots out of it than anyone thought possible. But your luck's run out. Buck ain't gonna talk. Neither is any other gang that comes looking for Old Man McCabe's silver. We don't stand up to them, they'll fire this town while people are still in their beds."

Saul tugged on his boots. "We'll stand up to them."

"Prayers and fine words won't do the trick, Marshal"

"They have so far."

"Not anymore." Jack was defiant. "It's time for the whip. It's time for the gun. It's time for the sword of the Lord and Gideon."

Saul put on his Boss of the Plains Stetson. "It's time for the Lord Jesus Christ."

Jack nodded. "Yeah. Riding the white horse and pulling out his sword like a Colt 45." He began to recite the Bible as if he were in a church meeting: "Now I saw heaven opened, and behold, a white horse. And he who sat on him was called

Faithful and True, and in righteousness he judges and makes war. His eyes were like a flame of fire, and on his head were many crowns. He had a name written that no one knew except himself. He was clothed with a robe dipped in blood, and his name is called The Word of God. And the armies in heaven, clothed in fine linen, white and clean, followed him on white horses. Now out of his mouth goes a sharp sword, that with it he should strike the nations. And he himself will rule them with a rod of iron. He himself treads the winepress of the fierceness and wrath of Almighty God. And he has on his robe and on his thigh a name written: King of Kings and Lord of Lords." Jack paused. "That's Revelation chapter nineteen and verses eleven to sixteen, marshal. And I know who I'm riding with at sunrise."

He left the room and they could hear his boots thumping down the staircase, through the marshal's office and out into the street. Andy stood staring at Saul along with Nate and Zacchaeus and Sam.

"They plan to kill everyone," Nate said.

"They're going to dynamite the town," added Zacchaeus. "I'll throw in my lot with the Lord and his white horse."

Nate and Zacchaeus left.

"I've got a Henry Rifle," Andy said again.

He went out of the room and down the stairs.

Sam stared at Saul. "What do you intend?"

"To ride out of town and meet them. Unarmed."

Sam nodded. "Reckon I'll join you."

"You're not even Amish."

Sam smiled. "Not till today."

They walked into the street together. It was half-six, but the light was coming. The east was silvering. They climbed on their horses just as the bell of the Methodist church began to ring. And ring. Everyone would know it meant fire or a bank robbery or an Indian attack or a twister. If the townspeople weren't up already they'd be tumbling out of their beds now. The two men began to walk their horses towards the edge of town and the dawn. No one entered Lone Star from the west. The only decent road snaked in out of the east.

"What're Jack and Nate and Zack gonna do, marshal?" Sam asked him.

"Convince the mayor and council to order folk to take up arms and resist," Saul replied.

Who'll listen?"

"Most."

"Most?"

Saul nodded. "I've felt it coming, Sam. Like a locomotive at full steam. It's like Jack said. We've played out our hand. You can't win jackpots forever. And you can't have summer forever. There's always a fall. Always a winter. Not just in Kansas. In the human heart, too."

SHERIFF

CHAPTER TEN

Saul knew she'd come.

He did not want her at risk, but he also knew she'd do whatever she wanted to do, no matter what he said.

Eve rode up on a buckskin in her men's wood-chopping clothes, and she was furious—her eyes narrowed, her teeth bared, her hair streaming loose behind her as she galloped, her mare kicking dust. "And you weren't going to tell me, Saul Miller?"

"I have no cause to put you in harm's way."

"You're not putting me in harm's way. You're not putting me anywhere. I'll decide for myself where I'll be and what I'll do, and no one is going to tell me otherwise."

"Understood."

"Just because you think I'm pretty as a flower doesn't mean I'm as fragile as one."

"Daisies are hardy," Saul replied, staring straight ahead and fighting back a grin. "I've seen them weather snowsqualls and frost that took down thistles and seedlings."

"What?"

"If you want to be here, I've no objection. But you know as well as I do that anything could happen."

She flared up again. "Your objections don't matter two cents to me, Saul Miller. If I want to remain here, I shall. I want to be with the man I … " She stumbled. "I want to be with you. And that's that."

"Here comes the sun," Sam said quietly. "And the Irish Gang with it, looks like."

Saul squinted into the gold. "I wouldn't know them but for being told they all got the green bandanas around their throats."

"I can't tell yet," Sam replied.

Eve was shading her eyes. "I can. They do."

Saul and Eve and Sam had stopped their horses about two hundred yards from the edge of town. The gang came in at a lope, not too fast, not too slow. There were ten of them. This got Saul's mind turning like a wagon wheel. He'd heard Buck O'Shea had at least fifteen riders. Where were the others? Minding house?

O'Shea was obvious. For no one else could be him, to Saul's way of thinking, except the man who walked his horse up to the three of them and looked to be ten feet tall in the saddle, especially with a Boss of the Plains hat exactly like Saul's. The man was layered in dust from the ride. Even his mustache and beard were chalk white with the powder. He nodded. "Marshal."

"O'Shea."

"I know that kid got in here ahead of us. This is the first time we've met."

"Yes, sir."

O'Shea had a distinctive accent. From the other side of the sea, Saul imagined. The outlaw held up his right hand, palm outwards. "I know you're not armed, Marshal. And I sure didn't come here to gun down any unarmed lawman or his deputies. McCabe was a skunk, and I'm sure he got what was coming to him. But his old man's money is good."

"How good?" asked Saul.

"Good enough."

"Good enough for blood money?"

O'Shea shook his head like a bull. "No, sir. None of us want a rep as child killers. We have no intention of putting anyone at all in the ground. And we sure aren't going to shoot women and children and orphans."

"What then?"

"This is what." O'Shea leaned forward in his saddle. "How many citizens you got? Two hundred? Three hundred?"

"So?"

"Get 'em out. We'll spare the train depot and tracks and stock pens. Next train's in six hours. Heading west to Wichita. You can probably get all the women and children on that one. In time, the town can be rebuilt. Look how fast Deadwood shot up."

"You expect three or four hundred men and women and children to live in tents all winter, O'Shea?"

"I'm pretty sure Kansas will do better than that. Ye'll be back here in new buildings long before Christmas, Marshal. The cattle trade demands it. There'll be tents here in less than a week. Big ones. The slaughter houses in Chicago will probably put 'em up. They can't let this place go. It's too important to them. Heck, New York and Boston and Philadelphia want their beef. They'll kick in. The railroad will kick in. Topeka will kick in—Lone Star is one of the state's golden eggs. The town'll probably be better off brand new than it is now. We're doing ye a favor."

"Some favor!" snapped Eve. "My mother worked her fingers to the bone to get her boarding house to pay. And you're going to burn a lifetime of dreams and hard work and God's blessings to the ground in less than an hour. You call that a favor? Where will you be after you've done us this favor, sir?"

O'Shea tipped his hat to Eve and smiled. "We shall have retired to Mexico, ma'am. What is a minor inconvenience to ye shall be the door to a new life for us with Old Man McCabe's silver."

"A minor inconvenience!" Eve's face was scarlet. "I thought Ireland produced poets and gentlemen. You put the lie to that myth, sir!"

Saul could see the words bit deep. O'Shea's face darkened, and sharp lines crackled all over it. The outlaw's hand rested on his six-gun. "I left Ireland the hard way. With only the clothes on my back and a British boot to kick me to America. No one's done me any favors, ma'am. I never got to be in a sweet little orphanage like ye have here."

"Yes. Until you turn the orphans into twice the orphans they are with your matches and your kerosene and your greed. God will judge."

O'Shea's eyes became slits. "Ye'd best control your little Missy here, Marshal."

"I am no one's Little Missy, you brute!" cried Eve.

"How about this, O'Shea?" Saul began calmly. "You turn around and go home and forget about all of it."

"No one's turning around and giving another gang McCabe's silver, Marshal," the outlaw growled.

"You know how it'll work if you stay," Saul went on. "I won't pull a gun. Sam here won't pull a gun. But you'll have to kill us to get past us. We swore an oath to protect the citizens of this town, and you're not going to make us break that oath. Letting you raze Lone Star isn't what I'd call protecting the women and children from harm."

"If ye want it that way, we can sure plant ye easy, marshal. Like to play god, do ye? Like to play hero? We'll oblige ye."

"Once you kill us, there'll be no one to tell the townsfolk to put away the Colts and Winchesters and Remingtons. You won't walk in and burn the town, O'Shea. The town will burn you. Without me and Sam here to keep the peace without guns, the guns will be back out, and they'll all be pointed at you and your men."

"I don't believe that, Marshal."

"Trust me."

"Who's that?" O'Shea squinted over Saul's shoulder. "More of your unarmed friends come to save the day?"

Saul turned in the saddle at the same time Eve and Sam turned in theirs. About two dozen riders were galloping towards them. Saul recognized Jack Stranger and Nate. He recognized the mayor too. A number were holding carbines as they rode. Saul glanced back at O'Shea, expecting to see anger. Instead the outlaw was smiling.

"Perfect," he said. "Armed citizens. Just perfect."

A crackle of gunfire suddenly erupted far back at the other end of town. The western end. O'Shea's smile grew. Saul swung back and stared over the heads of the riders coming towards them. He spotted clouds of gun smoke.

"Didn't ye know I have the fifteen men in my gang, Marshal Miller?" O'Shea was almost laughing. "Did ye not wonder where the other five were? So, now ye know. They've got things started in town. And with your lads coming upon us here with their pistols and rifles, it will make everything so much the easier for myself and my boys. We can kill every last man jack of ye and ne'er feel a twinge of guilt or be sent to hell for it when we die. For we shot to protect ourselves, didn't we, marshal? Ye left us no choice once ye'd armed your men, and we had to shoot you all in self-defense."

SHERIFF

CHAPTER ELEVEN

O'Shea's pistol was suddenly in his hand. Saul saw the Irish Gang whipping out revolvers and carbines. He threw up his arm and yelled. "No! Stop!"

"Why would we stop, marshal?" demanded O'Shea. "Your crew have already drawn their weapons."

Saul spun his horse around and saw Nate and Jack Stranger and many others with their six-guns out. He caught Jack's eye. "We've come this far. Don't do it."

"Get out of the way, Saul Miller," hissed Lucky Jack, "or I'll shoot clean through you. They don't get to burn down the town and shoot up the women and children for thirty pieces of silver."

"They won't. No killing. They promised me." Saul reined his horse back to face the Irish Gang. "Say it, O'Shea. No killing."

A blast rocked the morning air. As if it were some sort of signal, guns erupted all around Saul, and clouds of smoke from burnt powder choked out the sunlight. Sam was hit with shots from behind and hurled out of his saddle and over the head of his horse. Saul dove sideways and pitched into Eve, throwing them both to the ground. His horse reared and screamed as bullets cut into it from front and back. Saul kept his body over Eve, shielding her, pushing her further into the dirt and grit.

Men yelled and horses bellowed. Hooves slashed at Saul's head. Bodies fell into the dust, rolled and stopped. Horses lay on their backs, their legs thrashing wildly. There were more pistol shots, the crack of carbines, the hard thump of shotgun blasts. Then a final flurry of gunfire. And silence.

Hands turned Saul over.

Nate and the mayor and another man Saul recognized as one of the bartenders from The Cattleman's Saloon.

"You all right, Marshal?" asked the bartender.

"Yeah," grunted Saul, releasing Eve. "No blood."

"The lady all right?"

"I am all right, Mr. Flynn," said Eve, sitting up and shaking her head, her hair loose and snarled and filled with dirt. "Crushed, but all right." She glanced around at the bodies of men and horses and put her hand to her mouth. "I must get away. The carnage. The smell of blood and death." She quickly got to her feet and half-ran from the crowd of mounted men.

"No gunshot wounds, Miss Sorensen?" called one of the town councilors.

"No, sir. Thank you."

"No cuts or abrasions?"

"Certainly, some of those. Nothing like the dead have experienced."

Saul stood up. Prayers made their way through his heart and mind and soul as he looked at the tangled bodies of man and beast. Lucky Jack was dead nearby, pinned under his horse. The mare was shot to pieces. Nate was beside Jack and riddled with bullets. He saw several other townsmen who had been cut down, their horses long gone across the prairie. Others were wounded, sitting in the dust, friends bandaging their arms or legs or heads. Smoke still swirled in the air. Through it, Saul spotted a horseman galloping towards them from Lone Star. "Rider," he said.

Most of the townsmen were still mounted. They turned their horses. "It's Wil Sybard," someone spoke up. "He'll have news."

Sybard reined up by the mayor, his face dark from burnt powder. "Sir."

"What is it, Wil?" asked the mayor.

"It was just like you'd hoped it would be. We ambushed them at the edge of town. Shot down all five. No one else got hurt. It's just them, dead as coffin nails."

The mayor nodded. "Thank God." He turned to Saul. "Your job just got a whole lot easier, Marshal."

Saul stared at him. "How's that?"

"Once word of this gets around, every cowboy will go easy in Lone Star. Turn in their guns, avoid trouble, leave again as quiet as a mouse. Spilling blood was necessary if the town was going to prosper. Just like the spilling of blood at the slaughter houses in Chicago is necessary for the same reason. Cowpokes will have even more respect for law and order in Lone Star now. We can put our firearms away. We'll need them even less after this."

Saul shook his head. "You're mistaken. You will need your guns even more. No one will trust the town to keep them safe anymore. They will be inclined to believe their lives are in their own hands. And outlaws will learn a lesson from the massacre of the Irish Gang. Kill or be killed. The lawmen of Lone Star will not be able to quell crimes or violence without resort to the sword from this day forward."

"Well, Marshal, I trust you'll find that will not be the case."

"No marshal will. Not any longer. Not ever again." Saul unpinned the star from his shirt and placed it in the mayor's hand. "I've had my season. It was a short season. But it was miraculous. Thank God. Now the town and its lawmen will have to pray and act and thank God in different ways for different things."

He walked to where Eve was standing. "I'm grateful you were not hit."

She blinked at him through wet and shining eyes. “I would’ve been if you hadn’t knocked me off my high horse.” She tried to smile at her little joke but collapsed into his arms instead, her shoulders heaving. “This is a terrible thing, a terrible thing.”

“The burning of our town would have been a terrible thing, Miss Sorensen,” the mayor said quietly. “The shooting of our women and children and orphans would have been a terrible thing.”

Saul nodded. “There is no easy road, even with faith. I will come back with my wagon and collect the bodies of Lucky Jack and Nate. And Sam. I will bury them at my farm. With the permission of Nate’s and Sam’s kin.”

The mayor nodded. “Very well.”

Saul looked at Wil Sybard. “So, Zacchaeus is not hurt?”

Sybard shook his head. “No, sir. He was in charge of things, and he came out just fine. Everyone did.”

“The boy with the Henry rifle?”

“Right as rain, Marshal.”

Saul looked at Eve. “May I ride with you into town to gather up my things?”

“Of course.”

“Take Streams, Marshal.” The bartender, Tim Flynn, led Nate’s horse to Saul. “I’m sure your deputy would’ve wanted you to have his roan.”

“Thank you.”

Saul and Eve swung into the saddles of their horses at the same time and began to walk their mounts past the bodies scattered over the ground.

“Are you sure, Marshal?” asked the mayor, holding out the badge.

Saul glanced back and shook his head. “Summer’s over. I saw its end coming like a north wind bringing hail. Find yourselves lawmen for the long winter ahead. They will need to be just as brave as any in the county. Probably braver." He put Nate's horse into a trot. "I'll be back with the wagon."

SHERIFF

CHAPTER 12

Saul and Eve were wed in May of 1875 after she was baptized into the Amish faith. Eve made her new home at the Miller farmhouse that stood white and sturdy, three stories high, among the fields of spring corn. In time, they would raise six children, four from birth and two they'd adopted from the orphanage. Three boys and three girls. The farmstead became known as a place of laughter and happiness. Once he turned fifty, Saul was selected to be bishop over the Amish church of Lone Star.

Zacchaeus left the Amish faith rather than face church discipline and shunning for bearing arms and taking human life, and became marshal of Lone Star. He chose Andy, the boy with the Henry rifle, to be one of his deputies the day Andy turned fifteen. The town grew wilder as it prospered, and gunfights and brawls became common. Marshal Zack had his work cut out for him. And a six-gun on his hip. All the churches prayed for him and his men—the Amish church led by Saul Miller most of all.

Everything changed with the boom of Dodge City to the west. More drives wound up there, and soon enough, more trigger-happy cowpokes, gamblers, card sharks and gunslingers. Lone Star quieted down, and Zack went back to whittling. He'd enjoyed the whittling during slow afternoons as one of Saul Miller's deputies. Zack marshaled till he was sixty, and it was another century. Then he retired, still single, to a small house not far from Saul and Eve Miller. He took to wondering if the Amish church would have him back again.

Saul and Eve did not forget the summer of 1874. No one who experienced the miracle of a cow town kept safe without guns did, nor did they forget the tragic gunfight that ended the dream. Saul would go to the graveyard far back of the house and talk it over with Lucky Jack now and then. He was buried next to Nate and Sam, and those two were just a little way off from Saul's first wife, Mary, and his first child.

"I can't blame you for taking up the gun at the end," Saul said to Jack's grave one evening. "After all, you took it up to save life more than you took it up to end life. But here's the bigger mystery I still chew on. What made a gunslinger like you unbuckle his two-gun rig to begin with, throw in with an Amish marshal, and go unarmed against a world you'd always faced with two Colt 45s smoking in your fists? That went against everything you were. But, and this is the truth, I couldn't have done it without you. Men were in awe of an unarmed Jack Stranger. They didn't fool around with him in town, gun or no gun. You made a difference to everyone. Most of all, to me. No. Maybe most of all to God."

Once a month on Sunday afternoons, spring and summer, till about 1885, the orphans in town would visit accompanied by the ladies and madame from the Flamingo. They would picnic in the Millerses' yard, thank Saul yet again for protecting them without resorting to fists or gunplay, and place flowers at the graves of Jack and Nate and Sam. By 1882, none of the children who'd seen that summer unfold were at the orphanage anymore, but those who were knew the story. And a good number of the ladies from the Flamingo who'd been present in 1874 were still around a decade later. They'd seen the unarmed Amish marshal and his unarmed deputies protect the Flamingo and the orphanage with their lives. So had the boy and girl Eve and Saul had adopted. When the sun burned low in an August sky, the gold made them all think, wherever they were, of how unbelievable it had been, how improbable, how impossible. But even though they often called it a dream, it hadn't been a dream. It had been as real as the big blue Kansas sky and the long fields of tall bright summer corn. A miracle, yes. But a miracle you could touch.

"It was like we had a stairway to heaven," Eve said as she sat on the porch with Saul one of those golden evenings, paring green apples.

He smiled and shook his head. "That's an exaggeration, my love. But maybe a door to one of those heavenly mansions was left open a crack. Just a crack. Just enough for some of that good light to get out. And maybe, just for a while, the pearly gates were swung wide."

THE END

AMISH FOR THE SUMMER

By Amos Wyse

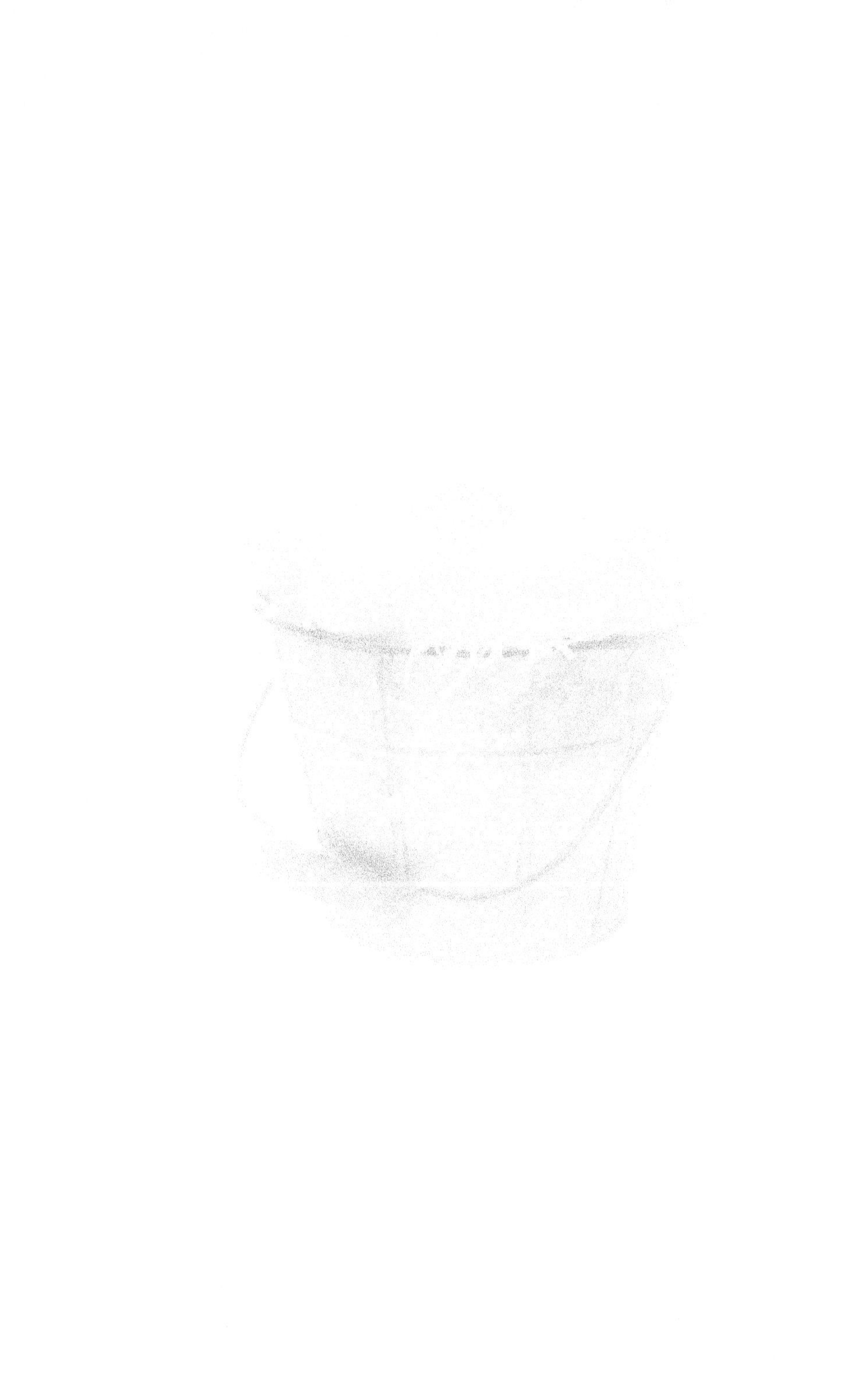

Prologue

Samuel Morse and Diane Sullivan were born the same day, in the same hospital, just outside Barnville, Pennsylvania. That was the only common thing they shared. Diane was born to a well-to-do family in the city. Her father was second in command at McManus Construction, the largest home builder in the area, and her mother ran a small bistro that was *the place* to have a coffee and biscotti in town. This young lady had never known hardship or hunger.

Samuel was a different story. The only reason he was born in a hospital was due to a buggy accident putting his mother's midwife in a room on a floor above her. He was born into the local Amish community. His days were filled with school and work. Eventually, the toil of labor would become his life and how he earned his keep. Samuel's father and mother both worked the *familye* farm for food and for the little coin his uncle had for their wages. You see, the land belonged to his Uncle John Beiler.

CHAPTER ONE

Diane

"Michael, did you hear that?" Diane's mother questioned, her voice rising in excitement. She rushed across the living room to stand by the bassinette.

Mr. Michael S. Sullivan put down his paper, folding it neatly across his knee while looking over at his wife. She still held the evidence of her youthful good looks, tempered by age and attitude.

The rattling of the paper appeared to startle Diane, and she began to cry loudly.

"Now see what you've done!" Rita remarked crossly, "She was saying her name."

"Children do not say their own names. They say mama or dada first." He crushed his cigarette in the ashtray. In doing so, he noticed the dish hadn't been emptied in days. "You need to have a good talking to with that maid. She refuses to clean the ashtrays despite my repeatedly telling her it is a part of her job. You take care of this, or I will!"

"Yes, dear." An elaborate sigh escaped her mouth, "But did you hear Diane? She said 'DeeDee'."

"And that makes you think she is saying her name?" Michael's scornful look was well-practiced on his crew leaders and in turn, the men who worked for them. He stood, "Let me show you."

He stretched, exiting the large, high-back, black upholstered chair like a man who captured and owned all that he pursued. Removing the scorn from his face, he now peered into the Sullivan family bassinette.

"Dada."

"Deedee," came the reply.

"Dada," he tried again.

"Deedee," the baby repeated.

Changing strategy, "Mama."

"Deedee," came the sing-song reply from the rosebud lips of his blonde angel.

Eventually, the mama and dada would come. Little did they know then the *Deedee* would stay. Deedee became Diane's nickname and the only name she would answer to.

At five, Deedee was excited to get her way and go to the store to pick out her birthday present. She wanted a bike, and that was what her parents would buy her. Nancy down the street had gotten one. Deedee's would be better.

"What about this," the man at the store asked, pointing out the prettiest pink bike with a white basket and training wheels.

"No," was her only answer. She wound her way down the line of bikes until they got to the one she wanted. This bike was far too big for her, but it went home, and she willed herself to ride it. Deedee got what Deedee wanted.

She was truly a difficult baby and went right on being a difficult child. She was as "pretty as a penny" those who met her would say. What they did not see were the numerous temper tantrums from not her getting her way. People who fawned over the cute little girl had no idea the number of experienced, battle-hardened nannies who simply said "no more." Strangers failed to see her wear her parents down until she became what she desired to be—spoiled.

Samuel

"*Gott,*" rang out clearly in the otherwise quiet Beiler home. There was nothing unusual about hearing the Lord's name in this home. What made this particular utterance unusual was the soul who made it. Baby Samuel. It was not only the clarity of the word, but that it was the very first word he had chosen to share with the world around him.

"Samuel, do you know what you have said?" asked his shock-faced *Mutti,* Violet.

"*Gott,*" he said again, then giggled so much that his tummy and plump legs jiggled with him.

"Such a happy baby," Violet laughed along with him, repeating a phrase heard from so many in her child's short life.

Samuel grew up not so different from any other Amish boy in his district, being taught to love *Gott und familye* and in that order. At five, he would go with his *daed* to milk the cows. In Barnville, even the Amish used machines to milk cows. However, that did not stop Samuel from learning how to milk by hand into a small unadorned white pitcher he would bring to his *mutti* for her breakfast each morning.

Young Samuel's parents bred Labrador puppies to help pay the bills, and despite their pleadings, he gave each puppy a name at birth and played with and loved them all. He cried as the first litter was sold off but came to understand quickly they were never really his. What surprised his parents was the love never stopped from boy to puppy even to the very next litter. By fifteen, he was a breeder himself, adding to the great reputation of Beiler Farms Labradors.

Holly was a puppy born with a slight wobble in her gait. The problem was as simple and as heartbreaking as a leg a tad longer than the other. All the puppies from that litter would be spayed and sold as *not for breeding*. The sire was put on a list of dogs he would not hire again. Holly would become Samuel's dog. He did not treat her as a crippled dog and she treated him the only way a dog knows how. She loved him unconditionally.

CHAPTER TWO

Deedee's phone rang. She rolled onto her side, sliding the newest miniature model from the tiny pocket of her designer jeans.

"Hello," she said absently, examining her manicure by her bedside light.

"Dee, we are going out to have some fun. Come with."

It was David. The only person who dared call Deedee anything else. He got by with his charm and good looks as much as she did. They were a true pair.

"It's already midnight," she said, tossing the magazine she'd been looking through onto her nightstand. "My father would have a fit!"

"When has that stopped you?"

She sat up. "I try not to make it happen every night for fear their heads might explode," her voice registering half-pity and half-contempt.

"I have a case of beer and a bottle of that wine you like."

"Get me at the bus stop. That motorcycle of yours is too loud to get any closer. You know they hate you and want me to stop hanging out with you guys."

"I don't care what they want, what do you want?"

"I don't care that you don't care." She put him in his place with a shake of her blonde hair. "You just better have that bottle of wine."

"See you in fifteen."

"Yeah-yeah, see you."

Deedee stood, fixing her face in her vanity mirror, then riffling through her closet, reaching for a sweatshirt for the cool Spring night. Her window was already open, so she slid the screen up and rolled the fire escape ladder out her second story window. It boggled her mind that her parents believed she wanted it in case of a fire.

The ladder swayed in the moonlight, and she enjoyed the thrill. Jumping the last two feet, she lightly jogged towards the Canfield Road bus stop several blocks away.

David sat beneath a streetlight on his idling bike. He might call her Dee, but he never kept her waiting.

"I got you that helmet you wanted—lipstick red with the sparkles."

That brought a smile to Deedee's lips, painted the same shade of crimson.

"About time you start treating me decently. I was thinking I'd have to start looking for an upgrade."

They both knew, that despite being presented as a joke, the words were a stark reality. She had left a path of dating destruction behind her full of boys who made promises they did not or could not keep.

She put the helmet on and climbed behind David. His leathers were a shock of cold, but she knew they would warm quickly. This was not her first ride. With a roar, the bike sprung to life, and Deedee hugged David tighter to keep from falling off. She knew he did the abrupt start for the close contact, but never called him out. She liked the way the bike ride made her feel wild, while the boy in front of her did all the work of keeping the cold wind off her.

An hour later, four beers were gone and a third of the bottle of wine. They sat on the swings in a park across town. This part of town was mostly Amish, so the odds of anyone being around were fairly slim. That said, the rumble of an exhaust system gave them enough warning to hide the alcohol before the red Ford pickup came into view.

Deedee rolled her eyes then looked over at David. "Did you invite the idiot patrol?"

"C'mon, hun. You know they're my friends. I have no idea why they're here, honest."

Her *fine* came with an inflection that said it was anything but. "And if you call me 'hun' one more time, I will show you how close to *Atilla the Hun* I can act."

"OK-OK, Deedee." David reverted to her full name in a purely defensive reaction.

The pickup came to a stop near the couple.

"Dude," a yell came from the open window. Two young men exited the truck.

David nodded to them as they walked closer to the swing set he and Deedee had made their night's entertainment.

"Mike, Sam, how's it goin'? What'cha doing in this part of town?"

"We'll tell ya if you give us some of those beers you hid so badly," Mike said, nodding at the exposed cardboard peeking out from behind a nearby bush. "Good thing for you we aren't cops. They'd send your butt to juvie."

"You seem to forget, I'm eighteen now."

"Okay, you win. They would send you straight to jail." Sam replied quickly.

The two red-headed friends burst into laughter, which quickly was taken up by Deedee and finally, David himself.

"Fine," David said, grabbing a full six pack and tossing it to Sam. It was clear from the spinning cans that David was less than thrilled with sharing his beer and the two of them crashing his plan to have Deedee alone and drunk.

The two seventeen-year-olds quickly chugged down the first beer then opened seconds, tossing the empties into the sand box near the swings.

"So, remember how that Morse kid out-benched you in gym?" Mike's statement was directed to David. "We're going to his uncle's farm and are gonna tip some cows and wake some Amish."

As David was about to say no, Deedee spoke up. "Is that really a thing?"

"You-bet," came out of the pair as if it were both one word and one voice.

"This, I have to see." Deedee decided, swaying slightly as she stood from the swing. She grabbed the half-empty wine bottle from its hiding spot and headed for the dirty truck.

David realized his plans were busted and rushed to catch up to her. She plopped herself into the passenger seat with Sam quickly jumping in to drive. David teetered and entered the bed of the truck with Mike, stepping haphazardly on a day-glow orange can of spray paint in the bed and falling hard.

"Good thing he isn't driving," Deedee yelled back through the sliding window. They all dissolved into another fit of laughter even as Sam threw the truck into gear.

Two miles down the road, they turned off their lights and spun around, leaving the truck headed in the getaway direction and killed the ignition.

"Where are the cows?" Deedee complained as the silence stretched. The boys had all taken a beer to drink. It was dark, and she was getting sleepy from too much alcohol.

"In the field behind this corn. You'll to have to come with us if you want to see," Mike said quietly.

"Fine. I was told there's no such thing, so I am going to watch you all make even bigger fools of yourselves." She laughed alone.

They made their way, leaving cornstalks bent and broken behind them, before finally arriving at the pasture. Looking around, Deedee got a smug look on her face.

"These cows aren't even asleep, not that one standing anyway."

"Nope, that one is awake but the mostly black one over there, she is asleep on her feet and about to meet the ground …"

With that, Mike made his way quietly next to the big milk cow and gave her a solid push with a bit of a lift. The two legs nearest him had little grab on the ground as the cow sprung to action a second too late and went crashing down. A loud mournful moo went up as close to fifteen-hundred pounds of cow hit the ground, bruising muscle on her side.

Deedee thought it was the best thing she had ever seen.

"So they are really asleep? Could I tag one with graffiti?" she asked, taking the can of orange paint from Sam's hand and shaking it.

"Uh, that seems a bit reckless, you aren't going to paint our names on them or anything are ya?" Mike asked, showing that he had some slight chance of surviving into adulthood one day.

"No, something better."

She worked her way toward another cow. It stood still flicking its tail back and forth. Deedee aimed the can and made an upside-down arrow on the beast.

"Your turn, champ," she held the can out to David.

"I'm not going to tip a big ol' cow," he answered.

"I'm not dating a chicken," came her cold reply.

"And I'm not letting you hurt any more of these cows," a deep male voice behind them said with conviction. The sheriff continued, planting his feet firmly in the dirt, "You must be the group that keeps harassing the Beiler farm cows. Third time this week was really stupid. You should have figured they'd be calling me."

"I'm just here because I don't have a ride home. I had no idea what they were doing or going to do," Deedee said in a plaintive voice. "These guys will swear to that in court."

"I bet your daddy would be willing to give everyone involved a fat envelope to make this go away," the sheriff pondered aloud. "Problem is, I did not actually catch you tipping the cow. I just have you all on trespass charges."

A deep sigh ran through the group. "Except you, miss. You, I have on vandalism charges as well."

Deedee's temper rose. "You just said you did not see anything that happened!"

"I did indeed. I might have said I failed to catch you all red-handed. You, however, I have caught orange-handed." He walked up and lifted her hand high enough for all to see the paint she had gotten on herself while painting the cow. "I bet that matches the color on the cow, and I'll find the can nearby with your prints."

Deedee had the street sense to stop talking as the handcuffs were put on her, and she was led to the side road and into the back of the car. Sitting there, she watched the sheriff take down statements from each of the boys, hearing them state Deedee had wanted to see cow tipping, and they just went along to be popular.

Smelling the beer on them, he asked one of them to call a parent to give them a ride home and took the keys to the truck. He'd grown up around here too and knew that beer was all too common among the local youth and was something the parents would deal with better than the law.

"Deedee, I can't just pay a judge and make this go away. You got caught vandalizing property, and that property was alive. You are lucky they did not add animal abuse charges."

"I can't get into college with an arrest record!" Deedee raised her voice at her father.

"Then you really should choose your friends and activities more wisely," her father said at just above a whisper for effect.

"If I tell you you're right, will you help me?"

"Only if I believe you when you say it."

"They all turned on me!"

"After you tried to throw them under the bus first is the way I hear it."

"Well, I was the only one there headed to college. Clearly my personal record is more important than a laborer's!"

Michael closed his eyes. His brow tensed and jaw clenched. He gave every sign of trying not to snap.

"Everything you have in your life comes from laborers. The men and women that build the houses pay for your arrogance and disdain."

"So you aren't going to help me?" Deedee interrupted.

"Oh, I am going to help you, but this will be the very last time. I am shutting off your phone, your credit card, and removing you from the car insurance policy. You want to drive, you bring me a policy of your own, paid up."

"But, but … Daddy," Deedee whined and rubbed at her eyes.

"Knock it off. You aren't five anymore, and I am not stupid. It is long past the time we treated each other as if we were. I know Judge Perkins and the Beiler family. Perhaps we can make some arrangement."

Deedee kept her smile hidden. She'd begun to think she wasn't getting away with this one. She'd have to work harder to make Daddy remember she was his girl.

Three days later, wearing a new outfit bought on a card her father had not remembered to cancel, Deedee stood before the judge at her arraignment.

"I understand the parties have come to a settlement, and the charges are being dropped," Judge Perkins stated as much as asked.

"Not exactly, Your Honor," came the reply from the prosecutor.

"Excuse me??!!" said the livid Deedee, looking from the judge to the prosecutor and then at her attorney.

The gavel rang hard three times, and the bailiff demanded order. One of the uniformed deputies assigned to the courthouse moved closer to Deedee to remind her that she was, for lack of a better phrase, property of the court.

The prosecutor continued, "Your honor, we were not made aware of the deal until fifteen minutes ago. We would like to stay the charges until the service is completed, so if the accused fails to appear or meet the terms of the deal, she will be under these same charges again at that time."

"Young lady, do you plan to follow this plan to keep you out of prison?"

"What plan is that?" Deedee responded without the courtesy title of "your honor."

"You know, Bob," the judge said to the prosecutor, "that sounds like a very good idea. Any issues, Ted? Good so be it. Rewrite the deal and have it on my desk this afternoon. The community service begins tomorrow at 6:00 a.m."

The judge had not paused enough to let Ted Wallace bring up an expected objection and none came after the sentence.

"I don't do six, *Your Honor,"* Deedee's voice dripped with anger.

"You don't seem to understand. You have exactly one choice in this. You will either do 6:00 a.m. at the Beiler farm, or you will do 6:00 a.m. at the Clover Junction Women's Prison. You have six seconds to tell me where to send you."

"Ugh! Fine! I will wash the paint off the stupid cow at six, even though it would be just as clean at ten." Deedee protested, watching the judge's eyes squint together in what appeared to be confusion.

Later that afternoon, Bob Maxwell brought the signed deal to the judge with the new provision. Picking it up to inspect and sign it, Judge Perkins asked the question that had nagged at him since that arraignment.

"She has no idea this is for the entire summer, does she?"

"Her father had a 'come to Jesus' talk with her, and you saw her attitude after that. He wants her to learn respect for hard work before she goes off to her private school and trust fund-type life. He actually recommended the addition to keep her feet to the fire."

"Good for him to recognize the need. Interesting approach. Keep me apprised on the progress on this."

"Will do, sir."

"Give my best to your wife, Bob."

"Will do on that task too, sir. You do the same to Wendy and the kids from us."

With that, the two men separated and went their own ways. One went to the local homeless shelter and the other home to his wife.

Judge Perkins just kept whispering the same words over and over as he ladled soup into bowls and added a piece of bread to the plate. "Amish for a summer. Her punishment is the dream of so many."

Finally, the line ended, and the time came for the judge to fill his own bowl and sit down to eat with everyone. He hoped being among those suffering would help prevent them from doing something that would put them into his courtroom. He also silently prayed he would be prevented from losing touch with these people whom prosperity had ignored and poverty had such a tight grip on.

CHAPTER THREE

The alarm went off at five, and Michael Sullivan smiled before getting out of bed. He stepped into his L.L. Bean plaid slippers and walked quietly down the hall to Deedee's room. Taking a deep breath, he knocked with a firm hand.

"Go away! It is the middle of the night."

"You have to go to the Beiler's and be there by six or face prison time. They don't let you sleep late in there either."

"Ughhh …"

A light thud of feet to the floor came from inside. Michael smiled and walked toward the kitchen to get his morning coffee.

As they neared the farm, Deedee gave up on her silent treatment of her father accidentally with a loud, "What on earth is that smell?"

"The Beiler's farm is primarily a dairy farm. That, dear Deedee, is the smell of money. This is one of the biggest Amish farms for miles, and its milk, cheeses, and yogurt are well-known, even outside the state.

"Only you would think this stench smells of money. It smells like the sewer it is. You allowed them to send me to a sewer to clean a cow!"

"About that ..."

Only at this point did Deedee become aware her sentence was sixty days of community service. One of the cows that had been tipped that week had cracked ribs and heavy vet bills, which her father had paid to get this arrangement agreed to.

"I will not stay here for two months and ruin my plans for summer!"

"Should I turn the car around then?"

Giving the alternative thought, a meek voice responded. "No, I guess I'll vacation in hell with these idiots. Did you at least bring my phone?"

"Nope, no phones, no electricity. Just honest work and no friends who think animal abuse is a funny thing. Ah, here we are."

Her father turned at a set of four mailboxes onto a dirt and gravel road. This headed toward the farm.

The large white farmhouse with no power cables and three large beautiful barns told this was an Amish farm. The people scurrying from here to there already doing the farm work wearing celery green colored frocks for the women and suspender-held dark pants with a white shirt for the men was so descriptive even a child could tell them as Amish.

Michael parked the car near the home and handed Deedee her bag. Before backing out, he told her he hoped she made him proud.

While she was standing dumbfounded that he had indeed left her at a stranger's home, two women exited the large farmhouse and walked towards her. One was a young woman barely older than Deedee, and the other appeared to be her mother. Neither was smiling, and Deedee was sure the look on their faces meant they were not happy to see her.

"Good morning. I am Lizzie Beiler. My husband, John, runs this farm," the younger woman greeted.

"I am Frau Beiler. My son and daughter-in-law are your hosts. I am the woman who will be making sure you do what is told and stay out of trouble here."

Lizzie wrung her hands. "Now, *mutti,* we agreed to give this young woman a chance."

"One chance," agreed Frau Beiler with a sniff.

Deedee lifted her chin higher. "Where is the cow I painted? I expect cleaning that will be first?"

"No, that was work for the men, done the next morning. Your father paid a great deal of money to have a veterinarian tend that cow and the others your friends hurt, as well as to check on the entire herd."

"Why would he do that? They said they had only done that once or twice before!"

"Part of it was to give us peace of mind that none of our herd had been harmed and not reported. Part of it was to secure your place here this summer," Frau Beiler replied.

"This was his idea?" Deedee said, shocked. *I hate him! I'll surely make him pay for this!*

"*Ja,* and he was a powerful advocate for you, young lady. We do not like to mix with you *Englishe.* Truth be told, we do not want our children to act like you. The less lazy *Englishe* they see, the healthier it is for them. Yours will never be the life of a godly Amish."

"I am not English," Deedee started to respond before being cut off.

"To us, you are all *Englishe.*" This response came from Lizzie. "Long ago, the Amish began calling any non-Amish person *Englishe.* I doubt we will change now."

Lizzie and her mother-in-law shared a brief chuckle at Deedee's expense, then Lizzie apologized. "I regret if that offended you. You are a guest in our home."

Deedee's eyes lit up at the word guest, then fell as Frau Beiler stated, "You will be assigned chores. There is no reason, sick or well, not to do them. If you fail to do them, your summer here ends. I understand there are other accommodations waiting for you in that event."

Deedee felt a chill run down her. She had been sold into slavery by her own father. No wonder he took her phone so she could not report him.

"Do you have a phone I can use?" she asked.

Frau Beiler turned to Lizzie, and the two of them held back the laughter.

"We have no electricity to power a phone," Lizzie explained.

"Cell phones use batteries," Deedee tried.

"*Mmm* and connect us to *Englishe* people wanting to sell us car warranties," laughed Frau Beiler.

"No. We keep one for business, but it is with my husband where it belongs," added Lizzie. "It is nearly time for breakfast, the men have been milking and working the cows for the morning and will be hungry. Help us serve."

"We will see to clothing you properly after breakfast. We cannot well have you running around half dressed," Frau Beiler added, getting a nod from Lizzie.

Deedee did not know what part of that statement to dislike more. That people had been up long enough to not call 7:00 a.m. morning, that she would be a waitress, or that they were going to make her look like them. Quickly weighing her options, she put on a fake smile and followed them into the home to help serve breakfast.

Grabbing a steaming plate of scrapple, she held her nose high and followed Lizzie into the dining room. She was doing fine until she saw him. She remembered being interested in him at Blount Middle School but was never able to get him alone. Samuel Morse. He now stood a bit over six foot, she guessed, from how he dwarfed the other grown men near him. His shoulders had those next to him leaning away for space. His white shirt showed off the muscles that would have made him a walk on for any football team he tried for. Well, had he not been Amish and unwilling to hit others.

Deedee felt her face grow warm as he looked up at her and nearly dropped her platter when he spoke:

"You are Diane … um … Sullivan, right?"

"That's me," she said acknowledging her given name perhaps for the first time in her life.

"Oh, I thought you were Deedee," Lizzie questioned behind her.

"That is just a childhood nickname," Deedee heard herself saying, trying to agree with Samuel.

"I thought this was the Beiler farm, Mr. Morse. How is it that you are here?" Deedee said with a hint of playfulness.

"My *mutti* … sorry, mother, is a Beiler. We are needed here to help run the farm part of the dairy," Samuel explained.

"Perhaps you can show me around when you have a free moment, so I can see what it is I'll be doing here." Deedee floated the sentence like a lure on still water. Much like that lure, the intended target is not always first to the hook.

"You won't need to know anything about the work the men do. We are not *Englishe* here. You will work with us women, and we will fill your hours well enough," Frau Beiler remarked, giving her a cold blank stare that could have been ill humor or premeditating her demise.

She would just have to learn what the "*women's work*" was and get it done faster than these protected freaks.

Being Monday, it was laundry day at the Beiler household. The women had her run all the clothes down to the washing area where two hand machines were set up. The machines were an odd stainless-steel looking contraption with a rounded bottom and a stainless lid with a large white handle. Next to those was a pair of even stranger machines with large cranks that seemed to be connected to two rolling pin-type devices held together with strong springs. Deedee had no way of knowing this was at least twice the laundry facilities as found in most Amish homes. Her lack of being impressed rubbed the Beiler women the wrong way.

"Perhaps you would prefer to dry the clothes than have to use the hand-crank washers?" Frau Beiler suggested.

With an audible sigh of relief, Deedee agreed. She failed to see the snickering faces around her.

The women made quick work of sorting and starting loads of laundry. After the scrubbing and washing, the clothes went through the wringers to remove the majority of the water, and then went into a basket. Once the first basket was filled, Deedee asked where the dryers were.

"Oh, we have three of those. We keep them outside," Frau Beiler said with feigned pride.

"Perhaps I can help you find a good used one in town," Deedee offered, trying to get on the good side of Frau Beiler before walking out the door and realizing what had been done to her.

There were dryers all right—each a long line of rope connected to a barn with a pulley at each end and a basket of clothespins awaiting her on the near post of each. She had been had.

Basket after basket of clothing came out for her to pin up and pull the rope to get new open line to hang things on. As the line filled, the strength needed to pull them got greater as well. It was all she could do to finish the line without giving up. Giving up was something she was not prepared to do.

Lizzie and Frau Beiler finished inside and pushed the water onto the floor towards the drain put there for just this reason. Deedee was halfway through the second line when they came out.

"This is all you managed to get hung?" Frau Beiler asked.

"Yes, ma'am," Deedee answered, too tired to fight.

"Well, for a spoiled *Englishe,* I guess I should not have expected better. Let's get the rest of this up, or we will surely be without clothing tomorrow."

With that command, the women grabbed the clothes and seemed to be throwing them onto the line. There was no stopping, no hard cranking of the line, just efficient work, done by women with smiling faces.

CHAPTER FOUR

Tired, sore, and humiliated, Deedee was ready to go lay down and cry. Frau Beiler had other plans. There were floors to sweep, shelves to dust, and meals to prepare. As the sun set, so did Deedee, only to be woken in what seemed like minutes later to start each new day.

There was bread to bake, and then breakfast to make as the men returned from the morning's milking. The only joy she had was the brief times she got to see Samuel and sometimes share a few words with him.

This pattern repeated itself day after day. By the second week's end, Deedee no longer felt tired when she woke up and no longer collapsed at the end of the day. A nonbiased observer would say she was getting better at the work she was doing. There were, however, no nonbiased observers at the Beiler farm. Frau Beiler was still not satisfied that Deedee was trying with all her heart.

There was a break on Sunday, of course, when Deedee was given the "*English*" Bible and assigned a book to read and explain. She was a bit surprised she did not find the hate and fearmongering in it she had been told was on every page.

She read about the prodigal son and how he was welcomed back. That made her wonder if it applied to prodigal daughters as well. She read further throughout the next week in the evenings and discovered Daniel, who had so much confidence in the Lord he did not fear even a night in the lion's den. She read of Jesus saving a woman who had done far worse than she herself had ever done. He saved that woman from a stoning with only a reprimand to "go and sin no more."

Was it really that easy, she wondered in her simple bed at night. She would need to ask someone but felt she had no friends in the Beiler household. That was the last thought that went through her head as sleep finally found her the end of her third week at the farm.

Monday morning, Deedee woke without assistance. She was, as a matter of fact, earlier rising than even Frau Beiler. Knowing it was wash day, she began filling pots with water and placing them on the stovetop. She threw small pieces of kindling on top of last night's embers in the tinder box of the stove, as she'd seen Lizzie do, which caught quickly. Then she added bigger sticks and logs.

She chuckled, realizing this was the peak of her kitchen skills, starting a fire and heating water. Her amusement was interrupted by the sound of a throat clearing behind her. Spinning around with a kettle in her hand, she saw Frau Beiler.

"Good morning, Frau Beiler."

"And a *gut* morning to you as well. What is this you are doing?"

The older woman peered down her nose at Deedee, who retreated a step back.

"We will need hot water for laundry, I ... I am just getting it ready."

"That is Lizzie's work, is it not?" The woman walked behind her, sniffing into the slowly stirring water inside the pots.

"Isn't all of our work the laundry? It isn't as if one of us will be done before the others."

"Who are you and what have you done with that whining *Englishe* girl?"

"I suppose I have that coming. I did do quite a bit of bellyaching. I figure I have a month left here, I can be miserable and fearful or be like Daniel and fearless."

"So, I am a lion now?" Frau Beiler asked, her brow furrowing fiercely.

"More so than a housecat," Deedee answered with a laugh, then froze as Frau Beiler did not laugh with her.

Their eyes met.

"Hmmmph," Frau Beiler said sounding indignant. "I suppose I had that coming."

A slight smile tugged at the corners of her mouth, then a deep rich laugh escaped her lips. Deedee would have sworn the woman never had laughter in her.

The older woman nodded towards the steaming pots. "It looks as if you have enough water. Go fetch the eggs in the hen house. I could use a hand with breakfast this morning."

"I fear you are looking at my only kitchen skill," Deedee said holding up the kettle that was still clutched in her hand.

"We shall have to fix that. Even *Englishe* girls need to cook for their men, *Ja*?"

"I confess, I'd not really thought that far ahead. I just assumed my future husband would cook or hire a cook for us. That seems silly now."

Frau Beiler hurried her from the room, taking the kettle from her hand. "Hurry along, the eggs will not gather themselves." Her voice back to her usual gruff tone.

So, there was a limit to the orneriness, and a sense of humor wasn't far below the surface! *But oh*, Deedee thought, *which way the wind blew was the difference between the two.*

The egg gathering was a new chore. Surely Deedee was moving up in the eyes of the family matriarch. She practically skipped from the kitchen and out through the hinged screen door. It slapped closed with a bang. She ducked her head and ran. Freedom nipped at her heels for a moment. She longed to run through the fields of grain in the distance.

However, she curbed her gusto and aimed towards the coop which was behind the house and closer to the barn. Deedee had followed the chickens' comings and goings with curiosity, passing them often in the yard.

They pecked at each other and at the tufts of grass, always busy and clucky, bantering with each other. Now, she would enter their domain. A chill ran up her spine.

She entered the little house. It was early enough that none had been let out yet for the day. They scattered at her entrance and flew up in a kerfuffle. Wisps of feathers clung in the air before her. Deedee sneezed loudly, *Achoo!* Another tumult ensued until only two chickens remained on their roosts.

Grabbing a pail by the door, she made quick work of gathering warm eggs from the straw beds. She considered passing up the chickens who were still roosting but wanted to make Frau Beiler proud.

Cautiously dipping a hand beneath, she was met with the underside of the chicken. All bones and feathers. Her fingers found two eggs quickly. Her confidence high, she strode before the perch of the last chicken, its face level with hers. She leaned in to dig for eggs.

The fowl's black eyes flashed. *Peck-peck.* Deedee jumped back. It screamed a single loud cluck at her, indignant. The old Deedee's temper flared. However, the brown hen then stood to its full height. Beneath her laid two pristine white eggs. Deedee licked her lips and advanced.

Another screeching cluck caused her to stop and retreat. The other hen locked eyes with Deedee, seemingly giving her a warning.

Deedee nodded, clearing her throat, and announced aloud, "We'll get them next time."

Leaving the dim coop, she clutched her bucket in one hand. Contritely, having been put in place by a chicken, she made her way back to the house.

Upon her return, she was taught how to scramble eggs. This helped to alleviate some of her pent-up frustration. She must've been a sight for Frau Beiler, and now Lizzie watched her with wide eyes. They taught her a trick to cook them, adding a bit of water to the bowl so the steam it made when cooking kept the eggs fluffy. Deedee thought herself a master of eggs after one quick lesson and again asked herself: Was it really that easy?

CHAPTER FIVE

Breakfast came and went. Laundry came and went. They finished early as the extra set of hands was now finally a help more than a hindrance. Frau Beiler let all of the girls have the afternoon off with directions to be back in the kitchen to help with dinner. Lizzie and the girls went off to work on a quilt they were making. They asked if Deedee wanted to join them but seemed relieved when she said no.

She retrieved her Bible, then sat in a corner of the front room in an upholstered high back chair. The room was in deep contrast to her own home, which had knick-knacks everywhere including shelving created just for that purpose. Tucking her feet beneath her, she began to read. After a few minutes, the door opened, and a voice called out for Lizzie.

"She is quilting in the other room," Deedee said not looking up.

"Could you possibly help me then?"

The voice belonged to Samuel, she realized, looking up. The telltale scamper of four feet followed him fully into the house.

"I don't know. What was it you needed?"

Despite herself, she could not remove the flirtation from her voice. That is, until Samuel held up his bleeding hand.

"Oh no! Get into the kitchen and over to the sink and stop bleeding on this clean floor!" Deedee had no idea how much she sounded like both Lizzie and Frau Beiler at that moment.

"Let's get this washed and see what we are working with," she exclaimed, holding his wrist and rinsing off the bloody hand. "Does Lizzie have a first aid kit in the house?"

She paused to look into Samuel's pale face. He had yet to find his words. "You are a near grown man, stop thinking about the blood and answer me."

"*Ja*, under the sink."

"Keep pumping that cold water over it." Deedee instructed, pushing the dog aside, and getting out the kit and opening it.

"Okay, get your hand out of there. We will dry it off and make sure that it's not infected."

With that sentence, Samuel's eyes grew larger.

"You great big lug," Deedee teased. "You work as a man and yet are still afraid like a boy."

"It is easier when it is not my own blood," Samuel hurried to explain, patting the chocolate lab at his side.

"Baby," Deedee scolded him as she put methylate on the cut.

"Aiiiiiieeeeeeee," came out of the man child sounding more child than man at that moment.

Deedee ignored him and wrapped the area with bandage. "Have Frau Beiler or your mother look at that after dinner."

"Yes, ma'am," Samuel said meekly, and Deedee instantly felt bad she had been so tough on him.

"You're right, you know. It is easier when it's someone else's blood." She hid a smile as he sheepishly went back outside.

It was barely past dinner and clean up when Samuel came to Deedee, holding his hand in front of him and the bandaging in the other.

"*Mutti* said you did a *gut* job on the bandaging and wants you to put a new one on tonight." Samuel explained. "It hurts, but I see the redness is not there any longer."

"You're welcome. I think you were trying to find a 'thank you' in there somewhere."

"*Ja*, sorry it did not come out by itself sooner. I am not so *gut* talking to women."

"Well, as a woman, that whole honesty thing is not a bad start. Have you been trying to speak to a certain young woman, Samuel?" Despite herself, Deedee struck a pose of innocence and anticipation.

Samuel's face reddened, and he clammed up, deflecting, "Can you do the bandage now, please?"

Deedee took her time on the bandage, but not another squeak came from this man turned mouse. She had time to give him, now she knew he was interested. She would try to make talking to her easier for him.

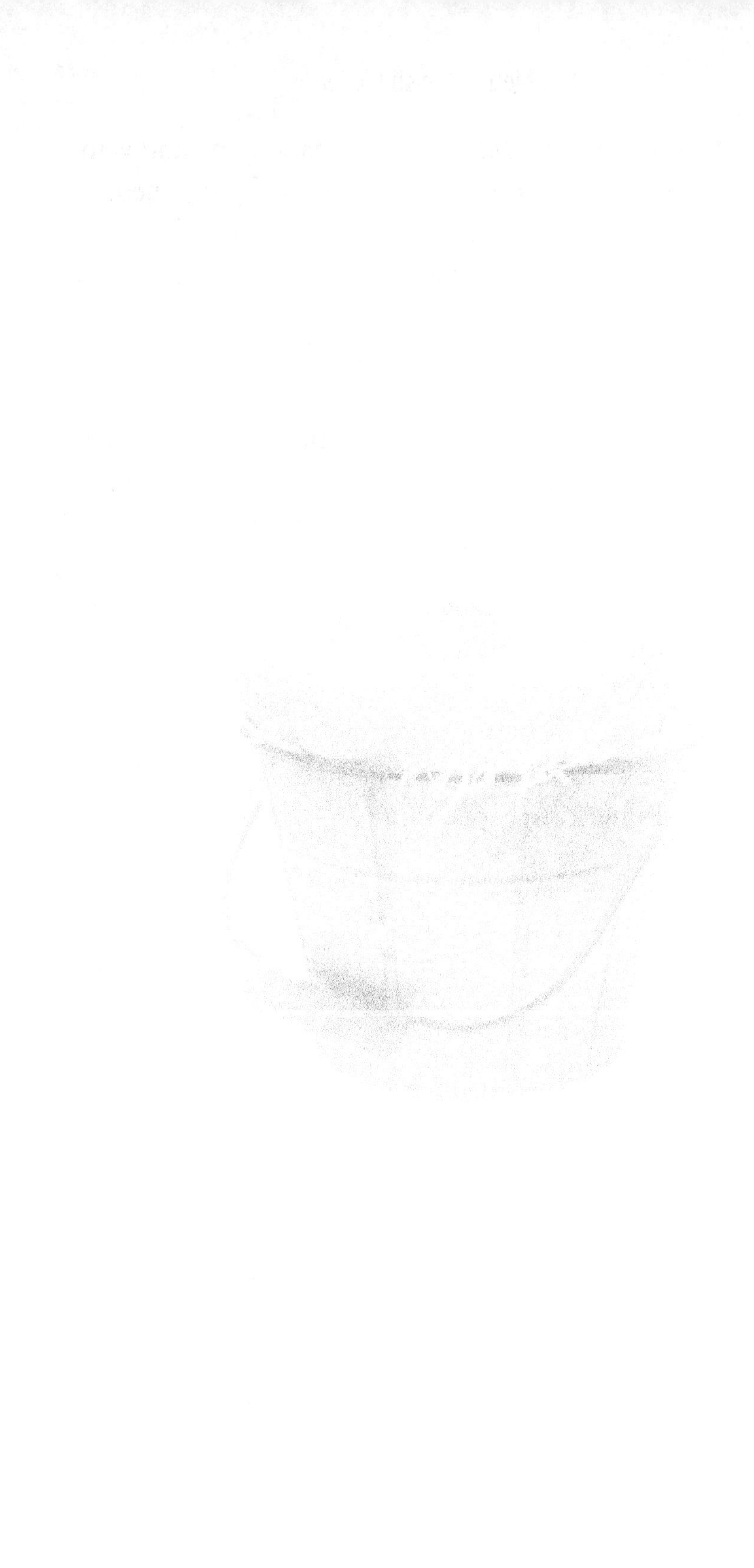

CHAPTER SIX

Morning again found her up early and feeling good about her surroundings. She felt her face warm when she thought of Samuel, and had there been a mirror, she was sure to have seen a bit of extra color that had not come from bottle nor brush. Breakfast was about to be set when there came a knock.

"I'll get it," Deedee said, heading for the door.

"Oh, that is my *schwester*, Naomi. She has come to breakfast with us and help with the quilting frolic," Lizzie called out from the *kich*.

Naomi was a striking young woman. She had enough of Lizzie's looks to know they were related but enough of something else to land her on a magazine cover. They made quick work of setting the table, before the men came back from milking, feeding and the other early morning chores for their repast.

They took to their normal seats, prayed and began the meal. When Deedee stole a glance at Samuel, his face looked as if he had been on a tropical beach, all red and flustered. Inwardly, Deedee liked she had that power over him. He had certainly been telling the truth—he made not uttered a single word of conversation all breakfast long.

As soon as the meal ended, he bolted up from his chair and made for the exit and the rest of his chores, his dog alongside him every step of the way. Then, Deedee saw a backward glance at Naomi and a renewed layer of red on both Samuel *and* Naomi's faces.

"Ohhhh . . ." Deedee said quietly, suddenly understanding.

Samuel was flustered by *Naomi's* presence, not her own. Her first thought was denial—that lasted merely a blink as the truth of it was undeniable for any who were looking for or at it.

Deedee thought for a moment. A month ago, had another woman caught the eye of a man in her sights, she would have made a quick decision to make that woman miserable and turn the man against her. She was repulsed by that thought now. Repulsed by who and what she had been.

That a change so large had come over her so quickly seemed too simple to her. What was so different now? She admitted to herself she was still very much jealous of Naomi's claim on Samuel's heart. She was just acting on the realization much differently than the previous version of herself would have.

"Progress?" she muttered to herself.

"Deedee, would you please reconsider and join us for the frolic?" Lizzie asked, the desire clear in her voice to have Deedee there.

"I can't so much as thread a needle," came the harsh honest truth in Deedee's reply.

"I had thought you could cut some for us so we can do more of the sewing, to be honest."

"I can't draw a straight line, never mind cut one," she answered, though this argument sounded weak.

"There is a tool that keeps lines straight and true while cutting. I can show you in moments how to use it."

"I'd just slow you down." This time the excuse did not sound like Deedee even wanted it to be true.

"I will make a deal with you. I will show you how to cut the shapes we need. If after a half-hour, you cannot find it in yourself to be useful, we will send you packing to make lunch or to read."

"I think that might be a deal I can take you up on," Deedee replied, grinning.

She followed Lizzie into the room the women used for quilting. There was a long table set up with several thick pads on top stamped with measurements along with cutting implements. The ladies sat in chairs in a loose circle, facing each other, and sewed on pieces stretched in a hand-held quilting hoop. There were two treadle sewing machines not in use against one wall.

Deedee took three tries to get the first cut right on the blue and yellow cotton calico. Lizzie patiently explained the measurements and within ten minutes, Deedee knew her job. She was to cut 110 of the small triangles.

She concentrated on her work at the table, listening to the women chatter about their husbands and their way of life, from harvesting to canning. The cadence in their speech eased the tension Deedee had been feeling and calmed her. They weren't so much different than people from outside world, except theirs was a slower pace with concentration on family and faith. In that moment, Deedee missed her parents.

"Deedee, a half-hour has passed," Lizzie said somberly. "I fear I have something to tell you."

Deedee stopped in her tracks, the cutting wheel halfway through a folded piece of cloth.

"We need more than the one color of those. Grab some other fabric and cut us some of that same shape and size in the unbleached muslin."

"Oh, of course you do! I'm sorry, I think I was daydreaming."

"Do not be so hard on yourself. You did exactly what was asked. We had no idea you would take to it so quickly," Frau Beiler added warmly. "Perhaps later, I can teach you how to thread one of these needles and let you make a square to keep for yourself."

"I could never ask you to waste so much time on me that way."

"In Isaiah, you will find the Lord tells us that when the time is right, He will make it happen. Perhaps now is the time the Lord Himself wants for you to learn how to thread a needle and sew."

"That seems a stretch, don't you think?"

"He who began a good work in you will bring it to completion," Naomi said from the circle.

"Is that from Philippians? I was just starting to read that book. I seem to be attracted to Paul's writings."

"Yes, it is Philippians 1:6. Look at you, remembering verses," Naomi remarked encouragingly.

"I also read Matthew. Your family did not take me in because I deserved a chance at redemption, you did it because I was the "least" of his brothers. You did it for the Lord's sake, didn't you?"

"That is a far better question for the bishop than for us women. It was after all, his decision in the end," Lizzie answered from her seat.

"Doesn't that bother you? Being told what to do?"

"I should think that if your presence would have been such a huge bother to us, the bishop would have said no."

"But my father bribed, I mean paid for me to be here, didn't he? Even as it was his decision to not get me out of trouble completely."

"He was acting biblically. 'Our father makes us lie down in green pastures'—he saw this as a green pasture you needed to spend time in. Seeing the changes that have come over you these last weeks, I think your father was correct." Frau Beiler replied, taking a rare break from her stitching.

She started again, then paused. "I do not want you think money played a part in the deacon's decision. He does not appear to be so, but he might be the richest man in this county. His farm is larger than ours, and he was one of the earliest providers of what you *Englishe* call organic milk in this area. Once he was sure of the market, he had us make the required changes in our process so we earned more for our milk as well."

"Why did you say earned as if it were a past tense thing? Organic milk still sells for more than regular milk."

"Because greedy *Englishe* corporate farms have ignored the guidelines for organic grazing and sold their milk cheaper while calling it organic anyway," Lizzie said. "Their costs are less than ours, and they undercut our prices. The real shame is people are paying more for something that is not what they think they are buying."

"Has anyone told the government about this? Surely there is an agency that regulates this," Deedee said taking up the cause. "I will make sure when I am out of here to contact our representatives and senators."

"Your politicians know two things, young lady. There are no punishments in the guidelines to stop the corporate farmers and, as a general rule, Amish stay away from the polls on your elections," Frau Beiler said ruefully. "As a child, roughly your age, I went out into your world and was appalled. Most of the people were kind enough, but the things you all worship … celebrities, television, money. It appeared as if you strap yourselves with anchors and then have some sort of contest as to who can have the most of them before they sink into oblivion."

Frau Beiler took a deep breath, exhaling slowly, "I am sorry. I rant. I made an *Englishe* friend. She died from drinking with drugs in her system while driving a very expensive car. I find it is hard to both miss and blame the same person."

"I'm sorry to hear that. It is a hard for me to imagine you had that sort of an English friend."

"She had a prescription for the drugs they found, just not for the quantity of what they found in her. Anyways, it is too bright a day to concentrate on so dark a topic."

Silence held sway in the room for a pregnant minute before Deedee spoke, "What about Samuel, what is his story?"

With the exception of Naomi, the room burst into laughter that took a while to die down.

"What did I say?" Deedee asked.

"Samuel catches all the ladies' eyes, it seems," Lizzie spoke first.

"He is a big, strong, fine-looking man," added Frau Beiler to giggles.

"He is a boy trapped in the body of a man, that is his story," huffed Naomi, who then shook her head as if dismissing him to return to her sewing. "And this quilt will not finish itself."

"Naomi Fisher, what has gotten into you?" Lizzie asked.

"Nothing. I just am not one to gossip about boys!"

"Since when?" Lizzie asked, and the whole room laughed again.

"Okay, so maybe I have in the past. I just want to get this done. Time is running out."

With unspoken agreement, the women got back to sewing and Deedee to cutting the quilt.

Not ten minutes went by, when Naomi spoke up again, "It isn't that he is ugly nor is he afraid of hard work. I am sure he will find a way to make a place for himself."

Lizzie broke in, gasping, "Is my little *schwester* interested in my brother-in-law?"

"No, I am not! I am just making conversation. Besides, that boy only cares for that limping dog of his. He is unaware how many in the district have thrown themselves at him."

"He is shy. I bandaged his hand, and his face was near as red as the blood from his cut. I think it was kind of cute," Deedee offered.

"I don't see him with an *Englishe* wife, so I would not be chasing that idea." Naomi said, meant jokingly, but with an edge to her voice. Her color now nearly matched the description of Samuel.

"I am neither," Deedee said, not taking offense, "interested, nor ready for anything of that sort. I am headed to college in the fall."

"That is where *Englishe* girls go to find their husbands," explained Frau Beiler to the small group.

The women nodded knowingly.

"Well, sometimes, but most of us go to learn. To become doctors or nurses or veterinarians or computer programmers. Not that finding a cute smart guy who can cook would be such a bad thing …"

The women laughed again and rejoined, in earnest, their quilting.

CHAPTER SEVEN

After dinner that evening, Deedee was somewhat surprised to have Samuel come to her to have his bandages changed.

"*Mutti* said you did a *gut* job with the bandage—could you do it again?"

Deedee brought his hand closer to her and unwrapped the cut.

"See how much less red and angry the skin is?" She asked him, then teased. "Wait, does Amish skin get angry?"

"It gets angry. It just doesn't fight back—kind of like poor cows that get knocked over in the night."

Deedee grimaced. "I guess I deserved that."

"*Englishe* think we don't get angry, and they take our pictures when we ask that they do not. They point and gawk at us as if we were puppies for sale, and they are picking their favorites."

"And why you can speak to me and not to say … Naomi?"

Immediately, Samuel pulled back his arm and spun around, looking to see if anyone else had heard her words.

"Why would you say that? What do you mean?" His agitation transferred to the chocolate brown dog laying nearby. The pup stood, and for the first time Deedee had seen, bared its teeth looking for whatever had vexed her master.

Samuel made a few quick hand gestures and the pup calmed, coming over and nuzzling his leg. This was rewarded with a quick scratch behind the ears, a weak spot on every

Labrador. Deedee wondered if she would be able to resist him if he were to rub her temples or cup her head with his large hands, then shook her head visibly to break that image.

"I saw you looking at her and she at you. Neither of you seem to be able to say anything to the other. That is usually a sign there is either good or bad blood between two people. You didn't get fresh with her, did you?"

The look of terror on Samuel's face was precious as he denied ever doing anything to make Naomi cross with him.

"Yet, you cannot speak with her?"

"She is so pretty. She would not be interested in talking with me."

Deedee was a bit offended by that and made a gesture with her hand starting at her forehead and swiftly running downward towards her feet.

"I am not considered ugly by most who know me. Yet, you speak with me easily enough."

"You do not count. You are *Englishe*, and I was angry with you."

"So, you are not angry with me now?"

"No, I can see you are a *gut* person inside. It must have been your friends who made you act that way."

Deedee digested his comment, then began to cry softly.

"It was me …" Her words came out between sobs. "*I was the one* who put paint on your cow. *I was the one* who tried to force my boyfriend, well ex-boyfriend now, into knocking that cow to the ground. *I am the* horrible person."

The words left her body like waves crashing on the shore from an open ocean. She expected anger and resentment to return alongside the echoes of her grief.

"I know for a fact you are not a horrible person," Samuel stated, not offering anything hateful or hurtful. "Holly likes you. She does not like bad people nor most *Englishe*."

Deedee felt the cold wet nose of love rub up against her ankle, then looked down at Holly who looked worried about Deedee's sadness.

Deedee bent down to the warm lab and through a mixture of laughter and tears, spoke. "You are such a good girl, Holly. What must I have ever done to earn your friendship?"

Holly's tail began to wag, lightening Deedee's mood. She rubbed the dog's head and the length of her red-brown coat.

"She is so soft. It feels like all of my sadness and anger are running out of my hands and into her fur." Deedee leaned forward and hugged Holly.

Holly, for her part was not sure what she had done, but was willing to be hugged for extended periods of time without complaint.

"Samuel Morse, I am going to help you," Deedee announced.

"You are already changing my bandage," Samuel said holding his half-bandaged hand up.

"Well, yes. I will finish that as well. I was talking about helping you to speak to Naomi."

"I do not know about that. I am hopeless when it comes to speaking with pretty girls."

"And yet you speak to me with kindness and care, a pretty English girl who has done you little good and much harm. Clearly, you can see the humor in this?"

Deedee straightened and went back to work on his hand.

"I would not call it humorous at all."

Deedee thought hard. "Do you think we can spend a half-hour a day together, perhaps after dinner. We can read the Bible and discuss it. Would you be willing to do that?"

"Do you really think that would help me?" Samuel questioned. "I fear someone with a better tongue in their head will speak to Naomi and turn her gaze from me forever."

"Then we will start this very evening." Deedee said as she finished wrapping up Samuel's hand.

"What? Wait, we cannot begin so soon …"

"Samuel."

"Yes."

"Haven't we been talking these past fifteen minutes?"

"Yes," he said, hesitantly.

"That was the start of us getting you comfortable with talking with girls. Tomorrow night, we will sit and discuss mighty David and Goliath. Okay?"

"Well, okay. I know that story."

"Good, then think about your fear being Goliath and you being David. That will have you ready to discuss the story tomorrow."

After a couple of nights, Samuel was able to lead the conversations during these meetings with Deedee with the same strength he showed elsewhere.

A whisper into Lizzie's ear brought Naomi to dinner the next week.

"Naomi," Deedee said during the meal "I do hope you can stay after dinner and read with Samuel and I."

Naomi's face flashed with anger and sadness, then set to its normal beauty. "I would love to. I hope my presence will not spoil it for you." Her eyes shot daggers at Deedee.

"It would only make the experience better," came Samuel's voice to the rescue.

With that both women looked at him, shock on their faces. Both were happy, but for different reasons.

After dinner, the three made their way to a quiet corner in the front room, to read and discuss the story of Esther.

The concepts of men and women being kept separate felt common to Samuel and Naomi, as well as the Jews being among a nation that did not follow their beliefs. This did not resonate as much with Deedee. She was more focused on how Esther had the king's favor in the end.

Samuel surprised them both by declaring his favorite part was that the king extended grace to Esther and to her uncle, Mordecai.

"A man must show honor to the woman who grabs his heart," he declared boldly, stealing a glimpse at Naomi as he said it.

The half-hour turned to an hour before Naomi said with regret clear in her voice, "I fear I must be getting home, there are chores to do in the morning, and *mutti* is surely waiting up for me."

"I can drive you home, if it pleases you," offered Samuel without shyness.

"What has gotten into you, Samuel Morse? Only weeks ago, I could not get you to so much as look at me, and now, you not only speak, but speak to me and perhaps for me?"

"If you are pleased, the credit goes to Deedee. If I am offending, it is my fault alone."

"I am not offended," Naomi replied, blushing a deep red and ducking her head.

"I will go hitch the horse. Stay inside where it is well-lit until I return."

"Such a gentleman," Deedee said, teasing Samuel as he exited.

Once he had closed the door, Deedee turned to Naomi. "I hope you do not hurt him. He is perhaps the best man I've ever known. He doesn't grovel before me, doesn't fear work, doesn't brag upon himself, despite doing more than many around him."

"It sounds as though he has grabbed your heart as tightly as he has grabbed mine," Naomi declared quietly. "I owe you thanks. I was beginning to think he would never speak to me."

"He is shy, like that silly dog of his. Once you get to know them, they are both protecting and loving."

"Do you think Samuel loves you?" Naomi asked with sadness in her voice.

"I think he likes me as a friend, more so because I helped him gain the courage to speak to you," Deedee stated matter-of-factly.

"Oh!" Naomi responded, a smile lighting her face. "Well, thank you then!"

The conversation silenced as the door opened and Samuel walked through.

"It seems someone took it upon themselves to hitch the buggy up. We are all set to go if you are ready."

Naomi stood as if to leave then turned suddenly and hugged Deedee.

"Thank you, thank you," she whispered, just loud enough for Deedee to hear.

"I am glad the two of you are becoming friends. I think you both share many traits over and above your obvious physical beauty," Samuel declared.

Naomi's head spun between the two, finally moving to stand beside Samuel, looking back to mouth "thank you" once again to Deedee.

The young couple went out the door, and minutes later, the sound of a horse walking away was heard in the Beiler home. Deedee looked at the door with a resigned appearance on her face.

"Do you regret helping them?" Lizzie asked, quietly entering the room and seeing the way of her thoughts.

"No. It is clear, even to *English* me, that they are a good pair. I hope they can find a way to let the love they both seem to have hidden come forward and surround them."

"Then why the down look?"

"I have only a week left here. I confess I came here kicking and screaming, and, I fear, I will leave the same way."

Lizzie came to stand at her side. "You have become a friend to more than Samuel in this household. I am sure many of us would be saddened if you did not come to visit. Especially on Monday."

With that last part, it was as much laughter as speech as Lizzie nearly fell over.

"I would be honored to teach you Amish women how to do laundry, I will definitely come back at least one Monday."

Deedee joined Lizzie in a fit of uncontrollable laughter. They continued until Frau Beiler came into the room and reminded them it was past time for bed.

CHAPTER EIGHT

The last week of Deedee's "punishment" went by quickly. Before she knew it, the Saturday of her leaving was upon her. She packed her belongings into her designer bag and began to walk to the kitchen to prepare the last breakfast she would share with the Beiler family.

In only two months, they had gone from people to make fun of, to family … for Deedee felt as much a part of this family as she did her own.

"Changes need to happen," she said to herself walking the short hallway for perhaps the last time.

Arriving in the *kich*, she was surprised to see the food was already on the table and an extra place set on the men's side of the table. As if to answer the barely formed question of who the place was set for, there came a knock on the door. Lizzie rushed to open it and welcome Mr. Michael Sullivan to her home.

He stepped in, took off his coat into the waiting arms of Lizzie, and then turned to speak with John and Samuel's father, Ernst, briefly. Finishing the pleasantries, he turned and made eye contact with Deedee and froze in place.

For her part, Deedee was not sure what to expect when seeing her father. She had been so very angry with him for so very long. That emotion was just not there when she saw him now. He seemed taller to her, bigger than he used to be. A quick inventory of his clothing said clearly, he was the same size. The coat he took off was a Christmas present from last year. The shirt was a birthday present from the year before.

Deedee realized her perspective was what had changed. She no longer saw him as another piece of her puzzle to put into place and be done with. She now saw her father the way others did. He was a leader of men and a savvy businessman. He was also radiating a near palpable mixture of love and fear towards Deedee.

"I'm surprised you came yourself to get me," Deedee broke the silence.

With that sentence, Michael's face fell.

"I deserve to have been made to walk home with all the trouble I've been."

Her dad's smile half returned with a noticeable glimmer of hope behind it.

"You are my daughter … my princess, and I could never do that to you."

"Can I not be your princess anymore? It will be more than enough to be your daughter."

"I am sure we can work out something."

"Well before you two sit down to negotiate, let's all pray and give thanks to *Gott*." John Beiler announced, waving them towards the large wooden table that had been in the Beiler family longer than any of the people who would sit at it today.

Michael knew woodcraft and commented on the simple beauty the person who crafted this all those years back had found in the wood.

"It was either my grandfather or my great-grandfather who built it. Perhaps they worked it together. Each pointed to the other when I was old enough to ask."

"I would think the auction houses would fight to list it, but I know that you would never think of parting with a family piece like this."

"No, I just keep having more chairs made to fit all the new family members who sit at it," John replied. "Why is it that every time I have you here, you try to get me to sell you something?"

"To be honest, I think it is because I like it when you say no and remind me there are things more valuable than money. Family is one of those." Michael Sullivan looked squarely at his daughter when he said the last.

Deedee stopped her path back to the stove to help serve the food and walked to her seat. Today she was company, not part of the family any longer. A pang of sadness tugged at her heart as she realized it.

"Can't I at least promise to help with the cleanup? I would hate to be a burden."

"Of course, dear. But first let us sit, eat, and enjoy." Frau Beiler stated, smiling at Deedee.

There were pancakes in plenty, whole hog sausage, fresh eggs from the henhouse, and biscuits with gravy passed around and enjoyed by all.

The women stood to clear the table after the meal.

Deedee brewed some coffee, then brought the large percolator to the table to refill the men's mugs.

Her one-word question, "Refill?" was filled with caring for all those who heard it.

She excused herself to go outside, and Michael turned to John, "Who is that and what have you done to my daughter?"

Laughter followed.

"I assure you, the changes in her did not happen all at once, but she is a good person. I think maybe she was hanging around with the wrong crowd."

"I assure you, *she* was the wrong crowd that other parents did not want their kids to hang out with. I like this version of her much better."

"The women have taken to her as well. She was not ready for the workload they gave to her, but she never quit."

"Well, that is my girl then, she never ever quits."

Outside, Deedee ran to the chicken coop and leaned against it. She'd never forget the sounds and smells of the farm. She'd miss the chickens and the cows and well … everything. She'd thought she was a city girl—all designer handbags and even sneakers. It turns out, a leopard can change their spots.

Deedee entered the coop for the last time. She hadn't revealed to the other women, but she'd named several of the chickens. Her favorite, Hildegard, was the stubborn little lady who refused every day to give up her eggs.

Today Deedee spoke softly to her, at eye height. She cooed to the momma and distracted it with one hand. While the hen was focusing on that, Deedee reached beneath and grabbed the three eggs that sat there warm and snug.

Hildegard clucked at her, but gone were the days of the shrill protest. They'd become friends of sorts. She patted the chicken's feathers flat, calming her and bidding her adieu. Her eyes stung. She'd miss every single thing here, but she was ready to start a new life for herself where she belonged.

Shortly after, Deedee returned, placing the eggs on the counter in a full basket.

Lizzie looked her up and down, smiling. "Diane Sullivan, we have seen a remarkable change in you. You started as the *Englishe* we fear and dislike and became as a part of the family."

"Well, we have traditions in this family, and we are not about to break them just for you," Frau Beiler said in her usual gruff tone, moving to Deedee's side.

With that, the kitchen door opened, and Naomi came through it with the quilt they had been working on. She handed it to Lizzie, then went and stood next to Samuel. The two shared a simple smile that spoke silent volumes.

"We had you make a quilt square. That is for us, this is for you." Lizzie said, handing the quilt to Deedee.

At this point, Deedee was reduced to tears. "It is not too much to hope that I might come to visit you once in a while?"

"Family does not need an invitation. Come anytime," Frau Beiler said in an uncharacteristically friendly tone.

The summer of Amish living was over for Deedee, but not the end of its effects.

On the ride home, Deedee turned to her father. "Dad, I'm sorry for the trouble I've brought you and … not just the cow. I'm so very grateful you did not just buy my way out of that responsibility."

"Well, it was not an inexpensive thing to have put you there. Frau Beiler drives a hard bargain."

"I'll make it up to you and want to come to work for you. I don't care if it's just filing, but I want to contribute to something bigger than myself. D-Do you think you could start calling me Diane? I don't want to be Deedee any longer—she was not a very good person."

"The good was always in you. You just were too good too early at manipulating people. Me included."

"I don't want to use that for selfish purposes the way I have in the past. I wonder if I have any real friends. I know most of them were just trying to stay on my good side. Maybe it's best to make a clean break."

"You've been away for two months. That's about as clean a break as you are going to get. You need to talk with these people and see who *they* really are. Once you do that, you can decide which are friends and which are hangers on."

"I'm not ready to date anyone. I need to figure out me before I try to make an *us* with someone. I've seen real love, and it isn't brash and bold. It is quiet and deep. It's the kind of love I want someday, like you and Mom."

"Love comes in lots of sizes and shapes. Sometimes, it is outrageous and loud. Your mom and I started that way, honest. We were young and foolish once, a long, long time ago."

"Diane Sullivan starts today. I want a binding promise from you that if Deedee ever starts to creep back, you will let me know."

"I will do just that. Ah, here we are, home sweet home."

"I never appreciated home, I certainly do now. I can't wait to get into my own bed."

As they walked from the car to the door, Diane ran to her father and gave him a huge hug.

"I have missed you," they both said at the same time.

FROM THE AUTHOR:

People ask me why there is a mention of a buggy crash or buggy crash victim in so many of my stories. The reason is altogether too easy: There are just way too many car or truck to buggy crashes. If you are doing fifty-five and the car ahead of you is doing fifty, you have time to adjust. When that vehicle is doing fifteen to twenty-five mph, you don't. Speeding is usually cited along with any other charges in buggy accidents.

The point? Please obey speed limits and drive safely in Amish country. The life you save could be your own or the main character in my next *Barnville* story.

—Amos Wyse

ABOUT THE AUTHORS

WILLARD CARPENTER

To know Wil, one would probably not think of him as an author. He is a husband, a father, a Christian, a veteran, a business owner, and a servant. He has led a life of bold and diverse experiences that immediately capture one's attention.

Getting to know him more deeply, I've learned that Willard has an unexpected artistic and creative side—something that might be considered uncommon, given his life's works.

Wil's greatest inner strength is his expression and creativity. His life's works give a credit to his writing that few other fiction authors possess. This generates a vivid degree of realism above and beyond other works of fiction.

Upon reading Wil's first book, *Prodigal*, which was first published at about the same time as the first edition of *The Boyertown Bulletin*, I was immediately struck by the quality of the story line, and immediately expressed my desire for him to join *The Boyertown Bulletin's* staff.

Since that time, he has been integral to our publication, frequently covering some of the most difficult topics in our modern society.

—**Eric J. Eidle**, President and Editor, *The Boyertown Bulletin*

Patrick E. Craig

Amazon bestselling author Patrick E. Craig is a lifelong writer and musician who left a successful music career to become a pastor in 1986. In 2007 he retired to concentrate on writing and publishing fiction books. In 2013, Harvest House Publishers published his first Amish series, *Apple Creek Dreams*. His latest Amish series, *The Amish Heiress, The Amish Princess*, and *The Mennonite Queen,* as well as the reprinted *Apple Creek Dreams* are published by Patrick's imprint, P&J Publishing.

In 2017, Harlequin Publishing purchased *The Amish Heiress* for their Walmart Amish series and released it in April 2019. He also recently signed a contract with Elk Lake Publishers to produce his middle grade/YA mystery series, *The Adventures of Punkin and Boo.* His latest release is *Far On The Ringing Plains,* a literary fiction work with Murray Pura, who also collaborated on *The Amish Menorah and Other Stories.* Patrick and his wife, Judy, live in Idaho. They have two daughters and five grandchildren. Patrick is represented by the Steve Laube Agency. His website is *www.patrickecraig.com*

Jerry Eicher

Jerry Eicher was born to Amish parents, and raised in an Amish settlement in Honduras, Central America. The family returned stateside in the late seventies, when Jerry was sixteen. He spent his youth with a beloved Amish youth group in Belle Center, Ohio, and was married in 1983 to Tina Schmucker, whose parents had moved to the community from Nappanee, Indiana.

Jerry and Tina left the Amish to join the Mennonites after the birth of their second son. He wrote his first work in the early twenties, a fictionalized version of his childhood in Central America. His second title was an Amish love story—*Sarah*. Since then Jerry has published over thirty fiction titles and sold nearly a million books.

Thomas Nye

Thomas Nye writes novels about Amish life, with a touch of romance, and a foundation of faith in Christ. He and his wife, Shari, live on her family farm where they raised five children. They have seven grandchildren and a team of draft horses. Thomas walks a mail route for the US Postal Service. It keeps him close to nature and affords many quiet hours in which to dream up novels. "Over three decades of friendships with Amish neighbors has revealed a simple wisdom that inspires my writing." To find out more about Thomas Nye and his books, visit: amishhorses.blogspot.com

Murray Pura

Murray Pura has over twenty-four novels to his credit and, in addition, has published dozens of short stories, novellas,,and poems along with numerous books of nonfiction. He has worked with Baker, Barbour, Zondervan, Harvest House, MillerWords, HarperCollins, Harlequin, Harper One and Elk Lake Publishing. His fiction has won or been short listed for a number of literary prizes. Pura has lived in the UK, the Middle East, the USA and Canada. He now makes his home in the Rocky Mountains of Alberta.

Amos Wyse

Amos Wyse was born in the Midwest. Spending a great deal of his youth around good, hard-working farmers, those who lived near them and worked with them. When writing, he keeps those people and the life lessons they taught close by.

www.ingramcontent.com/pod-product-compliance
Lightning Source LLC
Chambersburg PA
CBHW070643310726
48982CB00001B/396
9781649492326